The House of Silk

ANTHONY HOROWITZ

First published in Great Britain in 2011 by Orion Publishing. This educational edition of *The House of Silk* by Anthony Horowitz is published by arrangement with the Orion Publishing Group Limited, London.

Orion House, 5 Upper St Martin's Lane,
London WC2H 9EA
An Hachette UK company
www.orionbooks.co.uk

21, rue du Montparnasse
75283 Paris Cedex 06

HARRAP's® est une marque de Larousse SAS.
www.harrap.com

ISBN 978 2 81 870361 8

About the author

ANTHONY HOROWITZ is the author of the #1 *New York Times* bestselling[1] Alex Rider series of novels[2] and the award-winning[3] writer of PBS's *Foyle's War*, *Collision*, and *Injustice*, as well as many other film and television projects. He lives in London.

1. n°1 dans la liste des best-sellers du *New York Times*
2. série de romans
3. qui a reçu un prix

Direction de la publication : Carine Girac-Marinier

Direction éditoriale : Claude Nimmo

Notes en marge : Patricia Seixas

Révision des notes : Marianne Mouchot

Informatique éditoriale : Philippe Cazabet, Marie-Noëlle Tilliette

Conception graphique : Uli Meindl

Mise en pages : Cynthia Savage

Fabrication : Rebecca Dubois

Mot de l'Éditeur

Vous aimeriez lire en langue originale, mais le vocabulaire, les expressions figurées ou la syntaxe vous arrêtent parfois ?

Cette collection est faite pour vous !

Vous trouverez en effet, en note dans la marge, une traduction de certains mots et expressions qui vous permettra d'avancer facilement dans votre lecture.

Nous n'avons pas cherché à vous donner une traduction littéraire de l'ouvrage et nous nous sommes parfois écartés du sens littéral pour vous fournir celui qui convient le mieux à l'histoire. Aussi les mots sont-ils traduits dans le contexte du texte original.

Les expressions figées anglaises sont, bien entendu, rendues par une expression équivalente en français.

Les allusions à des réalités culturelles du monde anglo-saxon sont expliquées également dans la marge, pour vous aider à mieux comprendre la trame de l'histoire.

Vous aurez ainsi, en regard du texte original, tout le savoir-faire d'un dictionnaire rien que pour vous et adapté à ce livre !

Notre objectif est de vous mener jusqu'au mot FIN en vous donnant les clés nécessaires à la compréhension du récit.

Laissez-vous gagner par l'angoisse, l'humour et le suspense qui règnent chez les maîtres de la littérature anglo-saxonne.

Lire en VO ? You can indeed!

For my old friend, Jeffrey S. Joseph

Acknowledgments

My thanks to Lee Jackson who greatly helped with the research for this book. His excellent website, www.victorianlondon.org, is a brilliant (and free) resource for anyone interested in the period. Two books that I found particularly useful were *London in the 19th Century* by Jerry White and *Life in Victorian Britain* by Michael Paterson although I also borrowed[1] liberally[2] from contemporary authors including George Gissing, Charles Dickens, Anthony Trollope, Arthur Morrison and Henry Mayhew. Thanks also to the Sherlock Holmes Society who have (so far[3]) been genial[4] and supportive[5] and in particular to one of their number[6], Dr Marina Stajic, who kindly shared her knowledge of forensic[7] toxology[8] with me at the House of Commons. My agent, 'agent of the year' Robert Kirby, first suggested this book – and at Orion, Malcolm Edwards has been incredibly patient, waiting eight years for me to write it. Finally, above all, I must acknowledge[9] the genius of Sir Arthur Conan Doyle whom I first encountered when I was sixteen and whose extraordinary creation has inspired so much of my own work. Writing this book has been a joy and my one hope is that I will have done some justice to the original.

1. j'ai aussi emprunté
2. largement
3. jusqu'ici
4. cordiaux
5. d'un grand soutien
6. l'un d'entre eux
7. médico-légale
8. toxicologie
9. saluer

Coup de pouce pour vous aider à bien comprendre le début de l'histoire...

Fidèle biographe de Sherlock Holmes, c'est avec fierté que j'ai toujours narré ses aventures. Mais ce grand détective est mort il y a maintenant un an et je voudrais, au soir de ma vie, reprendre la plume une dernière fois en son hommage.

L'histoire est terrible mais vaut qu'on la raconte...

Dr Watson

Preface

I have often reflected upon[1] the strange series of circumstances that led me to my long association with one of the most singular and remarkable figures of my age[2]. If I were of a philosophical frame of mind[3] I might wonder to what extent[4] any one of us is in control of our own destiny, or if indeed we can ever predict the far-reaching consequences[5] of actions which, at the time, may seem entirely trivial[6].

For example, it was my cousin, Arthur, who recommended me as Assistant Surgeon[7] to the Fifth Northumberland Fusiliers[8] because he thought it would be a useful experience for me and he could not possibly have foreseen[9] that a month later I would be dispatched[10] to Afghanistan. At that time the conflict which came to be known as the Second Anglo-Afghan War[11] had not even commenced. And what of the[12] Ghazi[13] who, with a single twitch[14] of the finger, sent a bullet hurtling into my shoulder[15] at Maiwand[16]? Nine hundred British and Indian souls[17] died that day and it was doubtless his intention that I would be one of them. But his aim was awry[18], and although I was badly wounded[19], I was saved by Jack Murray, my loyal and good-hearted[20] orderly[21] who managed to carry me over two miles of hostile territory and back to British lines.

Murray died at Kandahar in September of that year so would never know that I was invalided home[22] and that I then devoted several months – small tribute to his efforts on my behalf[23] – to a somewhat wasteful[24] existence on the fringes of London society.

1. médité sur
2. personnages de mon époque
3. Si j'étais prédisposé à la philosophie,
4. dans quelle mesure
5. l'immense portée
6. insignifiantes
7. chirurgien
8. [régiment d'infanterie britannique]
9. prévoir
10. envoyé
11. [1878-1880]
12. que dire du
13. [soldat musulman combattant les infidèles]
14. d'une seule détente
15. m'expédia une balle dans l'épaule
16. [défaite britannique, juillet 1880]
17. Britanniques et Indiens
18. il avait mal visé
19. grièvement blessé
20. généreux
21. ordonnance
22. je fus démobilisé
23. piètre tribut à son dévouement pour moi
24. quelque peu dissolue

At the end of that time, I was seriously considering a move to the South Coast, a necessity forced on me by the stark[1] reality of my rapidly diminishing finances. It had also been suggested to me that the sea air might be good for my health. Cheaper rooms in London would have been a more desirable alternative and I did very nearly take lodgings[2] with a stockbroker[3] on the Euston Road. The interview did not go well and immediately afterwards I made my decision. It would be Hastings: less convivial perhaps, than Brighton, but half the price. My personal possessions were packed. I was ready to go.

But then we come to[4] Henry Stamford, not a close friend of mine[5] but an acquaintance[6] who had served as my dresser[7] at St Bart's. Had he not been drinking late the night before, he would not have had a headache and, but for the headache[8], he might not have chosen to take the day off[9] from the chemical laboratory where he was now employed. Lingering at Piccadilly Circus, he decided to stroll up[10] Regent Street to Arthur Liberty's East India House to purchase a gift for his wife. It is strange to think that, had he walked the other way[11], he would not have bumped into me[12] as I came out of the Criterion Bar and, as a result, I might never have met[13] Sherlock Holmes.

For[14], as I have written elsewhere, it was Stamford who suggested that I might share rooms[15] with a man whom he believed to be an analytical chemist[16] and who worked at the same hospital as he. Stamford introduced me to[17] Holmes who was then experimenting with a method of isolating bloodstains[18]. The first meeting between us was odd, disconcerting, and certainly memorable ... a fair indication[19] of all that was to come.

This was the great turning point of[20] my life. I had never had literary ambitions. Indeed, if anyone had suggested that I might be a published writer[21],

1. dure
2. je faillis prendre une chambre meublée
3. chez un agent de change
4. c'est là qu'intervient
5. ami très proche
6. connaissance
7. avait été mon infirmier panseur
8. sans ce mal de tête
9. prendre sa journée
10. flâner le long de
11. dans l'autre direction
12. ne serait pas tombé sur moi
13. je n'aurais peut-être jamais rencontré
14. Car
15. je partage un appartement
16. chimiste
17. me présenta à
18. les taches de sang
19. assez représentative
20. tournant dans
21. un auteur publié

I would have laughed at the thought. But I think I can say, in all honesty and without flattering myself, that I have become quite renowned[1] for the way I have chronicled[2] the adventures of the great man, and felt no small sense of honour[3] when I was invited to speak at his memorial service[4] at Westminster Abbey, an invitation which I respectfully declined. Holmes had often sneered at my prose style[5], and I could not help but feel that had I taken my place at the pulpit[6] I would have felt him standing at my shoulder, gently mocking whatever I might say from beyond the grave[7].

It was always his belief that I exaggerated his talents and the extraordinary insights[8] of his brilliant mind. He would laugh at the way I would construct my narrative[9] so as to leave to the end[10] a resolution which he swore he had deduced in the opening[11] paragraphs. He accused me more than once of vulgar romanticism, and thought me no better than any Grub Street[12] scribbler[13]. But generally I think he was unfair[14]. In all the time that I knew him, I never saw Holmes read a single work of fiction – with the exception, that is, of the worst items[15] of sensational literature – and although I cannot make any great claim for[16] my own powers of description, I am prepared to say that they did the job[17] and that he himself could have done no better. Indeed, Holmes almost admitted as much[18] when he finally took pen to paper[19] and set out, in his own words, the strange case of Godfrey Emsworth. This episode was presented as *The Adventure of the Blanched Soldier*[20], a title which in itself falls short of perfection[21] in my view, for blanching would surely be more appropriate to an almond.

I have, as I say, received some recognition for my literary endeavours[22] but that of course was never the point. Through the various twists of fate[23] which I have outlined, I was the one chosen to bring the

1. je suis devenu assez célèbre
2. dont j'ai relaté
3. j'ai été très honoré
4. à ses obsèques
5. raillé ma prose
6. si j'avais pris place au pupitre
7. depuis l'au-delà
8. perspicacité
9. récit
10. de façon à laisser pour la fin
11. jurait avoir trouvée dès les premiers
12. [ancienne rue de Londres peuplée d'auteurs sous-payés]
13. scribouillard
14. injuste
15. cela dit, des pires exemples
16. je ne puisse guère me vanter de
17. étaient corrects
18. le reconnut presque
19. prit la plume
20. Le Soldat blanchi
21. est loin d'être parfait
22. entreprises littéraires
23. les différents hasards

achievements[1] of the world's foremost consulting detective to light and presented no fewer than sixty adventures to an enthusiastic public. More valuable to me, though, was my long friendship with the man himself.

It is a year since[2] Holmes was found at his home on the Downs[3], stretched out and still[4], that great mind for ever silenced. When I heard the news, I realised that I had lost not just my closest[5] companion and friend but, in many ways, the very reason for my existence[6]. Two marriages, three children, seven grandchildren, a successful career in medicine and the Order of Merit awarded to me by[7] His Majesty King Edward VII in 1908 might be considered achievement enough for anyone. But not for me. I miss him to this day[8] and sometimes, in my waking moments[9], I fancy[10] that I hear them still, those familiar words: 'The game's afoot[11], Watson!' They serve only to remind me that I will never again plunge into the darkness and swirling fog[12] of Baker Street with my trusty service revolver[13] in my hand. I think of Holmes, often, waiting for me on the other side of that great shadow which must come to us all, and in truth I long to join him[14]. I am alone. My old wound[15] plagues me to the end[16] and as a terrible and senseless war rages on the Continent, I find I no longer understand the world in which I live.

So why do I take up my pen one final time to stir up memories[17] which might better be forgotten? Perhaps my reasons are selfish[18]. It could be that, like so many old men with their lives behind them, I am seeking some sort of solace[19]. The nurses who attend upon me[20] assure me that writing is therapeutic and will prevent me from falling into the moods[21] to which I am sometimes inclined. But there is another reason, too.

The adventures of *The Man in the Flat Cap*[22] and *The House of Silk*[23] were, in some respects[24], the

1. exploits
2. Il y a maintenant un an que
3. [collines du sud-est de l'Angleterre]
4. gisant inanimé
5. plus proche
6. ma raison de vivre
7. dont m'avait décoré
8. Il me manque aujourd'hui encore
9. alors que je suis éveillé
10. j'imagine
11. Allez, c'est parti
12. le brouillard tourbillonnant
13. fidèle revolver de l'armée
14. j'ai hâte de le rejoindre
15. blessure
16. me tourmente sans cesse
17. pour ranimer des souvenirs
18. égoïstes
19. je recherche un certain réconfort
20. prennent soin de moi
21. de sombrer dans les états d'âme
22. à la casquette
23. soie
24. à certains égards

most sensational of Sherlock Holmes's career but at the time it was impossible for me to tell them, for reasons that will become abundantly clear. The fact that they became inextricably tangled up[1], the one with the other, meant that they could not be separated. And yet it has always been my desire to set them down[2], to complete the Holmes canon[3]. In this I am like a chemist in pursuit of a formula[4], or perhaps a collector[5] of rare stamps[6] who cannot take full pride in[7] his catalogue, knowing there to be two or three specimens that have evaded his grasp[8]. I cannot prevent myself[9]. It must be done.

It was impossible before – and I am not just referring to Holmes's well-known aversion to publicity. No, the events[10] which I am about to describe were simply too monstrous, too shocking to appear in print[11]. They still are. It is no exaggeration to suggest that they would tear apart the entire fabric of society[12] and, particularly at a time of war, this is something I cannot risk. When I am done[13], assuming I have the strength for the task, I will have this manuscript packed up and sent to the vaults[14] of Cox and Co. in Charing Cross, where certain others of my private papers are stored[15]. I will give instructions that for one hundred years, the packet must not be opened. It is impossible to imagine what the world will be like then, what advances mankind[16] will have made, but perhaps future readers will be more inured to[17] scandal and corruption than my own would have been. To them I bequeath[18] one last portrait of Mr Sherlock Holmes, and a perspective that has not been seen before.

But I have wasted enough energy on my own preoccupations. I should have already opened the door of 221B Baker Street and entered the room where so many adventures began. I see it now, the glow[19] of the lamp behind the glass and the seventeen steps[20] beckoning me up[21] from the street. How far away

1. enchevêtrées
2. les coucher sur le papier
3. les aventures de Holmes
4. à la recherche d'une formule
5. collectionneur
6. timbres
7. être totalement fier de
8. qui lui ont échappé
9. m'en empêcher
10. événements
11. pour être publiés
12. ébranleraient la société
13. j'en aurai terminé
14. chambres fortes
15. d'autres papiers à moi sont conservés
16. quelles avancées l'humanité
17. habitués aux
18. lègue
19. lueur
20. marches
21. m'invitant à monter

they seem, how long ago since last I was there[1]. Yes. There he is, with pipe in hand. He turns to me. He smiles. 'The game's afoot ...'

1. que de temps écoulé depuis ma dernière visite

ONE

The Wimbledon Art Dealer[1]

'Influenza[2] is unpleasant,' Sherlock Holmes remarked, 'but you are right in thinking that, with your wife's help, the child will recover[3] soon.'

'I very much hope so,' I replied, then stopped and gazed at him[4] in wide-eyed astonishment[5]. My tea had been halfway to my lips[6] but I returned it to the table with such force that the cup and the saucer almost parted company[7]. 'But for Heaven's sake[8], Holmes!' I exclaimed. 'You have taken the very thoughts from my head. I swear I have not uttered a word about[9] the child nor his illness[10]. You know that my wife is away[11] – that much[12] you might have deduced from my presence here. But I have not yet mentioned to you the reason for her absence and I am certain that there has been nothing in my behaviour that could have given you any clue[13].'

It was in the last days of November, the year 1890, when this exchange took place. London was in the grip of a merciless winter[14], the streets so cold that the very gas lamps[15] seemed frozen solid[16] and what little light[17] they gave out subsumed[18] by the endless fog. Outside, people drifted along the pavements[19] like ghosts[20], with their heads bowed[21] and their faces covered, while the growlers[22] rattled past[23], their horses anxious[24] to be home. And I was glad to be in, with a fire blazing in the hearth[25], the familiar smell of tobacco in the air and – for all

1. marchand d'art
2. La grippe
3. guérira
4. le regardai,
5. sidéré
6. à mi-chemin de mes lèvres
7. faillit tomber de la soucoupe
8. pour l'amour du ciel
9. que je n'ai pas dit un seul mot de
10. ni de sa maladie
11. s'est absentée
12. ça, au moins,
13. le moindre indice
14. sous l'emprise d'un hiver redoutable
15. les réverbères eux-mêmes
16. gelés
17. le peu de lumière
18. était aspiré
19. erraient sur les trottoirs
20. des fantômes
21. la tête courbée
22. fiacres
23. passaient avec fracas
24. pressés
25. flambant dans l'âtre

the clutter[1] and chaos with which my friend chose to surround himself – a sense that everything was in its right place.

I had telegraphed my intention to take up my old room and stay with Holmes for a short while, and I had been delighted to receive his acquiescence by return[2]. My practice[3] could manage without me. I was temporarily alone. And I had it in mind to[4] watch over[5] my friend until I was certain that he was fully restored to health[6]. For Holmes had deliberately starved himself[7] for three days and three nights, taking neither food nor water, in order to persuade a particularly cruel and vengeful[8] adversary that he was close to death. The ruse had succeeded triumphantly, and the man was now in the capable hands of Inspector Morton of the Yard[9]. But I was still concerned about[10] the strain that Holmes had placed upon himself[11] and thought it advisable to keep an eye on him until his metabolism was fully restored.

I was therefore glad to see him enjoying a large plate of scones[12] with violet honey[13] and cream, along with a pound cake[14] and tea, all of which Mrs Hudson had carried in on a tray and served for the two of us. Holmes did seem to be on the mend[15], lying at ease in his big armchair, wearing his dressing gown[16] and with his feet stretched out in front of the fire. He had always been of a distinctly lean[17] and even cadaverous physique, those sharp eyes accentuated by his aquiline nose, but at least there was some colour in his skin and everything about his voice and manner pronounced him to be very much his old self[18].

He had greeted me warmly[19], and as I took my place opposite him, I felt the strange sensation that I was awakening from a dream. It was as if the last two years had never happened, that I had never met my beloved Mary, married her and moved to our

1. malgré le désordre
2. consentement par retour de courrier
3. clientèle
4. comptais
5. veiller sur
6. rétabli
7. s'était laissé mourir de faim
8. vindicatif
9. Scotland Yard
10. inquiet de
11. la grande fatigue que Holmes s'était infligée
12. [petits pains ronds pris à l'heure du thé]
13. miel de violettes
14. un quatre-quarts
15. en bonne voie de guérison
16. robe de chambre
17. maigre
18. confirmait qu'il était redevenu lui-même
19. m'avait accueilli avec chaleur

home in Kensington, purchased with the proceeds[1] of the Agra pearls. I could have still been a bachelor[2], living here with Holmes, sharing with him the excitement of the chase and the unravelling of[3] yet another mystery[4].

And it occurred to me that he might well have preferred it thus[5]. Holmes spoke seldom[6] about my domestic arrangements[7]. He had been abroad[8] at the time of my wedding[9] and it had occurred to me then that it might not have been entirely a coincidence. It would be unfair to say that the entire subject of my marriage was forbidden, but there was an unspoken agreement[10] that we would not discuss it at any length[11]. My happiness and contentment were evident to Holmes, and he was generous enough not to begrudge it[12]. When I had first arrived, he had asked after[13] Mrs Watson. But he had not requested any further information and I had certainly provided none, making his remarks all the more unfathomable[14].

'You look at me as if I were a conjuror[15],' Holmes remarked, with a laugh. 'I take it[16] you have given up on the works[17] of Edgar Allan Poe?'

'You mean his detective, Dupin?' I said.

'He used a method which he termed[18] ratiocination[19]. In his view, it was possible to read a person's innermost thoughts[20] without their even needing to speak. It could all be done from a simple study of their movements, by the very flicker of an eyebrow[21]. The idea impressed me greatly at the time but I seem to recall that you were somewhat scornful[22]—'

'And doubtless I will pay for it now,' I concurred[23]. 'But are you seriously telling me, Holmes, that you could deduce the sickness of a child you have never met, simply from my behaviour over a plate of scones?'

1. acquis grâce au produit de la vente
2. célibataire
3. de poursuivre et de démêler
4. un mystère de plus
5. qu'il aurait sans doute préféré que ce soit le cas
6. rarement
7. ma vie familiale
8. à l'étranger
9. mariage
10. accord tacite
11. n'en parlerions pas longuement
12. pour ne pas m'en vouloir
13. s'était enquis de
14. d'autant plus énigmatiques
15. comme si j'étais illusionniste
16. suppose que
17. renoncé à lire les œuvres
18. qu'il appelait
19. [raisonnement subtil]
20. les pensées les plus profondes
21. un simple mouvement de sourcil
22. quelque peu méprisant
23. renchéris-je

'That and rather more,' Holmes replied. 'I can tell that you have just returned from Holborn Viaduct. That you left your house in a hurry, but even so missed[1] the train. Perhaps the fact that you are currently[2] without a servant girl is to blame[3].'

'No, Holmes!' I cried. 'I will not have it![4]'

'I am wrong?'

'No. You are correct on every count[5]. But how is it possible ... ?'

'It is a simple matter of observation and deduction, the one informing the other[6]. Were I to[7] explain it to you, it would all seem painfully childish[8].'

'And yet I must insist that you do just[9] that.'

'Well, since you have been so good as to pay me this visit, I suppose I must oblige[10],' returned Holmes with a yawn[11]. 'Let us begin with the circumstance that brings you here. If my memory serves[12], we are approaching the second anniversary of your marriage, are we not?'

'Indeed so, Holmes. It is the day after tomorrow.'

'An unusual time then, for you to separate from your wife. As you yourself said just now, the fact that you have chosen to stay with me, and for a prolonged period of time, would suggest that there was a compelling[13] reason for her to part company with you. And what might that be? As I recall, Miss Mary Morstan – as she once was[14] – came to England from India and had no friends or family here. She was taken on as a governess[15], looking after the son of one Mrs Cecil Forrester, in Camberwell, which is of course how you met her. Mrs Forrester was very good to her, particularly in her time of need[16], and I would imagine that the two of them have remained close[17].'

'That is indeed[18] the case.'

'And so, if anyone were likely to call[19] your wife away from home[20], it might well be her[21]. I wonder then what reason might lie behind[22] such a

1. mais que malgré tout, vous avez raté
2. actuellement
3. en est la cause
4. Ça ne se passera pas comme ça !
5. à tous points de vues
6. l'une nourrissant l'autre
7. Si je devais
8. terriblement enfantin
9. précisément
10. que je vous dois bien ça
11. en bâillant
12. est bonne
13. impérieuse
14. de son nom de jeune fille
15. engagée comme gouvernante
16. dans les moments difficiles
17. sont restées proches
18. effectivement
19. s'il est une personne pour laquelle
20. votre épouse s'absenterait
21. c'est bien elle
22. pourrait motiver

summons[1], and in this cold weather the sickness of a child springs instantly to mind[2]. It would, I am sure, be very comforting for the afflicted lad[3] to have his old governess back.'

'His name is Richard and he is nine years old,' I concurred. 'But how can you be so confident[4] that it is influenza and not something altogether more serious[5]?'

'Were it more serious, you would surely have insisted upon attending yourself[6].'

'Your reasoning has so far been utterly straightforward[7] in every respect,' I said. 'But it does not explain how you knew that my thoughts had turned towards them[8] at that precise moment.'

'You will forgive me if I say that you are to me as an open book[9], my dear Watson, and that with every movement, you turn another page. As you sat there sipping[10] your tea, I noticed your eye drift[11] towards the newspaper on the table right beside you[12]. You glanced at the headline[13] and then reached out[14] and turned it face down[15]. Why? It was perhaps the report on the train crash[16] at Norton Fitzwarren a few weeks ago that disturbed you[17]. The first findings of the investigation into the deaths[18] of ten passengers were published today and it was, of course, the last thing you would wish to read just after leaving your wife at a station.'

'That did indeed remind me of[19] her journey[20],' I agreed. 'But the sickness of the child?'

'From the newspaper, your attention turned to the patch of carpet[21] beside the desk and I distinctly saw you smile to yourself. It was there, of course, that you once kept your medicine bag[22] and it was surely that association that reminded you of the reason for your wife's visit.'

'This is all guesswork[23], Holmes,' I insisted. 'You say Holborn Viaduct, for example. It could have been any station in London.'

1. un appel si pressant
2. vient immédiatement à l'esprit
3. le gamin malade
4. si sûr
5. de beaucoup plus grave
6. pour vous en occuper vous-même
7. remarquablement clair
8. je pensais à eux
9. je lis en vous comme dans un livre
10. à boire
11. votre regard glisser
12. juste à côté de vous
13. le gros titre
14. avez tendu le bras
15. pour le retourner
16. l'article sur l'accident de train
17. qui vous a affecté
18. découvertes de l'enquête sur la mort
19. m'a en effet rappelé
20. voyage
21. vers cet endroit du tapis
22. que vous laissiez votre sacoche de médecin
23. Il ne s'agit que d'hypothèses

'You know that I deplore guesswork. It is sometimes necessary to connect points of evidence[1] with the use of imagination, but that is not at all the same thing. Mrs Forrester lives in Camberwell. The London Chatham and Dover Railway has regular departures from Holborn Viaduct. I would have considered that the logical starting point, even if you had not obliged me by leaving[2] your own suitcase by the door. From where I am sitting, I can clearly see a label[3] from the Holborn Viaduct Left Luggage Office[4] attached to the handle[5].'

'And the rest of it?'

'The fact that you have lost your maid[6] and that you left the house in a hurry? The smudge of black polish[7] on the side of your left cuff[8] clearly indicates both. You cleaned your own shoes and you did so rather carelessly[9]. Moreover, in your haste[10], you forgot your gloves[11]—'

'Mrs Hudson took my coat from me. She could also have taken my gloves.'

'In which case[12], when we shook hands, why would yours have been[13] so cold? No, Watson, your entire bearing speaks of[14] disorganisation and disarray[15].'

'Everything you say is right,' I admitted. 'But one last mystery, Holmes. How can you be so sure that my wife missed her train?'

'As soon as you arrived, I noticed a strong scent[16] of coffee on your clothes. Why would you be drinking coffee immediately before coming to me for tea? The inference is[17] that you missed your train and were forced to stay with your wife for longer than you had intended[18]. You stowed your case[19] at the left luggage office and went with her to a coffee house. Might it have been Lockhart's? I'm told the coffee there is particularly good.'

There was a short silence and then I burst into laughter. 'Well, Holmes,' I said, 'I can see that I had

1. des éléments de preuve
2. ne m'aviez aidé en laissant
3. étiquette
4. la consigne
5. poignée
6. bonne
7. trace de cirage noir
8. manchette gauche
9. à la va-vite
10. dans votre hâte
11. gants
12. Mais alors
13. la vôtre était-elle
14. toute votre apparence dénote
15. la confusion
16. odeur
17. J'en déduis que
18. plus longtemps que prévu
19. avez entreposé votre valise

no reason to worry about your health. You are as remarkable as ever.'

'It was quite elementary,' returned[1] the detective with a languid[2] gesture of one hand. 'But perhaps something of greater interest now approaches. Unless I am mistaken[3], that is the front door ...'

Sure enough[4], Mrs Hudson came in once again, this time ushering in[5] a man who walked into the room as if he were making an entrance on the London stage[6]. He was formally dressed[7] in a dark tail coat[8], wing collar[9] and white bow tie[10] with a black cloak[11] around his shoulders, waistcoat[12], gloves and patent leather[13] shoes. In one hand he held a pair of white gloves and in the other a rosewood walking stick[14] with a silver tip and handle[15]. His dark hair was surprisingly long, sweeping back over a high forehead[16] and he had neither beard nor moustache. His skin was pale, his face a little too elongated to be truly handsome[17]. His age, I would have said, would have been in the mid-thirties[18] and yet the seriousness of his demeanour[19], his evident discomfort at finding himself here, made him appear older. He reminded me at once of some of the patients who had consulted me; the ones who had refused to believe they were unwell[20] until their symptoms persuaded them otherwise[21]. They were always the most gravely ill. Our visitor stood before us with equal reluctance[22]. He waited in the doorway, looking anxiously around him, while Mrs Hudson handed Holmes his card.

'Mr Carstairs,' Holmes said. 'Please take a seat.'

'You must forgive me arriving in this manner ... unexpected and unannounced.' He had a clipped, rather dry way of speaking[23]. His eyes still did not quite meet our gaze[24]. 'In truth, I had no intention of coming here at all. I live in Wimbledon, close to the green[25], and have come into town[26] for the opera – not that I'm in any mood for[27] Wagner. I have

1. riposta
2. indolent
3. Sauf erreur de ma part
4. Et en effet
5. faisant entrer
6. la scène londonienne
7. en tenue de soirée,
8. vêtu d'une queue-de-pie
9. d'un col cassé
10. d'un nœud papillon blanc
11. une cape noire
12. un gilet
13. en cuir verni
14. canne en bois de rose
15. avec embout et poignée en argent
16. repoussés à l'arrière d'un front haut
17. réellement beau
18. dans les 35 ans
19. attitude
20. souffrants
21. ne les persuadent du contraire
22. la même réticence
23. un débit saccadé
24. ne croisaient pas vraiment notre regard
25. près de la pelouse du village
26. à Londres
27. d'humeur à apprécier

just come from my club where I met with my accountant[1], a man I have known for many years and whom I now consider a friend. When I told him of the troubles I have been having, the sense of oppression that is making my life so damnably difficult, he mentioned your name and urged me[2] to consult you. By coincidence, my club is not far from here and so I resolved to come straight[3] from him to you.'

'I am happy to give you my full attention,' Holmes said.

'And this gentleman?' Our visitor turned to me.

'Dr John Watson. He is my closest adviser[4], and I can assure you that anything you have to say to me can be uttered[5] in his presence.'

'Very well. My name, as you see, is Edmund Carstairs and I am, by profession, a dealer in fine art[6]. I have a gallery, Carstairs and Finch on Albemarle Street, which has been in business now for six years. We specialise in the works[7] of the great masters, mainly from the end of last century and the early years of this present one: Gainsborough, Reynolds, Constable and Turner. Their paintings will be familiar to you, I am sure, and they command the very highest prices[8]. Only this week I sold two Van Dyck portraits to a private client for the sum of £25,000. Our business is a successful one and we have flourished[9], even with so many new – and I might say, inferior[10] – galleries sprouting[11] in all the streets around us. Over the years[12] we have built for ourselves[13] a reputation for sobriety and reliability[14]. Our clients include many members of the aristocracy and we have seen our works hung[15] in some of the finest mansions[16] in the country.'

'Your partner[17], Mr Finch?'

'Tobias Finch is rather older than myself, although we are equal[18] partners. If there is one disagreement between us it is that he is more cautious[19] and conservative[20] than I. For example, I have a strong

1. comptable
2. m'a vivement conseillé
3. j'ai décidé de venir directement
4. C'est mon plus proche conseiller
5. dit
6. marchand d'art
7. les œuvres
8. se vendent aux prix les plus élevés
9. prospéré
10. de second ordre
11. qui fleurissent
12. Au fil des ans,
13. nous nous sommes forgé
14. de sérieux et de fiabilité
15. exposés
16. plus belles demeures
17. associé
18. à parts égales
19. prudent
20. classique

interest in some of the new work coming in from the Continent. I refer to the painters who have become known as the *impressionistes*, such artists as Monet and Degas. Only a week ago I was offered a seaside scene[1] by Pissaro which I thought to be quite delightful and full of colour. My partner, alas, took the opposite view[2]. He insists that such works are little more than a blur[3], and although it is indeed the case that some of the shapes are indistinguishable at short range[4], I cannot persuade him that he is missing the point[5]. However, I will not tire you gentlemen with a lecture on art[6]. We are a traditional gallery and that, for now[7], is what we shall remain.'

Holmes nodded. 'Pray continue.[8]'

'Mr Holmes, two weeks ago I realised that I was being watched[9]. Ridgeway Hall, which is the name of my home, stands on one side of a narrow lane[10], with a cluster of almshouses[11] some distance away at the end. These are our closest neighbours. We are surrounded by common land[12], and from my dressing room I have a view of the village green[13]. It was here, on a Tuesday morning, that I became aware of[14] a man standing with his legs apart and his arms folded[15] – and I was struck at once by his extraordinary stillness[16]. He was too far away for me to be able to see him clearly, but I would have said that he was a foreigner[17]. He was wearing a long frock coat with padded shoulders[18] of a cut that was most certainly not English. Indeed, I was in America last year and if I were to guess I would say it was from this country that he had originated. What struck me most forcefully, however, for reasons that I will shortly explain, was that he was also wearing a hat, a flat cap[19] of the sort that is sometimes called a cheesecutter[20].

'It was this and the way that he stood there that first attracted my attention and so unnerved me[21]. If he had been a scarecrow[22], I swear he could not

1. une scène de bord de mer
2. fut d'avis contraire
3. ne sont que des images floues
4. vues de près
5. qu'il ne comprend pas de quoi il est question
6. une conférence sur l'art
7. pour l'instant
8. Je vous en prie, continuez.
9. surveillé
10. une petite rue étroite
11. un ensemble d'hospices
12. entourés de terrains communaux
13. la grande pelouse du village
14. j'ai aperçu
15. jambes écartées et bras croisés
16. immobilité
17. étranger
18. redingote à épaulettes
19. casquette
20. [casquette d'ouvrier]
21. m'a mis si mal à l'aise
22. épouvantail

have been more static. There was a light rain falling, swept by the breeze[1] across the common, but he didn't seem to notice it. His eyes were fixed on my window. I can tell you that they were very dark and that they seemed to be boring into me[2]. I gazed at him for at least a minute, perhaps longer, then went down to breakfast. However, before I ate, I sent the scullery boy[3] out to see if the man was still there. He was not. The boy reported back[4] that the green was empty.'

'A singular occurrence[5],' Holmes remarked. 'But Ridgeway Hall is, I am sure, a fine building. And a visitor to this country might well have found it merited his examination.'

'And so I told myself[6]. But a few days later, I saw him a second time. On this occasion, I was in London. My wife and I had just come out[7] of the theatre – we'd been to the Savoy – and there he was, on the other side of the road, wearing the same coat, again with the flat cap. I might not have noticed him, Mr Holmes, but, as before, he was unmoving and with the crowds passing round on either side of him[8]; he could have been a solid rock in a fast-flowing river[9]. I'm afraid I was unable to see him clearly, however, for although he had chosen a position in the full glow of a street lamp[10], it had thrown a shadow across[11] his face and acted like a veil[12]. Though perhaps that was his intent[13].'

'But you were sure it was the same man?'

'There could be no doubt of it.'

'Did your wife see him?'

'No. And I did not wish to alarm her by making any mention of it. We had a hansom waiting[14] and we left at once.'

'This is most interesting,' Holmes remarked. 'The behaviour of this man makes no sense at all[15]. He stands in the middle of a village green and beneath a street lamp. On the one hand[16], it's as if he is mak-

1. balayée par la brise
2. me transpercer
3. garçon de cuisine
4. En rentrant, le garçon m'a indiqué
5. Étrange
6. c'est ce que je me suis dit
7. sortions tout juste
8. la foule le contournait de chaque côté
9. une rivière à fort courant
10. bien éclairée par un réverbère
11. l'ombre de celui-ci voilait
12. le masquait
13. qu'il l'avait fait exprès
14. Un fiacre nous attendait
15. n'a aucun sens
16. D'un côté

ing every effort to be seen. And yet[1] he makes no attempt to approach you.'

'He did approach me,' Carstairs replied. 'The very next day[2], in fact, when I returned early to the house. My friend, Finch, was in the gallery, cataloguing a collection of drawings and etchings[3] by Samuel Scott[4]. He had no need of me and I was still uneasy after the two sightings[5]. I arrived back at Ridgeway Hall shortly before three o'clock – and it was just as well that I did[6], for there was the rogue[7], approaching my front door[8]. I called out to him[9] and he turned and saw me. At once, he began to run towards me and I was sure that he was about to strike me[10] and even lifted my walking stick to protect myself. But his mission was not one of violence. He came straight up to me[11] and for the first time I saw his face: thin lips, dark brown eyes and a livid[12] scar[13] on his right cheek, the result of a recent bullet wound. He had been drinking spirits[14] – I could smell them on his breath[15]. He didn't utter a word to me but instead lifted a note into the air and pressed it into my hand[16]. Then, before I could stop him, he ran off[17].'

'And the note?' Holmes asked.

'I have it here.'

The art dealer produced a square of paper, folded into four[18], and handed it to Holmes. Holmes opened it carefully. 'My glass, if you please, Watson.' As I handed him the magnifying glass[19], he turned to Carstairs. 'There was no envelope?'

'No.'

'I find that of the greatest significance[20]. But let us see ...'

There were just six words written in block capitals[21] on the page.

ST MARY'S CHURCH. TOMORROW. MIDDAY.

'The paper is English,' Holmes remarked. 'Even if the visitor was not. You notice that he writes in

1. Et pourtant,
2. Dès le lendemain
3. de gravures à l'eau-forte
4. [peintre du XVIIIe s. célèbre pour ses vues de la Tamise]
5. perturbé par ces deux apparitions
6. heureusement, d'ailleurs
7. cette fripouille
8. s'avançant vers ma porte d'entrée
9. Je l'ai interpellé
10. sur le point de me frapper
11. jusqu'à moi
12. noirâtre
13. cicatrice
14. de l'alcool
15. haleine
16. me l'a fourré dans la main
17. a décampé
18. plié en quatre
19. la loupe
20. c'est extrêmement important
21. en majuscules

capitals, Watson. What do you suggest his purpose might be?[1]'

'To disguise his handwriting[2],' I said.

'It is possible. Although since the man[3] had never written to Mr Carstairs, and is perhaps unlikely to[4] write to him again, you would have thought his handwriting would have been of no consequence. Was the message folded when it was handed to you[5], Mr Carstairs?'

'No. I think not. I folded it myself later.'

'The picture becomes clearer by the minute[6]. This church that he refers to[7], St Mary's. I assume[8] it is in Wimbledon?'

'It is on Hothouse Lane,' Carstairs replied. 'Just a few minutes' walk[9] from my home.'

'This behaviour is also lacking in logic[10], do you not think? The man wishes to speak with you. He places a message to that effect in your hand. But he does not speak. He does not utter a word.'

'My guess was that he wished to talk to me alone. And as it happened,[11] my wife, Catherine, emerged[12] from the house a few moments later. She had been standing in the breakfast room which looks out onto the drive[13] and she had seen what had just occurred[14]. "Who was that?" she asked.

' "I have no idea," I replied.

' "What did he want?"

'I showed her the note. "It's someone wanting money," she said. "I saw him out of the window just now[15] – a rough-looking fellow[16]. There were gypsies[17] on the common last week. He must have been one of them. Edmund, you mustn't go."

' "You need not concern yourself[18], my dear," I replied. "I have no intention of meeting with him." '

'You reassured your wife,' Holmes murmured. 'But you went to the church at the appointed time[19].'

'I did exactly that – and carried a revolver with me. He wasn't there. The church is not well at-

1. Pourquoi, à votre avis ?
2. Pour déguiser son écriture
3. puisque cet homme
4. ne va sans doute pas
5. lorsqu'il vous a été remis
6. à chaque minute
7. dont il parle
8. Je suppose
9. à quelques minutes à pied
10. manque également de logique
11. Or il se trouve que,
12. est sortie
13. qui donne sur l'allée
14. ce qui venait de se passer
15. à l'instant même
16. un type aux airs de voyou
17. des romanichels
18. Inutile de vous inquiéter
19. à l'heure dite

tended[1] and it was unpleasantly cold. I paced the flagstones[2] for an hour and then I came home. I have heard no more from him since, and I have not seen him again, but I have been unable to get him out of my mind[3].'

'The man is known to you[4],' Holmes said.

'Yes, Mr Holmes. You go right to the heart of it.[5] I do believe I know the identity of this individual, although I confess I do not quite see[6] the reasoning that has brought you to that conclusion.'

'It strikes me as self-evident[7],' Holmes replied. 'You have seen him only three times. He has asked for a meeting but failed to show up[8]. Nothing that you have described would suggest that this man is any threat to you[9], but you began by telling us of the sense of trouble and oppression that has brought you here[10] and would not even meet him without carrying a gun[11]. And you still have not told us the significance of the flat cap.'

'I know who he is. I know what he wants. I am appalled that he has followed me[12] to England.'

'From America?'

'Yes.'

'Mr Carstairs, your story is full of interest and if you have time before your opera begins, or perhaps if you will agree to forgo the overture[13], I think you should give us the complete history of this affair. You mentioned that you were in America a year ago. Was this when you met the man in the flat cap?'

'I never met him. But it was on his account[14] that I was there.'

'Then you will not object[15] if I fill[16] my pipe? No? So take us back with you[17] and tell us of your business[18] on the other side of the Atlantic. An art dealer is not the sort of man to make enemies, I would have thought. But you seem to have done just that[19].

1. n'est pas très fréquentée
2. J'ai arpenté le dallage
3. me le sortir de la tête
4. Vous connaissez cet homme
5. Vous allez droit à l'essentiel.
6. que je ne vois pas bien
7. Cela va de soi, il me semble
8. n'y est pas venu
9. vous menace de quelque façon que ce soit
10. qui vous a conduit ici
11. sans arme sur vous
12. horrifié à l'idée qu'il m'ait suivi
13. de renoncer à l'ouverture
14. à cause de lui
15. ne verrez pas d'inconvénient
16. à ce que je bourre
17. accordez-nous un retour en arrière
18. ce que vous alliez faire
19. on dirait que c'est précisément ce que vous avez fait

1. ennemi
2. je voudrais tant ne jamais avoir entendu
3. babouche
4. rangeait son tabac
5. prenait sa respiration
6. et voici l'histoire

'Indeed so. My foeman[1] is called Keelan O'Donaghue and I wish to Heaven that I had never heard[2] the name.'

Holmes reached for the Persian slipper[3] where he kept his tobacco[4] and began to fill his pipe. Meanwhile, Edmund Carstairs drew a breath[5] and this is the tale[6] that he told.

TWO

The Flat Cap Gang

'Eighteen months ago, I was introduced to a quite extraordinary man by the name of[1] Cornelius Stillman who was in London at the end of a lengthy European tour[2]. His home was on the East Coast[3] of America and he was what is termed a Boston Brahmin[4], which is to say that he belonged to one of their most elevated[5] and honoured families. He had made a fortune from the Calumet and Hecla mines and had also invested in the railroads[6] and the telephone companies. In his youth[7], he had apparently had ambitions to become an artist and part of the reason for his visit was to experience the[8] museums and galleries of Paris, Florence, Rome and London.

'Like many wealthy[9] Americans, he was imbued with a[10] sense of civic responsibility that did him great credit[11]. He had purchased land in the Back Bay area of Boston and had already begun work on the construction of an art gallery which he called The Parthenon and which he planned to fill with the finest works of art, purchased on his travels. I met him at a dinner party and found him to be a huge volcano of a man, brimming with energy[12] and enthusiasm. He was rather old-fashioned in his dress[13], bearded and affecting[14] a monocle, but he proved to be remarkably well informed[15], fluent in[16] French and Italian with a smattering[17] of ancient Greek. His knowledge of art[18], his aesthetic sensibility[19], also

1. appelé
2. à l'issue d'un tour d'Europe prolongé
3. Il résidait sur la côte est
4. « brahmane de Boston »
5. du plus haut rang
6. chemins de fer
7. jeunesse
8. d'aller à la découverte des
9. fortunés
10. avait un grand
11. qui était tout à son honneur
12. débordant d'énergie
13. Ses tenues étaient un peu désuètes
14. il était barbu et portait
15. cultivé
16. parlant couramment le
17. et ayant quelques notions
18. Sa connaissance de l'art
19. sens de l'esthétique

set him apart from many of his fellow citizens[1]. Do not think of me as unnecessarily chauvinistic[2], Mr Holmes. He himself told me of the many shortcomings[3] of the cultural life to which he had become accustomed[4] as he grew up[5] – how great paintings had been exhibited next to freaks of nature[6] such as mermaids[7] and dwarves[8]. He had seen Shakespeare performed[9] with interludes by tightrope walkers[10] and contortionists. Such was the way of things in Boston at the time. The Parthenon would be different, he said. It would, as its name implied, be a temple to art[11] and to civilisation.

'I was overjoyed when Mr Stillman agreed to come to my gallery in Albemarle Street. Mr Finch and I spent many hours in his company, taking him through[12] our catalogue and showing him some of the purchases[13] we had recently made in auctions[14] around the country. The long and the short of it was that[15] he bought from us works by Romney, Stubbs and Lawrence but also a series of four landscapes[16] by John Constable which were quite the pride of our collection. These were views of the Lake District, painted in 1806, and unlike anything else in the artist's canon[17]. They had a profundity of mood and spirit that was remarkable, and Mr Stillman promised they would be exhibited in a large and well-lit room that he would design specifically for them. We parted[18] on excellent terms. And in view of what happened, I should add that I banked[19] a substantial sum of money. Indeed, Mr Finch remarked that this was undoubtedly the most successful transaction of our lives.

'It now only remained to send the works to Boston. They were carefully wrapped, placed in a crate[20] and dispatched with[21] the White Star Line from Liverpool to New York. By one of those twists of fate that mean nothing at the time but which will later return to haunt you[22], we had intended to send them

1. le distinguaient de nombre de ses compatriotes
2. chauvin
3. nombreux défauts
4. il s'était habitué
5. en grandissant
6. de phénomènes de foire
7. des sirènes
8. des nains
9. des représentations de Shakespeare
10. avec, en intermède, des équilibristes
11. un temple voué à l'art
12. à lui faire découvrir tout
13. acquisitions
14. dans des ventes aux enchères
15. Enfin bref,
16. paysages
17. très différentes des autres œuvres de l'artiste
18. Nous nous sommes quittés
19. j'ai encaissé
20. emballées, placées dans une caisse
21. par
22. vous tarauder

directly to Boston. The RMS *Adventurer* made that journey but we missed it by a matter of hours[1] and so chose another vessel[2]. Our agent, a bright[3] young man by the name of James Devoy, met the package[4] in New York and travelled with it on the Boston and Albany Railroad – a journey[5] of one hundred and ninety miles.

'But the paintings never arrived.

'There were, in Boston at this time, a number of gangs, operating particularly in the south of the city, in Charlestown and Somersville. Many of them had fanciful names[6] such as the Dead Rabbits and the Forty Thieves[7] and had come originally[8] from Ireland. It is sad to think that, having been welcomed into that great country, their return to it should have been[9] lawlessness[10] and violence, but such was the case and the police had been unable to restrain them or bring them to justice[11]. One of the most active and most dangerous groups was known as the Flat Cap Gang, headed by a pair of Irish twins[12] – Rourke and Keelan O'Donaghue, originally from Belfast. I will describe these two devils to you as best as I can, because they are central[13] to my narrative.

'The two of them were never seen apart[14]. Although they were identical when they were born, Rourke was the larger of the two, square-shouldered and barrel-chested[15] with heavy fists[16] that he was always ready to use in a fight[17]. It is said that he beat a man to death[18] in a game of cards when he was barely sixteen[19]. By contrast, his twin stood very much in his shadow, smaller and quieter. Indeed, he seldom spoke at all – there were rumours that he was unable to. Rourke was bearded, Keelan clean-shaven[20]. Both wore flat caps and it was this that gave the gang its name. It was also widely believed that they carried each other's initials[21], tattooed[22] on their arms, and that in every aspect of their lives they were inseparable.

1. de quelques heures
2. navire
3. intelligent
4. récupéra le paquet
5. trajet
6. des noms farfelus
7. les Lapins morts et les Quarante Voleurs
8. étaient originaires
9. ils ne lui donnent en retour que
10. l'anarchie
11. de les maîtriser ni de les traduire en justice
12. dirigé par deux jumeaux irlandais
13. ce sont des personnages clés
14. inséparables
15. les épaules carrées et le torse puissant
16. des poings massifs
17. dans une bagarre
18. Il paraît qu'il a battu un type à mort
19. alors qu'il avait à peine 16 ans
20. rasé de près
21. chacun avait les initiales de l'autre
22. tatouées

'Of the other gang members, their names tell you perhaps as much as you would wish to know about them[1]. There was Frank "Mad Dog" Kelly and Patrick "Razors" Maclean. Another was known as "The Ghost" and was feared as much[2] as any supernatural being[3]. They were involved[4] in every conceivable form of street crime, robberies, burglaries[5] and protectionism[6]. And yet, at the same time, they were held in high regard by[7] many of the poorer inhabitants of Boston who seemed unable to recognise them as the foul pestilence[8] that they undoubtedly were to the community. They were the underdogs, waging war on an uncaring system[9]. I need hardly point out to you that twins have appeared in mythology since the very dawn[10] of civilisation. There are Romulus and Remus, Apollo[11] and Artemis and Castor and Pollux, for ever[12] immortalised as Gemini[13] in the night sky. Something of this attached itself to the O'Donaghues. There was a belief that they would never be caught, that they could get away with anything[14].

'I knew nothing about the Flat Cap Gang – I had never even heard of them – when I sent off the paintings at Liverpool but somehow, at exactly the same time, they were tipped off[15] that a large amount of currency[16] was about to be transferred from the American Bank Note Company in New York to the Massachusetts First National Bank in Boston a few days hence[17]. The sum in question was said to be one hundred thousand dollars and it was travelling on the Boston and Albany Railroad. Some say that Rourke was the brains[18] behind their operation. Others believe that Keelan was the more natural mastermind of the two[19]. In any event, between them[20] they arrived at the idea of holding up[21] the train before it could reach the city and making off[22] with the cash.

1. sont sans doute suffisamment évocateurs
2. aussi redouté
3. qu'une créature surnaturelle
4. impliqués
5. vols, cambriolages
6. racket
7. très estimés de
8. de voir en eux cet ignoble fléau
9. opprimés, en guerre contre un système indifférent
10. dès l'aube
11. Apollon
12. à jamais
13. les Gémeaux
14. tout se permettre
15. avertis
16. devises
17. quelques jours plus tard
18. le cerveau
19. des deux, c'était Keelan l'organisateur-né
20. à eux deux,
21. d'attaquer
22. de partir

'Train robberies were still prevalent[1] in the western frontiers of America, in California and Arizona, but for such a thing to take place[2] on the more developed eastern seaboard[3] was almost inconceivable and that is why the train left the Grand Central Terminal in New York with only one armed guard stationed in the mail car[4]. The banknotes were contained in a safe[5]. And by some wretched chance[6], the paintings were still in their crate, travelling in the same compartment. Our agent, James Devoy, was travelling in second class. He was always assiduous in his duties[7] and had taken a seat as close to the mail car as possible.

'The Flat Cap Gang had chosen an area just outside Pittsfield for the attempted raid. Here, the track climbed steeply upwards[8] before crossing the Connecticut River. There was a tunnel that ran for[9] two thousand feet and, according to railway regulations[10], the engineer was obliged to test his brakes at the exit[11]. The train was therefore travelling very slowly as it emerged and it was a simple matter for Rourke and Keelan O'Donaghue to jump down onto the roof[12] of one of the wagons. From here, they climbed over[13] the tender[14] and, to the astonishment of the driver and his brakeman[15], they suddenly appeared in the engine cab[16] with guns drawn[17].

'They ordered the train to come to a halt in a forest clearing[18]. They were surrounded by white pine trees that soared up[19] all around, forming a natural screen[20] behind which they might commit their crime. Kelly, Maclean and all the other members of the gang were waiting with horses – and with dynamite which they had stolen from a construction site. All of them were armed. The train drew in[21] and Rourke struck the driver with the side of his revolver, concussing him[22]. Keelan, who had not uttered a word, produced some rope and tied[23] the brakeman to a metal stanchion[24]. Meanwhile, the

1. monnaie courante
2. de là à ce qu'il y en ait un
3. la côte est
4. wagon postal
5. les billets étaient enfermés dans un coffre-fort
6. par un malheureux hasard
7. consciencieux dans son travail
8. les rails remontaient en pente raide
9. de
10. règlement
11. vérifier ses freins à la sortie
12. de sauter sur le toit
13. ils escaladèrent
14. [wagon avec réserve de charbon et d'eau]
15. garde-frein
16. cabine de conduite
17. les armes à la main
18. de stopper dans une clairière
19. se dressaient
20. écran
21. s'arrêta
22. le laissant assommé
23. sortit de la corde et ligota
24. à un montant métallique

rest of the gang had boarded[1] the train. Ordering the passengers to remain seated, they approached the mail car and began to set charges[2] around the door.

'James Devoy had seen what was happening and was in despair of the consequences[3]. He must have guessed that the robbers were here for reasons other than[4] the Constables. After all, very few people[5] knew of their existence, and even if they'd had the wit or the education[6] to recognise the work of an Old Master[7], there would have been no one to whom the paintings could be sold[8]. While the other passengers cowered[9] all around him, Devoy left his seat and climbed down, meaning to plead with[10] the gang. At least, I assume that was his intention. Before he could say a word, Rourke O'Donaghue turned on him and gunned him down[11]. Devoy was shot three times in the chest[12] and died in a pool of his own blood[13].

'Inside the mail car, the security guard had heard the shots and I can only imagine the terror he must have felt as he heard the gang members operating outside. Would he have unlocked the door if they had demanded it? We will never know. A moment later, a huge explosion rent the air[14] and the entire wall of the carriage was blown apart[15]. The guard was killed instantly. The safe with the money was exposed.

'A second, smaller charge sufficed to open it and now the band discovered that they had been misinformed. Only two thousand dollars had been sent to the Massachusetts First National Bank, a fortune perhaps to these vagabonds, but immeasurably less[16] than they had hoped for[17] and expected. Even so, they snatched up the notes[18] with whoops[19] and cries of exaltation, not caring that they had left two men dead behind them and unaware that their explosives had utterly destroyed[20] four

1. étaient montés dans
2. à installer des charges explosives
3. désespéré à l'idée des conséquences
4. n'étaient pas venus pour
5. très peu de gens
6. l'intelligence et la culture
7. grand peintre
8. à qui vendre les toiles
9. tremblaient dans leur coin
10. dans l'intention d'aller implorer
11. l'abattit
12. poitrine
13. en baignant dans son sang
14. retentit
15. wagon fut déchiqueté par le souffle
16. infiniment moins
17. qu'ils ne l'avaient espéré
18. s'emparèrent des billets
19. des cris de joie
20. totalement détruit

canvases[1] which alone were worth[2] twenty times what they had taken. These, and the other works, were and are an incalculable loss[3] to British culture. Even now I have to remind myself that a young and dutiful man died that day, but I would be lying to you if I did not say that, shameful to admit[4], I mourn the loss[5] of those paintings just as much.

'My friend, Finch, and I heard the news with horror. At first we were led to believe[6] that the paintings had been stolen and would have preferred it had this been the case, for at least the works would still have been appreciated by someone and there was always a chance that they might be recovered[7]. But such an unhappy accident of timing, wanton vandalism in pursuit of a handful of cash[8]! How bitterly we regretted the route we had chosen[9] and blamed ourselves for[10] what had occurred. There were also financial considerations[11]. Mr Stillman had paid a large deposit[12] for the paintings but, according to the contract[13], we were entirely responsible for them until they were delivered into his hands[14]. It was fortunate that[15] we were insured with Lloyd's of London or else we would have been wiped out[16], as eventually[17] I would have no choice but to repay[18] the money. There was also the matter of James Devoy's family. I now learned that he had a wife and a young child. Someone would have to take care of them.

'It was for these reasons that I resolved to travel to America and I left England almost at once, arriving first in New York. I met Mrs Devoy and promised her that she would receive some compensation[19]. Her son was nine years old and a sweeter[20], more good-looking child would be hard to imagine. I then travelled to Boston and from there to Providence, where Cornelius Stillman had built his summer house. I have to say that even the many hours I had spent in the company of the man had failed

1. toiles
2. qui valaient à elles seules
3. restent une perte inestimable
4. même si j'ai honte de l'admettre
5. je pleure la perte
6. tout nous porta à croire
7. l'on puisse les retrouver
8. ce vandalisme gratuit pour une poignée de billets
9. Nous avons amèrement regretté d'avoir choisi ce trajet
10. nous nous sommes reproché
11. les aspects financiers
12. un acompte considérable
13. selon le contrat
14. lui soient livrées en mains propres
15. Heureusement,
16. nous aurions tout perdu
17. en définitive
18. rembourser
19. des indemnités
20. plus gentil

to prepare me for the spectacle that met[1] my eyes. Shepherd's Point was huge, constructed in the style of a French chateau by the celebrated architect Richard Morris Hunt. The gardens alone[2] stretched out for[3] thirty acres[4] and the interior displayed an opulence beyond[5] anything I could have imagined. Stillman himself insisted on showing me round[6], and it is a journey[7] I will never forget. The magnificent wooden staircase[8] that dominated the Great Hall, the library[9] with its five thousand volumes, the chess set[10] that had once belonged to Frederick the Great, the chapel with its ancient organ once played by[11] Purcell ... by the time we reached the basement[12] with its swimming pool and bowling alley[13], I was quite exhausted[14]. And as for the art[15]! Well, I counted works by Titian, Rembrandt and Velasquez, and this before I had even reached the drawing room[16]. And it was while I was considering all this wealth, the limitless funds[17] on which my host must be able to draw[18], that an idea formed in my mind.

'Over dinner[19] that night – we were sitting at a vast, medieval banqueting table and the food was carried in by negro servants dressed in what you might call colonial style – I raised the subject of Mrs Devoy and her child. Stillman assured me that even though they were not resident in Boston, he would alert the city fathers[20] who would take care of them. Encouraged by this, I went on to the matter[21] of the Flat Cap Gang and asked if there was any way he could help bring them to justice, the Boston police having so far signally failed to make any progress. Might it not be possible, I suggested, to offer a sizeable reward[22] for information as to their whereabouts[23] and, at the same time, to hire[24] a private detective agency to apprehend them on our behalf[25]. In this way we would avenge the death of James Devoy and simultaneously punish them for the loss of the Constable landscapes.

1. qui s'offrit à
2. à eux seuls
3. s'étendaient sur
4. env. 15 ha
5. affichait une opulence dépassant
6. pour me le faire visiter
7. parcours
8. escalier en bois
9. la bibliothèque
10. le jeu d'échecs
11. son orgue ancien sur lequel avait joué
12. sous-sol
13. son bowling
14. franchement épuisé
15. quant aux œuvres d'art
16. salon
17. ces fonds illimités
18. pouvait sans doute puiser
19. Au cours du dîner
20. les édiles locaux
21. j'enchaînai sur la question
22. une belle récompense
23. permettant de savoir où ils se trouvaient
24. d'engager
25. en notre nom

'Stillman seized on[1] my idea with enthusiasm. "You're right, Carstairs!" he cried, bringing his fist crashing down[2]. "That's exactly what we'll do. I'll show these bums[3] that it was a bad day that they chose to hornswoggle[4] Cornelius T. Stillman!" This was not his customary manner of speech, but we had between us finished a bottle of particularly fine claret[5] and had moved on to the port[6] and he was in a more than usually relaxed mood[7]. He even insisted on funding the full cost[8] of the detectives and the reward himself, although I had offered to make a contribution. We shook hands on it and he suggested that I stay with him[9] while the arrangements were made, an invitation I was glad to accept. Art has been my life, both as a collector and as a dealer, and there was enough in Stillman's summer home to keep me entranced[10] for months.

'But in fact, events took a swifter course[11] than that. Mr Stillman contacted Pinkerton's and engaged a man called Bill McParland. I was not invited to meet him myself – Stillman was the sort of person who must do everything alone and in his own way. But I knew enough of McParland's reputation to be sure that he was a formidable investigator who would not give up[12] until the Flat Cap Gang had been delivered into his hands. At the same time, advertisements[13] were placed in the *Boston Daily Advertiser*[14] offering a reward of one hundred dollars – a considerable sum – for information leading to the arrests of[15] Rourke and Keelan O'Donaghue and all those associated with them[16]. I was glad to see that Mr Stillman had included my name along with his own beneath the announcement, even though the money was entirely his.

'I spent the next few weeks at Shepherd's Point and in Boston itself, a remarkably handsome and fast-growing[17] city. I travelled back to New York a few times and took the opportunity[18] to spend sev-

1. adopta
2. en tapant du poing sur la table
3. minables
4. ce n'était pas le bon jour pour rouler
5. d'excellent bordeaux
6. étions passés au porto,
7. il était donc particulièrement détendu
8. pour prendre entièrement à charge les frais
9. je séjourne chez lui
10. me fasciner
11. se déroulèrent plus rapidement
12. ne renoncerait pas
13. des annonces
14. [premier quotidien fondé à Boston, 1813-1929]
15. permettant d'arrêter
16. leurs comparses
17. en plein développement
18. en profitai

eral hours at the Metropolitan Museum of Art, a poorly designed[1] building, though containing a superb collection. I also visited Mrs Devoy and her son. It was while I was in New York that I received a telegram from Stillman, urging me[2] to return. The size of the reward had achieved its aim[3]. McParland had been given a tip-off[4]. The net was closing in[5] on the Flat Cap Gang.

'I returned at once, taking a room at a hotel on School Street. And it was there, in the evening, that I heard from[6] Cornelius Stillman what had occurred.

'The tip-off had come from the owner of a dramshop[7] – which is what the Americans call a saloon – in the South End, a less than salubrious part of Boston and one that was already home to[8] a large number of Irish immigrants. The O'Donaghue twins were holed up[9] in a narrow tenement house[10] close to the Charles River, a dark, squalid[11] building on three storeys[12] with dozens of rooms clustered together, no hallways[13] and just one privy serving each floor[14]. Raw sewage[15] ran through[16] the corridors and the stench[17] was only kept at bay[18] by the fumes of charcoal[19], burning in a hundred tiny stoves[20]. This hell-hole[21] was filled with screaming babies, drunken men and mumbling, half-crazed women[22], but a rough[23] construction, mainly of timber[24] with a few pressed bricks, had been added separately at the back and this the twins had managed to make their own[25]. Keelan had one room to himself. Rourke shared another with two of his men. A third room was occupied by the rest of the gang.

'The money they had stolen from the train was already gone, frittered away[26] on alcohol and gambling[27]. As the sun set that evening, they were crouched around the stove, drinking gin and playing cards. They had no look-out[28]. None of the families would have dared to peach on them[29] and they were sure that the Boston police had long ago lost any

1. à l'architecture médiocre
2. me demandant instamment
3. atteint son but
4. un tuyau
5. Les mailles du filet se resserraient
6. je sus par
7. du propriétaire d'un débit de boissons
8. où vivaient déjà
9. se terraient
10. immeuble
11. sordide
12. étages
13. agglutinées, sans couloirs
14. un seul cabinet d'aisances par étage
15. Les eaux usées
16. parcouraient
17. puanteur
18. atténuée
19. émanations de charbon
20. poêles minuscules
21. trou à rats
22. de femmes marmonnant, à moitié folles
23. sommaire
24. essentiellement en bois
25. réussi à se la réserver
26. gaspillé
27. en paris
28. pas de guetteur
29. osé les dénoncer

interest in the theft of two thousand dollars. And so they were oblivious[1] to the approach of McParland who was closing in on[2] the tenement, accompanied by a dozen armed men.

'The Pinkerton's agents had been instructed to take them alive if they could for it was very much Stillman's hope that he would see them in a court of law[3], besides which there were many innocent people in close proximity making an all-out gunfight[4] something to be avoided if at all possible[5]. When his men were in position, McParland took up the bullhorn[6] he had brought with him and called out a warning[7]. But if he had hoped that the Flat Cap Gang would surrender[8] quietly, he was disillusioned a moment later by a volley of shots[9]. The twins had allowed themselves to be taken by surprise, but they were not going to give up without a fight, and a cascade of lead poured out[10] into the street, fired not just out of windows but through holes punched in the very walls[11]. Two of the Pinkerton men were gunned down and McParland himself was wounded, but the others gave as good as they got[12], emptying their six-shooters[13] directly into the structure. It is impossible to imagine what it must have been like as hundreds of bullets tore through the flimsy wood[14]. There was no protection. There was nowhere to hide.

'When it was all over, they found five men lying together in the smoke-filled[15] interior, their bodies shot to pieces[16]. One had escaped. At first it seemed impossible, but McParland's informant had assured him that the entire gang would be assembled in that place and during the gunfight it had seemed to him that six men had returned their fire[17]. The room was examined and at last the mystery was solved. One of the floorboards[18] was loose[19]. It was pulled aside to reveal a narrow gulley, a drainage ditch[20] which sank below the surface of the ground[21] and con-

1. ne se doutaient pas
2. était en train d'encercler
3. passer devant un juge
4. fusillade générale
5. dans la mesure du possible
6. saisit le porte-voix
7. lança un avertissement
8. allait se rendre
9. une salve de tirs
10. un déluge de plomb s'abattit
11. pratiqués dans les murs mêmes
12. rendirent coup pour coup
13. revolvers [à six coups]
14. criblaient les minces parois de bois
15. envahi de fumée
16. criblés de balles
17. riposté
18. lames du plancher
19. disjointe
20. une étroite rigole, un fossé d'écoulement
21. s'enfonçait dans le sol

tinued all the way to the river. Keelan O'Donaghue had escaped by this means[1], although it must have been the devil of a tight squeeze[2] for the pipe[3] was barely large enough to contain a child, and certainly none of the Pinkerton's agents was willing to give it a try[4]. McParland led some of his men down to the river but by now it was pitch-dark[5] and he knew any search would be fruitless. The Flat Cap Gang was destroyed but one of its ringleaders had got away[6].

'This was the outcome[7] that Cornelius Stillman described to me in my hotel that night, but it is not by any means[8] the end of the story.

'I remained in Boston another week, partly in the hope that Keelan O'Donaghue might even now be found. For a slight concern had risen[9] in my mind. Indeed[10], it might have been there from the very start, but it was only now that I became conscious of it. It referred to that blasted advertisement[11] which I have already mentioned and which bore my name[12]. Stillman had made public the fact that I had been party to[13] the reward and to the posse[14] which had been sent after the Flat Cap Gang. At the time I had been gratified[15], thinking only of my sense of public duty[16] and, I suppose, the honour of being associated with the great man. It now occurred to me that to have killed one twin and to have left the other alive[17] might make me a target for revenge[18], particularly in a place where the very worst criminals could count on the support[19] of so many friends and admirers. It was with a sense of nervousness that I now walked in and out[20] of my hotel. I did not stray[21] into the rougher parts of the city. And I certainly didn't go out at night.

'Keelan O'Donaghue was not captured and there was even some doubt that he had actually survived. He could have been wounded and died of blood loss[22], like a rat, underground[23]. He could have drowned.[24] Stillman had certainly persuaded

1. par ce moyen
2. bien qu'il ait dû avoir un mal de chien à se faufiler
3. le conduit
4. n'avait envie de s'y risquer
5. à présent il faisait nuit noire
6. l'un des meneurs s'en était sorti
7. le résultat
8. ce n'est en aucun cas
9. Car une légère inquiétude avait surgi
10. En réalité
11. cette satanée annonce
12. mentionnait mon nom
13. j'aie été associé à
14. équipe policière
15. cela m'avait fait plaisir
16. devoir civique
17. en vie
18. faisait de moi la cible d'une éventuelle vengeance
19. soutien
20. désormais, j'entrais et sortais
21. Je ne m'aventurais pas
22. saigné à mort
23. sous terre
24. Peut-être s'était-il noyé.

himself that this was the case by the time we met for the last time, but then, he was the sort of man who never liked to admit failure[1]. I had booked passage back[2] to England on the SS[3] *Catalonia*, run by[4] the Cunard line. I was sorry not to be able to bid farewell[5] to Mrs Devoy and her son, but I did not have the time to return to New York. I left the hotel. And I remember that I had actually reached the gangplank[6] and was about to board the ship[7] when I heard the news[8]. It was being shouted out by a newsboy[9] and there it was, on the front page.

'Cornelius Stillman had been shot dead[10] whilst walking[11] in the rose garden[12] of his home in Providence. With a shaking hand[13], I purchased a copy[14] of the newspaper and read that the attack had happened the day before; that a young man wearing a twill jacket, scarf[15] and flat cap had been seen fleeing[16] from the scene. A manhunt[17] had already begun and would spread all over New England, for this was the murder of a Boston Brahmin and no effort could be spared in[18] bringing the perpetrator[19] to justice. According to the report[20], Bill McParland was assisting the police and there was a certain irony in this, as he and Stillman had fallen out[21] in the days before Stillman's death. Stillman had held back half the fee that he had agreed[22] with the Pinkerton man, arguing that the job would not have been fully completed[23] until the last body had been recovered. Well, that last body was up and walking[24], for there could be no doubt at all as to the identity of Stillman's assailant.

'I read the newspaper and then climbed the gangplank. I went directly to my cabin and remained there until six o'clock in the evening when there was a tremendous hoot[25] and the *Catalonia* lifted its moorings[26] and slipped out of port. Only then did I return to the deck[27] and watch as Boston dis-

1. admettre un échec
2. réservé ma traversée de retour
3. à bord du navire
4. affrété par
5. faire mes adieux
6. je venais d'atteindre la passerelle
7. monter à bord
8. la nouvelle
9. C'était un vendeur de journaux qui la criait
10. abattu
11. tandis qu'il se promenait
12. roseraie
13. D'une main tremblante
14. un exemplaire
15. une veste en sergé, une écharpe
16. en train de s'enfuir
17. Une chasse à l'homme
18. tous les moyens seraient mis en œuvre pour
19. l'auteur des faits
20. l'article
21. s'étaient brouillés
22. retenu la moitié des honoraires convenus
23. totalement achevé
24. bel et bien sur pied
25. mugissement [de sirène]
26. largua ses amarres
27. sur le pont

1. très soulagé
2. en reparler
3. bien avant
4. les mains croisées
5. Un morceau de charbon se détacha
6. fit des étincelles
7. le faire sortir
8. si secondaire
9. impoli
10. sursauta
11. une représentation
12. n'a eu d'effet sur vous
13. croyez de toute évidence qu'il s'agit de
14. se venger

appeared behind me. I was hugely relieved[1] to be away.

'That, gentlemen, is the story of the lost Constables and my visit to America. I of course told my partner, Mr Finch, what had occurred, and I have spoken of it with my wife. But I have never repeated it to anyone else. It happened more than a year ago. And until the man in the flat cap appeared outside my house in Wimbledon, I thought – I prayed – that I would never have to refer to it again[2].'

Holmes had finished his pipe long before[3] the art dealer came to the end of his narration, and had been listening with his long fingers clasped[4] in front of him and a look of intense concentration on his face. There was a lengthy silence. A coal tumbled[5] and the fire sparked[6]. The sound of it seemed to draw him out[7] of his reverie.

'What was the opera you intended to see tonight?' he asked.

It was the last question I had expected. It seemed to be of such trivial importance[8] in the light of everything we had just heard that I wondered if he was being deliberately rude[9].

Edmund Carstairs must have thought the same. He started back[10], turned to me, then back to Holmes. 'I am going to a performance[11] of Wagner – but has nothing I have said made any impression on you[12]?' he demanded.

'On the contrary, I found it of exceedingly great interest and must compliment you on the clarity and attention to detail with which you told it.'

'And the man in the flat cap ...'

'You evidently believe him to be[13] this Keelan O'Donaghue. You think he has followed you to England in order to exact his revenge[14]?'

'What other possible explanation could there be?'

'Offhand[1], I could perhaps suggest half a dozen. It has always struck me that any interpretation of a series of events is possible until all the evidence says otherwise[2] and even then[3] one should be wary[4] before jumping to a conclusion[5]. In this case, yes, it might be that this young man has crossed the Atlantic and found his way to your Wimbledon home. However, one might ask[6] why it has taken him more than a year to make the journey and what purpose he had in[7] inviting you to a meeting at the church of St Mary. Why not just shoot you down[8] where you stood[9], if that was his intent? Even more strange is the fact that he failed to turn up[10].'

'He is trying to terrorise me.'

'And succeeding.'

'Indeed.[11]' Carstairs bowed his head[12]. 'Are you saying that you cannot help me, Mr Holmes?'

'At this juncture[13], I do not see that there is a great deal I can do[14]. Whoever he may be[15], your unwanted[16] visitor has given us no clue[17] as to how we may find him. If, on the other hand[18], he should reappear, then I will be pleased to give you what assistance I can. But there is one last thing I *can* tell you, Mr Carstairs. You can enjoy your opera in a tranquil state of mind. I do not believe he intends to do you harm[19].'

But Holmes was wrong. At least, that was how it appeared the very next day. For it was then that the man in the flat cap struck again.

1. Spontanément
2. tout semble prouver le contraire
3. même dans ce cas,
4. il vaut mieux être prudent
5. d'en tirer une conclusion hâtive
6. on pourrait se demander
7. quel était son but en
8. vous abattre
9. sur place
10. qu'il ne soit pas venu
11. Effectivement.
12. baissa la tête
13. Pour l'instant
14. je ne pense pas que je puisse faire grand-chose
15. Qui que ce soit
16. indésirable
17. aucune indication
18. pourtant
19. qu'il ait l'intention de vous faire du mal

THREE

At Ridgeway Hall

The telegram arrived the next morning, while we were sitting together at breakfast.

1. fracturé
2. appelée

O'DONAGHUE CAME AGAIN LAST NIGHT. MY SAFE BROKEN INTO[1] AND POLICE NOW SUMMONED[2]. CAN YOU COME?

It was signed, Edmund Carstairs.

3. qu'en pensez-vous
4. en jetant le message sur la table
5. J'avais prévu
6. de très approchant
7. soi-disant
8. bredouillai-je
9. n'avez-vous pas averti M. Carstairs
10. À défaut de preuves supplémentaires
11. traversé la pelouse
12. une plate-bande
13. des traces de boue

'So what do you make of that[3], Watson?' Holmes asked, tossing the paper down onto the table[4].

'He has returned sooner, perhaps, than you had thought,' I said.

'Not at all. I was anticipating[5] something very much like this[6]. From the start, it occurred to me that the so-called[7] man in the flat cap was more interested in Ridgeway Hall than its owner.'

'You expected a burglary?' I stammered[8]. 'But, Holmes, why did you not give Mr Carstairs a warning[9]? At the very least you might have suggested the possibility.'

'You heard what I said, Watson. With no further evidence[10], there was nothing I could hope to achieve. But now our unwanted visitor has most generously decided to assist us. He has quite probably forced a window. He will have walked across the lawn[11], stood in a flower bed[12] and left muddy tracks[13] across the carpet. From this we will learn, at the very least, his height[1], his weight[2], his profession and any peculiarities he may have in his gait[3]. He may have been so kind as[4] to drop[5] some item[6] or leave something behind. If he has taken jewellery[7], it will have to be disposed of[8]. If it was money, that too may make itself known[9]. At least now he will have laid a track[10] that we can follow. Can I trouble you to pass the marmalade? There are plenty of trains to Wimbledon. I take it you will join me?'

'Of course, Holmes. I would like nothing better.'

'Excellent. I sometimes wonder how I will be able to find the energy or the will[11] to undertake[12] another investigation if I am not assured that the general public[13] will be able to read every detail of it in due course[14].'

I had grown accustomed to such ribaldry[15] and took it to be an indication of my friend's good humour, so did not respond. A short while later, when Holmes had finished smoking his morning pipe, we put on our coats and left the house. The distance to Wimbledon was not great, but it was close to eleven o'clock when we arrived and I wondered if Mr Carstairs might not have given up on us altogether[16].

My first impression of Ridgeway Hall was that it was a perfect jewel box of a house and one well suited to[17] a collector of fine art who would surely display many priceless things inside. Two gates, one on each side, opened from the public lane with a gravel drive[18], shaped like a horseshoe[19], sweeping round[20] a well-manicured[21] lawn and up to[22] the front door. The gates were framed by ornate pilasters[23], each one surmounted by a stone lion with a paw raised[24] as if warning visitors to stop and consider[25] before deciding to enter. A low wall ran between[26] the two. The house itself was set some distance back[27]. It was what I would have termed a villa, built in the classic Georgian[28] style, white and perfectly square, with elegant windows placed symmetrically on either

1. taille
2. poids
3. particularité dans sa démarche
4. Peut-être a-t-il eu l'amabilité
5. laisser tomber
6. quelque chose
7. des bijoux
8. il devra s'en débarrasser
9. se faire remarquer
10. laissé une piste
11. la volonté
12. entamer
13. le grand public
14. le moment venu
15. ce genre de plaisanteries
16. ne s'attendait plus du tout à nous voir
17. cette maison était une petite merveille et l'endroit rêvé pour
18. par une allée de gravier
19. en forme de fer à cheval
20. contournant
21. impeccable
22. menant à
23. encadrées de pilastres ouvragés
24. une patte levée
25. de réfléchir
26. séparait
27. un peu en retrait
28. [des règnes des 4 rois George, 1714-1830]

side of the front entrance. This symmetry even extended to the trees, of which there were many fine specimens but which had been planted so that one side of the garden almost formed a mirror image of the other[1]. And yet, at the very last moment it had all been spoiled[2] by an Italian fountain which, though beautiful in itself, with cupids[3] and dolphins[4] playing in the stone and the sunlight sparkling[5] off a thin veneer of ice[6], had nonetheless been positioned slightly out of kilter[7]. It was quite impossible to see it without wishing to pick it up[8] and carry it two or three yards[9] to the left.

It turned out[10] that the police had come and gone. The door was opened by a manservant, smartly dressed[11] and grim-faced[12]. He led us along a wide corridor with rooms leading off on both sides[13], the walls hung with paintings and engravings[14], antique mirrors and tapestries. A sculpture showing a shepherd boy leaning on his staff[15] stood on a little table with curved legs[16]. An elegant longcase clock[17], white and gold, stood at the far end, the gentle sound of its ticking[18] echoing through the house. We were shown into the drawing room where Carstairs was sitting on a chaise longue[19], talking to a woman a few years younger than himself. He was wearing a black frock coat, silver-coloured waistcoast and patent leather shoes. His long hair was neatly combed back[20]. To look at him, one might think he had just lost a hand[21] at bridge. It was hard to believe that anything more untoward[22] had occurred. However, he sprang to his feet[23] the moment he saw us.

'So! You have come! You told me yesterday that I had no reason to fear the man whom I believe to be Keelan O'Donaghue. And yet last night he broke[24] into this house. He has taken fifty pounds and jewellery from my safe. But for[25] the fact that my wife is a light sleeper[26] and actually surprised him in the

1. était presque le reflet de l'autre
2. gâché
3. des chérubins
4. des dauphins
5. scintillant
6. sur une fine couche de givre
7. avec un léger décalage
8. la soulever
9. à env. 2,5 m
10. Il s'avéra
11. chic
12. à la mine lugubre
13. s'ouvrant de chaque côté
14. couverts de tableaux et de gravures
15. un jeune berger penché sur son bâton
16. au piètement recourbé
17. horloge
18. le bruit léger de son tic-tac
19. méridienne
20. soigneusement peignés en arrière
21. une manche
22. quelque chose de plus fâcheux
23. se leva d'un bond
24. s'est introduit
25. N'eût été
26. a le sommeil léger

middle of his larceny[1], who knows what he might have done next?'

I turned my attention to the lady who had been sitting beside him. She was a small, very attractive person of about thirty years of age, and she impressed me at once with her bright, intelligent face and her confident demeanour[2]. She had fair[3] hair, drawn back and tied in a knot[4]; a style that seemed designed to accentuate the elegance and femininity of her features[5]. Despite the alarms[6] of the morning I guessed that she had a quick[7] sense of humour, for it was there in her eyes, which were a strange shade[8] between green and blue, and her lips, which were constantly on the edge of a smile[9]. Her cheeks were lightly freckled[10]. She was wearing a simple dress with long sleeves[11], untrimmed and unbraided[12]. A necklace[13] of pearls hung around her neck. There was something about her that[14] reminded me, almost at once, of my own, dear Mary. Even before she had spoken, I was sure that she would have the same disposition[15]; a natural independence and yet a keen sense of duty[16] to the man whom she had chosen to marry.

'Perhaps you should begin by introducing us,' Holmes remarked.

'Of course. This is my wife, Catherine.'

'And you must be Mr Sherlock Holmes. I am very grateful to you for replying so quickly to our telegram. I told Edmund to send it. I said you would come.'

'I understand that you have had a very unsettling experience[17],' Holmes said.

'Indeed so.[18] It is as my husband told you. I was woken up last night and saw from the clock that it was twenty past three. There was a full moon shining[19] through the window. I thought at first that it must have been a bird or an owl[20] that had disturbed me, but then I heard another sound, coming

1. en plein cambriolage
2. assurance
3. blonds
4. tirés en arrière et noués en chignon
5. ses traits
6. inquiétudes
7. vif
8. de couleur étrange
9. sur le point de sourire
10. parsemées de taches de rousseur
11. à manches longues
12. sans aucune garniture
13. collier
14. Quelque chose en elle
15. caractère
16. un grand sens du devoir
17. venez de vivre un incident pénible
18. En effet.
19. La pleine lune brillait
20. un hibou

from inside the house, and I knew that I was wrong. I rose from my bed, drew on[1] a dressing gown and went downstairs.'

'It was a foolish thing to do[2], my dear,' Carstairs remarked. 'You could have been hurt.'

'I didn't consider myself to be in any danger. To be honest, it didn't even occur to me[3] that there might be a stranger[4] in the house. I thought it might be Mr or Mrs Kirby – or even Patrick. You know I don't completely trust[5] that boy. Anyway, I looked briefly in the drawing room. Nothing had been disturbed. Then, for some reason, I was drawn to[6] the study.'

'You had no light with you?' Holmes asked.

'No. The moon was enough. I opened the door and there was a figure, a silhouette perched on the window sill[7], holding something in his hand. He saw me and the two of us froze[8], facing each other across the carpet[9]. At first, I didn't scream. I was too shocked. Then it was as if he simply fell backwards[10] through the window, dropping down onto the grass, and at that very moment I was released from my spell[11]. I called out and raised the alarm[12].'

'We will examine the safe and the study momentarily[13],' Holmes said. 'But before we do so, Mrs Carstairs, I can tell from your accent that you are American. Have you been married long?'

'Edmund and I have been married for almost a year and a half.'

'I should have explained to you how I met Catherine,' Carstairs said. 'For it is very much connected with the narrative that I related[14] yesterday. The only reason that I chose not to do so was because I thought it had no relevance[15].'

'Everything has a relevance,' remarked Holmes. 'I have often found that the most immaterial aspect[16] of a case can be at the same time its most significant[17].'

1. j'ai enfilé
2. Ce n'était pas raisonnable
3. il ne m'est même pas venu à l'esprit
4. un inconnu
5. que je ne fais pas vraiment confiance à
6. quelque chose m'a attirée vers
7. le rebord de la fenêtre
8. nous sommes restés figés
9. face à face, de part et d'autre du tapis
10. s'il était juste tombé à la renverse
11. je suis sortie de ma transe
12. j'ai donné l'alerte
13. dans un instant
14. l'histoire que j'ai racontée
15. qu'elle n'avait pas de rapport
16. le côté le plus anodin
17. le plus important

'We met on the *Catalonia* the very day that it left Boston,' Catherine Carstairs said. She reached out[1] and took her husband's hand. 'I was travelling alone, apart, of course, from a girl whom I had employed to be my companion[2]. I saw Edmund as he came on board and I knew at once that something dreadful had happened. It was obvious from[3] his face, from the fear in his eyes. We passed each other on the deck that evening. Both of us were single[4]. And by a stroke of good fortune[5] we found ourselves seated next to each other at dinner.'

'I do not know how I would have lasted the crossing[6] if it had not been for Catherine.' Carstairs continued the tale. 'I have always been of a nervous disposition and the loss of the paintings, the death of Cornelius Stillman, the terrible violence ... it had all been too much for me. I was quite unwell[7], in a fever. But from the very first[8] Catherine looked after me and I found my feelings towards her growing even as the coast of America slipped away behind me. I have to say that I have always sneered at[9] the concept of "love at first sight[10]", Mr Holmes. It is something I may have read in yellow-back novels[11] but which I have never believed. Nonetheless, that is what occurred. By the time we arrived in England, I knew that I had found the woman with whom I wished to spend the rest of my life.'

'And what, may I ask, was the reason for your visit to England?' Holmes asked, turning to the wife.

'I was married briefly in Chicago, Mr Holmes. My husband worked in real estate[12], and although in business he was well respected in the community, and a regular churchgoer[13], he was never kind to me. He had a dreadful temper[14] and there were times when I even feared for my safety. I had few friends and he did everything in his power to keep it that way. In the last months of our marriage he actually confined me[15] to the house, afraid perhaps

1. tendit le bras
2. engagée comme compagne de voyage
3. Cela se voyait sur
4. célibataires
5. heureux hasard,
6. j'aurais survécu à la traversée
7. Je me sentais très mal
8. dès le départ
9. je me suis toujours moqué
10. coup de foudre
11. les romans de gare
12. dans l'immobilier
13. très pratiquant
14. très mauvais caractère
15. est allé jusqu'à m'enfermer

that I might speak out against him[1]. But then, quite suddenly, he became ill with tuberculosis and died. Sadly, his house and much of his wealth[2] went to his two sisters. I was left with little money, no friends and no reason to wish to stay in America. And so I left. I was coming to England for a new start.' She glanced down[3] and added, with a look of humility, 'I had not expected[4] to come across it[5] so soon, nor to find the happiness that had for so long been missing from my life.'

'You mentioned a travelling companion who was with you on the *Catalonia*,' Holmes remarked.

'I hired her[6] in Boston. I had never met her before – and she left my employ[7] soon after we arrived.'

Outside, in the corridor, the clock chimed the hour[8]. Holmes sprang to his feet with a smile on his face and that sense of energy and excitement that I knew so well. 'We must waste no further time[9]!' he exclaimed. 'I wish to examine the safe and the room in which it is contained. Fifty pounds has been taken, you say. Not a very large sum of money, all things considered[10]. Let us see what, if anything, the thief has left behind.'

But before we could make a move, another woman came into the room and I saw at once that, though part of the household[11], she was as different from Catherine Carstairs as could be imagined. She was plain[12] and unsmiling[13], dressed in grey, with dark hair tightly bound[14] at the back of her neck. She wore a silver cross[15] and her hands were knotted together as if in prayer[16]. From her dark eyes, her pale skin and the shape of her lips, I surmised[17] that she must be related to[18] Carstairs. She had none of his theatricality but was more like the prompter[19], for ever cast into the shadows[20], waiting for him to forget his lines[21].

'What now?[22]' she demanded. 'First I am disturbed in my room by police officers asking absurd ques-

1. craignant peut-être que je ne le dénonce
2. l'essentiel de sa fortune
3. baissa les yeux
4. Je ne m'attendais pas
5. à ce que cela m'arrive
6. l'ai engagée
7. a quitté mon service
8. l'heure sonna à l'horloge
9. ne devons plus perdre un instant
10. en fin de compte
11. bien qu'elle fasse partie de la famille
12. sans charme
13. austère
14. tirés avec sévérité
15. une croix en argent
16. étaient jointes, comme pour une prière
17. je supposai
18. une parente de
19. le souffleur
20. toujours dans l'ombre
21. ses répliques
22. Quoi encore ?

tions to which I cannot possibly know the replies. And that is not enough? Are we to invite the whole world in to invade our privacy?[1]'

'This is Mr Sherlock Holmes, Eliza,' Carstairs stammered. 'I told you that I consulted with him yesterday.'

'And much good did it do you.[2] There was nothing he could do; that was what he told you. A fine consultation, Edmund, I am sure. We could all of us have been murdered in our beds.'

Carstairs glanced at her fondly[3] but at the same time with exasperation. 'This is my sister, Eliza,' he said.

'You reside in this house?' Holmes asked her.

'I am tolerated[4], yes,' replied the sister. 'I have an attic room[5] where I keep myself to myself[6] and everyone seems to prefer it that way. I reside here, but I am not part of this family. You might as well speak[7] to the servants as to me.'

'You know that's not fair[8], Eliza,' Mrs Carstairs said.

Holmes turned to Carstairs. 'Perhaps you might tell me how many people there are in the house.'

'Apart from myself and Catherine, Eliza does indeed occupy the top floor[9]. We have Kirby, who is our footman[10] and man-of-all-work[11]. It was he who showed you in.[12] His wife acts as our housekeeper[13] and the two of them reside downstairs. They have a young nephew, Patrick, who came to us recently from Ireland and who acts as the kitchen boy and runs errands[14], and there is a scullery maid[15], Elsie. In addition, we have a coachman and groom[16] but they live in the village.'

'A large household and a busy one,' Holmes remarked. 'But we were about to examine the safe.'

Eliza Carstairs remained where she was. The rest of us went out of the living room, down the corridor and into Carstairs's study, which was at the

1. Allons-nous laisser entrer tout le monde dans notre intimité ?
2. Pour ce que ça t'a servi !
3. la regarda tendrement
4. On m'y tolère
5. Je dispose d'une mansarde
6. j'ai l'habitude de m'isoler
7. Autant parler
8. que ce n'est pas vrai
9. le dernier étage
10. valet de pied
11. homme à tout faire
12. C'est lui qui vous a fait entrer.
13. nous sert de gouvernante
14. garçon de cuisine et de courses
15. une fille de cuisine
16. un cocher et un palefrenier

very back[1] of the house with a view of[2] the garden and, in the distance, an ornamental pond[3]. This turned out to be a comfortable, well-appointed[4] room with a desk framed by two windows, velvet curtains[5], a handsome fireplace[6] and some landscapes which, from[7] their bright colours and the almost haphazard way the paint had been applied[8], I knew must belong[9] to the impressionist school of which Carstairs had spoken. The safe, a solid enough affair[10], was tucked away[11] in one corner. It was still open.

'Is this how you found it?' asked Holmes.

'The police have examined it,' Carstairs replied. 'But I felt it best[12] to leave it open until you arrived.'

'You were right,' Holmes said. He glanced at[13] the safe. 'The lock[14] does not appear to have been forced which would suggest that a key has been used,' he remarked.

'There was only one key and I keep it with me all the time,' Carstairs returned. 'Although I asked Kirby to make a copy of it some six months ago. Catherine keeps her jewellery in the safe and when I am away – for I still travel to auctions[15] all over the country and sometimes to Europe – she felt she should have a key of her own[16].'

Mrs Carstairs had followed us into the room and was standing by the desk. She brought her hands together. 'I lost it,' she said.

'When was that?[17]'

'I cannot really say, Mr Holmes. It may have been a month ago, it may have been longer. Edmund and I have been through this[18]. I wanted to open the safe a few weeks ago and could not find it. The last time I used it was on[19] my birthday, which is in August. I have no idea what happened to it after that. I am not normally so careless.[20]'

'Could it have been stolen?'

1. tout à l'arrière
2. vue sur
3. au loin, une pièce d'eau
4. bien aménagée
5. des rideaux de velours
6. cheminée
7. vu
8. l'application presque aléatoire des touches de couleur
9. devaient, selon moi, appartenir
10. paraissant pourtant solide
11. en retrait
12. j'ai pensé qu'il valait mieux
13. observa
14. serrure
15. je vais encore à des ventes aux enchères
16. sa propre clé
17. À quand cela remonte-t-il ?
18. nous en avons déjà parlé
19. le jour de
20. Je ne suis pas aussi étourdie d'habitude.

'I kept it in a drawer[1] beside my bed and nobody comes into the room apart from the servants. As far as I know[2], the key never left this house.'

Holmes turned to Carstairs. 'You did not replace the safe.'

'It was always in my mind to do so.[3] But it occurred to me that if the key had somehow been dropped[4] in the garden or even in the village, nobody could possibly know what it opened. If, as seemed more likely[5], it were somewhere amongst my wife's possessions[6], then it was unlikely to fall into the wrong hands[7]. Anyway, we cannot be sure that it was my wife's key which was used to open the safe. Kirby could have had a second copy made.'

'How long has he been with you?'

'Six years.'

'You have had no cause to complain[8] about him?'

'None whatsoever.[9]'

'And what of[10] this kitchen boy, Patrick? Your wife says she mistrusts him[11].'

'My wife dislikes him because he is insolent and can be a little sly[12]. He has been with us for only a few months and we only took him on[13] at the behest[14] of Mrs Kirby, who asked us to help him find employment. She will vouch for[15] him, and I have no reason to think him dishonest.'

Holmes had taken out his glass and examined the safe, paying particular attention to the lock. 'You say that some jewellery was stolen,' he said. 'Was it your wife's?'

'No. As a matter of fact it was a sapphire[16] necklace belonging to my late mother[17]. Three clusters[18] of sapphires in a gold setting[19]. I imagine it would have little financial value to the thief but it had great sentimental value to me. She lived with us here until a few months ago until ...' He broke off[20] and his wife went over to him, laying a hand[21] on his arm. 'There was an accident, Mr Holmes. She had a

1. tiroir
2. À ma connaissance
3. Je n'ai cessé de me dire que j'allais le faire.
4. avait été égarée d'une façon ou d'une autre
5. comme cela semblait plus probable
6. parmi les affaires de ma femme
7. qu'elle tombe dans de mauvaises mains
8. aucun motif de vous plaindre
9. Pas la moindre.
10. quid de
11. qu'elle se méfie de lui
12. se montrer sournois
13. avons accepté de le prendre
14. à la demande
15. se porte garante de
16. de saphirs
17. ma défunte mère
18. grappes
19. serties en or
20. Sa voix se brisa
21. posant une main

gas fire[1] in her bedroom. Somehow the flame blew out[2] and she was asphyxiated in her sleep.'

'She was very elderly[3]?'

'She was sixty-nine. She always slept with the window closed, even in the summer. Otherwise she might have been saved.'

Holmes left the safe and went over to the window. I joined him there as he examined the sill, the sashes[4] and the frame[5]. As was his habit[6], he spoke his observations aloud[7] – not necessarily for my benefit[8]. 'No shutters[9],' he began. 'The window is snibbed[10] and some distance from the ground. It has evidently been forced from the outside. The wood is splintered[11], which may explain the sound that Mrs Carstairs heard.' He seemed to be making a calculation. 'I would like, if I may, to speak to your man, Kirby. And after that I will walk in the garden, although I imagine the local police will have trampled over anything[12] that might have furnished me with[13] any clue as to what has taken place. Did they give you any idea of their line of investigation[14]?'

'Inspector Lestrade returned and spoke to us shortly before you arrived.'

'What? Lestrade? He was here?'

'Yes. And whatever opinion you may have of him, Mr Holmes, he struck me as being both thorough and efficient[15]. He had already ascertained[16] that a man with an American accent took the first train from Wimbledon to London Bridge at five o'clock this morning. From the way he was dressed[17] and the scar on his right cheek, we are certain that it is the same man that I saw outside my house.'

'I can assure you that if Lestrade is involved[18], you can be quite certain that he will come to[19] a conclusion very quickly, even if it is completely the wrong one! Good day, Mr Carstairs. A pleasure to meet you, Mrs Carstairs. Come, Watson ...'

1. poêle à gaz
2. s'est éteinte
3. âgée
4. les châssis [de la fenêtre à guillotine]
5. cadre
6. Comme à son habitude
7. fit ses observations à voix haute
8. pas forcément à mon intention
9. Pas de volets
10. fermée
11. fendu
12. a sûrement piétiné tout
13. aurait pu me fournir
14. de la piste qu'ils poursuivent
15. aussi rigoureux qu'efficace
16. établi
17. D'après sa tenue vestimentaire
18. s'en occupe
19. parviendra à

We retraced our footsteps down[1] the corridor to the front door where Kirby was already waiting for us. He had seemed barely welcoming[2] on our arrival but it may have been that he saw us as an impediment[3] to the smooth running[4] of the house. He still appeared square-jawed[5], with a hatchet face[6], a man unwilling to speak more words than were truly necessary, but at least he was a little more amenable[7] as he answered Holmes's questions. He confirmed that he had been at Ridgeway Hall for six years. He was from Barnstaple originally, his wife from Belfast. Holmes asked him if the house had changed very much during his time there.

'Oh yes, sir,' came the reply. 'Old Mrs Carstairs was very fixed in her ways[8]. She would certainly let you know[9] if there was anything that was not to her liking[10]. The new Mrs Carstairs could not be more[11] different. She has a very cheerful disposition[12]. My wife considers her a breath of fresh air[13].'

'You were glad that Mr Carstairs married?'

'We were delighted, sir, as well as surprised.'

'Surprised?'

'I wouldn't wish to speak out of turn[14], sir, but Mr Carstairs had formerly[15] shown no interest in such matters, being devoted to his family and to his work. Mrs Carstairs rather burst in on the scene[16] but we are all agreed that the house has been better for it[17].'

'You were present when old Mrs Carstairs died?'

'Indeed I was, sir. In part I blame myself. The lady had a great fear of draughts[18], as a result of which I had – at her insistence – stopped up every crevice[19] by which air might enter the room. The gas, therefore, had no way of escaping. It was the maid, Elsie, who discovered her in the morning. By then the room was filled with fumes[20] – a truly dreadful business[21].'

'Was the kitchen boy, Patrick, in the house at the time?'

1. reprîmes
2. très peu cordial
3. une entrave
4. à la bonne marche
5. avait toujours cette mâchoire carrée
6. ce visage en lame de couteau
7. affable
8. avait ses manies
9. n'hésitait pas à vous faire savoir
10. n'était pas à son goût
11. est on ne peut plus
12. un tempérament très enjoué
13. une bouffée d'air pur
14. tenir des propos déplacés
15. auparavant
16. est arrivée de façon plutôt inopinée
17. s'en porte mieux
18. courants d'air
19. comblé chaque interstice
20. Les émanations avaient déjà envahi la pièce
21. c'était horrible

'Patrick had arrived just one week before. It was an inauspicious start[1], sir.'

'He is your nephew, I understand.'

'On my wife's side, yes, sir.'

'From Belfast?'

'Indeed. Patrick has not found it easy, being in service[2]. We had hoped to give him a good start in life but he has yet to learn the correct attitude for one befitting his station[3], particularly in the way he addresses the master of the house. It may well be, though, that the early calamity of which we have spoken and the disruption that followed[4] may in some way be responsible. He is not such a bad young man and I hope that in time[5] he will prosper[6].'

'Thank you, Kirby.'

'My pleasure[7], sir. I have your coat and your gloves ...'

Out in the garden, Holmes showed himself to be in an unusually[8] jaunty mood[9]. He strode across the lawn[10], inhaling the afternoon air and rejoicing in[11] this brief escape from the city, for none of the fogs[12] of Baker Street had followed us here. At this time, there were parts of Wimbledon which were still very much akin to being[13] in the country. We could see sheep[14] huddled together[15] on a hillside[16] beside a grove of ancient oaks[17]. There were but a few houses dotted[18] around us and we were both struck by the tranquillity of the landscape and the strange quality of the light which seemed to throw everything into sharp focus[19]. 'This is a wholly[20] remarkable case, do you not think?' he exclaimed, as we made our way[21] towards the lane.

'It strikes me as quite trivial[22],' I replied. 'The sum of fifty pounds has been taken along with an antique necklace. I can't call this[23] the most testing of your challenges[24], Holmes.'

1. fâcheux, pour un début
2. d'être un employé de maison
3. pour quelqu'un dans sa position [sociale]
4. les bouleversements consécutifs
5. qu'avec le temps
6. il s'améliorera
7. Je vous en prie
8. manifesta, chose inhabituelle,
9. une humeur légère
10. Il arpenta la pelouse
11. savourant
12. brouillards
13. donnaient encore l'impression d'être presque
14. des moutons
15. blottis les uns contre les autres
16. le flanc d'un coteau
17. d'un bosquet de chênes ancestraux
18. de ci de là
19. tout faire ressortir
20. à tous égards
21. nous dirigions
22. banal
23. Je ne dirais pas
24. que parmi vos défis, ce soit le plus difficile

'I find the necklace particularly fascinating, given[1] everything we have heard about this household. You have already arrived, then, at the solution?'

'I would suppose that it all hinges on whether[2] the unwanted visitor to this house was indeed the twin brother from Boston.'

'And if I were to assure you[3] that he was almost certainly not[4]?'

'Then I would say that, not for the first time, you are being thoroughly perplexing[5].'

'Dear old Watson. How good it is to have you at my side. But I think this is where the intruder arrived last night . . .' We had come to the bottom of the garden where the drive met the lane[6], with the village green on the other side. The continuing[7] cold weather and the well-tended[8] lawn had together created a perfect canvas[9] on which all the comings and goings[10] of the preceding twenty-four hours had been, in effect, frozen. 'There, if I am not mistaken[11], goes the thorough and efficient Lestrade.' There were footprints all around[12], but Holmes had pointed to one set[13] in particular.

'You cannot possibly know they are his[14].'

'No? The length of the stride[15] would suggest a man of about five foot six inches in height[16], the same as Lestrade. He was wearing square-toed[17] boots, such as I have often seen on Lestrade's feet. But the most damning evidence[18] is that they are heading in quite the wrong direction[19], missing everything of importance – and who else could that be but[20] Lestrade? He has, you will see, entered and left by the gate on the right. It is a perfectly natural choice for, on approaching the house, it is the first gate that you come to. The intruder, however, surely came in the other way.'

'Both gates seem identical to me, Holmes.'

'The gates are indeed identical, but the one to the left is less conspicuous[21] due to the position of the

1. étant donné
2. tout dépend si
3. si je vous assurais
4. ce n'était vraisemblablement pas lui
5. je vous trouve déroutant
6. débouchait sur la route
7. persistant
8. bien entretenue
9. toile de fond
10. allées et venues
11. si je ne m'abuse
12. des empreintes de pas partout
13. désignait une série
14. si ce sont les siennes
15. la longueur du pas
16. mesurant env. 1,67 m
17. à bouts carrés
18. la preuve la plus incriminante
19. exactement dans la mauvaise direction
20. si ce n'est
21. moins visible

fountain. If you were to approach[1] the house without wishing to be seen[2], this is the one you would choose, and as you will observe, we have only one set of footprints here with which to concern ourselves[3]. Halloa! What have we here?' Holmes crouched down[4] and seized hold of the butt of a[5] cigarette which he showed to me. 'An American cigarette, Watson. There is no mistaking the tobacco.[6] You will notice that there is no ash[7] in this immediate area.'

'The stub[8] of a cigarette but no ash?'

'Meaning that although he was careful not to be seen, he did not linger long[9]. Do you not find that significant?'

'It was the middle of the night, Holmes. He could see that the house was in darkness. He had no fear of being noticed.'

'Even so[10] ...' We followed the tracks across the lawn and round the side of the house to the study. 'He was walking at a steady pace[11]. He could have paused at the fountain to make sure that he was safe but he chose not to.' Holmes examined the window that we had already examined from within. 'He must have been a man of uncommon strength.'

'The window would not have been so difficult to force.'

'Indeed not, Watson. But consider the height of it[12]. You can see where he jumped down when he was finished[13]. He has left two deep imprints[14] in the grass. But there is no sign of a ladder[15], nor even a garden chair. It is just possible that he could have found a toehold[16] on the wall. The mortar is loose[17] and some of the edges are exposed[18]. But he would still have had to use one hand to cling to the sill[19] while he jemmied open[20] the window with the other. We must also ask ourselves if it was a coincidence that he chose to break into the very room in which the safe was contained.'

1. Si vous deviez accéder à
2. sans être vu
3. à observer
4. s'accroupit
5. s'empara d'un mégot de
6. Ce tabac est très reconnaissable.
7. cendres
8. mégot
9. ne s'est pas éternisé
10. Tout de même
11. d'un pas régulier
12. à quelle hauteur elle se trouve
13. après son forfait
14. marques profondes
15. échelle
16. une prise pour son pied
17. Le ciment s'effrite
18. certains bords sont saillants
19. pour se cramponner au rebord
20. forçait

'Surely he came round the back[1] of the house because it was more secluded[2] and there was less chance of his being seen? He then chose a window at random[3].'

'In which instance he was remarkably fortunate[4].' Holmes had concluded his examination. 'But it is exactly as I hoped, Watson,' he went on. 'A necklace with three clusters of sapphires in a gold setting should not be hard to trace[5], and that should lead us directly to our man. Lestrade has at least confirmed that he took the train to London Bridge. We must do the same. The station is not far and it's a pleasant day. We can walk.'

We made our way across[6] the front of the house, following the drive. But before we could reach the lane, the front door of Ridgeway Hall opened and a woman hurried out[7], stopping in front of us. It was Eliza Carstairs, the art dealer's sister. She had drawn a shawl across her[8] shoulders, which she clutched to her chest[9], and it was clear from her features[10], her staring eyes[11] and the wisps[12] of dark hair that flew around her forehead, that she was in a state of consternation.

'Mr Holmes!' she cried.

'Miss Carstairs.'

'I was rude[13] to you inside and for that you must forgive me. But I must tell you now that nothing is as it seems[14] and that unless you help us, unless you can lift the curse that has fallen[15] on this place, we are doomed[16].'

'I beg of you[17], Miss Carstairs, to compose yourself[18].'

'She is the cause of all this!' The sister flung an accusatory finger in the direction of the house. 'Catherine Marryat – for that was her name by her first marriage. She came upon Edmund when he was at his lowest ebb[19]. He has always had a sensitive nature[20], even as a boy, and it was inevitable that his

1. a fait le tour par l'arrière
2. retiré
3. au hasard
4. Lequel a bien fait les choses
5. difficile à retrouver
6. passâmes par
7. se précipita dehors
8. s'était mis un châle sur les
9. le tenant serré sur sa poitrine
10. à son expression
11. la fixité de son regard
12. les mèches
13. Je me suis montrée impolie
14. les apparences sont trompeuses
15. lever la malédiction qui s'est abattue
16. perdus
17. Je vous en prie
18. reprenez vos esprits
19. au plus bas
20. été de nature sensible

nerves would be unable to stand up[1] to the ordeal he had been through[2] in Boston. He was exhausted, infirm and – yes, in need of someone to take care of him. And so she threw herself at him[3]. What right did she have, an American nobody[4] with barely any money to her name[5]? Out at sea[6], with days on board that ship, she spun a web[7] around him so that when he returned home, it was too late. We could not dissuade him.'

'You would have looked after him yourself.'

'I love him as only a sister can. My mother too. And do not believe for a single minute that she died as a result of an accident. We are a respectable family, Mr Holmes. My father was a printseller[8] who came to London from Manchester and it was he who opened the picture-dealership[9] in Albemarle Street. Alas, he died when we were quite young and since then the three of us have lived together in perfect harmony. When Edmund announced his determination to ally himself with[10] Mrs Marryat, when he argued with us and refused to listen to reason, it broke my mother's heart. Of course we would have liked to see Edmund married. His happiness was all that mattered to us in the world. But how could he marry her? A foreign adventuress we had never met and who, from the start, was clearly interested only in his wealth and position, in the comfort and protection he could give her. My mother killed herself, Mr Holmes. She could not live with the shame[11] and the unhappiness of this accursed[12] marriage and so, six months after the wedding day[13], she turned on the gas tap[14] and lay on her bed until the fumes had done their work[15] and the kindness of oblivion[16] had taken her from us[17].'

'Did your mother communicate her intentions to you?' Holmes asked.

'She didn't need to. I knew what was in her mind and I was hardly[18] surprised when they found her.

1. ne puissent résister
2. à l'épreuve qu'il avait traversée
3. c'est ainsi qu'elle l'a séduit
4. une moins que rien d'Américaine
5. quasiment sans le sou
6. En mer, loin de tous
7. a tissé sa toile
8. marchand de gravures
9. la galerie d'art
10. s'unir à
11. cette honte
12. maudit
13. le jour du mariage
14. a ouvert le robinet du gaz
15. aient fait leur office
16. que le réconfort de l'oubli
17. nous l'enlève
18. n'ai guère été

She had made her choice. This has not been a pleasant household[1] from the day that the American woman arrived, Mr Holmes. And now this latest business[2], this intruder who has broken into our home and stolen Mama's necklace, our most cherished memory[3] of that dear, departed soul[4]. It is all part of the same evil business[5]. How do we not know that this stranger has not come here on her account[6] rather than to pursue[7] some vendetta against my brother? She was with me in the sitting room when he first appeared. I saw him from the window. Perhaps he is an old acquaintance who has followed her here. Perhaps he is more. But this is only the beginning of it, Mr Holmes. So long as this marriage continues, we will none of us be safe.'

'Your brother seems perfectly content[8],' Holmes responded, with a degree of[9] indifference. 'But setting that aside, what would you have me do? A man can choose whom he marries without the blessing[10] of his mother. Or, indeed, of his sister.'

'You can investigate her.'

'It is none of my business[11], Miss Carstairs.'

Eliza Carstairs gazed at him with contempt[12]. 'I have read of your exploits, Mr Holmes,' she replied. 'And I have always considered them to be exaggerated. You yourself, for all your cleverness[13], have always struck me as someone with no understanding of the human heart. Now I know that to be true.' And with that, she wheeled round[14] and went back into the house.

Holmes watched her until the door had closed. 'Most singular[15],' he remarked. 'This case becomes increasingly[16] curious and complex.'

'I have never heard a woman speak with such fury,' I observed.

'Indeed, Watson. But there is one thing I would particularly like to know, for I am beginning to see

1. L'ambiance est détestable dans cette famille
2. ce tout dernier incident
3. précieux souvenir
4. chère disparue
5. la même entreprise néfaste
6. à cause d'elle
7. et non pour exercer
8. satisfait
9. une relative
10. bénédiction
11. Cela ne me regarde pas
12. mépris
13. malgré votre grande intelligence
14. Sur ces paroles, elle tourna les talons
15. Voilà qui est singulier
16. de plus en plus

1. silhouettes de pierre
2. le disque d'eau gelée

great danger in this situation.' He glanced at the fountain, at the stone figures[1] and the frozen circle of water[2]. 'I wonder if Mrs Catherine Carstairs is able to swim?'

FOUR

The Unofficial Police Force

Holmes slept in late[1] the next morning and I was sitting on my own, reading *The Martyrdom of Man*, by Winwood Reade[2], a book that he had recommended to me on more than one occasion but which, I confess, I had found heavy going[3]. I could see, however, why the author had appealed to[4] my friend with his hatred of 'idleness[5] and stupidity', his reverence[6] for 'the divine intellect[7]', his suggestion that 'It is the nature of man to reason from himself[8] outwards[9].' Holmes could have written much of it himself, and although I was glad to turn the last page and set it aside[10], I felt it had at least provided me with some insight into the[11] detective's mind. The morning post had brought a letter from Mary. All was well in Camberwell; Richard Forrester was not so ill that he could not take delight in[12] seeing his old governess again, and she was evidently enjoying the companionship[13] of the boy's mother who was treating her, quite correctly, as an equal[14] rather than a former[15] employee.

I had picked up my pen to reply to her when there was a loud ring[16] at the front door, followed by the patter[17] of many feet on the stairs. It was a sound that I remembered well, so I was fully prepared when about half a dozen street Arabs[18] burst into[19] the room and formed themselves into something resembling an orderly line[20], with the tallest and oldest of them shouting them into shape[21].

1. dormit tard
2. [explorateur et penseur britannique, XIXe s.]
3. fastidieux
4. plu à
5. haine de l'oisiveté
6. vénération
7. l'intelligence divine
8. en partant de soi
9. vers l'extérieur
10. de le mettre de côté
11. m'avait au moins offert un aperçu de
12. malade au point de ne pouvoir se réjouir de
13. compagnie
14. sur un pied d'égalité
15. ancienne
16. un violent coup de sonnette
17. trottinement
18. de gosses des rues
19. firent irruption dans
20. formèrent un semblant de rang
21. leur criant comment faire

'Wiggins!' I exclaimed, for I remembered his name. 'I had not expected to see you again.'

'Mr 'olmes sent us a message, sir, summoning us on a matter of the greatest hurgency[1],' Wiggins replied. 'And when Mr 'olmes calls, we come, so 'ere we are!'

Sherlock had once named them the Baker Street division[2] of the detective police force[3]. At other times he referred to them as the Irregulars. A scruffier, more ragged bunch[4] would be hard to imagine, boys between the ages of eight and fifteen, held together by[5] dirt and grime[6], their clothes so cut about[7] and stitched back together[8] that it would be impossible to say to how many other children they must have at some time[9] belonged. Wiggins himself was wearing an adult jacket that had been cut in half, a strip removed[10] from the middle and the top, and the bottom put together again. Several of the boys were barefooted[11]. Only one, I noted, was a little smarter[12] and better fed[13] than the others, his clothes slightly less threadbare[14], and I wondered what wickedness[15] – pickpocketing, perhaps, or burglary – had furnished him with the means[16] not just to survive but, in his own way, to prosper. He could not have been more than thirteen years old and yet, like all of them, he was already quite grown up[17]. Childhood[18], after all, is the first precious coin that poverty steals from a child.

A moment later, Sherlock Holmes appeared and with him, Mrs Hudson. I could see that our landlady[19] was flustered and out of sorts[20] and she did not attempt to hide her thoughts. 'I won't have it, Mr Holmes. I've told you before. This is a respectable house in which to invite a gang of ragamuffins[21]. Heaven knows what diseases[22] they'll have brought in with them – nor what items of silver or linen[23] will be gone when they depart.'

1. nous convoquant de toute urgence
2. section
3. police judiciaire
4. Pire troupe de loqueteux dépenaillés
5. ne faisant qu'un avec
6. la boue et la crasse
7. déchirés
8. raccommodés
9. en d'autres temps
10. une bande retirée
11. pieds nus
12. plus élégant
13. mieux nourri
14. élimés
15. quel mauvais coup
16. lui avait permis
17. il faisait déjà très mûr
18. L'enfance
19. logeuse
20. nerveuse et de mauvaise humeur
21. galopins
22. maladies
23. quelles pièces d'argenterie ou de linge de maison

'Please calm yourself, my good Mrs Hudson,' Holmes laughed. 'Wiggins! I've told you before. I will not have the house invaded[1] in this way. In future, you alone will report to me. But since you are here and have brought with you the entire gang, listen carefully to my instructions. Our quarry[2] is an American, a man in his mid-thirties who occasionally wears a flat cap. He has a recent scar on his right cheek and, I think we can assume, is a stranger to London. Yesterday, he was at London Bridge Station and has in his possession a gold necklace set with three clusters of sapphires which, needless to say, he came by illicitly[3]. Now, where do you think he would go to dispose of it?'

'Fullwood's Rents!' one boy shouted out.

'The Jews[4] on Petticoat Lane[5],' cried another.

'No! He'll get a better price at the hell houses[6],' suggested a third. 'I'd go to Flower Street or Field Lane.'

'The pawnbrokers[7]!' interjected the better-dressed boy who had first caught my attention.

'The pawnbrokers!' Holmes agreed. 'What's your name, boy?'

'It is Ross, sir.'

'Well, Ross, you have the makings[8] of a detective. The man that we seek is new to the city[9] and will not know Flower Street, Fullwood's Rents or any of the more esoteric corners[10] where you boys find trouble for yourselves[11]. He will go to the most obvious place and the symbol of the three golden balls[12] is known throughout the world. So that's where I want you to begin. He arrived at London Bridge, and let us assume that he chose to reside in a hotel or a lodging house[13] close to there. You must visit every pawnbroker in the district, describing the man and the jewellery which he may have attempted to sell.' Holmes reached[14] into his pocket. 'My rates[15] are the same as always. A shilling each[16] and a guinea[17] for whoever finds what I'm looking for.'

1. Je vous interdit d'envahir
2. Celui que nous recherchons
3. qu'il s'est procuré en toute illégalité bien entendu
4. juifs
5. [célèbre marché londonien depuis le XVIIIe s.]
6. [logements collectifs des déshérités de ce quartier]
7. prêteurs sur gages
8. tu as l'étoffe
9. est un nouveau venu dans cette ville
10. ces recoins obscurs
11. vous autres commettez vos méfaits
12. [symbole des prêteurs sur gages]
13. pension
14. fouilla
15. tarifs
16. pour chacun
17. [21 shillings à l'époque]

1. aboya un ordre
2. d'agitation
3. sous l'œil d'aigle de
4. les couverts
5. tapa des mains
6. s'affala
7. sûr et certain
8. quasiment
9. allons trouver
10. se renseignera aussi auprès des

Wiggins snapped a command[1] and, with a great deal of noise and bustle[2], our unofficial police force marched out, watched by a hawk-eyed[3] Mrs Hudson who would spend the rest of the morning counting the cutlery[4]. As soon as they had gone, Holmes clapped his hands[5] and sank[6] into a chair. 'Well, Watson,' he proclaimed. 'What do you make of that?'

'You seem to have every confidence[7] that we will find O'Donaghue,' I said.

'I am fairly[8] certain that we will locate[9] the man who broke into Ridgeway Hall,' he replied.

'Do you not think that Lestrade will also be enquiring at the[10] pawnbrokers?'

'I somehow doubt it. It is so obvious that it will not have crossed his mind. However, we have the whole day ahead of us and nothing to fill it so, since I have missed breakfast, let's take lunch together at Le Café de l'Europe beside the Haymarket Theatre. Despite the name, the food is English and first rate[11]. After that, I have it in mind[12] to visit the gallery of Carstairs and Finch in Albemarle Street. It might be interesting to acquaint ourselves with[13] Mr Tobias Finch. Mrs Hudson, should Wiggins return[14], you might direct him there[15]. But now, Watson, you must tell me what you thought of *The Martyrdom of Man*. I see that you have finally finished it.'

11. excellente
12. je prévois
13. faire la connaissance de
14. si Wiggins revient
15. envoyez-le directement là-bas
16. était posé, inoffensif
17. image [offerte autref. avec le paquet de cigarettes]
18. marque-page
19. enfin libéré de son dur labeur

I glanced at the book which was lying innocuously[16] on its side. 'Holmes ... ?'

'You have been using a cigarette card[17] as a bookmark[18]. I have watched its tortuous progress from the first page to the last and I see it is now lying on the table, finally released from its labours[19]. I will be interested to hear your conclusions. Some tea, perhaps, Mrs Hudson, if you will be so kind?'

20. pour nous diriger tranquillement
21. s'était levé

We left the house and strolled down[20] to the Haymarket. The fog had lifted[21] and, although still very cold, it was another brilliant day with crowds of people pouring in and out[1] of the department stores[2] and street sellers wheeling their barrows[3] and calling out their wares[4]. At Wimpole Street a great throng had gathered[5] round an organ grinder[6], an old Italian playing some mournful Neapolitan tune[7] which had also drawn in[8] an assortment of shammers[9] who moved among the spectators, relating their pitiful[10] stories to anyone who would listen[11]. There was barely a corner that did not have a street performer[12] and, for once, nobody was inclined to move them on[13]. We ate at Le Café de l'Europe where we were served an excellent raised game pie[14] and Holmes was in an effusive mood[15]. He did not speak of the case, at least, not directly, but I remember him musing on[16] the nature of pictorial art and its possible use in the solving of crime.

'You remember Carstairs telling us of the four lost Constables,' he said. 'They were views of the Lake District painted at the start of the century when, apparently, the artist was sombre and depressed. The oils on the canvas[17], therefore, become a clue to his psychology[18] and it follows[19] that if a man chooses to hang such a work on the wall of his drawing room, we may also learn a great deal about his own state of mind. Did you remark, for example, on the art on display[20] at Ridgeway Hall?'

'A great deal of it was French. There was a view of Brittany[21], another of a bridge crossing the River Seine. I thought the works very fine.'

'You admired them but you learned nothing from them.'

'You mean in respect of the character[22] of Edmund Carstairs? He prefers the countryside to the city. He is drawn to[23] the innocence of childhood. He is a man who likes to be surrounded by colour. I suppose that something of his personality could have been surmised[24] from the pictures we saw on his walls. But then again, we cannot be sure that every

1. entrant et sortant
2. grands magasins
3. poussant leurs charrettes à bras
4. faisant l'article à tue-tête
5. une foule se pressait
6. joueur d'orgue de Barbarie
7. une complainte napolitaine
8. attiré
9. d'imposteurs
10. pitoyables
11. à qui voulait bien écouter
12. sans son saltimbanque
13. n'avait envie de les faire partir
14. tourte levée au gibier
15. d'humeur expansive
16. méditant sur
17. Les huiles de cette toile
18. révèlent son état psychologique
19. il s'ensuit
20. exposé
21. la Bretagne
22. quant à la personnalité
23. attiré par
24. déduit

piece had been chosen by Carstairs himself. His wife or his late mother could have been responsible.'

'That is very true.'

'And even a man who kills his wife may have a gentler side to his nature which finds expression in his choice of art. You will recall[1] that business with the Abernetty family. Horace Abernetty had hung his walls with many fine studies of local flora[2], as I recall[3]. And yet he himself was an individual of the most loathsome and thuggish sort[4].'

'My own memory is that much of the fauna depicted[5] was of the poisonous variety, since you mention it.'

'And what of Baker Street, Holmes? Are you telling me that a visitor to your sitting room will find clues to your psychology through a contemplation of the works that hang around you?'

'No. But they might tell you a great deal[6] about my predecessor, for I can assure you, Watson, that there is hardly a single picture[7] in my own lodgings which was not there when I arrived. Do you seriously imagine that I went out and purchased[8] that portrait of Henry Ward Beecher which used to stand over your books? An admirable man by all accounts[9] and his views on slavery and bigotry[10] are to be recommended, but it was left behind[11] by whomever[12] had the room before me and I simply chose to leave it in its place.'

'Did you not purchase the picture of General Gordon?'

'No. But I had it mended[13] and reframed[14] after I accidentally fired a bullet into it. That was at the insistence of Mrs Hudson. You know, I may very well write a monograph[15] on this subject; the use of art in matters of detection.'

'Holmes, you insist upon seeing yourself as a machine,' I laughed. 'Even a masterpiece[16] of Impressionism is to you nothing more[17] than a piece

1. Rappelez-vous
2. de la flore locale
3. si mes souvenirs sont bons
4. de l'espèce la plus répugnante et la plus brutale qui soit
5. la faune représentée
6. vous en dire long
7. qu'il n'y a presque aucun tableau
8. je sois allé acheter
9. au dire de tous
10. opinion sur l'esclavage et le sectarisme
11. laissé là
12. celui qui
13. je l'ai fait restaurer
14. réencadrer
15. monographie
16. chef-d'œuvre
17. ne représente rien de plus, pour vous

of evidence[1] to be used in the pursuit of a crime. Perhaps an appreciation of art is what you need to humanise you. I shall insist that you accompany me on a visit to the Royal Academy.'

'We already have the gallery of Carstairs and Finch on our agenda[2], Watson, and I think that will be enough. The cheeseboard, waiter[3]. And a glass of Moselle, I think, for my friend. Port[4] is too heavy for the afternoon.'

It was but a short distance to the gallery[5], and once again we strolled together. I have to say that I took immense satisfaction in these moments of quiet sociability and felt myself to be[6] one of the luckiest men in London to have shared in[7] the conversation which I have just described and to be walking in such a leisurely manner[8] at the side of so great a personage as Sherlock Holmes. It was about four o'clock and the light was already fading[9] when we arrived at the gallery which was not, in fact, in Albemarle Street itself, but in an old coaching yard[10] just off it[11]. Apart from a discreet sign, written in gold letters, there was little to indicate that this was a commercial enterprise. A low door led into a rather gloomy interior with two sofas, a table and a single canvas – two cows in a field painted by the Dutch[12] artist Paulus Potter – mounted on an easel[13]. As we entered, we heard two men arguing[14] in the adjoining room. One voice I recognised. It belonged to Edmund Carstairs.

'It's an excellent price,' he was saying. 'And I am certain of it, Tobias. These works are like good wine. Their value can only rise[15].'

'No, no, no!' replied the other voice in a high-pitched whine[16]. 'He calls them seascapes[17]. Well, I can see the sea ... but precious little else[18]. His last show was a fiasco and now he has taken refuge in Paris where, I hear, his reputation is in rapid decline. It's a waste of money[19], Edmund.'

1. élément de preuve
2. à l'ordre du jour
3. Le plateau de fromages, garçon
4. Le porto
5. La galerie était à deux pas
6. j'avais conscience d'être
7. d'avoir pris part à
8. de marcher ainsi, tranquillement
9. jour baissait déjà
10. l'ancienne cour d'un relais
11. débouchant dessus
12. hollandais
13. posé sur un chevalet
14. en train de se disputer
15. ne peut qu'augmenter
16. d'une plainte aiguë
17. des paysages marins
18. guère plus
19. de l'argent gaspillé

'Six works by Whistler—'

'Six works we shall never be rid of[1]!'

I was standing at the door and closed it more heavily than was strictly necessary, wishing to signal[2] our presence to the two men inside. It had the desired effect. The conversation broke off[3] and a moment later a thin, white-haired individual, immaculately dressed in a dark suit[4] with a wing collar and black tie[5], appeared from behind a curtain. A gold chain hung across his waistcoat[6] and a pair of pince-nez, also gold, rested at the very tip[7] of his nose. He must have been at least sixty years old, but there was still a spring in his step[8] and a certain nervous energy that manifested itself in his every move[9].

'I take it you are Mr Finch,' Holmes began.

'Yes, sir. That is indeed my name. And you are ... ?'

'I am Sherlock Holmes.'

'Holmes? I don't believe we are acquainted and yet the name is familiar[10]—'

'Mr Holmes!' Carstairs had also come into the room. The contrast between the two men was striking[11]; the one old and wizened[12], belonging almost to another age[13], the other younger and more dandified[14], his features still displaying the anger[15] and frustration that were doubtless the result of the conversation we had overheard[16]. 'This is Mr Holmes, the detective I was telling you about,' he explained to his partner.

'Yes, yes. Of course I know. He has just introduced himself.'

'I did not expect to see you here,' Carstairs said.

'I came because it interested me to see your professional place of work,' Holmes explained. 'But I also have a number of questions for you, relating to the Pinkerton's men whom you employed in Boston.'

'A dreadful affair![17]' Finch interjected. 'I won't recover[18] from the loss of those paintings, not until the end of my days. It was the single great-

1. dont nous ne nous débarrasserons jamais
2. indiquer
3. s'interrompit
4. d'un costume sombre
5. cravate
6. ornait son gilet
7. reposait tout au bout
8. avait toujours une démarche dynamique
9. dans tous ses gestes
10. ce nom me dit quelque chose
11. frappant
12. l'un vieux et rabougri
13. presque d'une autre époque
14. aux allures de dandy
15. trahissant encore la colère
16. que nous avions surprise
17. Une épouvantable histoire !
18. Je ne me remettrai pas

est calamity[1] of my career. If only we had sold him a few of your Whistlers, Edmund. They could have been blown to pieces[2] and no one would give a jot[3]!' Once the old man had started, there seemed to be no stopping him[4]. 'Picture-dealing[5] is a respectable business[6], Mr Holmes. We deal with a great many aristocratic clients. I would not wish it to be known that we have been involved with gunmen[7] and murder!' The old man's face fell as he saw[8] that he was involved with more besides[9], for the door had just opened and a boy had rushed in[10]. I at once recognised Wiggins, who had been in our room only that morning[11], but to Finch it was as if the worst assault were being committed[12]. 'Go away! Get out of here!' he exclaimed. 'We have nothing for you.'

'You need not concern yourself, Mr Finch,' Holmes said. 'I know the boy. What is it, Wiggins?'

'We've found 'im, Mr 'olmes!' Wiggins cried, excitedly. 'The cove[13] you was looking for. We saw 'im with our own eyes, me and Ross. We was about to go in the jerryshop[14] on Bridge Lane – Ross knows the place for 'e's in and out of there often enough 'imself – when the door opens and there 'e is, clear as daylight[15], wiv 'is face cut livid by a scar[16].' The boy drew a line down[17] his own cheek. 'It was me what[18] saw 'im. Not Ross.'

'Where is he now?' Holmes asked.

'We followed 'im to 'is 'otel, sir. Will it be a guinea each if we take you there?'

'It will be the end of you[19] if you don't,' replied Holmes. 'But I have always played you fair[20], Wiggins. You know that. Tell me, where is this hotel?'

'In Bermondsey, sir. Mrs Oldmore's Private 'otel. Ross will be there now. I left 'im there to act as crow[21] while I 'iked all the way to your rooms[22] and then 'ere to find you. If your man steps out again[23], 'e'll watch where 'e goes. Ross is new to the game[24] but 'e's as canny as they come[25]. Are you going to

1. le plus grand désastre
2. réduits en miettes
3. personne ne s'en soucierait
4. rien ne semblait pouvoir l'arrêter
5. La vente de tableaux
6. activité
7. des gangsters
8. s'assombrit en voyant
9. ce qui l'attendait encore
10. venait de faire irruption
11. pas plus tard que ce matin-là
12. comme s'il subissait la pire agression
13. Le type
14. prêteur sur gage
15. pleinement visible
16. le visage balafré d'une cicatrice noirâtre
17. traça une ligne sur
18. qui
19. C'est fini pour toi
20. été fair-play avec toi
21. pour faire le guet
22. je retournais jusque chez vous
23. ressort
24. Pour Ross, c'est nouveau tout ça
25. y'a pas plus rusé que lui

1. fiacre
2. Je peux faire le trajet
3. les sourcils froncés
4. se concentraient sur ce qui allait suivre
5. à portée de main
6. nous glisser entre les doigts
7. c'est bien moi
8. de savoir comment ça finit
9. il est juste
10. d'en finir avec ça
11. de discuter
12. nous regarder partir, bouche bée
13. montâmes dedans
14. grimpant pour aller s'asseoir
15. puis se radoucit
16. lui laissa un pan de sa couverture
17. D'un coup de fouet,
18. Chalands et saltimbanques
19. une espèce totalement différente
20. d'hommes miteux et de femmes tapageuses
21. d'agir dans l'ombre
22. avait sa part d'ombre

come back with me, Mr 'olmes? Will you take a four-wheeler[1]? Can I ride[2] with you?'

'You can sit up with the driver.' Holmes turned to me and I saw at once the contracted eyebrows[3] and the intensity of expression that told me that all his energies were focused on what lay ahead[4]. 'We must leave at once,' he said. 'By a lucky chance, we have the object of our investigation in our grasp[5]. We must not let him slip between our fingers[6].'

'I will come with you,' Carstairs announced.

'Mr Carstairs, for your own safety—'

'I have seen this man. It was I who described him to you, and if anyone can be sure that these boys of yours have correctly identified him, it is I[7]. And I have a personal desire to see this out[8], Mr Holmes. If this man is whom I believe he is, then I am the cause of his presence here and it is only right[9] I see it to the end[10].'

'We have no time for argument[11],' Holmes said. 'Very well. The three of us will leave together. Let us not waste another minute.'

And so we hurried out of the gallery, Holmes, Wiggins, Carstairs and myself, leaving Mr Finch gaping after us[12]. A four-wheeler was located and we climbed in[13], Wiggins scrambling up[14] beside the driver who glanced at him disdainfully but then relented[15] and allowed him one fold of his blanket[16]. With a crack of the whip[17] we were away, as if something of our urgency had communicated itself to the horses. It was almost dark and with the coming of the night the sense of ease that I had felt had quite dissipated, and the city had once again turned cold and hostile. The shoppers and the entertainers[18] had all gone home and their places had been taken by a different species altogether[19], shabby men and gaudy women[20] who needed shadows in which to conduct their business[21] and whose business, in truth, carried shadows of its own[22].

The carriage took us over Blackfriars Bridge where the wind was at its iciest[1] and cut into us[2] like a knife. Holmes had not spoken since we had left, and I felt that in some way he'd had a presentiment of what was to come[3]. This was not something he had ever admitted and had I ever suggested it[4] I know he would have been annoyed. No soothsayer he![5] For him it was all intellect, all systematised common sense, as he once put it[6]. And yet still I was aware of something that defied explanation and which might even be considered supernatural. Like it or not, Holmes knew that the evening's events were going to provide a fulcrum[7], a turning point[8] after which his life – both our lives – would never be quite the same.

Mrs Oldmore's Private Hotel advertised a bed[9] and sitting room at thirty shillings a week, and was exactly the sort of establishment you would expect at that price; a mean, dilapidated[10] building with a slop house[11] on one side and a brick kiln[12] on the other. It was close to the river and the air was damp and grimy[13]. Lamps burned behind the windows, but the glass was so dirt-encrusted[14] that barely any light seeped through[15]. Ross, the companion of Wiggins, was waiting for us, shivering with cold[16] despite the thick padding of newspaper[17] with which his jacket was lined[18]. As Holmes and Carstairs climbed out of the carriage, he stepped back[19] and I saw that something had greatly frightened him. His eyes were filled with alarm and his face, in the glow of the street lamp, was ashen white[20]. But then Wiggins leapt down and grabbed hold of him[21] and it was as if the spell was broken[22].

'It's all right, my boy!' Wiggins cried. 'We are both of us to 'ave a guinea. Mr 'olmes 'as promised it.'

'Tell me what has happened in the time that you have been alone,' Holmes said. 'Has the man you recognised left the hotel?'

1. des plus glacés
2. nous transperçait
3. pressenti la suite
4. si jamais je l'avais suggéré
5. Il était tout sauf devin !
6. comme il l'avait dit, une fois
7. constitueraient un palier
8. un tournant
9. une chambre
10. misérable, délabré
11. atelier de travail à la journée
12. four à briques
13. humide et chargé
14. incrusté de crasse
15. la lumière passait à peine
16. tremblant de froid
17. l'épais matelas de journaux
18. doublée
19. recula
20. livide
21. descendit d'un bon et l'empoigna
22. le charme fut rompu

'Who are these gentlemen?' Ross pointed first at[1] Carstairs, then at me. 'Are they jacks[2]? Are they coppers[3]? Why are they 'ere?'

'It's all right, Ross,' I said. 'You have no need to be concerned.[4] I am John Watson, a doctor. You saw me this morning when you came to Baker Street. And this is Mr Carstairs who has a gallery in Albemarle Street. We mean you no harm[5].'

'Albemarle Street – in Mayfair?' The boy was so cold that his teeth were chattering[6]. Of course all the street Arabs in London were accustomed[7] to the winter, but he had been standing out here for at least two hours on his own.

'What have you seen?' Holmes asked.

'I ain't seen nothing[8],' Ross replied. His voice had changed. There was something about his manner[9] now that might almost have suggested that he had something to hide. Not for the first time it occurred to me that all these children had reached a sort of adulthood[10] long before their tender age should have allowed[11]. 'I been 'ere, waiting for you. 'e ain't come out. No one 'as gone in. And the cold, it's gone right through my bones.'

'Here is the money that I promised you – and you, too, Wiggins.' Holmes paid both the boys. 'Now take yourselves home[12]. You have done enough tonight.' The boys took the coins[13] and ran off[14] together, Ross casting one last look[15] in our direction. 'I suggest we enter the hotel and confront this man,' Holmes went on. 'God knows, I have no wish to linger[16] here any longer than I have to. That boy, Watson. Did it occur to you that he was dissembling[17]?'

'There was certainly something he was not telling us,' I concurred[18].

'Let us hope that he has not acted in some way so as to betray us[19]. Mr Carstairs, please stand well back[20]. It is unlikely that our target will attempt violence, but we have come here without prepar-

1. désigna tout d'abord
2. des poulets
3. des flics
4. Inutile de t'inquiéter.
5. ne te voulons aucun mal
6. claquaient
7. habitués
8. J'ai rien vu
9. dans son attitude
10. atteint une maturité d'adultes
11. que leur jeune âge ait dû le permettre
12. rentrez chez vous
13. pièces de monnaie
14. détalèrent
15. jetant un ultime regard
16. aucune envie de m'attarder
17. dissimulait quelque chose
18. acquiesçai-je
19. ne nous a pas trahi d'une façon ou d'une autre
20. restez bien en arrière

ation. Dr Watson's trusty revolver is doubtless lying wrapped up[1] in cloth[2] in some drawer in Kensington and I, too, am unarmed. We must live on our wits.[3] Come on!'

The three of us entered the hotel. A few steps led up to the front door which opened into a public hallway with no carpets, little light, and a small office to one side. An elderly man was sitting there, propped up[4] in a wooden chair, half-asleep, but he started[5] when he saw us. 'God bless you[6], gentlemen,' he quavered[7]. 'We can offer you good, single beds[8] at five shillings a night—'

'We are not here for accommodation[9],' Holmes replied. 'We are in pursuit of[10] a man who has recently arrived from America. He has a livid scar on one cheek. It is a matter of the greatest urgency, and if you do not wish to land yourself in trouble[11] with the law, you will tell us where he can be found.'

The Boots[12] had no desire to be in trouble with anyone. 'There is but one[13] American here,' he said. 'You must be referring to Mr Harrison from New York. He has the room at the end of the corridor on this floor. He came in a while ago and I think he must be asleep as I haven't heard a sound.'

'The number of the room?' Holmes demanded.

'It's number six.'

We set off[14] at once, down a bare corridor[15] with doors so close together[16] that the rooms behind them must be little more than cupboards[17] and gas-jets[18] turned so low that we had almost to feel our way through[19] the darkness. Number six was indeed at the end. Holmes raised his fist, meaning to knock[20], then stepped back, a single gasp escaping from his lips[21]. I looked down and saw a streak[22] of liquid, almost black in the half-light[23], curling out from beneath[24] the door and forming a small pool[25] against the skirting[26]. I heard Carstairs give a cry and saw him recoiling[27], his hands covering his eyes. The

1. bien enveloppé
2. un linge
3. Nous devrons compter sur notre intelligence.
4. bien calé
5. sursauta
6. Dieu vous bénisse
7. dit-il d'une voix chevrotante
8. des chambres individuelles
9. pour nous loger
10. recherchons
11. vous attirer des ennuis
12. [porteur et cireur de chaussures, à l'hôtel]
13. Il n'y a qu'un seul
14. partîmes
15. le long d'un couloir nu
16. si rapprochées
17. devaient s'apparenter à des placards
18. les brûleurs à gaz
19. avancer à tâtons dans
20. pour frapper à la porte
21. poussant un cri de surprise
22. un filet
23. demi-jour
24. serpentant par-dessous
25. flaque
26. contre la plinthe
27. se reculer

1. sur le point d'apparaître
2. Impossible de l'ouvrir.
3. le fragile verrou vola en éclats
4. s'était sérieusement aggravé
5. avait été mise à sac
6. lové, un couteau planté dans le cou

Boots was watching us from the end of the corridor. It was as if he had already been expecting the horror that was about to unveil itself[1].

Holmes tried the door. It wouldn't open.[2] Without saying a word, he brought his shoulder up against it and the flimsy lock shattered[3]. Leaving Carstairs in the corridor, the two of us went in and saw at once that the crime, which I had once considered trivial, had taken a turn for the worse[4]. The window was open. The room was ransacked[5]. And the man we had been pursuing was curled up with a knife in the side of his neck[6].

FIVE

Lestrade Takes Charge[1]

Quite recently I saw George Lestrade again for what was to be the last time.

He had never fully recovered from the bullet wound he had sustained[2] whilst investigating[3] the bizarre murders that had become known in the popular press as the Clerkenwell Killings, although one of them had taken place in neighbouring Hoxton[4], and another turned out to be a suicide. By then, he had, of course, long retired[5] from the police force, but he had the kindness to come and seek me out[6] in the home into which I had just moved and we spent the afternoon together, reminiscing[7]. My readers will hardly be surprised to learn that it was the subject of Sherlock Holmes that occupied much of our discourse, and I felt a need to apologise[8] to Lestrade on two counts[9]. First, I had never described him in perhaps the most glowing terms[10]. The words 'rat-faced' and 'ferret-like'[11] spring to mind[12]. Well, as unkind as it must seem, it was at least accurate[13], for Lestrade himself had once joked that a capricious Mother Nature had given him the looks[14] of a criminal rather than a police officer and that, all in all[15], he might have made himself a richer man had he chosen the former profession[16]. Holmes, too, often remarked that his own skills[17], particularly in matters of lock-picking[18] and forgery[19], might have made him as equally successful a criminal as

1. prend les choses en main
2. reçue
3. alors qu'il enquêtait sur
4. dans le voisinage, à Hoxton
5. pris sa retraite depuis longtemps
6. de venir me voir
7. à nous remémorer le passé
8. faire des excuses
9. à deux égards
10. les termes les plus élogieux
11. « face de rat » et « tel un furet »
12. sont les exemples qui me viennent à l'esprit
13. exact
14. le physique
15. somme toute
16. la première profession
17. compétences
18. pour ce qui est de forcer des serrures
19. de fabriquer des faux

1. mais comme délinquants
2. j'étais peut-être injuste avec Lestrade
3. disait du mal de lui
4. si doué, intellectuellement
5. capable de rivaliser avec lui
6. dénigrait tout autant
7. confiance
8. mise à rude épreuve
9. En bref
10. pratiquement impossible
11. s'imposer
12. archives
13. affaires résolues
14. tout de même
15. commissaire divisionnaire adjoint
16. police judiciaire
17. reposait
18. dont le mérite lui était revenu
19. n'est plus
20. révèle ses secrets
21. rends à César ce qui est à César
22. finalement
23. En tout cas

he was a detective, and it is amusing to think that, in another world, the two men might have worked together on the wrong side of the law[1].

But where I perhaps did Lestrade an injustice[2] was in suggesting that he had no intelligence or investigative skill whatsoever. It's fair to say that Sherlock Holmes occasionally spoke ill of him[3], but then Holmes was so unique, so intellectually gifted[4] that there was nobody in London who could compete with him[5] and he was equally disparaging about[6] almost every police officer he encountered, apart perhaps from Stanley Hopkins, and his faith[7], even in that young detective, was often sorely tested[8]. Put simply[9], next to Holmes, any detective would have found it nigh on impossible[10] to make his mark[11] and even I, who was at his side more often than anyone, sometimes had to remind myself that I was not a complete idiot. But Lestrade was in many ways a capable man. Were you to look in the public records[12] you would find many successful cases[13] that he investigated quite independently and the newspapers always spoke well of him. Even Holmes admired his tenacity. And, when all is said and done[14], he did finish his career as Assistant Commissioner[15] in charge of the CID[16] at Scotland Yard, even if a large part of his reputation rested[17] on the cases that Holmes had, in fact, solved, but for which he took the credit[18]. Lestrade suggested to me, during our long and pleasant conversation, that he may well have been intimidated when he was in the presence of Sherlock Holmes, and that this might have caused him to function less than effectively. Well, he is gone now[19] and won't mind, I am sure, if I break his confidence[20] and give him credit where it's due[21]. He was not a bad man. And at the end of the day[22], I knew exactly how he felt.

At any event[23], it was Lestrade who arrived at Mrs Oldmore's Private Hotel the next morning. And yes, he was as always pale-skinned[1] with bright, sunken eyes[2] and the general demeanour[3] of a rat who has been obliged to dress up[4] for lunch at the Savoy. After Holmes had alerted the constables[5] in the street, the room had been closed off[6] and kept under police guard until the cold touch of light[7] could dispel the shadows[8] and lend itself to[9] a proper investigation, along with the general surroundings[10] of the hotel.

'Well, well, Mr Holmes,' he remarked with a hint[11] of irritation. 'They told me you were expected when I was at Wimbledon and here you are again now.'

'We have both been following in the footsteps[12] of the unfortunate wretch[13] who has ended his days here,' retorted Holmes.

Lestrade took one look at the body. 'This would indeed seem to be the man we have been seeking.' Holmes said nothing and Lestrade glanced at him sharply[14]. 'How did you come to find him?'

'It was absurdly simple. I knew, thanks to the brilliance of your own enquiries[15], that he had returned on the train to London Bridge. Since then, my agents have been scouring the area[16] and two of them were fortunate enough to come across him[17] in the street.'

'I assume that you are referring to that gang of urchins[18] you have at your beck and call[19]. I'd keep my distance if I were you, Mr Holmes. No good will come of it.[20] They're all thieves and pickpockets when they are not being encouraged by you. Is there any sign of the necklace?'

'There seems to be no obvious sign of it – no. But then I have not yet had a chance[21] to search the room in its entirety.'

'Then maybe we should start by doing just that.'

Matching his actions to his words[22], Lestrade examined the room carefully. It was a fairly dismal place[23] with tattered curtains, a mouldering carpet[24] and a bed that looked more exhausted than anyone who might have attempted to sleep in it. A cracked[25]

1. pâle, comme toujours,
2. les yeux brillants, enfoncés dans leurs orbites
3. l'allure
4. s'endimancher
5. agents de police
6. interdite d'accès
7. le jour blafard,
8. ayant dissipé les ombres,
9. [la chambre] se prête à
10. ainsi que les alentours
11. un soupçon
12. suivi la trace
13. l'infortuné
14. vivement
15. grâce à l'excellence de vos propres recherches
16. ont ratissé cette zone
17. ont eu la chance de tomber sur lui
18. garnements
19. qui vous obéissent au doigt et à l'œil
20. Il n'en ressortira rien de bon.
21. l'occasion
22. Joignant le geste à la parole
23. un endroit assez lamentable
24. un tapis en proie à la moisissure
25. fêlé

mirror hung on one wall. A washstand[1] stood in the corner with a soiled basin[2] and a single, misshapen[3] lump of cast-iron soap[4]. There was no view. The window looked over[5] a narrow alley to a brick wall opposite, and although it was out of sight and some distance away, the River Thames had permeated[6] the place with its dampness and smell[7]. Next he turned his attentions to the dead man who was dressed as Carstairs had first described him, in a frock coat that came down to his knees[8], a thick waistcoat and a shirt buttoned to the neck. All of these were saturated with blood[9]. The knife that had killed him had buried itself up to the hilt[10], penetrating the carotid artery. My training told me that he would have died instantly[11]. Lestrade searched his pockets but found nothing. Now that I was able to scrutinise him more carefully, I saw that the man who had followed Carstairs to Ridgeway Hall was in his early forties, well built[12], with thickset[13] shoulders and muscular arms. He had close-cropped[14] hair that had begun to turn grey[15]. Most striking of all[16] was the scar which began at the corner of his mouth and slanted over his cheekbone[17], narrowly missing his eye[18]. He had come close to death once.[19] He had been less fortunate the second time.

'Can we be sure that this is the same man who imposed himself on[20] Mr Edmund Carstairs?' Lestrade asked.

'Indeed so. Carstairs was able to identify him.'

'He was here?'

'Briefly, yes. Sadly, he was compelled to leave[21].' Holmes smiled to himself[22] and I recalled how we had been compelled to bundle[23] Edmund Carstairs into a cab[24] and send him on his way to Wimbledon. He had barely glimpsed[25] the body but it had been enough to send him into a fainting fit[26] and I had understood how he must have been on board the *Catalonia* following his experiences with the Flat

1. table de toilette
2. une cuvette sale
3. difforme
4. morceau de savon durci
5. donnait sur
6. imprégné
7. de son humidité et de son odeur
8. lui allait jusqu'aux genoux
9. imprégnés de sang
10. était enfoncé jusqu'à la garde
11. avait dû mourir instantanément
12. bien bâti
13. larges
14. coupés très court
15. grisonnaient
16. Le plus frappant
17. barrait sa joue
18. évitant l'œil de peu
19. Il avait frôlé la mort une fois.
20. a importuné
21. a dû partir
22. sourit dans sa barbe
23. pousser
24. fiacre
25. à peine entrevu
26. pour qu'il manque s'évanouir

Cap Gang in Boston. It may be that he had[1] the same sensitivity as some of the artists whose works he displayed. It was certainly the case that the blood and grime of Bermondsey were not for him.

'Here is further evidence[2] if you need it.' Holmes gestured at[3] a flat cap, lying on the bed.

Lestrade had meanwhile turned his attention to a packet of cigarettes lying on a table nearby. He examined the label. 'Old Judge ...'

'Manufactured, I think you will find, by Goodwin and Company of New York. I found the stub of one such cigarette[4] at Ridgeway Hall.'

'Did you now?[5]' Lestrade let out a silent exclamation. 'Well,' he said, 'I suppose we can discard[6] the idea that our American friend was the victim of a random attack[7]? Though there have been plenty of those in this neighbourhood[8], and it is always possible that this fellow returned to his room and surprised someone as they were ransacking the place. A fight ensued.[9] A knife was drawn. And there's the end of it ...'

'I think it is unlikely,' Holmes agreed. 'It would seem too much of a coincidence that a man who arrived recently in London and who was clearly up to no good[10] should suddenly meet his end[11] in this way. What happened in this hotel room can only be a direct result of his activities in Wimbledon. And then there is the position of the body and the angle at which[12] the knife was driven[13] into his neck. It seems to me that the attacker was waiting for him beside the door in the darkened room, for there was no candle burning here[14] when we arrived. He walked in[15] and was seized[16] from behind. Looking at him, you can see that he was a powerful man, capable of looking after himself[17]. But in this instance he was taken by surprise and killed with a single blow[18].'

1. Peut-être avait-il
2. une preuve supplémentaire
3. indiqua
4. d'une cigarette de ce genre
5. Vraiment ?
6. écarter
7. d'une attaque au hasard
8. dans ces parages
9. Cela a provoqué une bagarre.
10. de toute évidence, ne mijotait rien de bon
11. trouve soudain la mort
12. selon lequel
13. planté
14. car aucune bougie n'y brûlait
15. est entré
16. empoigné
17. se défendre
18. du premier coup

1. Le vol
2. à retrouver
3. le principal mobile du
4. portefeuille
5. actuel
6. se renfrogna
7. originaire de Boston
8. que vous le contestez
9. j'acquiesçai d'un signe de tête
10. Ce qui concorde
11. sommes parvenus au terme
12. désolant
13. blessé
14. lors de la fusillade
15. Ça, au moins,
16. c'est clair comme de l'eau de roche
17. À mon avis, rien n'est moins sûr au contraire

'Theft[1] might still be the motive,' Lestrade insisted. 'There are the fifty pounds and the necklace to be accounted for[2]. If they are not here, where are they?'

'I have every reason to believe you will find the necklace in a pawnbroker on Bridge Lane. Our man had just come from there. It would certainly appear that whoever killed him took the money, but I would suggest that was not the primary reason for the[3] crime. Perhaps you should ask yourself what else was taken from the room. We have a body with no identity, Lestrade. You would think that a visitor from America might have a passport or letters of introduction, perhaps, to recommend him to a bank. His wallet[4], I notice, is absent. You know what name he used on entering the hotel?'

'He called himself Benjamin Harrison.'

'Which is of course the current[5] American president.'

'The American president? Of course. I was aware of that.' Lestrade scowled[6]. 'But whatever name he chose, we know exactly who he is. He is Keelan O'Donaghue, late of Boston[7]. You see the mark on his face? That's a bullet wound. Don't tell me you'll argue with that[8]!'

Holmes turned to me and I nodded[9]. 'It is certainly a gun wound,' I said. I had seen many similar injuries in Afghanistan. 'I would say it is about a year old.'

'Which ties in[10] exactly with what Carstairs told me,' Lestrade concluded, triumphantly. 'It seems to me that we have come to the end[11] of this whole sorry[12] episode. O'Donaghue was injured[13] in the shoot-out[14] at the Boston tenement. At the same time, his twin brother was killed and he came to England on a mission of revenge. That much[15] is as plain as a pikestaff.[16]'

'To my eyes, it could hardly be less plain if a pikestaff had been used as the murder weapon[17],'

Holmes demurred[1]. 'Perhaps you can explain to us, then, Lestrade: who killed Keelan O'Donaghue – and why?'

'Well, the most obvious suspect would be Edmund Carstairs himself.'

'Except that Mr Carstairs was with us at the time of the murder. Also, having been witness to[2] his reaction on discovering[3] the body, I really don't think he would have had the nerve or the willpower[4] to strike the blow himself. Besides, he did not know where his victim was staying[5]. As far as we know, nobody at Ridgeway Hall had that information for we ourselves were only told[6] at the very last moment[7]. I might also ask you why, if this really is Keelan O'Donaghue, he has a cigarette case[8] marked with the initials WM?'

'What cigarette case?'

'It is on the bed, partly covered by the sheet[9]. That would doubtless explain why the killer missed it[10], too.'

Lestrade found the object in question and briefly examined it. 'O'Donaghue was a thief,' he said. 'There is no reason why he might not have stolen this.'

'Is there any reason why he *would* have stolen it? It is not a valuable item[11]. It is made of tin[12] with the letters painted on.'

Lestrade had opened the case. It was empty. He snapped it shut.[13] 'This is all the merest moonshine[14],' he said. 'The trouble with you, Holmes, is that you have a way of[15] complicating things. I sometimes wonder if you don't do it deliberately. It's as if you need the crime to rise to the challenge[16], as if it has to be unusual enough for it to be worth solving[17]. The man in this room was American. He had been wounded in a gunfight. He was seen once in the Strand and twice in Wimbledon. If he did visit this pawnshop of yours, then we will

1. objecta
2. témoin de
3. à la découverte
4. le cran ou la volonté
5. logeait
6. car nous-mêmes ne l'avons su
7. qu'au tout dernier moment
8. étui à cigarettes
9. recouvert par le drap
10. ne l'a pas vu
11. un objet de valeur
12. fer-blanc
13. Il le referma d'un coup sec
14. Ce ne sont que des fadaises
15. le don de
16. soit à la hauteur du défi
17. pour qu'il vaille la peine d'être résolu

1. alors nous saurons que c'est lui
2. de cerner
3. se sont disputés
4. nous éclairer
5. précédemment
6. à l'air revêche
7. se protégeant le buste de ses bras,
8. à moins de rester le plus loin possible
9. une étole en fourrure
10. (je frémis en pensant à l'animal d'où elle provenait)
11. il avait trouvé la mort
12. Mort de faim
13. une hypothèse vraisemblable
14. fraîchement débarqué
15. Il m'a dit au moins ça
16. parce qu'il savait pas trouver son chemin
17. un coin chic
18. de belles maisons, pour sûr
19. peu de bagages, des vêtements miteux
20. me doit
21. j'ai bien l'intention de le récupérer

know him to be[1] the thief who broke into Carstairs's safe. From there, it is easy enough to construe[2] what took place here. Doubtless O'Donaghue would have had other criminal contacts here in London. He may well have recruited one of them to help him in his vendetta. The two of them fell out[3]. The other pulled a knife. This is the result!'

'You are certain of that?'

'I am as certain as I need to be.'

'Well, we shall see. But there is nothing more to be gained from discussing the matter here. Perhaps the owner of the hotel will be able to enlighten us[4].'

But Mrs Oldmore, who was now waiting in the small office that had formerly[5] been occupied by the Boots, had little to add. She was a grey-haired, sour-faced[6] woman who sat with her arms wrapped around her[7] as if she were afraid that the building would contaminate her unless she could keep herself as far away as possible[8] from its walls. She was wearing a small bonnet and had a fur stole[9] across her shoulders, although I shuddered to think what animal had provided it[10] or how it had met its end[11]. Starvation[12] seemed a likely option[13].

''e took the room for the week,' she said. 'And paid me a guinea. An American gentleman, just off a ship[14] at Liverpool. That much 'e told me[15], though not much more. It was 'is first time in London. 'e didn't say so, but I could tell for 'e 'ad no idea 'ow to find 'is way around[16]. 'e said there was someone 'e 'ad come to see in Wimbledon and 'e asked me 'ow to get there. "Wimbledon," I said. "That's a posh area[17] and plenty of rich Americans with fancy 'omes, and no mistake[18]." Not that there was anything fancy about 'im – 'e 'ad little luggage, 'is clothes were tatty[19], and then there was that nasty wound on 'is face. "I will go there tomorrow," 'e said. "For there is someone who owes me[20] something and I mean to collect it[21]." From the way 'e talked, I could tell 'e was up to no good and I thought to myself then and there – whoever this person is, maybe 'e should look out for 'imself[1]. I was expecting trouble, but what can you do? If I turned away[2] every suspicious-looking[3] customer[4] who came knocking at my door, I'd 'ave no business at all[5]. And now this American, Mr 'arrison, is murdered! Well, it's to be expected[6], I suppose. It's the world we live in, isn't it, where a respectable woman can't run a 'otel[7] without 'aving blood on the walls and corpses spread out on the floorboards[8]. I should never 'ave stayed in London. It's an 'orrible place. Utterly[9] 'orrible!'

We left her sitting in misery[10] and Lestrade took his leave[11]. 'I'm sure we'll run into each other again, Mr Holmes,' he said. 'And if you need me, you know where to find me.'

'If I should ever find myself in need of Inspector Lestrade,' Holmes muttered[12] after he had gone, 'then things will have come to a pretty pass[13]. But let us step into the alleyway[14], Watson. My case is complete and yet there is still one small point which must be addressed[15].'

We went out of the front of the hotel into the main street and then entered the narrow, litter-strewn[16] alleyway that ran past[17] the room in which the American had met his end. The window was clearly visible about halfway down, with a wooden crate set[18] just beneath it[19]. It was evident that the killer had used this as a step to gain entrance[20]. The window itself had not been locked and would have opened easily from outside. Holmes glanced at the ground in a perfunctory way[21], but there seemed to be nothing there to attract his attention. Together we followed the alley to the point at which it ended with a high wooden fence[22] and an empty yard[23] beyond. From there, we returned to the main road. By now, Holmes was deep in thought[24] and I could see the unease[25] in his pale, elongated face.

'You remember the boy – Ross – last night,' he said.

1. il f'rait bien de se méfier
2. je refusais
3. à l'air louche
4. client
5. j'aurais plus un seul client
6. fallait s'y attendre
7. peut pas tenir un hôtel
8. des cadavres sur le parquet
9. Vraiment
10. la laissâmes à ses lamentations
11. prit congé
12. marmonna
13. la situation serait bien désespérée
14. rendons-nous dans la ruelle
15. à examiner
16. pleine de détritus
17. longeait
18. une caisse en bois placée
19. au-dessous
20. entrer
21. d'un œil rapide
22. clôture
23. cour
24. plongé dans ses pensées
25. l'inquiétude

'You thought that there was something he was holding back[1].'

'And now I am certain of it. From where he was standing, he had a clear view of both[2] the hotel and the alleyway, the end of which[3], as we have both seen, is blocked. The killer can only have entered, therefore, from the road[4], and Ross may well have had a sight of who it was[5].'

'He certainly seemed ill at ease. But if he saw something, Holmes, why did he not tell us?'

'Because he had some plan of his own[6], Watson. In a way, Lestrade was right. These boys live on their wits[7] every hour of their lives. They must learn to do so if they are to survive[8]. If Ross thought that there was money to be made, he would take on the devil himself[9]! And yet there is something here that I don't understand at all. What is it that this child could possibly have seen? A figure caught in the gas-light[10], flitting down a passageway[11] and disappearing from sight, perhaps he hears a cry as the blow is struck[12]. Moments later, the killer appears a second time, hurrying away[13] into the night. Ross remains where he is and a short while later the three of us arrive.'

'He was afraid,' I said. 'He mistook[14] Carstairs for a police officer.'

'It was more than fear. I would have said the boy was in the grip[15] of something close to terror[16], but I assumed[17] ...' He struck a hand against his brow. 'We must find him again and speak with him. I hope I have not been guilty of a grave miscalculation[18].'

We stopped at a post office on the way back to Baker Street and Holmes sent another wire[19] to Wiggins, the chief lieutenant of his little army of Irregulars. But twenty-four hours later, Wiggins had still not reported back to us[20]. And it was a short while after that that we heard the worst possible news[21].

Ross had disappeared.

1. qu'il ne disait pas
2. voyait aussi bien
3. dont l'extrémité
4. n'a donc pu entrer que par la rue
5. a très bien pu voir qui c'était
6. son propre plan
7. doivent savoir se débrouiller
8. C'est un apprentissage indispensable pour survivre
9. s'en prendrait au diable en personne
10. Une silhouette aperçue à la lueur du réverbère
11. au détour d'une ruelle
12. au moment où le coup est porté
13. filant
14. Il a pris
15. sous l'emprise
16. s'apparentant à de la terreur
17. j'ai cru
18. erreur de jugement
19. télégramme
20. n'avait toujours pas répondu à notre convocation
21. nous sûmes le pire

SIX

Chorley Grange School for Boys

In 1890, the year of which I write, there were some five and a half million people in the six hundred square miles[1] of the area known as the Metropolitan Police District of London[2] and then, as always, those two constant neighbours[3] wealth[4] and poverty were living uneasily side by side[5]. It sometimes occurs to me now, having witnessed[6] so many momentous changes across the years[7], that I should have described at greater length[8] the sprawling[9] chaos of the city in which I lived, perhaps in the manner of Gissing[10] – or Dickens fifty years before. I can only say in my own defence that I was a biographer, not a historian or a journalist, and that my adventures invariably led me[11] to more rarefied walks of life[12] – fine houses, hotels, private clubs, schools and offices of government. It is true that Holmes's clients came from all classes, but (and perhaps someone might one day have pause[13] to consider the significance of this) the more interesting crimes, the ones I chose to relate, were nearly always committed by the well-to-do[14].

However, it is necessary now to reflect upon[15] the lower depths of the great cauldron[16] of London, what Gissing called 'the nether world[17]', to understand the impossibility of the task that faced us[18]. We had to find one child, one helpless tatterdemalion[19] among so many others, and if Holmes was

1. env. 1 500 km²
2. [zone couverte par la police de Londres, à partir de 1829]
3. voisins perpétuels
4. la richesse
5. coexistaient péniblement
6. été témoin de
7. tant de bouleversements au fil des ans
8. plus en détail
9. tentaculaire
10. [romancier de la fin du XIXᵉ s. influencé par Dickens]
11. me conduisaient
12. à des couches plus raffinées de la société
13. prendre le temps
14. les nantis
15. de se pencher sur
16. les bas-fonds du grand chaudron
17. le monde des ténèbres
18. qui nous attendait
19. un va-nu-pieds sans défense

right, if there was danger abroad[1], we had no time to spare[2]. Where to begin? Our enquiries would be made no easier[3] by the restlessness[4] of the city, the way its inhabitants moved from house to house and street to street in seemingly perpetual motion so that few knew so much as[5] the names of those who lived next door. The slum clearances[6] and the spread[7] of the railways were largely culpable, although many Londoners seemed to have arrived with a restlessness of spirit that simply would not allow them to settle long[8]. They moved like gypsies, following whatever work they could find; fruit-picking[9] and bricklaying[10] in the summer, bunkering down[11] and scurrying for[12] coal and scraps[13] once the cold weather arrived. They might stay a while in one place, but then, once their money had run out[14], they would bolt the moon[15] and be off again.

And then there was the greatest curse[16] of our age, the carelessness that had put tens of thousands of children out onto the street; begging[17], pickpocketing, pilfering[18] or, if they were not up to the mark[19], quietly dying unknown and unloved[20], their parents indifferent if indeed those parents were themselves alive. There were children who shared threepenny[21] lodging houses, provided they could find their share of the night's rent[22], crammed together[23] in conditions barely fit for animals. Children slept on rooftops, in pens[24] at Smithfield market, down in the sewers[25] and even, I heard, in holes scooped out of the dust-heaps[26] on Hackney Marshes. There were, as I shall soon describe, charities[27] that set out to help them, to clothe and to educate them. But the charities were too few, the children too many and even as the century drew to a close[28], London has every reason to be ashamed.

1. le danger rôdait
2. pas de temps à perdre
3. ne seraient pas facilitées
4. agitation
5. ne serait-ce que
6. La destruction des quartiers insalubres
7. la progression
8. rester longtemps
9. récoltant des fruits
10. travaillant comme maçons
11. se terrant
12. furetant à la recherche de
13. de restes
14. une fois l'argent épuisé
15. déménageaient à la cloche de bois
16. malédiction
17. mendiant
18. chapardant
19. à la hauteur
20. anonymes et délaissés
21. de quatre sous
22. leur part de loyer pour la nuit
23. entassés
24. sur les toits, dans les enclos
25. au fond des égouts
26. des trous creusés dans les tas d'ordures
27. des œuvres caritatives
28. touchait à sa fin

Come, Watson, that's quite enough of this. Get back to the story. Holmes would never have stood for it[1] had he been alive!

Holmes had been in a mood of constant disquiet[2] from the moment we had left Mrs Oldmore's Private Hotel. During the day, he had paced up and down[3] the room like a bear[4]. Although he had smoked incessantly, he had barely touched his lunch or dinner and I was concerned to see him glance once or twice at the smart morocco case[5] that he kept on his mantelpiece[6]. It housed[7], I knew, a hypodermic syringe[8], but it would have been unheard of for[9] Holmes, in the middle of a case, to indulge in[10] the seven-per-cent solution of cocaine[11] that was, without doubt, his most egregious habit[12]. I do not think he slept at all. Late into the night, before my own eyes closed, I heard him picking out a tune[13] on his Stradivarius, but the music was ragged[14] and full of discords[15] and I could tell[16] that his heart wasn't in it[17]. I understood all too well the nervous energy that afflicted my friend. He had spoken of a grave miscalculation. The disappearance of Ross suggested that he had been proved right[18] and, if this were the case, he would never forgive himself.

I thought we might go back to Wimbledon. From what he had said at the hotel, Holmes had made it clear[19] that the adventure of the man in the flat cap was over, the case solved and all that remained was for him to launch[20] into one of those explanations that would leave me wondering[21] how I could have been so obtuse as to have not seen it for myself from the start. However, breakfast brought a letter from Catherine Carstairs, informing us that she and her husband had gone away for a few days, staying with friends in Suffolk. Edmund Carstairs, with his fragile nature, needed time to regain his composure[22] and

1. ne l'aurait jamais toléré
2. tracas
3. arpenté
4. comme un ours en cage
5. l'élégant coffret en maroquin
6. le dessus de sa cheminée
7. contenait
8. seringue
9. il aurait été inédit que
10. s'accorde
11. de la cocaïne diluée à 7 %
12. son accoutumance dominante
13. jouer un morceau
14. irrégulière
15. dissonances
16. je voyais bien
17. que le cœur n'y était pas
18. eu raison
19. clairement dit
20. qu'il ne lui restait plus qu'à se lancer
21. après laquelle je me demanderais
22. pour se ressaisir

1. en l'absence d'un auditoire
2. deux jours s'écoulèrent
3. comment, franchement

Holmes would never reveal what he knew without an audience[1]. I would therefore have to wait.

In fact, it was another two days[2] before Wiggins returned to 221B Baker Street, this time on his own. He had received Holmes's wire (quite how[3], I do not know, I never learned where Wiggins lived or in what circumstances) and since then he had been searching for Ross, but without success.

''e came to London at the end of the summer,' Wiggins explained.

'Came to London from where?'

4. à neuf dans deux pièces
5. J'ai l'impression
6. qu'il veut se faire oublier
7. me chercher
8. pendant deux ou trois heures
9. était partant
10. Je l'ai pas forcé.
11. Ce n'est pas du tout ce que je veux dire.
12. je vous ai congédiés
13. de son côté

'I've no idea. When I met 'im, 'e was sharing a kitchen in King's Cross with a family – nine of them in two rooms[4] – and I spoke to them but they ain't seen 'im since that night at the 'otel. No one's seen 'im. It sounds to me[5] like 'e's lying low[6].'

'Wiggins, I want you to tell me what happened that night,' Holmes said, sternly. 'The two of you followed the American from the pawnbroker to the hotel. You left Ross watching the place while you came for me[7]. He must have been alone there for a couple of hours[8].'

'Ross was game[9]. I didn't make 'im.[10]'

'I'm not suggesting that for a moment.[11] Finally, we returned, Mr Carstairs, Dr Watson, you and I. Ross was still there. I gave you both money and dismissed you[12]. You left together.'

'We didn't stay together long,' Wiggins replied. ''e went 'is way[13] and I went mine.'

'Did he say anything to you? Did the two of you speak?'

'Ross was in a strange mood and no mistake. There was something 'e'd seen ...'

14. Ça lui a fichu la frousse.
15. il est à la coule
16. il était chamboulé

'At the hotel? Did he tell you what it was?'

'There was a man. That was all. It put the wind up 'im.[14] Ross is only thirteen but 'e normally knows what's what[15]. You know? Well, 'e was shook to the core[16].'

'He saw the killer!' I exclaimed.

'I don't know what 'e saw but I can tell you what 'e said. "I know 'im and I can make something from 'im[1]. More than the guinea I got from bloody Mr 'olmes." Forgive me, sir. But them were 'is words[2] exactly. I reckon 'e was all set to put the squeeze on someone[3].'

'Anything else?'

'Only that 'e was in an 'urry to be off[4]. 'e ran into the night. 'e didn't go to King's Cross. I don't know where 'e went. The only thing[5] is that nobody saw 'im no more[6].'

As Holmes listened to this, he was as grave as I had ever seen him. Now he moved closer to the boy and crouched down. Wiggins seemed very small beside him. Malnourished and sickly[7], with matted hair[8], rheumy eyes and skin befouled[9] by London dirt, it would have been impossible to distinguish him in a crowd[10]. It may be that this was why it was so easy to ignore the plight[11] of these children. There were so many of them. They all looked the same.[12] 'Listen to me, Wiggins,' Holmes said. 'It seems to me that Ross could be in great danger—'

'I looked for 'im! I searched everywhere!'

'I'm sure of it. But you must tell me what you know of his past. Where did he come from before you met him. Who were his parents?'

''e never 'ad no parents.[13] They were dead, long ago. 'e never said where 'e come from and I never asked. Where do you think any of us come from? What does it matter?[14]'

'Think, boy. If he found himself in trouble, is there anyone he would turn to[15], any place where he might seek refuge[16]?'

Wiggins shook his head. But then he seemed to think again. 'Is there another guinea in it for me?' he asked.

1. en tirer quelque chose
2. c'est ce qu'il a dit
3. À mon avis, il se préparait à faire chanter quelqu'un
4. il était pressé de partir
5. Tout ce que je sais,
6. ne l'a plus vu
7. Sous-alimenté et maladif
8. les cheveux emmêlés
9. l'œil chassieux et la peau salie
10. de le distinguer dans la foule
11. détresse
12. Ils se ressemblaient tous.
13. Il a jamais eu de parents.
14. Quelle importance ?
15. vers qui il pourrait se tourner
16. un endroit où il pourrait se réfugier

1. Holmes plissa les yeux
2. qu'il luttait pour garder son calme
3. il n'était rien pour moi
4. disparaissait à jamais
5. continuait de le regarder avec colère
6. se radoucit
7. Des gens se sont occupés de lui
8. en tout cas
9. qui l'a recueilli
10. sur la route de Hamworth
11. qu'il avait détesté être là-bas
12. si quelque chose lui a fait peur
13. lui voulait du mal
14. Là, au moins, il savait à quoi s'attendre
15. se redressa
16. la lui donna
17. vous nourrira
18. nous déposa
19. au bord d'un chemin étroit
20. grimpait en pente raide
21. maison de campagne
22. de tuiles rouges
23. tout autour
24. façade
25. de plantes grimpantes
26. nues et grêles

Holmes's eyes narrowed[1] and I could see he was struggling to compose himself[2]. 'Is the life of your compatriot worth as little as that?' he demanded.

'I don't understand "compatriot". 'e was nothing to me[3], Mr 'olmes. Why would I care if 'e lived or died? If Ross were never seen again[4], there are twenty more that would take 'is place.' Holmes was still glaring at him[5] and Wiggins suddenly softened[6]. 'All right. 'e was looked after[7], for a while anyway[8]. There was a charity what took 'im in[9]. Chorley Grange, up 'amworth way[10]. It's a school for boys. 'e told me once that 'e'd been there but 'e 'ated it[11] and ran away. That was when 'e set up in King's Cross. But, I suppose, if 'e was scared[12], if someone was after 'im[13], maybe 'e could 'ave gone back. Better the devil you know[14]...'

Holmes straightened up[15]. 'Thank you, Wiggins,' he said. 'I want you to keep looking for him. I want you to ask anyone you meet.' He took out a coin and handed it over[16]. 'If you find him, you must bring him here at once. Mrs Hudson will feed you[17] both and look after you until I return. Do you understand me?'

'Yes, Mr 'olmes.'

'Good. Watson, I trust you will accompany me? We can take the train from Baker Street.'

One hour later, a cab dropped us off[18] in front of three handsome buildings that stood next to one another on the edge of a narrow lane[19] which climbed steeply[20] for at least half a mile from the village of Roxeth up to Hamworth Hill. The largest of these, the one at the centre, resembled an English gentleman's country home[21] of perhaps a hundred years ago, with a red-tiled[22] roof and a veranda running its full length[23] at the level of the first floor. The face[24] of the house was covered in vines[25] which might be luxuriant in the summer but which were bare and spindly[26] now, and the entire habitation was surrounded by farmland[1], with a lawn slanting down to an orchard[2] filled with ancient apple trees. It was hard to believe that we were so close to London, for the air was fresh and the surrounding countryside most attractive, or it would have been had the weather been more clement, for it was very cold again and had begun to drizzle[3]. The buildings on each side were either barns[4] or brewhouses[5] but had presumably[6] been adapted to the school's needs. There was a fourth structure on the other side of the lane, this one surrounded by an ornate metal fence with an open gate. It gave the impression of being empty for there was no light or movement there. A wooden sign[7] read[8]: CHORLEY GRANGE SCHOOL FOR BOYS. Looking across the fields, I noticed a small group of boys attacking a vegetable patch[9] with spades and hoes[10].

We rang the front bell and were admitted by a man who was sombrely dressed in a dark grey suit and who listened in silence as Holmes explained who we were and on what mission we had come. 'Very good, gentlemen. If you would like to wait here ...' He admitted us into the building and left us standing in an austere, wood-panelled hall[11] with nothing on the walls apart from a few portraits, so faded[12] as to be almost indecipherable[13], and a silver cross[14]. A long corridor with several doors stretched into the distance[15]. I could imagine classrooms on the other side, but not a sound came from within[16]. It struck me that the place was more like a monastery than a school.

Then the servant[17], if that was what he was, returned, bringing with him a short, round-faced man[18] who had to take three steps[19] for every one of his companion's[20] and panted loudly[21] in his efforts to keep up[22]. Everything about this new arrival was circular. In shape, he reminded me of the snowmen[23] that I might see any time now in Regent's Park, for his head was one ball and his body

1. des terres agricoles
2. en pente menant à un verger
3. un crachin commençait à tomber
4. des granges
5. des brasseries [fabriques]
6. probablement
7. panneau
8. indiquait
9. un potager
10. à la bêche et au sarcloir
11. une entrée ornée de boiseries
12. si fanés
13. qu'on ne distinguait plus grand chose
14. croix en argent
15. allait vers l'intérieur
16. pas un bruit n'en sortait
17. le domestique
18. un homme de petite taille, au visage rond
19. devait faire trois pas
20. là où son compagnon en faisait un
21. haletait bruyamment
22. en essayant de suivre
23. Sa silhouette me rappelait les bonshommes de neige

another and there was a simplicity about his face that could have been suggested with a carrot and several lumps of coal. He was about forty years old, bald[1], with just a little dark hair around his ears. He was dressed in the manner of a clergyman[2], complete with dog collar[3], which formed another circle around his neck. As he walked towards us, he beamed[4] and spread his arms in welcome[5].

'Mr Holmes! You do us a great honour. I have of course read of your exploits, sir. The greatest consulting detective in the country[6], here at Chorley Grange! It is really quite remarkable. And you must be Dr Watson. We have read your stories in class. The boys are delighted by them. They will not believe that you are here. Might you have time to address them[7]? But I am running ahead of myself[8]. You must forgive me, gentlemen, but I cannot contain my excitement[9]. I am the Reverend Charles Fitzsimmons. Vosper tells me that you are here on serious business[10]. Mr Vosper helps to administer this establishment and also teaches maths and reading. Please, come with me to my study. You must meet my wife and perhaps we can offer you some tea?'

We followed the little man down a second corridor and through a door into a room which was too large and too cold to be comfortable even though some effort had been made with bookcases[11], a sofa and several chairs arranged around a fireplace. A large desk, piled high with[12] documents, had been positioned so as to look out through a set of picture windows[13] on to the lawn and the orchard beyond. It had been cold in the corridor, and it was colder here, despite the fire in the grate[14]. The red glow[15] and the smell of burning coal gave the illusion of warmth[16] but little more[17]. The rain was hammering now against[18] the windows and running down the glass[19]. It had drained the colour out of the fields[20].

1. chauve
2. d'un ecclésiastique
3. jusqu'au col romain
4. fit un sourire radieux
5. ouvrit les bras en signe de bienvenue
6. du pays
7. de leur parler
8. je vais trop vite en besogne
9. je ne peux contenir mon enthousiasme
10. concernant quelque chose de grave
11. des rayonnages
12. où s 'empilait une montagne de
13. fenêtres panoramiques
14. qui brûlait dans l'âtre
15. rougeoiement
16. chaleur
17. guère plus
18. martelait à présent
19. ruisselait sur les vitres
20. avait ôté toute couleur aux champs

Although it was only the middle of the afternoon, it could just as well have been night.

'My dear,' exclaimed our host. 'This is Mr Sherlock Holmes and Dr Watson. They have come to ask us for our help. Gentlemen, may I present my wife, Joanna?'

I had not noticed the woman who had been sitting in an armchair in the darkest corner of the room, reading a volume of several hundred pages which was balanced on her lap[1]. If this was Mrs Fitzsimmons, then the two of them made an odd couple[2], for she was quite remarkably tall and, I would have said, several years older than him. She was dressed entirely in black, an old-fashioned[3] satin dress that fitted high around the neck[4] and tight around the arms[5], with beaded[6] passementerie across the shoulders. Her hair was tied in a knot behind her and her fingers were long and thin. Were I a boy, I might have thought her witch-like[7]. Certainly, looking at the two of them, I had the perhaps unworthy thought[8] that I could understand why Ross had chosen to run away. Had I been in his shoes[9], I might very well[10] have done the same[11].

'Will you have some tea?' the lady asked. Her voice was as thin as the rest of her[12], her accent deliberately refined[13].

'We will not inconvenience you[14],' Holmes replied. 'As you are aware[15], we are here on a matter of some urgency. We are looking for a boy, a street urchin whom we know only by the name of Ross.'

'Ross? Ross?' The reverend searched in his mind. 'Ah yes! Poor, young Ross! We have not seen him for quite a while[16], Mr Holmes. He came to us from a very difficult background[17], but then so do[18] many of the charges in our care[19]. He did not stay with us long.'

1. tenait en équilibre sur ses genoux
2. un couple étrange
3. démodée
4. dont le col remontait très haut
5. aux manches étroites
6. ornée de perles
7. qu'elle ressemblait à une sorcière
8. cette pensée peut-être indigne
9. À sa place
10. j'aurais très bien pu
11. de même
12. que le reste de sa personne
13. sophistiqué
14. ne voulons pas vous déranger
15. Comme vous le savez
16. depuis assez longtemps
17. était issu d'un milieu difficile
18. c'est le cas de
19. de nos élèves

'He was a difficult and a disagreeable child,' his wife cut in[1]. 'He would not obey the rules. He disrupted[2] the other boys. He refused to conform[3].'

'You are too hard, too hard, my dear. But it is true, Mr Holmes, that Ross was never grateful for the help that we tried to give him and did not settle into our ways[4]. He had only been here for a few months before he ran away. That was last summer ... July or August. I would have to consult my notes to be sure. May I ask why you are looking for him? I hope he has not done something amiss[5].'

'Not at all. A few nights ago he was the witness[6] to certain events in London. I merely[7] wish to know what he saw.'

'It sounds most mysterious, does it not, my dear? I will not ask you to elucidate further[8]. We do not know where he came from. We do not know where he has gone.'

'Then I will not take up any more of your time[9].' Holmes turned to the door, then seemed to change his mind. 'Though perhaps before we leave, you might like to tell us something about your work here. Chorley Grange is your property[10]?'

'Not at all, sir. My wife and I are employed by the Society for the Improvement of London's Children.' He pointed at a portrait of an aristocratic gentleman leaning against a pillar[11]. 'That is the founder[12], Sir Crispin Ogilvy, now deceased[13]. He purchased this farm fifty years ago, and it is thanks to his bequest[14] that we are able to maintain it[15]. We have thirty-five boys here, all taken from the streets of London and saved from a future picking oakum[16] or wasting their hours on the treadmill[17]. We give them food and shelter[18] and, more important than either, a good, Christian education. In addition to reading, writing and basic mathematics, the boys are taught shoemaking, carpentering[19] and tailoring[20]. You will have noticed the fields. We have a hundred

1. intervint
2. dissipait
3. de se plier aux règles
4. ne s'est jamais fait à nos habitudes
5. de mal
6. a été témoin
7. simplement
8. de donner plus d'explications
9. vous faire perdre plus de temps
10. vous appartient
11. appuyé contre un pilier
12. fondateur
13. décédé
14. grâce à son legs
15. en mesure de l'entretenir
16. fabrication de filasse [activité alors pour détenus]
17. [roue actionnant le métier à filer]
18. de la nourriture et un toit
19. apprennent la cordonnerie, la menuiserie
20. la confection

acres and grow[1] almost all our own food. In addition, the boys learn how to breed pigs and poultry[2]. When they leave here, many of them will go to Canada, Australia and America to begin a new life. We are in contact with a number of farmers who will be pleased to welcome them and give them a fresh start[3].'

'How many teachers do you have?'

'There are just the four of us[4], along with my wife, and we divide the responsibilities between us[5]. You met Mr Vosper at the door. He is the porter[6] and teaches maths and reading, as I think I said. You have arrived during afternoon lessons and my other two teachers are in class.'

'How did Ross come to be here[7]? '

'Doubtless he would have been picked up in one of the casual wards[8] or night shelters[9]. The society has volunteers[10] who work in the city and who bring the boys to us. I can make enquiries[11] if you wish, although it has been so long since we had any news of him that I rather doubt[12] we can be of any help.'

'We cannot force the boys to stay,' Mrs Fitzsimmons said. 'The great majority of them will choose to do just that[13], and will grow up to be a credit[14] to themselves and to the school. But there are the occasional troublemakers[15], boys with no gratitude whatsoever.'

'We have to believe in every child, Joanna.'

'You are too soft-hearted[16], Charles. They take advantage of you.[17]'

'Ross cannot be blamed for[18] what he was. His father was a slaughterman[19] who came into contact with a diseased sheep[20] and died very slowly as a result[21]. His mother turned to alcohol[22]. She's dead too. For a time Ross was looked after by an elder sister but we don't know what became of her[23]. Ah yes! I remember now. You asked how he came here. Ross

1. nous cultivons
2. à élever des porcs et de la volaille
3. un nouveau départ
4. Nous ne sommes que quatre
5. nous nous répartissons les rôles
6. portier
7. s'est-il retrouvé ici
8. dortoirs temporaires [dans les hospices]
9. des refuges de nuit
10. des bénévoles
11. me renseigner
12. que je doute fort
13. choisissent de rester
14. font honneur, en grandissant
15. fauteurs de trouble
16. vous laissez trop attendrir
17. Ils en profitent.
18. On ne peut reprocher à Ross
19. travaillait dans un abattoir
20. un mouton malade
21. en est mort à petit feu
22. s'est mise à boire
23. ce qu'elle est devenue

1. vol à l'étalage
2. nous l'a confié
3. Je tremble à l'idée
4. que vous ayez perdu
5. à quoi bon le faire
6. Vous m'avez abandonné
7. et moi je vous ai aussi abandonné [Bible]
8. jeunes vagabonds
9. une idée lui était soudain venue à l'esprit
10. nous cacher
11. très aimable de votre part
12. la tête enfouie
13. son pesant ouvrage
14. qu'elle se consacre entièrement à
15. la religion
16. la lessive
17. les soigne
18. n'ai-je pas été assez clair
19. de notre chair et de notre sang

was arrested for shoplifting[1]. The magistrate took pity on him and handed him to us[2].'

'A last chance.' Mrs Fitzsimmons shook her head. 'I shudder to think[3] what will become of him now.'

'So you have no idea at all where we might be able to find him.'

'I am sorry you have wasted[4] your time, Mr Holmes. We do not have the resources to search for boys who have chosen to leave us, and in truth, what would be the point of it[5]? "*Ye have forsaken me*[6] *and therefore have I also left you*[7]." Can you tell us what it is that he witnessed and why it is so important for you to find him?'

'We believe him to be in danger.'

'All these homeless boys[8] are in danger.' Fitzsimmons clapped his hands together as if struck by a sudden thought[9]. 'But might it help you to speak to some of his former classmates? It is always possible that he may have told one of them something that he would have preferred to keep from us[10]. And if you would like to accompany me, it will give me an opportunity to show you the school and to explain a little more about our work.'

'That would be most kind of you[11], Mr Fitzsimmons.'

'The pleasure would be entirely mine.'

We left the study. Mrs Fitzsimmons did not join us but remained in her seat in the corner, her head buried[12] in her weighty tome[13].

'You must forgive my wife,' the Reverend Fitzsimmons muttered. 'You may think her a little severe but I can assure you that she lives for[14] these boys. She teaches them divinity[15], helps with the laundry[16], nurses them[17] when they are ill.'

'You have no children of your own?' I asked.

'Perhaps I have not made myself clear[18], Dr Watson. We have thirty-five children of our own, for we treat them exactly as if they were our flesh and blood[19].'

He took us back down the corridor I had first noticed and into one of the rooms, which smelled strongly of leather and new hemp[1]. Here were eight or nine boys, all clean and well groomed[2], dressed in aprons[3], silently concentrating on the shoes that were laid out in front of them[4] while the man we had met at the door, Mr Vosper, watched over them. They all rose[5] as we came in and stood in respectful silence but Fitzsimmons waved them down cheerfully[6]. 'Sit down, boys! Sit down! This is Mr Sherlock Holmes from London who has come to visit us. Let us show him how industrious we can be[7].' The boys went on with their work. 'All well, Mr Vosper?'

'Indeed so, sir.'

'Good! Good!' Fitzsimmons positively beamed with approval. 'They have two more hours' work and then an hour of leisure[8] before tea. Our day finishes at eight o'clock with prayers and then bed[9].'

He set off again, his short legs working hard to propel himself forward[10], this time leading us upstairs to show us a dormitory, a touch spartan[11] but decidedly clean and airy[12], with beds lined up like soldiers, each one a few feet apart[13]. We saw the kitchens, the dining room, a workshop[14] and finally came to a classroom with a lesson in progress. It was a square room with a single, small stove[15] in one corner, a chalkboard[16] on one wall and an embroidered text with the first line of a psalm[17] on another. There were a few books neatly stacked on shelves, an abacus[18] and a scattering of objects – pine cones[19], rocks and animal bones[20] – which must have been collected from field trips[21]. A young man sat marking a copybook[22] while a boy of about twelve or thirteen, acting as the class monitor[23], stood reading to his fellows from a well-worn[24] Bible. The boy stopped the moment we walked in. Fifteen students had been sitting in three rows[25],

1. le cuir et le chanvre frais
2. à la tenue soignée
3. vêtus de blouses
4. disposées devant eux
5. se levèrent tous
6. avec bonhomie, leur fit signe de s'asseoir
7. comme nous travaillons dur
8. de détente
9. les prières, puis le coucher
10. peinant à soutenir sa marche
11. un peu spartiate
12. résolument propre et spacieux
13. avec env. 1 m entre chacun
14. atelier
15. un seul petit poêle
16. un tableau noir
17. une broderie de la première ligne d'un psaume
18. empilés sur des étagères, un boulier
19. des pommes de pin
20. des ossements d'animaux
21. lors d'excursions
22. assis, corrigeait un cahier
23. chef de classe
24. éculée
25. sur trois rangées

listening intently[1], and once again they stood up respectfully, gazing at us with pale, serious faces.

'Sit down, please!' exclaimed the reverend. 'Forgive the interruption, Mr Weeks. Was that the Book of Job[2] I heard just now, Harry? "*Naked I came out of my mother's womb*[3] *and naked shall I return*[4]..." '

'Yes, sir.'

'Very good. A fine choice of text.' He gestured at the teacher who alone had remained seated. He was in his late twenties[5], with a strange, twisted[6] face and a tangle of brown hair[7] that sprawled lopsidedly[8] on one side of his head. 'This is Robert Weeks, a graduate[9] of Balliol College[10]. Mr Weeks was building a successful career[11] in the city but has chosen to join us for a year to help those less fortunate than himself[12]. Do you remember the boy Ross, Mr Weeks?'

'Ross? He was the one who ran away.'

'This gentleman here is none other than[13] Mr Sherlock Holmes, the well-known detective.' This caused a certain tremor of recognition among some of the boys.[14] 'He is afraid that Ross may have got himself into trouble.'

'Not surprising,' muttered Mr Weeks. 'He was not an easy child.'

'Were you a companion of his, Harry?'

'No, sir,' the monitor replied.

'Well, surely there must have been someone in this room who befriended him[15] and who perhaps spoke with him and can now help us find him? You will recall[16], boys, that we talked a great deal[17] after Ross left here. I asked you all where he might have gone and you were unable to tell me anything. I beseech you all[18] to consider the matter one last time.'

'My desire is only to help your friend,' Holmes added.

There was a brief silence. Then a boy in the back row[19] put up his hand. He was fair-haired[20] and very

1. attentivement
2. le livre de Job
3. Nu je suis sorti du sein de ma mère
4. nu je retournerai
5. proche de la trentaine
6. tordu
7. une tignasse brune
8. retombait asymétriquement
9. diplômé
10. [à l'université d'Oxford]
11. entamait une belle carrière
12. ceux qui n'ont pas eu sa chance
13. en personne
14. Un frisson parcourut les garçons qui le reconnurent.
15. était ami avec lui
16. Souvenez-vous
17. beaucoup
18. Je vous implore tous
19. au dernier rang
20. blond

fragile and I guessed about eleven. 'Are you the man in the stories[1]?' he asked.

'That's right[2]. And this is the man who writes them.' It was rare for me to hear Holmes introduce me in this manner and I have to say I was extremely pleased to hear it. 'Do you read them?'

'No, sir. There are too many long words. But sometimes Mr Weeks reads them to us.'

'We must let you return to your studies,' Fitzsimmons said and began to usher us[3] towards the door.

But the boy at the back had not finished yet. 'Ross has a sister, sir,' he said.

Holmes turned[4]. 'In London?'

'I think so. Yes. He spoke about her once. Her name is Sally. He said that she worked at a public house[5], The Bag of Nails[6].'

For the first time, the Reverend Fitzsimmons looked angry, a dull red patch[7] spreading into the round of his cheeks[8]. 'This is very wrong of you[9], Daniel,' he said. 'Why did you not tell me before?'

'I had forgotten, sir.'

'Had you remembered[10], we might have been able to find him, to protect him from whatever trouble has come his way.'

'I'm sorry, sir.'

'We'll say no more of it.[11] Come, Mr Holmes.'

The three of us walked back towards the main door of the school. Holmes had paid the cab driver to wait for us and I was glad to see he was there, for it was still raining heavily[12].

'The school does you credit[13],' Holmes said. 'I find it remarkable how quiet and well disciplined the boys seem to be.'

'I am very grateful to you,' returned[14] Fitzsimmons, relaxing once again into his more congenial self[15]. 'My methods are very simple, Mr Holmes. The stick[16] and the carrot – quite literally so[17]. When the boys misbehave[18], I flog them[19]. But if they work

1. le héros des histoires
2. exact
3. nous raccompagner
4. se retourna
5. un pub
6. clous
7. une tache rouge diffuse
8. gagnant le gras de ses joues
9. très mal de ta part
10. Si tu te l'étais rappelé
11. N'en parlons plus.
12. à verse
13. est tout à votre honneur
14. répondit
15. retrouvant son côté avenant
16. bâton
17. au sens propre
18. se conduisent mal
19. je sévis avec le bâton

hard and abide by our rules[1], then they find that they are well fed. In the six years that my wife and I have been here, two boys have died, one with congenital heart disease[2], the other of tuberculosis. But Ross is the only one who has run away. When you find him, for I am sure that you will, I hope you will prevail upon him[3] to return. Life here is not as austere as it may seem in this vile weather[4]. When the sun shines and the boys can run wild[5] in the open air[6], Chorley Grange can be a cheerful place too.'

'I am sure of it. One last question, Mr Fitzsimmons. The building opposite. That is part of the school?'

'Indeed so, Mr Holmes. When we first came here it was a coach-builder's factory[7] but we have adapted it to our own needs and now use it for public performances[8]. Did I mention to you that every boy in the school is a member of a band[9]?'

'You have had a performance recently.'

'Only two nights ago. You have doubtless noticed the many wheel tracks[10]. I would be honoured if you came to our next recital, Mr Holmes – and you too, Dr Watson. Indeed, might you consider becoming benefactors[11] of the school? We do the best we can, but we also need all the help that is available[12].'

'I will certainly consider it[13].' We shook hands and left. 'We must go straight[14] to The Bag of Nails, Watson,' Holmes said the moment[15] we had climbed into the cab. 'There is not a second to be lost[16].'

'You really think ... ?'

'The boy, Daniel, told us what he had refused to tell his masters but only because he knew who we were and thought we could save his friend. For once, Watson, I am being guided by my instinct and not by my intellect. What is it, I wonder, that gives me such cause for alarm[17]? Whip[18] the horses, driver, and take us to the station! And let us just pray[19] that we're not too late[20].'

1. respectent nos règles
2. maladie cardiaque
3. que vous le convaincrez
4. par ce temps horrible
5. courir en toute liberté
6. en plein air
7. une fabrique de calèches
8. les représentations
9. un orchestre
10. traces de roues
11. bienfaiteurs
12. disponible
13. Je ne manquerai pas d'y penser
14. directement
15. dès que
16. une seconde à perdre
17. qui m'inquiète tant
18. Fouettez
19. prions
20. qu'il ne soit pas trop tard

SEVEN

The White Ribbon

How differently things might have turned out had there not been[1] two public houses[2] in London with the name The Bag of Nails. We knew of one[3] in Edge Lane in the heart of[4] Shoreditch and, believing this to be a likely place of employment[5] for the orphaned[6] sister of a penniless[7] street child, made our way directly there. It was a small, squalid place on a corner, with the stink[8] of old beer and cigarette smoke seeping out of the very woodwork[9], and yet the landlord was amicable enough[10], wiping[11] his huge hands on a soiled apron[12] as he examined us across the bar.

'There's no Sally working in this place,' he said, after we had introduced ourselves. 'Nor has there ever been.[13] What makes you gentlemen think you might find her here?'

'We're looking for her brother, a boy called Ross.'

He shook his head. 'I know no Ross, neither. You're sure you've been directed to[14] the right place? There's a Bag of Nails over in Lambeth, I believe. Maybe you should try your luck[15] there.'

We were back out in the street immediately and soon crossing London in a hansom, but already it was late in the day[16] and by the time we reached the lower quarter of Lambeth it was almost dark. The second Bag of Nails was more welcoming than the first, but conversely[17], its landlord was less so[18],

1. s'il n'y avait pas eu
2. pubs
3. en connaissions un
4. au cœur de
5. un lieu de travail vraisemblable
6. orpheline
7. sans le sou
8. une puanteur
9. imprégnant les boiseries
10. le tenancier se montra assez aimable
11. essuyant
12. sur un tablier taché
13. Il n'y en a jamais eu, d'ailleurs.
14. que l'on vous a indiqué
15. tenter votre chance
16. il se faisait tard
17. à l'inverse
18. l'était moins

a surly, bearded fellow[1] with a broken nose that had set badly[2] and a scowl to match[3].

'Sally?' he demanded. 'What Sally would that be?'

'We know only her first name[4],' Holmes responded. 'And the fact that she has a younger brother[5], Ross.'

'Sally Dixon? Is that the girl you want? She has a brother. You'll find her round the back[6] but you'll tell me what you want with her[7] first.'

'We wish only to speak with her,' Holmes replied. Once again, I could feel the tension burning within him, the unremitting sense of energy[8] and drive[9] that propelled him through his every case[10]. There was never a man who felt it more when circumstances conspired to frustrate him. He slid a few coins onto the bar. 'This is to recompense you for her time.'

'There's no need for that,' returned the landlord but he took the money anyway. 'Very well. She'll be in the yard. But I doubt you'll get very much from her. She's not the most talkative of girls[11]. I'd get better company employing a mute[12].'

There was a courtyard behind the building, its stones still wet and glistening from the rain[13]. It was filled with scrap of every description[14], the different pieces rising high up the walls that surrounded the place, and I could not help but wonder how it had come here. I saw a broken piano, a child's rocking horse[15], a birdcage, several bicycles, half-chairs, half-tables ... all manner of furniture[16], but nothing whole[17]. A pile of broken crates stood on one side, old coal bags stuffed with[18] Lord knows what on the other. There was smashed glass[19], great piles of paper, twisted fragments of metal[20] and, in the middle of it, barefoot[21] and in a dress too thin[22] for this weather, a girl of about sixteen, sweeping[23] what space was still available[24], as if it would make any difference. I recognised in her the same looks as her

1. un barbu hargneux
2. mal replacé
3. l'air renfrogné allant avec
4. prénom
5. frère cadet
6. derrière
7. ce que vous lui voulez
8. cet inlassable élan
9. ce dynamisme
10. tout au long d'une affaire
11. une fille des plus bavardes
12. une muette
13. trempées et luisantes de pluie
14. toutes sortes de rebuts
15. cheval à bascule
16. toutes sortes de meubles
17. d'entier
18. sacs à charbon bourrés de
19. verre brisé
20. des bouts de métal tordu
21. pieds nus
22. vêtue d'une robe trop légère
23. balayant
24. le peu d'espace restant

younger brother. Her hair was fair, her eyes blue and, but for the circumstances in which she found herself[1], I would have said she was pretty. But the cruel touch of poverty and hardship[2] was also evident in the sharp line[3] of her cheekbones[4], the arms as thin as sticks and the grime embedded[5] in her hands and cheeks. When she looked up[6], her face showed only suspicion and contempt. Sixteen! And what had her life been[7] to bring her here?

We stood in front of her, but she continued with her work, ignoring us both.

'Miss Dixon?' Holmes asked. The brushes of the broom[8] swept back and forth, the rhythm unbroken[9]. 'Sally?'

She stopped and slowly raised her head, examining us. 'Yes?' I saw that her hands had closed around the broom handle[10], clutching it as if it were a weapon.

'We don't wish to alarm you,' Holmes said. 'We mean you no harm.'

'What do you want?' Her eyes were fierce[11]. Neither of us was standing close to her. We would not dare to.[12]

'We wish to speak to your brother, to Ross.'

Her hands tightened[13]. 'Who are you?'

'We are his friends.'

'Are you from the House of Silk? Ross is not here. He has never been here – and you will not find him.'

'We want to help him.'

'Of course you would say that[14]. Well, I'm telling you, he's not here. You can both go away! You make me sick. Go back where you came from.'

Holmes glanced at me and, hoping to be of service, I took one step[15] towards the girl. I had thought I would reassure her but I had made a grievous mistake[16]. I am still not sure what happened. I saw the broom fall and heard Holmes cry out[17]. Then the girl seemed to punch the air[18] in front of me and I felt

1. si sa condition avait été autre
2. la trace cruelle de la pauvreté et des épreuves
3. visible dans les lignes anguleuses
4. pommettes
5. la saleté incrustée
6. leva les yeux
7. quelle vie avait-elle eue
8. balai
9. à un rythme ininterrompu
10. le manche du balai
11. Elle lançait un regard furieux
12. Nous n'osions pas.
13. se crispèrent
14. vous n'allez pas dire le contraire
15. je fis un pas
16. je me trompais lourdement
17. pousser un cri
18. frapper le vide

1. d'incandescent me lacérer la poitrine
2. Je reculai en chancelant
3. du sang goutter
4. je mis un moment à me rendre compte
5. poignardé
6. un tesson
7. grondant
8. le regard enflammé
9. les lèvres retroussées
10. se précipita auprès de moi
11. un seul hurlement guttural
12. un étroit passage voûté
13. L'épaisseur
14. lame
15. pu faire
16. je nettoierais
17. En y repensant à présent
18. aussi étrange que cela paraisse
19. intégrité physique
20. signifiait au moins quelque chose
21. indifférent
22. égratignure
23. tachées de sang
24. devriez plutôt demander
25. la moindre rancœur
26. m'avait frappé

something white hot slice across my chest[1]. I staggered back[2], pressing my hand against the front of my coat. When I looked down, I saw blood trickling[3] between my fingers. So shocked was I, it took me a moment to realise[4] that I had been stabbed[5], either with a knife or a shard of glass[6]. For a moment, the girl stood in front of me, not a child at all but snarling[7] like an animal, her eyes ablaze[8], her lips drawn back[9] in a ferocious grimace. Holmes rushed to my side[10]. 'My dear Watson!' Then there was a movement behind me.

'What's going on here?' The landlord had appeared. The girl let out a single, guttural howl[11], then turned and fled through a narrow archway[12] leading out into the street.

I was in pain, but I already knew that I had not been seriously injured. The thickness[13] of my coat and my jacket underneath had protected me from the worst of what the blade[14] might have achieved[15], and later that evening I would dress[16] and disinfect a relatively minor wound. Thinking back now[17], I remember that there would be another occasion, ten years later, when I would be hurt while in the company of Sherlock Holmes and, strange though it may sound[18], I felt almost a sense of gratitude towards both my attackers who demonstrated that my physical well-being[19] did at least mean something[20] to the great man and that he was not as coldly disposed[21] towards me as he sometimes pretended.

'Watson?'

'It's nothing, Holmes. A scratch[22].'

'What's happened?' the landlord demanded. He was staring at my bloodstained[23] hands. 'What did you do to her?'

'You might ask[24] what she has done to me,' I grunted, although even in the shock of the moment I was unable to feel any rancour[25] towards this poor, malnourished child who had struck out at me[26] in fear[1] and incomprehension and who had not really wished me any harm[2].

'The girl was frightened,' Holmes said. 'Are you sure you are not hurt, Watson? Come inside. You need to sit down.'

'No, Holmes. I assure you, it is not as bad as it seems.'

'Thank heaven for that.[3] We must call at once for a hansom. Landlord, it was the girl's brother that we came here to find. A boy of thirteen, fair-haired also, shorter than her and better fed.'

'You mean Ross?'

'You know him?'

'I told you. He has been working here with her. You should have asked for him in the first place.'

'Is he here now?'

'No. He came a few days ago, needing a roof[4] above his head[5]. I said he could share with[6] his sister in return for work[7] in the kitchen. Sally has a room beneath the stairs and he went in[8] with her. But the boy was more trouble than he was worth[9], never around[10] when he was needed. I don't know what he was up to, but he had some sort of business in his mind[11], that I can tell you. He hurried out[12] just before you arrived.'

'Do you have any idea where he went?'

'No. The girl might have told you. But now she's gone too.'

'I must see to[13] my friend. But should either of them[14] return, it is urgent that you send a message to my lodgings[15] at 221B Baker Street. Here is further money[16] for your pains. Come, Watson. Lean on me.[17] I think I hear an approaching[18] cab ...'

And so the day's adventure ended with the two of us sitting close by the fire[19], I with a restorative brandy and soda[20], Holmes smoking furiously. I took a moment to reflect on the circumstances that had brought us to this point, for it seemed to

1. par frayeur
2. du mal
3. Dieu merci.
4. à la recherche d'un toit
5. où s'abriter
6. loger avec
7. en échange de son travail
8. il s'est installé
9. m'a plus posé problème que rendu service
10. jamais là
11. il avait bien un projet en tête
12. est sorti précipitamment
13. m'occuper de
14. si l'un ou l'autre
15. mes appartements
16. de l'argent en plus
17. Appuyez-vous sur moi.
18. qui arrive
19. au coin du feu
20. un cognac [à l'eau gazeuse] revigorant

me that we had strayed a great distance[1] from our original quarry[2], the man with the flat cap or indeed the identity of the person who had killed him. Was this the person that Ross had seen outside Mrs Oldmore's Private Hotel, and if so, how could the boy have possibly recognised him? Somehow, that chance encounter[3] had led him to[4] believe that he could make some money for himself[5], and since then he had vanished from sight[6]. He must have told his sister something of his intentions, for she had been afraid on his behalf[7]. It was almost as if she had been expecting us[8]. Why else[9] would she have been carrying a weapon? And then there were those words of hers[10]. 'Are you from the House of Silk?' On our return Holmes had searched through his index[11] and the various encyclopaedias that he kept on his shelves but we were none the wiser[12] as to what she had meant[13]. We did not speak of any of this together. I was exhausted, and I could see that my friend was preoccupied with his own thoughts. We would just have to wait and see what the next day would bring.

What it brought was a police constable, knocking at our door just after breakfast.

'Inspector Lestrade sends his compliments, sir. He is at Southwark Bridge and would be most grateful if you could join him.'

'On what business[14], officer?'

'Murder, sir. And a very nasty one.'

We put on our coats and left at once, taking a cab over Southwark Bridge, crossing the three great cast-iron[15] arches that spanned[16] the river from Cheapside. Lestrade was waiting for us on the south bank[17], standing with a group of policemen who were clustered around[18] what looked, from a distance, like a small heap of discarded rags[19]. The sun was shining, but it was once again bitterly cold[20] and the Thames water had never been crueller, the

1. énormément dévié
2. celui que nous cherchions au départ
3. rencontre fortuite
4. l'avait amené à
5. en tirer de l'argent
6. disparu de la surface de la terre
7. pour lui
8. comme si elle s'attendait à nous voir
9. Sinon, pourquoi
10. sa question
11. consulté son fichier
12. nous n'étions pas plus avancés
13. ce qu'elle avait voulu dire
14. À quel sujet
15. en fonte
16. enjambaient
17. berge
18. entouraient
19. tas de vieilles guenilles
20. il faisait à nouveau un froid mordant

grey waves beating monotonously at the shore[1]. We descended a spiral staircase of grey metal that twisted down from the road, and walked over the mud and shingle[2]. It was low tide[3] and the river[4] seemed to have shrunk back[5], as if in distaste at[6] what had happened here. There was a steamboat pier[7] jutting out[8] a short distance away with a few passengers waiting, stamping their feet[9], their breath frosting[10] in the air. They seemed utterly divorced from[11] the scene that presented itself to us. They belonged to life. Here there was only death.

'Is he the one you were looking for?' Lestrade asked. 'The boy from the hotel?'

Holmes nodded. Perhaps he did not trust himself to speak.

The boy had been beaten brutally. His ribs[12] had been smashed[13], his arms, his legs, each one of his fingers. Looking at those dreadful injuries[14], I knew at once that they had all been inflicted methodically, one at a time[15], and that death, for Ross, would have been one long tunnel of pain. Finally, at the end of it all, his throat had been cut[16] so savagely that his head had almost been separated from his neck. I had seen dead bodies before, both with Holmes and during my time as an army surgeon, but I had never seen anything as dreadful as this, and I found it far beyond understanding[17] that any human being could have done this to a thirteen-year-old boy.

'It's a bad business,' Lestrade said. 'What can you tell me about him, Holmes? Was he in your employ?[18]'

'His name was Ross Dixon,' Holmes replied. 'I know very little about him, Inspector. You might ask at the Chorley Grange School for Boys in Hamworth, but there may not be much that they are able to add[19]. He was an orphan, but he has a sister who worked until recently at The Bag of Nails public house in Lambeth. You may yet find her there. Have you examined the body?'

1. la rive
2. la boue et les galets
3. marée basse
4. fleuve
5. s'être rétracté
6. comme dégoûté par
7. embarcadère de bateaux à vapeur
8. qui se détachait
9. en tapant des pieds
10. leur souffle se givrant
11. détonaient complètement avec
12. côtes
13. broyées
14. blessures terrifiantes
15. une par une
16. on lui avait tranché la gorge
17. qu'il dépassait l'entendement
18. Il travaillait pour vous ?
19. ils ne devraient pas être en mesure d'en dire plus

'We have. His pockets were empty. But there is something strange that you should see, though heaven knows what it signifies. It made me sickish[1] – I'll tell you that much.'

Lestrade nodded and one of the policemen knelt down[2] and took hold of one of the small, broken, arms. The sleeve of his shirt fell back[3] to reveal a white ribbon, knotted[4] around the boy's wrist. 'The fabric[5] is new,' Lestrade said. 'It's a good-quality silk from the look of it[6]. And see – it is untouched by blood[7] or by any of this Thames filth[8]. I would say, therefore, that it was placed on the boy after he was killed, as some sort of sign.'

'The House of Silk!' I exclaimed.

'What's that?'

'Do you know of it[9], Lestrade?' Holmes asked. 'Does it mean anything to you?'

'No. The House of Silk? Is it a factory? I've never heard of it.'

'But I have[10].' Holmes stared into the distance[11], his eyes filled with horror and self-reproach[12]. 'The white ribbon, Watson! I have seen it before.' He turned back to Lestrade. 'Thank you for calling me out[13] and for informing me of this.'

'I hoped you might be able to shed some light on the matter[14]. It may be, after all, that this is your fault.'

'Fault?' Holmes jerked round[15] as though he had been stung[16].

'I warned you about mixing with[17] these children. You employed the boy. You set him on the trail[18] of a known criminal. I grant you[19], he may have had his own ideas and they may have been the ruin of him[20]. But this is the result.'

I cannot say if Lestrade was being deliberately provocative but his words had an effect on Holmes that I was able to witness for myself[21] on the journey back to Baker Street. He had sunk[22] into the corner

1. J'en ai eu la nausée
2. s'agenouilla
3. se retroussa
4. noué
5. tissu
6. à première vue
7. il n'y a pas de sang dessus
8. ni aucune immondice de la Tamise
9. En avez-vous entendu parler
10. moi, oui
11. fixa le lointain
12. trahissant son sentiment de culpabilité
13. de m'avoir fait venir
14. d'éclaircir un peu cette affaire
15. fit volte-face
16. comme si quelque chose l'avait piqué
17. Je vous avais dit le risque qu'il y avait à fréquenter
18. l'avez lancé sur la piste
19. Je vous l'accorde
20. signé sa perte
21. vérifier par moi-même
22. s'était affalé

of the hansom and for much of the way he sat in silence[1], refusing to meet my eyes[2]. His skin seemed to have stretched itself[3] over his cheekbones and he appeared more gaunt than ever[4], as if he had been struck down[5] by some virulent disease[6]. I did not try to speak to him. I knew he needed no consolation from me. Instead, I watched and waited as he brought[7] that enormous intellect of his to bear on[8] the terrible turn that this adventure had taken.

'It may be that Lestrade was right,' he said at length[9]. 'Certainly, I have used my Baker Street Irregulars without much thought or consideration. It amused me to have them lined up in front of me, to give them a shilling or two, but I have never wantonly put them in harm's way[10], Watson. You know that. And yet I stand accused[11] of dilettantism and must plead guilty[12]. Wiggins, Ross and the rest of them were nothing to me, just as they are nothing to the society that has abandoned them to the streets, and it never occurred to me[13] that this horror might be the result of my actions. Do not interrupt me! Would I have allowed[14] a young boy to stand alone outside a hotel in the darkness had it been[15] your son or mine? And the logic of what has taken place seems inescapable[16]. The child saw the killer enter the hotel. We both saw how it afflicted him. Even so, he thought he could turn the situation to his advantage. He attempted to do so and he died. For that I must hold myself responsible.

'And yet! And yet! How does the House of Silk fit[17] into this conundrum[18] and what are we to make of the strip of silk around the boy's wrist? That is the crux of the matter[19] and once again I am blameworthy[20]. I was warned! That's the truth of it. Honestly, Watson, there are times when I wonder if I shouldn't leave this profession and seek my fortune[21] elsewhere. There are a few monographs I would still like to write. I have always had

1. resta silencieux
2. croiser mon regard
3. s'être tendue
4. plus émacié que jamais
5. frappé
6. maladie foudroyante
7. tandis qu'il forçait
8. à s'appesantir sur
9. finalement
10. n'ai jamais cherché à les mettre en danger
11. pourtant on m'accuse
12. plaider coupable
13. il ne m'est jamais venu à l'esprit
14. Aurais-je laissé
15. s'il avait été
16. imparable
17. Que vient faire la Maison de la soie
18. casse-tête
19. nœud de l'affaire
20. mérite des reproches
21. tenter ma chance

a fancy to keep bees[1]. Certainly, on the strength of my achievements[2] so far in the investigation of this case, I have no right to call myself a detective. A child is dead. You saw what they did to him. How am I to live with that?'

'My dear chap[3] ...'

'Say nothing. There is something I must show you. I was forewarned.[4] I could have prevented it ...'

We had arrived back. Holmes plunged[5] into the building, taking the stairs two at a time[6]. I followed more slowly, for although I had said nothing, the wound I had sustained the day before was hurting far more[7] than it had at the time it was inflicted. As I arrived in our sitting room, I saw him lean forward[8] and seize hold[9] of an envelope. It was one of my friend's many singularities that, although he lived in surroundings of extreme clutter[10] and even chaos[11], with letters and documents piled up everywhere, he could find whatever he was looking for without a second thought[12]. 'Here it is!' he announced. 'The envelope tells us nothing. My name is written on the front but not the address. It was hand-delivered[13]. Whoever sent it made no attempt to disguise his handwriting and I would certainly recognise it again. You will notice the Greek *e* in *Holmes*. That unusual top flourish[14] will not slip my mind[15] easily.'

'And what is inside it?' I asked.

'You can see for yourself[16],' replied Holmes, and passed me the envelope.

I opened it and, with a shiver that I could not disguise, drew out a short length[17] of white, silk ribbon. 'What is the meaning of this, Holmes?' I asked.

'I asked myself the same when I received it. In retrospect, it would seem to have been a warning[18].'

'When was it sent?'

1. envie d'élever des abeilles
2. si l'on en croit mes performances
3. Mon cher ami
4. J'avais été prévenu.
5. s'engouffra
6. grimpant les marches quatre à quatre
7. me faisait bien plus mal
8. se pencher
9. s'emparer
10. un désordre extrême
11. voire chaotique
12. sans même réfléchir
13. remise par porteur
14. fioriture insolite, au-dessus
15. ne me sortira pas de la tête
16. Voyez vous-même
17. un petit morceau
18. avertissement

'Seven weeks ago. At the time I was involved in a[1] bizarre affair that involved a pawnbroker, Mr Jabez Wilson, who had been invited to join[2]—'

'—the red-headed league[3]!' I interrupted, for I remembered the case well and had been fortunate enough to see it to its conclusion[4].

'Exactly. That was a three-pipe[5] problem if ever there was one, and when this envelope arrived, my mind was elsewhere. I examined the contents and tried to work out their significance[6] but, being otherwise engaged[7], I set it aside and forgot it. Now, as you can see, it has come back to haunt me[8].'

'But who would have sent it to you? And to what purpose[9]?'

'I have no idea, but for the sake[10] of that murdered child, I intend to find out.' Holmes reached out and took the strip of silk from me. He laced it through[11] his skeletal fingers and held it in front of him, examining it in the way that a man might a poisonous snake[12]. 'If this was directed to me as a challenge[13], it is one I now accept[14],' he said. He punched at the air, his fist closing[15] on the white ribbon. 'And I tell you, Watson, that I shall make them rue the day that[16] it was sent.'

1. je m'occupais d'une
2. à intégrer
3. la ligue des rouquins
4. d'y assister jusqu'à la fin
5. qui demande réflexion [Holmes s'accorde de fumer 3 pipes l'une après l'autre pour y réfléchir à loisir]
6. d'en deviner le sens
7. absorbé par ailleurs
8. cela revient me hanter
9. dans quel but
10. en souvenir
11. le passa entre
12. serpent venimeux
13. S'il m'a été envoyé pour me jeter un défi
14. alors je l'accepte
15. en serrant le poing
16. je vais leur faire regretter le jour où

EIGHT

A Raven[1] and Two Keys

1. corbeau
2. Ce n'était pas étonnant
3. étant donné
4. craignait sûrement
5. était à présent relatée
6. que c'était lui
7. avaient le chic pour se répandre comme une traînée de poudre
8. s'insinuant dans
9. sous-sol sordide
10. insidieuses
11. marquant tout ce qu'elles touchaient
12. n'était peut-être pas grand-chose
13. ses bras m'étaient bien utiles
14. la police
15. sur place
16. que vous ne soyez jamais venus
17. les problèmes

Sally had not returned to her place of work that night nor the following morning. This was hardly surprising[2], given[3] that she had attacked me and would surely be in fear of[4] the consequences. In addition, the death of her brother had now been reported[5] in the newspapers and although his name had not been mentioned, it was quite possible that she would know it was he[6] who had been found beneath Southwark Bridge, for that was how it was in those days, particularly in the poorer parts of the city. Bad news had a way of spreading like smoke from a fire[7], trickling its way through[8] every crowded room, every squalid basement[9], soft and insistent[10], smearing everything it touched[11]. The landlord of The Bag of Nails knew that Ross was dead – he had already been visited by Lestrade and he was even less pleased to see us than he had been the day before.

'Have you not caused enough trouble already?' he demanded. 'That girl may not have amounted to much[12] but she was still a good pair of hands[13] and I'm sorry to have lost her. And it's not good for business, having the law[14] about the place[15]! I wish the two of you had never shown up[16].'

'It was not we who brought the trouble[17], Mr Hardcastle,' Holmes replied, for he had read the landlord's name – Ephraim Hardcastle – above the door.

'It was here already[1] and we merely followed[2]. It seems likely that you were the last person to see the boy alive. Did he tell you nothing before he left?'

'Why would he speak to me or I to him?'

'But you said that he had some business on his mind.'

'I knew nothing of that.'

'He was tortured to death[3], Mr Hardcastle, his bones broken one at a time. I have sworn[4] to find his killer and bring him to[5] justice. I cannot do so if you refuse to help.'

The landlord nodded slowly and when he spoke again it was in more measured tones[6]. 'Very well. The boy turned up[7] three nights ago with some story about having fallen out[8] with his neighbours and needing a crib[9] until he could sort himself out[10]. Sally asked my permission and I gave my assent[11]. Why not? You've seen the yard. There's a whole load of rubbish[12] to be cleared out[13] and I thought he could help. He did a little work too, on that first day, but in the afternoon he went out, and when he came back, I saw he was very pleased with himself[14].'

'Did his sister know what he was doing?'

'She might have, but she said nothing to me.'

'Pray continue.[15]'

'I have little more to add, Mr Holmes. I saw him only one more time and that was in the minutes[16] before you arrived. He came into the public bar while I was carrying up the casks[17] and asked me the time[18], which only showed how ill-educated[19] he was, because you can read it as clear as day[20] on the church across the road.'

'Then he was on his way to a fixed appointment[21].'

'I suppose it's possible.'

'It's certain. What use would a child such as Ross have with the time unless he had been asked to present himself in a certain place at a certain time? You said that he spent three nights here with his sister.'

1. Ils étaient déjà là
2. nous n'avons fait que les suivre
3. torturé à mort
4. Je me suis juré
5. de le traîner devant
6. d'une voix plus mesurée
7. est arrivé
8. en racontant qu'il s'était disputé
9. un coin où crécher
10. le temps de se retourner
11. accord
12. tout un tas d'ordures
13. à déblayer
14. content de lui
15. Poursuivez, je vous prie.
16. quelques minutes
17. je remontais les fûts
18. m'a demandé l'heure
19. mal élevé
20. parfaitement la voir
21. rendez-vous

'He shared her room.'

'I would like to see it.'

'The police have already been there. They searched it and found nothing.'

'I am not the police.' Holmes placed a few shillings on the bar. 'This is for your inconvenience[1].'

'Very well. But I will not take your money this time. You are on the trail of a monster and it will be enough if you do[2] as you say and make sure he can't hurt anyone else.'

He showed us round the back[3] and along a narrow corridor between the taproom[4] and the kitchen. A flight of stairs[5] led down to the cellars[6] and, lighting a candle, the landlord led us to a dismal[7] little room that was tucked away beneath them[8], small and windowless[9], with a bare wooden floor[10]. This was where Sally, exhausted after her long day's labours, would have taken herself[11], sleeping on a mattress[12] on the floor, covered by a single blanket[13]. Two objects lay in the middle of this makeshift bed[14]. One was a knife, the other a doll[15] which she must have rescued from some rubbish tip[16]. Looking at its broken limbs[17] and stark white[18] face, I could not help but think of her brother who had been discarded[19] just as casually[20]. A chair and a small table with a candle stood in one corner. It would not have taken the police long to search the place for, the doll and the knife aside[21], Sally had no possessions[22], nothing she could call her own[23] beyond her name[24].

Holmes swept his eyes across the room[25]. 'Why the knife?' he murmured.

'To protect herself,' I suggested.

'The weapon that she used to protect herself she carried with her, as you know better than anyone. She will have taken that with her. This second knife is almost blunt[26].'

'And stolen from the kitchen!' Hardcastle murmured.

1. le dérangement
2. je me contenterai que vous fassiez
3. nous emmena derrière
4. le comptoir
5. volée de marches
6. aux caves
7. lugubre
8. cachée en dessous
9. sans fenêtre
10. un parquet nu
11. se rendait
12. matelas
13. d'une seule couverture
14. ce lit de fortune
15. une poupée
16. repêchée probablement dans quelque dépotoir
17. membres disloqués
18. d'une blancheur extrême
19. dont on s'était débarrassé
20. tout aussi négligemment
21. mis à part
22. n'avait rien
23. qui soit à elle
24. à part son nom
25. balaya la pièce du regard
26. émoussé

'The candle, I think, is of interest[1].' It was the unlit[2] candle on the table to which Holmes referred. He picked it up, then crouched down[3] and began to shuffle along the floor[4]. It took me a moment to realise that he was following a trail of melted wax droplets[5] which were almost invisible to the human eye. He, of course, had seen them at once. They led him to the corner furthest away[6] from the bed. 'She carried it to this far corner ... again to what purpose? Unless ... The knife please, Watson.' I handed it to him and he pressed the blade[7] into one of the cracks[8] between the wooden floorboards. One of the boards was loose and he used the knife to prise it up[9], then reached inside[10] and withdrew a bunched-up handkerchief[11]. 'If you could be so kind, Mr Hardcastle ...'

The landlord brought over his own, lit candle. Holmes unfolded the handkerchief, and by the light of the flickering flame[12], we saw that there were several coins inside – three farthings[13], two florins[14], a crown[15], a gold sovereign[16] and five shillings. For two destitute[17] children, it was a veritable treasure trove[18], but to which of them had the money belonged?

'This is Ross's,' Holmes said, as if reading my thoughts. 'The sovereign, I gave him.'

'My dear Holmes! How can you be sure it's the same sovereign?'

Holmes held it to the light[19]. 'The date is the same. But look also at the design. Saint George rides his horse but has a gash[20] across his leg. I noticed it as I handed it over. This is part of the guinea that Ross earned for his work with the Irregulars. But what of the rest of it?'

'He got it from his uncle,' Hardcastle muttered. Holmes turned to him. 'When he came here and asked to stay the night, he said he could pay for the room. I laughed at him and he said that he had

1. intéressante
2. éteinte
3. s'accroupit
4. avancer [en restant accroupi]
5. de gouttelettes de cire fondue
6. le plus éloigné
7. enfonça la lame
8. fentes
9. pour faire levier
10. engagea la main à l'intérieur
11. un mouchoir noué en baluchon
12. à la lueur de la flamme vacillante
13. [pièces d'un quart de penny]
14. [pièces de 2 shillings]
15. [pièce de 5 shillings]
16. [souverain britannique : pièce frappée en or]
17. indigents
18. trésor
19. le regarda à la lumière
20. entaille

been given money by his uncle but I didn't believe him and said he could work in the yard instead. If I'd known the boy had as much as this[1], I'd have offered him decent lodgings[2] upstairs.'

'The thing takes shape.[3] It becomes coherent. The boy decides to use the information that he has gleaned[4] from his presence[5] at Mrs Oldmore's Hotel. He goes out once, presents himself and makes his demands[6]. He is invited to a meeting ... a certain place at a certain time. It is at this meeting that he will be killed. But he has at least taken some precautions, leaving all his wealth behind with his sister. She hides it beneath the floorboards. How wretched she must now be[7], knowing that she was unable to retrieve it[8] when you and I chased her away[9], Watson. One last question for you, Mr Hardcastle, and then we will be on our way[10]. Did Sally ever mention the House of Silk to you?'

'The House of Silk? No, Mr Holmes. I have never heard of it. What am I to do with these coins?'

'Keep them. The girl has lost her brother. She has lost everything. Perhaps one day she will come back to you, needing help, and at the very least[11] you will be able to give them back.'

From The Bag of Nails we followed the sweep of the Thames[12], heading back towards[13] Bermondsey. I wondered aloud[14] if Holmes intended to revisit the hotel. 'Not the hotel, Watson,' he said. 'But nearby. We must find the source of the boy's wealth. It may prove central to the reason he was killed[15].'

'He got it from his uncle,' I said. 'But if his parents are dead, how are we to find any other of his relatives[16]?'

Holmes laughed. 'You surprise me, Watson. Are you really so unfamiliar with[17] the language of at least half the population in London? Every week thousands of labourers and itinerant workers[18] visit their uncles, by which they mean the pawnbrokers.

1. tant d'argent que ça
2. un logement correct
3. Les choses se précisent.
4. qu'il a glanées
5. en étant présent
6. donne ses exigences
7. Comme elle doit être malheureuse
8. n'a pu le récupérer
9. l'avons fait fuir
10. partirons
11. au moins
12. la courbe de la Tamise
13. pour regagner
14. à voix haute
15. C'est peut-être une piste capitale de son meurtre
16. d'autres parents à lui
17. Connaissez-vous si mal
18. de travailleurs et d'ouvriers itinérants

That is where Ross received his ill-gotten[1] gains. The only question is – what did he sell to receive his florins and shillings?'

'And where did he sell it?' I added. 'There must be hundreds of pawnbrokers in this part of London alone[2].'

'That is certainly the case. On the other hand, you will recall that Wiggins followed our mysterious assailant from a pawnbroker in Bridge Lane to the hotel and mentioned that Ross was frequently in and out of it[3] himself. Perhaps that is where his "uncle" is to be found.'

What a place of broken[4] promises and lost hopes[5] the pawnbroker proved to be! Every class, every profession, every walk of life[6] was represented in its grubby windows[7], the detritus of so many lives pinned like butterflies[8] behind the glass. Overhead, a wooden sign with three red balls on a blue background hung on rusty chains[9], refusing to swing in the breeze[10] as if to assert that nothing here would ever move, that once the owners had lost their possessions, they would never see them again. 'Money advanced on plate, jewels, wearing apparel[11] and every description of property[12]' read the notice below and so it was, for even Aladdin in his cave[13] would have been unlikely to stumble upon[14] such a treasure trove. Garnet brooches[15] and silver watches, china[16] cups and vases, pen holders[17], teaspoons and books, fought for space[18] on the shelves with such disparate objects as a clockwork[19] soldier and a stuffed jay[20]. Linen squares[21] from tiny handkerchiefs to tablecloths[22] and brightly embroidered bedcovers[23] dangled[24] at the sides. A whole army of chessmen[25] stood guard over[26] a battlefield of rings and bracelets laid out on green baize[27]. What workman had sacrificed his chisels and saws[28] for beer and sausages at the weekend? What little girl managed without her Sunday dress while her parents

1. mal acquis
2. rien que dans ce quartier
3. y allait souvent
4. non tenues
5. espoirs perdus
6. tous les milieux
7. sa vitrine crasseuse
8. épinglés comme des papillons
9. pendaient à une chaîne rouillée
10. se balancer à la brise
11. de la vaisselle, des bijoux, des vêtements
12. n'importe quel objet
13. Aladin dans sa grotte
14. tomber sur
15. Des broches en grenat
16. en porcelaine
17. des pots à crayons
18. s'entassaient
19. mécanique
20. geai empaillé
21. Du linge de maison
22. nappes
23. des dessus-de-lit aux broderies vives
24. pendaient
25. pièces d'échecs
26. veillait sur
27. disposés sur de la feutrine verte
28. ses burins et ses scies

struggled to find food for the table? The window was not just a display[1] of human degradation[2]. It was a celebration. And it was here, perhaps, that Ross had come.

I had seen pawnbrokers in the West End and knew that it was customary for them[3] to provide a side door[4] through which it was possible to enter without being seen, but that was not the case here, for the people who lived around Bridge Lane had no such scruples[5]. There was one main door and it was open. I followed Holmes into a darkened interior where a single man perched on a stool[6], reading a book with one hand, while the other rested[7] on the counter, the fingers rolling slowly inwards[8] as if turning some invisible object over[9] in his palm. He was a slim, delicate-looking man of about fifty, thin of face, wearing a shirt buttoned to the neck, a waistcoat and a scarf. There was something neat[10] and meticulous in his manner[11] that put me in mind of a watchmaker[12].

'And how may I help you, gentlemen?' he enquired[13], his eyes barely leaving[14] the page. But he must have scrutinised us as we came in for he continued: 'It looks to me as if[15] you are here on official business. Are you from the police? If so[16], I cannot help you. I know nothing about my customers. It is my practice[17] never to ask questions. If you have something you wish to leave with me, I will offer you a fair price[18]. Otherwise I must wish you a good day.'

'My name is Sherlock Holmes.'

'The detective? I am honoured. And what brings you here, Mr Holmes? Perhaps it has something to do with a gold necklace, set with sapphires, a nice little piece? I paid five pounds for it and the police took it back again, so I gained nothing at all. Five pounds and it might have brought me twice that[19] if it were not redeemed[20]. But there you are[21].

1. étalage
2. déchéance
3. l'usage chez eux
4. de ménager une porte sur le côté
5. n'avaient pas ce genre d'états d'âme
6. tabouret
7. était posée
8. s'enroulant lentement
9. comme s'ils faisaient tourner un objet invisible
10. de soigné
11. dans sa mise
12. horloger
13. demanda
14. quittant à peine
15. J'ai comme une idée que
16. Si c'est le cas
17. J'ai pour habitude
18. un prix honnête
19. aurait pu me rapporter le double
20. s'il n'avait pas été racheté
21. enfin, voilà

We're all on the road to ruin[1] but some are further ahead[2] than others.'

I knew that in at least one respect he was lying[3]. Whatever Mrs Carstairs's necklace was worth[4], he would have paid only a fraction of its true value for it was on this basic injustice that his livelihood was based[5]. Perhaps the farthings that we had found had come from here.

'We have no interest in the necklace,' said Holmes. 'Nor in the man who brought it here.'

'Which is just as well[6], for the man who brought it here, an American, is dead, or so the police tell me.'

'We are interested in another of your customers. A child by the name of Ross.'

'I hear that Ross has also left this vale of tears[7]. Poor odds[8], would you not say, to lose two pigeons in so short a space of time[9]?'

'You paid Ross money, recently.'

'Who told you so?'

'Do you deny it?[10]'

'I do not deny it nor do I affirm it. I merely say that I am busy and would be most grateful if you would leave.'

'What is your name?'

'Russell Johnson.'

'Very well, Mr Johnson. I will make you a proposition. Whatever Ross brought to you, I will purchase and I will pay you a good price, but only on the condition that you play fair with me[11]. I know a great deal about[12] you, Mr Johnson, and if you attempt to lie to me[13], I will see it and I will return with the police and take what I want and you will find you have made no profit at all.'

Johnson smiled but it seemed to me that his face was filled with melancholy. 'You know nothing about me at all, Mr Holmes.'

'No? I would say you were brought up in a wealthy family[14] and were well educated. You might have

1. courons tous à notre perte
2. certains ont plus d'avance
3. qu'il mentait au moins sur un point
4. valait
5. qu'il gagnait sa vie
6. Ce qui n'est pas plus mal
7. vallée de larmes
8. Les chances étaient maigres
9. en si peu de temps
10. Vous le niez ?
11. que vous jouiez le jeu avec moi
12. J'en sais énormément sur
13. me mentir
14. avez grandi dans une famille aisée

been a successful pianist for such was your ambition. Your downfall was due to[1] an addiction[2], probably gambling, quite possibly dice[3]. You were in prison earlier this year for receiving stolen goods[4] and were considered troublesome[5] by the warders[6]. You served a sentence[7] of at least three months but were released[8] in September and since then you have done brisk business[9].'

For the first time, Johnson gave Holmes his full attention. 'Who told you all this?'

'I did not need to be told, Mr Johnson. It is all painfully apparent.[10] And now, if you please, I must ask you again. What did Ross bring you?'

Johnson considered[11], then nodded slowly. 'I met this boy, Ross, two months ago,' he said. 'He was newly arrived in London, living up in King's Cross, and was brought here by a couple of[12] other street boys. I remember very little about him, except that he seemed well fed and better dressed than the others and that he carried with him a gentleman's pocket watch, stolen I have no doubt[13]. He came in a few more times after that, but he never brought in anything as good again.' He went over to a cabinet, rummaged about and produced[14] a watch on a chain, set in a gold casing[15]. 'This is the watch, and I gave the boy just five shillings for it although it's worth at least[16] ten pounds. You can have it for what I paid.'

'And in return?[17]'

'You must tell me how you know so much about me. You are a detective, I know, but I will not believe you can have plucked so much out of the air[18] on the basis of this one brief meeting.'

'It is a matter of such simplicity that if I explain it to you, you will see you have made a bad bargain[19].'

'But if you don't, I'll never sleep.'

'Very well, Mr Johnson. The fact of your education[20] is obvious from the manner of your speech[21]. I also note the copy[22] of Flaubert's letters to George

1. Votre ruine a été causée par
2. un penchant
3. les jeux de hasard, très probablement les jeux de dés
4. pour recel
5. difficile
6. gardiens
7. avez purgé une peine
8. avez été libéré
9. vos affaires marchent bien
10. Tout est absolument flagrant.
11. réfléchit
12. deux ou trois autres
13. j'en suis sûr
14. fouilla dedans et en sortit
15. boîtier [de la montre à gousset]
16. bien qu'elle vaille au moins
17. En échange de quoi ?
18. je ne peux croire que vous ayez sorti tout ça de nulle part
19. une mauvaise affaire
20. Votre instruction
21. se voit à votre façon de vous exprimer
22. l'exemplaire

Sand, untranslated[1], which you were reading as we came in. It is a wealthy family that gives a child a solid grounding in French[2]. You also practised long hours at the piano. The fingers of a pianist are easily recognised. That you should find yourself working in this place suggests some catastrophe in your life and the rapid loss of your wealth and position. There are not so many ways that could have happened; alcohol, drugs, a poor business speculation[3] perhaps. But you speak of odds[4] and refer to your customers as[5] pigeons, a name often given to novice gamblers[6], so that is the world that springs to mind[7]. You have a nervous habit, I notice. The way you roll your hand – it suggests the dice table.'

'And the prison sentence?'

'You have been given what I believe is called a terrier crop[8], a prison haircut[9], although you are displaying a further growth[10] of about eight weeks, suggesting that you were released in September. This is confirmed by the colour of your skin. Last month was unusually warm and sunny[11] and it is evident that you were at liberty at that time. There are marks on both your wrists that tell me you wore shackles[12] while you were in jail[13] and that you struggled against them[14]. The receipt of stolen goods is the most obvious[15] crime for a pawnbroker. As to this shop, the fact that you have been absent for a lengthy[16] period is immediately apparent from the books in the window which have faded in the sunlight[17], and from the layer of dust[18] on the shelves. At the same time, I notice many objects – this watch among them – which are dust-free[19] and so have been added recently, indicating a brisk trade.'

Johnson handed over the prize[20]. 'Thank you, Mr Holmes,' he said. 'You are quite correct in every respect. I come from a good family in Sussex and did hope once to be a pianist. When that failed, I went into the law[21] and might well have prospered ex-

1. non traduites
2. de solides notions de français
3. une malheureuse spéculation financière
4. chances [dans un pari]
5. qualifiez vos clients de
6. parieurs débutants
7. l'univers qui vient à l'esprit
8. coupe de la territoriale
9. coupe à ras pour détenus
10. bien que l'on remarque une repousse
11. chaud et ensoleillé pour la saison
12. que vous avez porté des chaînes
13. en prison
14. vous êtes débattu
15. le plus logique
16. prolongée
17. pâli à la lumière
18. la couche de poussière
19. qui ne sont pas poussiéreux
20. le trophée
21. j'ai fait du droit

cept that I found it so damnably dull[1]. Then, one evening, a friend introduced me to[2] the Franco-German Club in Charlotte Street. I don't suppose you know it. There's nothing French or German about it; the place is actually run by a Jew. Well, the moment I saw it – the unmarked[3] door with its little grating[4], the windows painted out[5], the dark staircase leading to the brightly lit rooms above – I was doomed[6]. Here was the excitement that was so missing from my life[7]. I paid my two and sixpence subscription[8] and was introduced to baccarat, to roulette, to hazard and, yes, to dice. I found myself slogging through the day[9] simply to arrive at the enticements[10] of the night. Suddenly I was surrounded by brilliant new friends, all of them delighted to see me and all of them, of course, bonnets[11], which is to say they were paid by the proprietor to entice me[12] to play. Sometimes I won. More often I lost. Five pounds one night. Ten pounds the next. Need I tell you more? My work became careless.[13] I was sacked from my job[14]. With the last of my savings[15] I set myself up in these premises[16], thinking that a new profession, no matter how low and wretched[17], would occupy my mind. Not a bit of it![18] I still go back, night after night. I cannot prevent myself and who knows what the future holds for me[19]? I am ashamed to think what my parents would say if they could see me. Fortunately, they are both dead. I have no wife or children. If I have one consolation, it is that nobody in this world cares about me. I therefore have no reason to be ashamed[20].'

Holmes paid him the money and together we returned to Baker Street. However, if I had thought we had come to the end of our day's labours[21], I was very much mistaken. Holmes had examined the watch in the cab. It was a handsome piece, a minute repeater[22] with a white enamel face[23] in a gold case manufactured by Touchon & Co. of Geneva. There

1. si terriblement ennuyeux
2. m'a fait connaître
3. anonyme
4. grille
5. occultées de peinture
6. c'en était fait de moi
7. qui manquait tant à ma vie
8. droit d'entrée
9. à trimer toute la journée
10. dans la seule perspective de l'excitation
11. des gens de main
12. pour m'inciter
13. Je me suis mis à négliger mon travail.
14. renvoyé
15. mes dernières économies
16. dans ces locaux
17. même vile
18. Pas le moins du monde !
19. ce que l'avenir me réserve
20. d'avoir honte
21. au bout de nos peines pour la journée
22. une montre à répétition minutes
23. un cadran en émail blanc

was no other name or inscription, but on the reverse[1] he found an engraved[2] image: a bird perching[3] on a pair of crossed keys.

'A family crest?[4]' I suggested.

'Watson, you are scintillating[5],' replied he. 'That is exactly what I believe it to be. And hopefully my encyclopaedia will enlighten us further[6].'

Sure enough, the pages revealed a raven and two keys to be the crest of the Ravenshaws, one of the oldest families in the kingdom with a manor house[7] just outside the village of Coln St Aldwyn in Gloucestershire. Lord Ravenshaw, who had been a distinguished Foreign Minister[8] in the current Administration[9], had recently died at the age of eighty-two. His son, the Honourable[10] Alec Ravenshaw, was his only heir[11] and had now inherited both the[12] title and the family estate[13]. Somewhat to my dismay[14], Holmes insisted on leaving London at once, but I knew him only too well, and, in particular, the restlessness[15] that was so much part of his character. I did not attempt to argue[16]. Nor, for that matter, would I have considered staying behind.[17] Now that I come to think of it, I was as assiduous in my duties as his biographer as he was in the pursuit of his various investigations. Perhaps that was why the two of us got on so well[18].

I just had time to pack a few things for an overnight stay[19], and by the time the sun set we found ourselves in a pleasant inn[20], dining on a leg of lamb[21] with mint sauce and a pint of quite decent claret. I forget now what we talked about over the meal[22]. Holmes asked after my practice and I think I described to him some of Metchnikoff's interesting work on cellular theory. Holmes always took a keen[23] interest in matters to do with medicine or science, although, as I have related elsewhere, he was careful not to clutter his mind[24] with information which, in his opinion, had no material value[25].

1. sur l'envers
2. gravée
3. perché
4. Des armoiries familiales ?
5. époustouflant
6. nous en dira plus
7. possédant un manoir
8. éminent secrétaire des Affaires étrangères
9. au sein du gouvernement actuel
10. vicomte [titre des enfants de la haute aristocratie]
11. seul héritier
12. hérité à la fois du
13. domaine familial
14. Quelque peu à ma consternation
15. cette agitation
16. discuter
17. Mais je n'aurais pas non plus envisagé de ne pas l'accompagner.
18. nous nous entendions si bien
19. séjour de 24 heures
20. agréable auberge
21. gigot d'agneau
22. pendant le repas
23. vif
24. de ne pas s'encombrer l'esprit
25. peu de valeur

Heaven protect the man[1] who tried to have a conversation with him about politics[2] or philosophy. A ten-year-old child would know more. One thing I can say about that evening: at no time did we discuss the business at hand[3] and, though the time passed in the easy conviviality[4] that the two of us had so often enjoyed, I could tell that this was quite purposeful[5]. Inwardly[6], he was still uneasy[7]. The death of Ross preyed on him[8] and would not let him rest.

Before he had even taken breakfast, Holmes had sent his card up to Ravenshaw Hall, asking for an audience[9], and the reply came soon enough. The new Lord Ravenshaw had some business to take care of, but would be pleased to see us at ten o'clock. We were there as the local church struck the hour, walking up the driveway to a handsome Elizabethan[10] manor house built of Cotswold stone[11] and surrounded by lawns that sparkled with the morning frost[12]. Our friend, the raven with two keys, appeared in the stonework[13] beside the main gate and again in the lintel[14] above the front door. We had come on foot, a short and pleasant walk from our inn, but as we approached we noticed that there was a carriage parked outside, and suddenly a man came hurrying out of the house, climbed into it and swung the door shut[15] behind him. The coachman whipped on[16] the horses and a moment later he was gone, rattling past us[17] on the drive. But I had already recognised him.

'Holmes,' I said. 'I know that man!'

'Indeed so, Watson. It was Mr Tobias Finch, was it not? The senior partner[18] in the picture gallery Carstairs and Finch of Albemarle Street. A very singular coincidence, do you not think?'

'It certainly seems very strange.'

'We should perhaps broach[19] the subject with a certain delicacy. If Lord Ravenshaw is finding it necessary to sell off[20] some of his family's heirlooms[21]—'

'He could be buying.'

1. Que le Ciel protège celui
2. sur la politique
3. de l'affaire en cours
4. dans l'ambiance détendue
5. à dessein
6. Intérieurement
7. mal à l'aise
8. le tourmentait
9. demandant à être reçu
10. [du temps d'Élisabeth Ire, 1558-1603]
11. [pierre couleur miel de cette région d'Angleterre]
12. étincelaient de gelée matinale
13. maçonnerie
14. linteau
15. claqua la porte
16. fouetta
17. nous frôlant avec fracas
18. associé principal
19. aborder
20. est contraint de liquider
21. objets de famille

'That is also a possibility.'

We rang the doorbell and were admitted by a footman[1] who led us through the hall and into a drawing room of truly baronial proportions[2]. The walls were partly wood-panelled with family portraits hanging above, and a ceiling so high that no visitor would dare raise his voice[3] for fear of the echo. The windows were mullioned[4] and looked out onto a rose garden with a deer park beyond[5]. Some chairs and sofas had been arranged around a massive stone fireplace[6] – there was the raven once again, carved into the lintel – with green logs crackling[7] in the flames. Lord Ravenshaw was standing there, warming his hands. My first impression was not entirely favourable. He had silver hair, combed back[8], and a ruddy, unattractive[9] face. His eyes protruded quite conspicuously[10] and it struck me that this might be due to some abnormality of the thyroid gland. He was wearing a riding coat[11] and leather boots and carried a crop tucked under his arm[12]. Even before we had introduced ourselves, he seemed impatient and keen to be on his way[13].

'Mr Sherlock Holmes,' he said. 'Yes, yes. I think I have heard of you. A detective? I cannot imagine any circumstances in which your business would connect with mine.'

'I have something that I believe may belong to you, Lord Ravenshaw.' We had not been invited to sit down. Holmes took out the watch and carried it over to the master of the estate[14].

Ravenshaw weighed it in his hand[15], as if he couldn't be sure that the watch was even his. Slowly, it dawned on him[16] that he was indeed holding his own property. He wondered how Holmes had come upon it[17]. He was glad to have it back. He spoke not a word but all these emotions passed across his face and even I found them easy to read. 'Well, I am very much obliged to you[18],' he said, at length. 'I am very

1. accueillis par un valet de pied
2. aux proportions tout à fait seigneuriales
3. n'aurait osé élever la voix
4. à meneaux
5. et, au-delà, un parc aux cerfs
6. une énorme cheminée en pierre
7. des bûches de bois vert crépitant
8. plaqués
9. rougeaud et ingrat
10. étaient très globuleux
11. une veste d'équitation
12. avait une cravache glissée sous le bras
13. désireux de partir
14. l'apporta au maître des lieux
15. la soupesa
16. il comprit enfin
17. avait bien pu la trouver
18. Je vous suis extrêmement reconnaissant

fond of this watch. It was given to me by my sister. I never thought I would see it again.'

'I would be interested to know how you lost it, Lord Ravenshaw.'

'I can tell you exactly, Mr Holmes. It happened in London during the summer; I was there for the opera.'

'Can you remember the month?'

'It was June. As I climbed out of my carriage, a young street urchin ran into me[1]. He couldn't have been more than twelve or thirteen. I thought nothing of it[2] at the time, but during the interval[3] I looked to see the time and of course discovered that I had been pickpocketed.'

'The watch is a handsome one, and you obviously value it[4]. Did you report[5] the incident to the police?'

'I do not quite understand the purpose of these questions, Mr Holmes. For that matter[6], I'm rather surprised that a man of your reputation should have troubled[7] to have come all this way from London to return it. I take it you are hoping for a reward?[8]'

'Not at all. The watch is part of a wider investigation[9] and I hoped you might be able to help.'

'Well, I'm afraid I must disappoint you. I know nothing more. And I didn't report the theft, knowing that there are thieves and scoundrels[10] on every street corner[11] and doubting that there was anything the police would be able to do, and so why waste their time[12]? I am very grateful to you for returning the watch to me, Mr Holmes, and I am perfectly happy[13] to pay you for your travel expenses[14] and time. But other than that[15], I think I must wish you a good day.'

'I have just one last question, Lord Ravenshaw,' Holmes said, with equanimity[16]. 'There was a man leaving here as we arrived. Unfortunately, we just missed him. I wonder if I was right[17] in recognising an old friend of mine, Mr Tobias Finch?'

1. m'a bousculé
2. Je n'y ai pas prêté attention
3. l'entracte
4. de toute évidence, elle vous est précieuse
5. Avez-vous déclaré
6. D'ailleurs
7. se donne le mal
8. J'imagine que vous espérez une récompense ?
9. d'une enquête plus large
10. des vauriens
11. à tous les coins de rue
12. à quoi bon leur faire perdre du temps
13. je serais ravi
14. frais de déplacement
15. sinon
16. sérénité
17. si j'avais vu juste

'A friend?' As Holmes had suspected, Lord Ravenshaw was not pleased to have been discovered in the company of the art dealer.

'An acquaintance.[1]'

'Well, since you ask, yes, it was he. I do not enjoy discussing family business[2], Mr Holmes, but you might as well know that my father had execrable taste in art[3] and it is my intention to rid myself[4] of at least part of his collection. I have been speaking to several galleries in London. Carstairs and Finch is the most discreet.'

'And has Mr Finch ever mentioned to you the House of Silk?'

Holmes asked the question and the silence that ensued[5] happened to coincide with the snapping[6] of a log in the fire so that the sound came almost as a punctuation mark[7].

'You said you had one question, Mr Holmes. That is a second[8] and I have had enough[9], I think, of your impertinence. Am I to call for my servant[10] or will you now leave?'

'I am delighted to have met you, Lord Ravenshaw.'

'I am grateful to you for returning my watch, Mr Holmes.'

I was glad to be out of that room, for I had felt almost trapped in the midst of[11] so much wealth and privilege. As we stepped onto the path[12] and began to walk back down to the gate, Holmes chuckled[13]. 'Well there's another mystery for you, Watson.'

'He seemed unusually hostile, Holmes.'

'I refer to the theft[14] of the watch. If it was taken in June, Ross could not have been responsible, for as far as we know[15], he was at the Chorley Grange School for Boys at that time. According to Johnson, it was pawned[16] two months ago, in September. So what had happened to it in the three months in-between[17]? If it was Ross who stole it, why did he hold on to it[18] for so long?'

1. Une connaissance.
2. des affaires de famille
3. un goût artistique exécrable
4. de me débarrasser
5. qui suivit
6. le craquement
7. ponctuer son propos
8. Il s'agit là de la seconde
9. j'en ai assez
10. domestique
11. piégé, au milieu de
12. Alors que nous nous engagions dans l'allée
13. eut un petit rire
14. Je parle du vol
15. d'après nos informations
16. donnée en gage
17. d'intervalle
18. l'a-t-il gardée

1. vola au-dessus de nos têtes
2. une corneille
3. regarder à nouveau vers le manoir
4. hanches
5. globuleux
6. bien que j'aie pu me tromper
7. plein de haine

We had almost reached the gate when a black bird flew overhead[1], not a raven but a crow[2]. I followed it with my eye and as I did so, something made me turn and glance back at the hall[3]. And there was Lord Ravenshaw, standing at the window, watching us leave. His hands were on his hips[4] and his round, bulging[5] eyes were fixed on us. And although I could have been mistaken[6] for we were some distance away, his face, it seemed to me, was filled with hate[7].

NINE

The Warning[1]

1. avertissement

'There is no helping it[2],' Holmes said with a sigh[3] of irritation. 'We are going to have to call upon[4] Mycroft.'

I had first met Mycroft Holmes when he had asked for help on the behalf of a neighbour of his[5], a Greek interpreter who had fallen in with[6] a vicious pair of criminals[7]. Until that moment, I had not the remotest idea[8] that Holmes had a brother seven years older than himself. Indeed, I had never thought of him as having any family at all. It may seem strange that a man whom I could quite reasonably call my closest[9] friend and one in whose company I had spent many hundreds of hours had never once mentioned his childhood, his parents, the place where he was born[10] or anything else relating to his life before Baker Street. But, of course, that was his nature. He never celebrated his birthday and I only discovered the date when I read it in his obituaries[11]. He once mentioned to me that his ancestors had been country squires[12] and that one of his relations[13] was a quite well-known artist but in general he preferred almost to pretend that[14] his family had never existed, as if a prodigy such as himself had sprung unaided onto the world stage[15].

When I first heard that Holmes had a brother, it humanised him – or at least, it did until I met the brother. Mycroft was, in many ways, as

2. Impossible de faire autrement
3. soupir
4. faire appel à
5. l'un de ses voisins
6. fréquenté
7. deux odieux criminels
8. ignorais totalement
9. le plus proche
10. son lieu de naissance
11. nécrologies
12. des propriétaires terriens
13. qu'un membre de sa famille
14. faire comme si
15. acquis tout seul la célébrité

peculiar as he[1]: unmarried[2], unconnected[3], existing in a small world of his own creation. This was largely defined by the Diogenes Club[4] in Pall Mall where he was to be found every day from a quarter to five until eight o'clock. I believe he had an apartment somewhere closc by[5]. The Diogenes Club, as is well known, catered to[6] the most unsociable and unclubbable[7] men in town. Nobody ever spoke to each other. In fact, talking was not allowed at all, except in the Stranger's Room[8], and even there the conversation hardly flowed[9]. I remember reading in a newspaper that the hall porter had once wished a member good evening and had been promptly dismissed[10]. The dining room had all the warmth and conviviality of a Trappist monastery, although the food was at least superior[11] as the club employed a French chef of some renown[12]. That Mycroft enjoyed his food[13] was evident from his frame[14], which was quite excessively corpulent. I can still see him wedged into a chair[15] with a brandy on one side and a cigar on the other. It was always disconcerting to meet him, for I would glimpse in him, just for a moment, some of the features[16] of my friend: the light grey[17] eyes, the same sharpness of expression[18], but they would seem strangely out of place[19], translated, as it were, to[20] this animated mountain of flesh[21]. Then Mycroft would turn his head and he would be a complete stranger to me, the sort of man who somehow warned you to keep your distance. I did sometimes wonder what the two of them might havc been like[22] as boys[23]. Had they ever fought together, read together, kicked a ball[24] between them[25]? It was impossible to imagine, for they had grown up to become the sort of men who would like you to think that they had never been boys at all.

When Holmes first described Mycroft to me, he had said that he was an auditor[26], working for a number of government departments. But actually

1. aussi bizarre que lui
2. célibataire
3. isolé
4. le club Diogène
5. non loin de là
6. accueillait
7. les moins sociables
8. la salle des visiteurs
9. on ne conversait guère
10. renvoyé sur-le-champ
11. de premier ordre
12. d'un certain renom
13. Le goût de Mycroft pour les plaisirs de la table
14. se voyait à sa silhouette
15. calé dans un fauteuil
16. certains traits
17. gris clair
18. air sagace
19. incongrus
20. ainsi insérés dans
21. montagne de graisse
22. comment étaient ces deux-là
23. quand ils étaient enfants
24. joué au ballon
25. ensemble
26. conseiller

this was only half the truth and I later learned that his brother was much more important and influential. I refer, of course, to the adventure of the Bruce-Partington plans when the blueprints for a top secret submarine[1] were stolen from the Admiralty[2]. It was Mycroft who was charged with getting them back[3], and that was when Holmes admitted to me[4] that he was a vital figure[5] in government circles, a human repository of arcane facts[6], the man whom every department consulted when something needed to be known. It was Holmes's opinion that, had he chosen to be a detective he might have been his equal[7] or even, I was astonished to hear him admit, his superior[8]. But Mycroft Holmes suffered from a singular character flaw[9]. He had a streak of indolence so ingrained[10] that it would have rendered him unable to solve any crime, for the simple reason that he would have been unable to interest himself in it. He is still alive, by the way. When I last heard[11], he had been knighted[12] and was the chancellor[13] of a well-known university, but he has since retired.

'Is he in London?' I asked.

'He is seldom anywhere else[14]. I will inform him that we intend to visit the club.'

The Diogenes was one of the smaller clubs on Pall Mall, designed rather like a Venetian palazzo[15] in the Gothic style, with highly ornate[16], arched[17] windows and small balustrades. This had the effect of making the interior rather gloomy. The front door led to an atrium which rose the full length[18] of the building with a domed window high above[19] but the architect had cluttered the place with[20] too many galleries, columns and staircases and the result was that very little light was able to disseminate its way through[21]. Visitors were permitted only on the ground floor[22]. According to the rules[23], there were two days of the week when they could accompany a member to the dining room above, but in the seventy years since

1. les plans d'un sous-marin top secret
2. l'amirauté
3. de les retrouver
4. m'avoua
5. un acteur incontournable
6. le dépositaire vivant d'un savoir obscur
7. il l'aurait peut-être égalé
8. surpassé
9. défaut
10. un côté indolent si ancré en lui
11. Aux dernières nouvelles
12. anobli
13. président
14. rarement ailleurs
15. un palais vénitien
16. très ornementées
17. cintrées
18. prenait toute la hauteur
19. coupole vitrée tout en haut
20. surchargé les lieux de
21. très peu de lumière parvenait à s'y infiltrer
22. rez-de-chaussée
23. le règlement

1. rayonnages en chêne, ployant
2. différents bustes en marbre
3. [sorte de balcon clos]
4. errant
5. n'aie jamais bien saisi ce que pouvait vouloir dire l'un ou l'autre
6. en entrant de son pas dandinant
7. du poids
8. je vois
9. que tu es redevenu toi-même
10. la grippe
11. Ce n'était qu'un léger accès.
12. sur les tatouages
13. désagréablement
14. acheté un perroquet
15. Emprunté.
16. j'espère qu'elle va bien
17. s'est absentée
18. cuisinière
19. a démissionné
20. À cause
21. à cran
22. tournoi
23. pivotant
24. nous désigna
25. s'affala

the club had been founded, this had never yet occurred. Mycroft received us, as always, in the Stranger's Room, with its oak bookshelves bowing[1] under the weight of so many books, its various marble busts[2], its bow window[3] with views across Pall Mall. There was a portrait of the Queen above the fireplace, painted, it was said, by a member of the club who had insulted her by including a stray[4] dog and a potato, although I was never able to grasp the significance of either[5].

'My dear Sherlock!' Mycroft exclaimed as he waddled in[6]. 'How are you? You have recently lost weight[7], I notice[8]. But I'm glad to see you restored to your old self[9].'

'And you have recovered from influenza[10].'

'A very mild bout.[11] I enjoyed your monograph on tattoos[12]. Written during the hours of the night, evidently. Have you been troubled by insomnia?'

'The summer was unpleasantly[13] warm. You did not tell me you had acquired a parrot[14].'

'Not acquired, Sherlock. Borrowed.[15] Dr Watson, a pleasure. Although it has been almost a week since you saw your wife, I trust she is well[16]. You have just returned from Gloucestershire.'

'And you from France.'

'Mrs Hudson has been away[17]?'

'She returned last week. You have a new cook[18].'

'The last one resigned[19].'

'On account[20] of the parrot.'

'She always was highly strung[21].'

This exchange took place with such rapidity that I felt myself to be a spectator at a tennis tournament[22], my head swivelling[23] from one to the other. Mycroft waved us to[24] the sofa and settled his own bulk[25] on a chaise longue. 'I was very sorry to hear of the death of the boy, Ross,' he said, suddenly more serious. 'You know, I have advised you against the use of[1] these street children, Sherlock. I hope you didn't place him in harm's way.'

'It is too early to say with any certainty. You read the newspaper reports?'

'Of course. Lestrade is handling the investigation[2]. He's not such a bad man. This business of the white ribbon, though. I find that most disturbing[3]. I would say that, allied with the extremely painful and protracted manner of the death[4], it was placed there as a warning. The principal question you should be asking yourself is whether that warning was a general one, or whether it was directed towards you[5].'

'I was sent a piece of white ribbon seven weeks ago.' Holmes had brought the envelope with him. He produced it[6] and handed it to his brother who examined it.

'The envelope tells us little,' he said. 'It was pushed through your letter box in a hurry for you see the end is scuffed[7]. Your name written by a right-handed, educated man[8].' He drew out the ribbon. 'This silk is Indian. Doubtless you will have seen that for yourself[9]. It has been exposed to sunlight, for the fabric has weakened[10]. It is exactly nine inches[11] in length[12], which is interesting. It was purchased from a milliner's[13] and then cut a second time. You can see that one end has been cut professionally with a pair of sharp[14] scissors while[15] the other was sliced, roughly[16], with a knife. I cannot add very much more than that, Sherlock.'

'Nor did I expect you to[17], brother Mycroft. But I did wonder if you might be able to tell me what it signifies. Have you heard of a place or an organisation called the House of Silk?'

Mycroft shook his head. 'The name means nothing to me. It sounds like a shop. Indeed, now I think of it, I seem to remember there being[18] a gentleman's outfitter[19] of that name in Edinburgh. Could it not be where this ribbon was purchased?'

1. déconseillé d'employer
2. est chargé de l'enquête
3. tout à fait troublant
4. cette mort très lente
5. il t'était destiné
6. la montra
7. le bord est éraflé
8. quelqu'un de cultivé, un droitier
9. par toi-même
10. n'a plus de tenue
11. [22,8 cm]
12. de long
13. chez un(e) modiste
14. coupants
15. alors que
16. coupée grossièrement
17. Je n'en demandais pas tant, non plus
18. qu'il y a
19. une boutique de confection pour hommes

'That seems unlikely, given the circumstances. We heard it first mentioned by a girl who had most probably lived her whole life in London. It filled her with such fear that she struck out at[1] Dr Watson here[2], inflicting a knife wound on his chest.'

'Goodness!'

'I mentioned it also to Lord Ravenshaw—'

'The son of the former Foreign Minister?'

'The very same.[3] His reaction, I thought, was one of alarm[4], although he did his best[5] not to show it.'

'Well, I can ask a few questions for you, Sherlock. Would it trouble you to call on me[6] at the same time tomorrow? In the meantime, I will hang on to this[7].' He gathered the white ribbon into his pudgy[8] hand.

But in fact we did not have to wait twenty-four hours for the result of Mycroft's enquiries. The following morning, at about ten o'clock, we heard the rattle of approaching wheels[9] and, Holmes, who happened to be standing at[10] the window, glanced outside. 'It's Mycroft!' he said.

I came over and joined him[11] in time to see Holmes's brother being helped down from a landau. I realised at once that this was a remarkable occurrence[12], for Mycroft had never visited us at Baker Street before and only ever came once again. Holmes himself had fallen silent and there was a very sombre expression on his face, from which I understood[13] that something quite sinister must have introduced itself into the affair to have caused such a momentous event[14]. We had to wait some time for Mycroft to join us in the room. The front stairs were narrow and steep[15], doubly unsuited[16] to a man of his bulk[17]. Eventually he appeared[18] in the doorway, took one look around him and sat down in the nearest chair. 'This is where you live?' he asked.

Holmes nodded.

'It is exactly as I imagined it. Even the position of the fire – you sit on the right and your friend on the

1. a attaqué
2. ici présent
3. Lui-même.
4. dénotait de l'inquiétude
5. bien qu'il ait fait de son mieux
6. de venir me voir
7. je conserve ceci
8. potelée
9. le bruit d'un attelage qui approchait
10. se tenait devant
11. Je vins le rejoindre
12. un évènement exceptionnel
13. d'où je conclus
14. un moment aussi historique
15. Les marches du perron étaient étroites et raides
16. inadaptées
17. corpulence
18. Il finit par apparaître

left, of course. Strange, is it not, how we fall into these patterns[1], how we are dictated to[2] by the space that surrounds us.'

'Can I offer you some tea?'

'No, Sherlock. I do not intend to stay long.' Mycroft took out the envelope and handed it to him. 'This is yours. I am returning it to you with some advice which I very much hope you will take[3].'

'Pray continue.'

'I do not have the answer to your question. I do not have any idea what the House of Silk is or where it may be found. Believe me when I say that I wish it were otherwise[4], for then you might have more reason to accept what I am about to say. You must drop[5] this investigation immediately. You must make no further enquiries[6]. Forget the House of Silk, Sherlock. Never mention those words again.'

'You know I cannot do that.'

'I know your character. It is the reason why I have crossed London and come to you[7] personally. It occurred to me that, if I tried to warn you, it would only make you turn this into a personal crusade[8] and I hoped that my coming here would underline the seriousness[9] of what I say. I could have waited until this evening and then informed you that my enquiries had led me nowhere[10] and left you to get on with it[11]. But I could not do that because I am concerned[12] that you are putting yourself into the gravest danger, you and Dr Watson too. Let me explain to you what has happened since our meeting at the Diogenes Club. I approached[13] one or two people whom I knew in certain government departments. At the time, I assumed that this House of Silk must refer to some sort of criminal conspiracy and I only wished to discover if anyone in the police or one of the intelligence services[14] was investigating it. The people I spoke to were unable[15] to help. At least, that is what they said.

1. prenons nos petites habitudes
2. conditionnés
3. que tu voudras bien suivre, j'espère
4. j'aimerais qu'il en soit autrement
5. abandonner
6. arrêter toute recherche
7. que je suis venu te voir
8. croisade personnelle
9. soulignerait la gravité
10. n'avaient rien donné
11. te laisser continuer
12. j'ai peur
13. J'ai contacté
14. des services du renseignement
15. n'ont pas été en mesure

'What happened next[1], however, came as a very unpleasant surprise. As I left my lodgings this morning, I was greeted by a carriage and taken[2] to an office in Whitehall[3] where I met a man whom I cannot identify[4], but whose name would be known to you and who works in close association with the[5] prime minister himself. I should add that this is a person whom I know well and whose wisdom and judgement I would never question[6]. He was not at all pleased to see me and came straight to the point[7], asking me why I had been asking about the House of Silk and what I meant by it[8]. His manner, I have to say, Sherlock, was singularly hostile and I had to think very carefully before I replied. I decided at once not to mention your name – otherwise it might not be me who was now knocking at your door. Having said that[9], it may make no difference anyway, for my relationship with you is well known and you may already be suspected. At any event[10], I told him merely that one of my informers had mentioned it in relation to a murder in Bermondsey, and that it had piqued my curiosity. He asked for the name of the informer and I made something up[11], trying to give the impression that it was a trivial affair[12] and that my original enquiry had been nothing more than casual[13].

'He seemed to relax a little, although he continued to weigh[14] his words with great caution[15]. He told me that the House of Silk was indeed the subject[16] of a police investigation, and it was for this reason that my sudden request had been referred to him[17]. Things were at a delicate stage[18] and any intervention from an outside party[19] could do untold damage[20]. I don't think a single word of this was true, but I pretended to acquiesce, regretting that my chance enquiry[21] should have prompted such alarm[22]. We spoke for a few minutes more and, after an exchange of pleasantries[23] and a final apol-

1. Ce qui s'est passé ensuite
2. une calèche m'attendait pour m'emmener
3. un ministère
4. dont je ne peux révéler l'identité
5. est un proche collaborateur du
6. dont je ne saurais remettre en question la sagacité
7. est allé droit au but
8. où je voulais en venir
9. Cela dit
10. En tout cas
11. j'ai inventé quelque chose
12. un point anodin
13. si j'avais posé des questions, c'était sans y attacher d'importance
14. choisir
15. soin
16. faisait en effet l'objet
17. lui avait été signalée
18. en étaient à un stade délicat
19. d'un tiers
20. occasionner d'immenses dégâts
21. questions fortuites
22. aient pu susciter tant d'inquiétude
23. civilités

ogy from myself for wasting this gentleman's time, I took my leave. But the point is, Sherlock, that politicians at this very senior level[1] have a way of saying a lot whilst giving away very little[2] and this particular gentleman managed to impress upon me[3] what I am now trying to tell you. You must leave it alone[4]! The death of a street child, as tragic as it may be[5], is completely insignificant when set against the wider picture[6]. Whatever the House of Silk is, it is a matter of national importance[7]. The government is aware of it[8] and is dealing with it[9] and you have no idea of the damage you may do and the scandal you may cause if you continue to be involved. Do you understand me?'

'You could not have been more lucid[10].'

'And will you heed[11] what I have said?'

Holmes reached for a cigarette. He held it for a moment as if wondering whether to light it. 'I cannot promise that,' he said. 'While I feel myself responsible for the death of the child, I owe it to him[12] to do all I can to bring his killer – or killers – to justice. His task was simply to watch over a man in a hotel. But if this inadvertently drew him[13] into some wider conspiracy[14], then I fear I have no choice but to pursue the matter.'

'I thought you might say that, Sherlock, and I suppose your words do you credit. But let me add this.' Mycroft got to his feet. He was anxious[15] to be on his way. 'If you do ignore[16] my advice and go ahead with[17] this investigation, and if it does lead you into peril, which I believe it may, you cannot come back to me for there will be nothing I can do to help you. The very[18] fact that I have exposed myself by asking questions on your behalf means that my hands are now tied[19]. At the same time, I urge you[20] once more to think again[21]. This is not one of your petty puzzles of the police court[22]. If you upset[23] the

1. de ces hautes sphères
2. tout en se livrant très peu
3. me faire comprendre
4. abandonner
5. soit-elle
6. vue dans un contexte plus vaste
7. une question d'intérêt national
8. en est conscient
9. s'en occupe
10. limpide
11. tiendras-tu compte de
12. je lui dois
13. l'a embarqué
14. dans quelque vaste complot
15. avait hâte
16. ne tiens pas compte de
17. que tu poursuis
18. simple
19. qu'à présent j'ai les mains liées
20. je te conjure
21. bien réfléchir
22. une petite énigme pour la correctionnelle
23. déranges

wrong people, it could be the end of your career ... and worse.'

There was nothing more to be said. Both brothers recognised it. Mycroft bowed slightly[1] and left. Holmes leant over the gasogene and lit his cigarette. 'Well, Watson,' he exclaimed. 'What do you make of that?'

'I very much hope you will consider what Mycroft had to say,' I ventured[2].

'I have already considered it.'

'I rather feared as much.[3]'

Holmes laughed. 'You know me too well, my boy. And now I must leave you. I have an errand to run[4] and must hurry if I am to make[5] the evening editions.'

He rushed out, leaving me alone with my misgivings[6]. At lunchtime he returned but did not eat, a sure sign[7] that he was engaged upon[8] some stimulating line of enquiry[9]. I had seen him so often like this before. He put me in mind of a foxhound[10], running upon breast-high scent[11], for just as[12] an animal will devote[13] its entire being[14] to one activity, so could he allow events to absorb him to the extent[15] that even the most basic human needs – food, water, sleep – could be set aside. The arrival of the evening newspaper showed me what he had done. He had placed an advertisement in the personal columns[16].

> **£20 REWARD** – Information relating to[17] The House of Silk. To be treated in the strictest confidence[18]. Apply[19] 221B Baker Street.

'Holmes!' I exclaimed. 'You have done the very opposite[20] of what your brother suggested. If you were going to pursue your investigation, and I can understand your desire to do so, you could at least have proceeded[21] with discretion.'

1. fit un léger salut
2. hasardai-je
3. C'est bien ce que je craignais.
4. une course à faire
5. si je ne veux pas rater
6. doutes
7. signe évident
8. s'engageait dans
9. une piste exaltante
10. chien de chasse [à courre]
11. après avoir flairé une piste
12. de même qu'
13. se consacre
14. de tout son être
15. au point
16. passé une petite annonce
17. Toute information concernant
18. Sera traitée en toute confidentialité
19. S'adresser au
20. tout le contraire
21. auriez au moins pu agir

'Discretion will not help us, Watson. It is time to seize[1] the initiative. Mycroft inhabits[2] a world of whispering men[3] in darkened rooms. Well, let us see how they react to a little provocation.'

'You believe you will receive an answer?'

'Time will tell.[4] But we have at least set our calling card[5] on this affair, and even if nothing comes of it[6], no harm has been done.'

Those were his words. But Holmes had no idea of the type of people with whom he was dealing[7] nor the lengths to which they would go[8] to protect themselves. He had entered[9] a veritable miasma of evil[10], and harm, in the worst possible way, was to come to us all too soon[11].

1. prendre
2. vit dans
3. chuchoteurs
4. Le temps nous le dira.
5. abattu notre carte maîtresse
6. cela ne donne rien
7. à qui il avait affaire
8. ni jusqu'où ils étaient prêts à aller
9. mis le pied dans
10. un univers maléfique
11. n'allait pas tarder à s'abattre sur nous

TEN

Bluegate Fields

'Ha, Watson! It would appear that our bait[1], cast though it was over unknown waters[2], may have brought in a catch[3]!'

So spoke Holmes a few mornings later, standing at our bow window in his dressing gown, his hands thrust deep[4] into his pockets. I joined him at once and looked down into Baker Street, at the crowds passing[5] on either side.

'Who do you mean?' I asked.

'Do you not see him?'

'I see a great many people[6].'

'Yes. But in this cold weather very few of them wish to linger[7]. There is one man, however, who is doing precisely that. There! He is looking our way.'

The man in question was wrapped[8] in a coat and a scarf with a broad-brimmed[9], black felt[10] hat and hands tucked beneath his arms so that beyond the fact that he *was* a man, and did indeed seem to be rooted to the spot[11], unsure whether to continue or not, there was very little of him that I could see to describe with any degree of accuracy[12]. 'You think he has come in response to our advertisement?' I asked.

'It is the second time he has passed[13] our front door,' Holmes replied. 'I noticed him the first time fifteen minutes ago, walking up from the Metropolitan Railway. He then returned, and since then he

1. appât
2. bien que jeté comme une bouteille à la mer
3. une prise
4. enfoncées
5. l'affluence de passants
6. beaucoup de gens
7. ont envie de s'attarder
8. emmitouflé
9. à larges bords
10. en feutre noir
11. s'être figé sur place
12. me permettant une description précise
13. qu'il passe devant

has barely moved[1]. He is making sure[2] that he is not observed. Finally, he has made up his mind[3]!' As we watched him, standing back[4] so that he could not see us himself, the man crossed the road. 'He should be with us in a moment,' Holmes said, returning to his seat.

Sure enough, the door opened and Mrs Hudson introduced[5] our new visitor, who peeled off[6] the hat, the scarf and the coat to reveal a strange-looking[7] young man whose face and physique displayed so many contradictions[8] that I was sure even Holmes would find it difficult to pin him down[9]. I say he was young – he could not have been past thirty – and he was built like a prizefighter[10] and yet his hair was thin[11], his skin grey and his lips cracked[12], all of which made him seem much older. His clothes were expensive and fashionable[13] but they were also dirty. He seemed nervous to be here, yet regarded us with a bullish self-confidence[14] that was almost aggressive. I stood waiting for him to speak, for until then I would be unsure whether I was in the presence of an aristocrat or a ruffian of the lowest sort[15].

'Please take a seat,' said Holmes, at his most congenial. 'You have been outside for a while and I would hate to think that you have caught a chill[16]. Would you like some hot tea?'

'I'd prefer a tot of rum[17],' he replied.

'We have none. But some brandy?' Holmes nodded at me and I poured a good measure[18] into a glass and handed it over[19].

The man drained it at once[20]. A little colour returned to his face and he sat down. 'Thank you,' he said. His voice was hoarse[21] but educated. 'I've come here for the reward. I shouldn't have. The people that I deal with would cut my throat if they knew I was here, but I need the money, that's the long and the short of it[22]. Twenty pounds will keep the de-

1. c'est à peine s'il a bougé
2. s'assure
3. s'est décidé
4. nous tenant en retrait
5. fit entrer
6. retira
7. à l'étrange apparence
8. étaient si disparates
9. aurait du mal à le cerner
10. boxeur professionnel
11. clairsemés
12. gercées
13. à la mode
14. un air sûr de lui
15. vaurien de la pire espèce
16. pris froid
17. un petit rhum
18. j'en versai une bonne dose
19. le lui tendis
20. le vida d'un trait
21. rauque
22. c'est aussi simple que ça

mons away for a good while[1] and that's worth sticking my neck out for[2]. Do you have it here?'

'You will have the payment when we have your information,' Holmes replied. 'I am Sherlock Holmes. And you ... ?'

'You may call me Henderson, which is not my real name but it will do as well as any other[3]. You see, Mr Holmes, I have to be careful. You placed an advertisement asking for information about the House of Silk, and from that moment[4] this house will have been watched[5]. Anyone coming, anyone leaving will have been noted, and it may well be that one day you will be asked to provide[6] the names of all your visitors. I made sure that my face was hidden before I crossed your threshold[7]. You will understand if I do the same for my identity.'

'You will still have to tell us something about yourself before I part with any money[8]. You are a teacher are you not?'

'What makes you say that?'

'There is chalk dust[9] on the edge of your cuff[10] and I notice a red ink stain[11] on the inside of your third finger.'

Henderson, if that was what I was to call him, smiled briefly, showing stained, uneven teeth[12]. 'I am sorry to have to correct you, but I am in fact a tidewaiter[13], although I do use chalk to mark the packages before they are unloaded[14] and enter[15] the numbers in a ledger[16] using red ink. I used to work with the customs officer at[17] Chatham but came to London two years ago. I thought a change of scene[18] would be good for my career, but in fact it has almost ruined me. What else can I tell you about myself? I come originally[19] from Hampshire and my parents live there still. I am married but have not seen my wife for a while. I am a wretch[20] of the very worst sort, and although I would like to blame others for my misfortune[21], I know that at the end

1. pour un bon moment
2. le risque en vaut la peine
3. il fera l'affaire
4. dès lors
5. a dû être placée sous surveillance
6. on vous demande
7. de franchir votre seuil
8. que je vous remette de l'argent
9. de la poudre de craie
10. le bord de votre manchette
11. une tache d'encre rouge
12. une dentition inégale et tachée
13. douanier en zone portuaire
14. déchargés
15. j'inscris
16. un registre
17. à la douane de
18. qu'un dépaysement
19. suis originaire
20. un misérable
21. rendre les autres responsables de mes malheurs

of the day[1] it is entirely my own doing[2]. Worse still, there is no turning back[3]. I would sell my mother for your twenty pounds, Mr Holmes. There is nothing I would not do.[4]'

'And what is the cause of your undoing[5], Mr Henderson?'

'Will you give me another brandy?' I poured him a second glass and this time he examined it briefly. 'Opium,' he said, before swallowing it down. 'That is my secret. I am addicted to[6] opium. I used to take it because I liked it. Now I cannot live without it.

'Here is my story. I left my wife in Chatham until I had established myself[7] and took up lodgings[8] in Shadwell to be close to my new place of work. Do you know the area? It is inhabited by seamen[9], of course, as well as dock workers[10], Chinamen, lascars[11] and blacks. Oh, it's a colourful neighbourhood and there are enough temptations – pubs and dancing saloons – to part any fool and his money[12]. I could tell you I was lonely[13] and missed my family[14]. I could simply say that I was too stupid to know any better[15]. What difference does it make? It was twelve months ago that I paid my first fourpence for the little pellet of brown wax to be drawn[16] from the gallipot[17]. How low the price seemed then! How little did I know! The pleasure it gave me was beyond anything I had experienced[18]. It was as if I had never truly lived. Of course I went back. First a month later, then a week later, then suddenly it was every day and soon it was as if I had to be there every hour. I could no longer think about my work. I made mistakes and flew into an incoherent rage[19] when I was criticised. My true friends fell away[20]. My false ones encouraged me to smoke more and more. It wasn't very long before my employers recognised the state into which I had fallen and they have threatened to dismiss me[21], but I no longer care. The desire for opium fills my every waking moment[22] and does

1. qu'en fin de compte
2. tout est ma faute
3. je ne puis revenir en arrière
4. Je suis capable de tout.
5. votre perte
6. me drogue à l'
7. le temps que je sois installé
8. j'ai emménagé
9. des marins
10. des dockers
11. des [matelots] indiens
12. pour inciter un crétin à la dépense
13. que je me sentais seul
14. que ma famille me manquait
15. pour tenter de résister
16. en échange d'une boulette de cire brune
17. pot à onguents [d'apothicaire]
18. allait au-delà de tout ce que j'avais connu
19. j'ai eu des accès de rage folle
20. m'ont abandonné
21. menacent de me renvoyer
22. occupe tous mes moments de veille

1. brumes de l'oubli
2. chez lui
3. n'avait que faire de ma compassion
4. de l'intérieur
5. une fumerie d'opium
6. Moins, paraît-il
7. carrefour
8. dans n'importe quelle direction
9. cette drogue
10. pubs de nuit
11. lui tendit
12. billets
13. les lui prit des mains
14. Une lueur
15. la bête tapie en lui
16. se réveillait
17. lieux de vente
18. baissent
19. de cette toile qui couvre
20. à très grande échelle

so even now. It's been three days since I've had a smoke. Give me the reward so that I can again lose myself in the mists of oblivion[1].'

I looked on the man with horror and pity, and yet there was something about him[2] that scorned my sympathy[3], that seemed almost proud of what he had become. Henderson was sick. He was being destroyed, slowly, from within[4].

Holmes was also grave. 'The place where you go to take this drug – is it the House of Silk?' he asked.

Henderson laughed. 'Do you really think I would have been so afraid or taken so many precautions if the House of Silk were merely an opium den[5]?' he cried. 'Do you know how many opium dens there are in Shadwell and Limehouse? Fewer, they say[6], than ten years ago. But you can still stand at a crossroads[7] and find one whichever direction you take[8]. There's Mott's and Mother Abdullah's and Creer's Place and Yahee's. I'm told you can buy the stuff[9] if you want to at night-houses[10] in the Haymarket and Leicester Square.'

'Then what is it?'

'The money!'

Holmes hesitated, then passed across[11] four five-pound notes[12]. Henderson snatched them up[13] and caressed them. A dull gleam[14] had come into his eyes as his addiction, the lingering beast within him[15], awoke again[16]. 'Where do you think the opium comes from that supplies London and Liverpool and Portsmouth and all the other outlets[17] in England – and Scotland and Ireland for that matter? Where do Creer or Yahee go when their stocks run low[18]? Where is the centre of the web that stretches across[19] the entire country? That is the answer to your question, Mr Holmes. They go to the House of Silk!

'The House of Silk is a criminal enterprise that operates on a massive scale[20] and I have heard it said

– rumour, only rumour – that it has friends in the very highest places[1], that its tentacles have spread out to ensnare[2] government ministers and police officers. We are talking of an import and export business, if you like, but one worth[3] many thousands of pounds a year. The opium comes in from the East[4]. It is transported to this central depot and from there it is distributed but at a much inflated price[5].'

'Where is it to be found?'

'In London. I do not know exactly where.'

'Who runs it?'

'I cannot say. I have no idea.'

'Then you have hardly helped us, Mr Henderson. How can we even be sure that what you say is true?'

'Because I can prove it.' He coughed unpleasantly[6] and I recalled that cracked lips and a dry mouth were both symptoms of the long-term use[7] of the drug. 'I have long been a customer[8] at Creer's Place. It's done up to be Chinese[9], with a few tapestries and fans[10], and I see a few Orientals in there sometimes, coiled up together on the floor[11]. But the man who runs it[12] is as English as you or I and a more vicious and uncharitable sort[13] you wouldn't want to meet[14]. Black eyes and a head like a dead man's skull[15]. Oh, he'll smile and call you his friend when you have your fourpence, but you ask favours from him or try to cross him[16] and he'll have you beaten and thrown in a ditch[17] without a second thought[18]. Even so, he and I rub along well enough[19]. Don't ask me why. He has a little office off[20] the main room and sometimes he'll invite me in to smoke with him – tobacco not opium. He likes to hear stories about life down at the docks. Well, it was while sitting with him that I first heard the House of Silk mentioned. He uses boys to bring in his supplies and also to search out[21] new customers in the saw mills[22] and the coal yards[23]—'

1. dans les plus hautes sphères
2. ses tentacules ont atteint
3. qui pèse
4. l'Orient
5. bien plus cher
6. eut une quinte de mauvaise toux
7. d'un usage prolongé
8. Je suis client depuis longtemps
9. C'est décoré à la chinoise
10. des éventails
11. lovés par terre, les uns contre les autres
12. le gérant
13. le genre de brute
14. qu'on préfère ne pas croiser
15. une tête de mort
16. de le contrecarrer
17. un fossé
18. sans aucun scrupule
19. on ne s'entend pas trop mal
20. qui donne sur
21. rechercher
22. scieries
23. dépôts de charbon

'Boys?' I interrupted. 'Did you ever meet any of them? Was one of them called Ross?'

'They have no names and I don't speak to any of them. But listen to what I'm saying! I was there a few weeks ago and one of these lads came in, evidently late. Creer had been drinking and was in an ill-humour. He grabbed[1] the boy, struck him and knocked him to the ground[2]. "Where have you been?" he demanded.

' "The House of Silk," the boy replied.

' "And what do you have for me?"

'The boy handed over a packet and slunk out of the room[3]. "What is the House of Silk?" I asked.

'That was when Creer told me what I have told you now. Had it not been for the whisky, he would not have been so loose-tongued[4], and when he had finished he realised what he had done and suddenly turned ugly[5]. He opened a little bureau[6] beside his desk and the next thing I knew[7], he was pointing a gun at me[8]. "Why do you want to know?" he cried. "Why do you ask me these questions?"

' "I have no interest at all," I assured him, both startled[9] and afraid. "I was making idle conversation.[10] That's all."

' "Idle conversation? There is nothing idle about it[11], my friend. You ever repeat a word of what I have just said to anyone, they'll be hauling your remains out of the Thames[12]. Do you understand me? If I don't kill you, they will." Then he seemed to think a second time. He lowered the gun, and when he spoke again it was in a softer tone of voice[13]. "You can take your pipe with no payment tonight," says he. "You're a good customer. We know each other well, you and I. We have to look after you[14]. Forget I ever spoke to you and never mention the subject again[15]. Do you hear me?"

'And that was the end of it. I had almost forgotten the incident, but then I saw your advertisement and

1. a empoigné
2. l'a envoyé à terre
3. s'est éclipsé
4. aussi bavard
5. il est devenu mauvais
6. secrétaire
7. tout d'un coup
8. m'a menacé d'une arme
9. stupéfait
10. Je disais ça comme ça.
11. Il n'y a pas de « comme ça » qui tienne
12. on repêchera tes restes dans la Tamise
13. d'un ton plus calme
14. prendre soin de toi
15. n'en reparle jamais

of course it brought it back to mind[1]. If he knew I had come to you, I have no doubt he would be as good as his word[2]. But if you are seeking the House of Silk, you must begin with his office for he can lead you there.'

'Where is it to be found?[3]'

'In Bluegate Fields. The house itself is on the corner[4] of Milward Street; a low, dirty place with a red light burning in the doorway.'

'Will you be there tonight?'

'I am there every night, and thanks to your beneficence[5] I will be there for many nights to come.'

'Does this man, Creer, ever leave his office?'

'Frequently. The den[6] is cramped[7] and smoke-filled[8]. He goes out to take the air.'

'Then you may see me tonight. And if all goes well and I find what I am looking for, I will double your reward.'

'Do not say you know me. Do not acknowledge my presence.[9] Do not expect any further assistance if things go awry[10].'

'I understand.'

'Then good luck to you, Mr Holmes. I wish you success – for my sake[11], not for yours.'

We waited until Henderson had left, then Holmes turned to me with a gleam in his eyes. 'An opium den! And one that does business with the House of Silk. What do you think, Watson?'

'I don't like the sound of it one bit[12], Holmes. I think you should stay well away[13].'

'Pshaw![14] I think I can look after myself.' Holmes strode over to his desk[15], opened a drawer[16] and took out a pistol. 'I'll go armed.'

'Then I shall go with you.'

'My dear Watson, I cannot possibly allow it. As much as I am grateful to you for your consideration, I have to say that the two of us together would look anything but the sort of[17] customers who might be

1. ça m'est revenu
2. qu'il tiendrait parole
3. Où est-ce ?
4. à l'angle
5. grâce à vos largesses
6. fumerie
7. exigue
8. enfumée
9. Faites comme si vous ne me connaissiez pas.
10. tournent mal
11. dans mon intérêt
12. Tout cela ne me dit rien qui vaille
13. rester en dehors de tout ça
14. Peuh !
15. se dirigea à grands pas vers son bureau
16. un tiroir
17. aurions l'air de tout sauf de

1. en quête d'
2. fumerie d'opium
3. un seul coup tiré et j'accours
4. malfrats
5. être sûrs qu'
6. ne va pas vous trahir
7. C'est juste.
8. Aucune importance.
9. la délectation
10. nous verrons bien
11. à nouveau du brouillard
12. reporter
13. que cela ait pu servir à quelque chose
14. en lame de couteau
15. rien ne le détournerait du chemin
16. où il s'était engagé
17. explicitement
18. qui le motivait
19. Car, tant qu'il se considérerait comme
20. nous déposait
21. ruelle
22. envahissait
23. étouffant le moindre bruit
24. reniflant dans le noir
25. cherchant sa proie
26. allions nous fourrer dans sa gueule
27. ruisselants d'humidité

seeking out[1] an East London opium den[2] on a Thursday night.'

'Nonetheless, Holmes, I insist. I will remain outside, if you wish. We must surely be able to find somewhere nearby. Then, if you are in need of assistance, a single shot will bring me to the scene[3]. Creer may have other thugs[4] working for him. And can we trust[5] Henderson not to betray you[6]?'

'You have a point.[7] Very well. Where is your revolver?'

'I did not bring it with me.'

'No matter.[8] I have another.' Holmes smiled and I saw the relish[9] in his face. 'Tonight we shall pay Creer's Place a visit and we shall see what we shall see[10].'

There was another fog[11] that night, the worst one of the month so far. I would have urged Holmes to postpone[12] his visit to Bluegate Fields if I had thought it would do any good[13] but I could see from his pale and hawk-like[14] face that he would not be deterred from the course of action[15] to which he had committed himself[16]. Although he had not said as much[17], I knew that it was the death of the child, Ross, that compelled him[18]. For as long as he held himself[19] even partly responsible for what had occurred, he would not rest and all thoughts of his own safety he would willingly set aside.

And yet how oppressed I felt as the cab dropped us[20] beside an alleyway[21] near the Limehouse Basin. The fog, thick and yellow, was unfolding through[22] the streets, deadening every sound[23]. Vile, it seemed, like some evil animal snuffling through the darkness[24] in search of its prey[25] and as we made our way forward it was as if we were delivering ourselves into its very jaws[26]. We passed through the alley, trapped between red brick walls dripping with moisture[27] and rising up so high that, but for the faint silvering of the moon[1], they might have completely blotted out[2] the sky. At first, our own footsteps were the only sounds we heard, but then the passage widened and the whinny[3] of a horse, the soft rumble of a steam engine[4], the rippling[5] of water and the shrill cry[6] of a sleepless baby echoed out from different directions, each in its own way defining the obscurity all around. We were by a canal. A rat, or some other creature, scuttled[7] in front of us and slipped over the edge of the footpath, falling into the black water with a splash. A dog barked[8]. We walked past a barge[9], tied to one side, chinks of light[10] just visible behind the curtained windows, smoke billowing out[11] of its chimney. Beyond was a dry dock[12], a tangle[13] of ships barely visible, hanging like prehistoric skeletons[14], their ropes and rigging[15] trailing down[16], awaiting repairs. We turned a corner and all of this was swallowed up[17] immediately by the fog which fell like a curtain behind us, so that when I turned round it was as if I had just emerged from nowhere. Ahead, too, there was nothing, and if we had been about to step off the edge of the world[18], we would have been no wiser[19]. But then we heard the jangle[20] of a piano, one finger picking out a tune[21]. A woman suddenly loomed up[22] in front of us and I glimpsed a wrinkled[23] face, hideously painted, a gaudy[24] hat and a feathered scarf[25]. I caught[26] her scent which reminded me of flowers dying in a vase. She laughed briefly and then was gone. And finally, in front of us, I saw lights; the windows of a public house. This was from where the music was coming.

It was called The Rose and Crown. We could only read the name when we were standing directly beneath its sign. It was a strange little place, a construction of bricks held together by a patchwork of wooden planks but which still tottered awkwardly[27] as if about to collapse[28]. None of the windows was

1. sans la lueur argentée de la Lune
2. cacher
3. hennissement
4. grondement d'un moteur à vapeur
5. clapotis
6. le cri perçant
7. détala
8. aboya
9. péniche
10. des rais de lumière
11. sortant en tourbillons
12. cale sèche
13. une masse
14. des squelettes
15. cordages et gréements
16. traînant par terre
17. englouti
18. tomber dans le vide, une fois arrivés au bout du monde
19. n'aurions pas été plus avancés
20. tintamarre
21. un air joué d'un seul doigt
22. surgit
23. ridé
24. criard
25. boa
26. perçus
27. l'air chancelant malgré tout
28. comme si elle allait s'écrouler

quite straight[1]. The door was so low that we would have to bend down[2] to go in.

'We are here[3], Watson,' Holmes whispered and I could see his breath frosting in front of his lips. He pointed. 'There is Milward Street, and I would imagine that to be Creer's Place. You see the red light in the doorway.'

'Holmes, I beg of you[4] one last time to let me accompany you.'

'No, no. It is better for one of us to remain on the outside for if it turns out[5] that I am expected, you will be in the stronger position to come to my aid.'

'You think Henderson was lying to you?'

'His story struck me as in every way improbable[6].'

'Then, for heaven's sake, Holmes—'

'I cannot be entirely certain, Watson, not without entering. It is just possible that Henderson spoke the truth. But if this is a trap[7], we will spring it[8] and see where it takes us[9].' I opened my mouth to protest but he continued: 'We have touched[10] something very deep[11], old friend. This is a business of the greatest singularity and we will not get to the bottom of it[12] if we refuse to take risks. Wait for me one hour. I would suggest you avail yourself of what[13] comfort this public house has to offer. If I have not reappeared by then, you must come after me[14] but take the greatest care. And if you hear gunfire[15], then come at once.'

'Whatever you say, Holmes.'

But it was still with the gravest misgivings[16] that I watched him cross the road, momentarily disappearing from sight as the fog and the darkness embraced him[17]. He emerged on the other side, standing in the glow of the red light, framed by the doorway[18]. In the far distance, I heard a clock strike the hour, the bell sounding eleven times. Before the first chime had faded[19], Holmes had gone.

1. vraiment droite
2. nous baisser
3. Nous y sommes
4. je vous supplie
5. car, s'il s'avère
6. m'a semblée peu crédible à tous points de vue
7. piège
8. allons le déclencher
9. cela nous mène
10. touché à
11. de très obscur
12. n'irons pas au fond de l'affaire
13. que vous profitiez du
14. venir à ma recherche
15. des coups de feu
16. les doutes les plus sérieux
17. l'enveloppaient
18. dans l'encadrement de la porte
19. la fin du premier carillon

Even in my greatcoat[1] it was too cold to stand outside for an hour, and I felt ill at ease, out in the street[2] in the middle of the night, particularly in a neighbourhood[3] whose inhabitants were well known to be of the lowest class[4], vicious, and semi-criminal. I pushed open the door of The Rose and Crown and found myself in a single room divided into two halves[5] by a narrow bar punctuated by ale taps[6] with handles[7] of painted porcelain and two shelves with an array[8] of bottles. To my surprise, between fifteen and twenty people had braved the weather[9] to gather in this small space. They were huddled together[10] at tables, playing cards, drinking and smoking. The air was thick with[11] cigarette and pipe smoke and smelled strongly also of the burning peat[12] which came from a battered cast-iron stove[13] in the corner. Apart from a few candles, this was the only source of light in the room but it seemed to be having almost the opposite effect for, looking at the red glow behind the thick, glass window, it was almost as if the fire was somehow sucking the light into itself[14], consuming it, and then spewing[15] black smoke and ashes up the chimney and into the night. A worn-out[16] piano stood next to the door and there was a woman sitting in front of it, idly prodding the keys[17]. This was the music I had heard outside.

I crossed to the bar where an old, grizzled[18] man with cataracts on his eyes poured me a glass of ale for a couple of pence and I stood there, not drinking, ignoring my own worst imaginings[19], trying not to think about Holmes. The majority of the men around me were sailors and dockworkers and many of them were foreign[20] – Spanish and Maltese. None of them took any notice of me, and for that I was glad. In fact, they barely spoke to each other, and the only real sound in the room was that made by the card players. A clock on the wall showed the passing hour[21] and it seemed to me that the

1. Même avec mon pardessus,
2. en pleine rue
3. quartier
4. pour appartenir à la classe la plus défavorisée
5. en deux
6. robinets à bière
7. des poignées
8. rangée
9. bravé le mauvais temps
10. agglutinés
11. était chargé de
12. la tourbe qui brûlait
13. poêle en fonte délabré
14. aspirait la lumière
15. recrachant ensuite
16. vétuste
17. tapotant négligemment les touches
18. grisonnant
19. scénarios les plus noirs
20. étrangers
21. égrenait l'heure

minute hand[1] was deliberately dragging itself[2], ignoring the laws of time. I had often waited, with and without Holmes, for a villain to show himself[3], whether it was on the moors[4] near Baskerville Hall, on the banks of the Thames or in the gardens of many a suburban[5] home. But I will never forget the fifty-minute vigil[6] that I spent in that little room with the slap, slap, slap[7] of the cards against the table, the out-of-tune notes[8] picked out on the piano, the dark faces gazing into their glasses as if all the answers to the mystery of life might there be found[9].

Fifty minutes exactly, for it was at ten to midnight that the still[10] of the night was suddenly shattered[11] by two gunshots[12] and, almost immediately, by the shrill cry of a police whistle[13] and the sound of voices shouting out in alarm[14]. I was instantly out in the street, bursting through the doors[15], sick with[16] myself and angry that I had ever let Holmes talk me into this dangerous scheme[17]. That he had fired the shots himself I never doubted. But had he fired them as a warning, for me, or was he in some sort of peril, forced to defend himself? The fog had lifted slightly and I hurled myself across[18] the street and up to[19] the entrance of Creer's Place. I turned the handle. The door was unlocked. Drawing[20] my own weapon from my pocket, I rushed in.

The dry, burning smell of opium greeted my nostrils[21] and at once brought irritation to my eyes and a sharp, stabbing pain[22] to my head, to the extent that I was unwilling to breathe[23] for fear of falling under the spell[24] of the drug myself. I was standing in a dank[25], gloomy room that had been decorated in the Chinese style with patterned rugs[26], red paper lampshades[27] and silk hangings on the walls, just as Henderson had described. Of the man himself there was no sign. Four men lay stretched out[28] on mattresses with their japan trays[29] and opium lamps on low tables nearby. Three of them were unconscious

1. l'aiguille des minutes
2. se traînait délibérément
3. qu'un méchant survienne
4. sur la lande
5. des faubourgs
6. attente
7. bruit
8. fausses notes
9. avaient pu s'y trouver
10. le calme
11. brisé
12. coups de feu
13. le son strident d'un sifflet de police
14. cris d'effroi
15. passant la porte en trombe
16. furieux contre
17. m'embarquer dans ce plan périlleux
18. je me ruai de l'autre côté de
19. jusqu'à
20. Tirant
21. assaillit mes narines
22. une douleur brutale
23. au point que je craignais de respirer
24. tomber sous l'emprise
25. froide et humide
26. des tapis à motifs
27. des abat-jour
28. étaient étendus
29. plateaux laqués

and could indeed have been corpses[1]. The last was resting his chin on one hand, gazing at me with unfocused eyes[2]. One mattress was empty.

A man came rushing towards me and I knew that this must be Creer himself. He was completely bald, his skin paper-white and stretched so tightly over his bones that, with his black, deep-set eyes[3], he seemed to have a dead man's skull instead of a living head. I could see that he was about to speak, to challenge me[4], but then he saw my revolver and fell back[5].

'Where is he?' I demanded.

'Who?'

'You know who I mean[6]!'

My eyes travelled past him[7] to an open doorway at the far end of the room and a corridor, lit by a gas lamp, beyond. Ignoring Creer, anxious to be out of this dreadful place before the fumes overcame me[8], I pushed my way forward. One of the wretches[9] lying on the mattresses called out to me and reached out with a begging hand[10], but I ignored him. There was another door at the far end[11] of the corridor and, as Holmes could not have possibly left by the front, he must surely have come this way. I forced it open and felt the rush[12] of cold air. I was at the back of the house. I heard more shouting, the clatter of a horse and carriage[13], the blast[14] of a police whistle. I knew already that we had been tricked[15], that everything had gone wrong[16]. But still I had no idea what to expect. Where was Holmes? Had he been hurt?

I ran down a narrow street, through an archway[17], around a corner[18] and into a courtyard[19]. A small crowd had gathered here. Where could they all have come from at this time of the night? I saw a man in evening dress[20], a police constable, two others. They were all staring at a tableau[21] that presented itself in front of them, none of them daring to move

1. des cadavres
2. les yeux dans le vague
3. ses yeux noirs enfoncés
4. m'interpeller
5. se ravisa
6. qui je veux dire
7. Je balayai du regard derrière lui
8. que les émanations n'aient raison de moi
9. épaves
10. tendit une main suppliante
11. tout au bout
12. le souffle
13. bringuebalement d'une calèche
14. le son strident
15. dupés
16. tout avait mal tourné
17. franchis un passage voûté
18. tournai à l'angle
19. pour arriver dans une cour
20. en tenue de soirée
21. Tous fixaient la scène

1. n'osant s'avancer
2. prendre les choses en main
3. Je me frayai un chemin parmi eux.
4. il y avait de quoi
5. reçu deux coups de feu
6. poitrine
7. les pavés
8. mare
9. semblait
10. gisait, inconscient

forward[1] and take charge[2]. I pushed my way through them.[3] And never will I forget what I then saw.

There were two figures. One was a young girl whom I recognised at once – and with good cause[4], for she had tried to kill me only a few days before. It was Sally Dixon, the older sister of Ross, who had been working at The Bag of Nails. She had been shot twice[5], in the chest[6] and in the head. She was lying on the cobblestones[7] in a pool[8] of liquid which showed[9] black in the darkness but which I knew to be blood. I also knew the man who lay unconscious[10] in front of her, one hand stretched out, still holding the gun that had shot her.

It was Sherlock Holmes.

ELEVEN

Under Arrest

I have never forgotten that night and its consequences.

Sitting here on my own[1], twenty-five years later, I still have every detail of it printed on my mind and although I sometimes have to strain through the distorting lens of time[2] to recall the features[3] of friends and foemen alike[4], I have only to blink[5] and there they all are: Harriman, Creer, Ackland and even the constable ... what was his name? Perkins! The fact is that I had many adventures with Sherlock Holmes and frequently saw him in dire straits[6]. There were times when I thought him dead[7]. Only a week before, indeed, I had observed him helpless[8] and delirious, supposedly[9] the victim of a coolie disease[10] from Sumatra. Then there was that time at Poldhu Bay in Cornwall where, had I not dragged him from[11] the room, he would certainly have succumbed to madness and self-destruction. I recall my vigil with him in Surrey when a deadly swamp adder[12] came slithering out of the darkness[13]. And how could I complete this brief list without reminding myself of the utter[14] despair, the sense of emptiness that I felt when I returned, alone, from the Reichenbach Falls[15]? And yet, all of these pale in comparison with[16] that night in Bluegate Fields. Poor Holmes. I see him now, recovering consciousness[17] to find himself surrounded[18], under arrest and quite unable to explain to himself or to anyone else what had just

1. tout seul
2. fouiller mes souvenirs déformés par le temps
3. traits
4. des amis comme des ennemis
5. cligner des yeux
6. dans une mauvaise passe
7. où je l'ai cru mort
8. cloué au lit
9. soi-disant
10. [maladie affectant les coolies]
11. traîné hors de
12. vipère des marais [cf. Le Ruban moucheté, aventure de Holmes]
13. surgit de l'obscurité en ondulant
14. total
15. [chutes d'eau où l'on croit qu'ont péri Holmes et Moriarty]
16. ne sont rien comparées à
17. reprenant connaissance
18. encerclé

taken place. It was he who had chosen, willingly[1], to walk into a trap[2]. This was the unhappy result.

A constable had arrived. I did not know from where. He was young and nervous but all in all[3] he went about his business with commendable[4] efficiency. First, he checked[5] that the girl was dead, then turned his attention to[6] my friend. Holmes looked dreadful. His skin was as white as paper and although his eyes were open he seemed unable to see clearly ... he certainly didn't recognise me. Matters were not helped by the crowd[7], and once again I asked myself who they were and how they could possibly have chosen such a night to congregate[8] here. There were two women, similar to the dreadful old crone[9] who had passed us by the canal, and with them two sailors, leaning against each other and reeking of ale[10]. A negro stared with wide eyes[11]. A couple of my Maltese drinking companions from The Rose and Crown stood next to him. And even a few children had appeared, ragged[12] and barefoot, watching the spectacle as if it were being played out for their benefit[13]. As I took this all in[14], a tall man, red-haired[15] and elegantly dressed, called out and gesticulated with his stick.

'Take him up[16], officer! I saw him shoot the girl. I saw it with my own eyes.' He had a thick[17] Scottish accent that sounded almost incongruous, as if this were all a play[18] and he[19] a member of the audience[20] who had, unbidden[21], wandered onto the stage[22]. 'God help her, the poor creature[23]. He killed her in cold blood[24].'

'Who are you?' the constable demanded.

'My name is Thomas Ackland. I was on my way home. I saw exactly what happened.'

I could not stand on the sidelines[25] any longer but pushed my way forward[26] and knelt beside my stricken[27] friend. 'Holmes!' I cried. 'Holmes, can you hear me? For God's sake tell me what has happened.'

1. volontairement
2. de se jeter dans le piège
3. tout compte fait
4. louable
5. s'assura
6. s'intéressa à
7. La foule n'arrangeait rien
8. pour se rassembler
9. vieille bique
10. empestant la bière
11. les yeux écarquillés
12. en guenilles
13. se déroulait à leur intention
14. Alors que j'observais tout cela
15. roux
16. Emparez-vous de lui
17. fort
18. n'était qu'une pièce de théâtre
19. lui,
20. spectateur
21. s'était, sans y être invité
22. retrouvé sur scène
23. petite
24. de sang-froid
25. demeurer à l'écart
26. m'avançai
27. prostré

But Holmes was still incapable of reply and now I found[1] the constable examining me[2]. 'You know this man?' he demanded.

'Indeed I do. He is Sherlock Holmes.'

'And you?'

'My name is John Watson and I am a doctor. Officer, you must allow me to attend upon[3] my friend. However black and white the facts may appear[4], I can assure you that he is innocent of any crime.'

'That is not true. I saw him shoot the girl. I saw the bullet fired by his own hand[5].' Ackland took a step forward[6]. 'I, too, am a doctor,' he continued. 'And I can tell you at once that this man is under the influence of opium. It is evident from his eyes[7] and from his breath[8] and you need seek no further motive[9] for this vile and senseless[10] crime.'

Was he right? Holmes lay there, unable to speak. He was certainly in the grip of some sort of narcotic[11] and, given that he had been in Creer's Place for the past hour, it was absurd to suggest that anything was responsible other than the drug that the doctor had named. And yet there was something about the diagnosis that puzzled me. I looked closely at Holmes's eyes and although I would have had to agree that the pupils were dilated[12], they lacked[13] the ugly pinpricks of light[14] which I would have expected to find. I felt his pulse[15] and found it almost too sluggish[16], suggesting that he had just been aroused[17] from a deep sleep rather than involved in the strenuous[18] activity of first chasing and then shooting down his victim. And since when had opium ever caused an event such as this? Its effects might include euphoria, total relaxation, freedom from physical pain. But never had I heard of a user being driven to[19] acts of violence, and even had Holmes been in the grip of the most profound paranoia, what possible motive[20] could his muddled[21] consciousness have come up with[22] for kil-

1. à présent, je vis que
2. me dévisageait
3. m'occuper de
4. Même si tout a l'air évident
5. Je l'ai vu tirer de sa propre main
6. avança d'un pas
7. Cela se voit à ses yeux
8. à sa respiration
9. il est inutile de chercher un autre mobile
10. ignoble et insensé
11. sous l'emprise d'un narcotique
12. les pupilles étaient dilatées
13. étaient dépourvues de
14. ces vilains points clairs
15. Je tâtai son pouls
16. lent
17. venait de sortir
18. éprouvante
19. à ma connaissance, cela n'avait conduit un usager à
20. quelle raison
21. embrumée
22. aurait-elle pu inventer

ling the one girl he had been most eager[1] to find and protect? How, for that matter, had she come to be here? Finally, I doubted that Holmes would have been able to shoot with any accuracy[2] had he been under the influence of opium. He would have had difficulty even holding the gun steady[3]. I set this all out here[4] as though I was able to deliberate at length on the evidence in front of me, and yet, in actual fact[5], it was the work of but a second[6] born out of[7] my many years in the medical profession and my intimate knowledge of the man accused.

'Did you accompany this person here tonight?' the constable asked me.

'Yes. But we were briefly apart[8]. I was at The Rose and Crown.'

'And he?'

'He ...' I stopped myself. The one thing I could not do was reveal where Holmes had been. 'My friend is a celebrated[9] detective and he was in pursuit of a case. You will discover that he is well known to Scotland Yard[10]. Call for[11] Inspector Lestrade who will vouch for him[12]. As bad as this looks[13], there must be another explanation.'

'There is no other explanation,' Dr Ackland interjected. 'He came staggering[14] from round that corner. The girl was in the street, begging[15]. He took out a gun and he shot her.'

'There is blood on his clothing[16],' the constable agreed, although he seemed to speak with a degree of reluctance[17]. 'He was evidently close to her[18] when she was killed. And when I arrived in this courtyard, there was nobody else in sight[19].'

'Did you see the shot fired?' I asked.

'No. But I arrived moments later[20]. And nobody ran from the scene.'

'He did it!' somebody shouted in the crowd and this was followed by a murmur of assent[21],

1. qu'il voulait à tout prix
2. avec une quelconque précision
3. ne serait-ce qu'à tenir son arme sans trembler
4. Je décris cela en détail
5. quand, en réalité
6. ce ne fut l'affaire que d'une seconde,
7. grâce à
8. avons été séparés brièvement
9. de renom
10. Scotland Yard le connaît bien
11. Demandez
12. se portera garant de lui
13. Même si les apparences jouent contre lui
14. en titubant
15. en train de mendier
16. ses vêtements
17. une certaine réticence
18. près d'elle
19. personne d'autre en vue
20. quelques instants plus tard
21. d'approbation

taken up[1] by the children who were all delighted to find themselves in the front row[2] for this spectacle.

'Holmes!' I cried, kneeling beside him and attempting to support his head[3] in my hands. 'Can you tell me what happened here?'

Holmes made no response and a moment later, I became aware[4] of another man who had approached silently and was now standing over me[5], next to the Scottish doctor. 'Please will you get to your feet[6],' he demanded, in a voice as cold as the night itself.

'This man is my friend—' I began.

'And this is the scene of a crime in which you have no business to interfere. Stand up and move back[7]. Thank you. Now, if anyone here saw anything, give your name and place of address[8] to the officer. Otherwise, return to your homes. You children[9], get out of here before I put the whole lot of you under arrest[10]. Officer? What's your name? Perkins! Are you in charge here?'

'Yes, sir.'

'This is your beat[11]?'

'It is, sir.'

'Well, you seem to have done reasonably good work[12] so far. Can you tell me what you saw and what you know? Try to keep it concise[13]. It's a damned cold night and the sooner we have it wrapped up[14], the sooner we can be in bed.' He stood in silence as the constable gave his version of events which added up to little more than I already knew[15]. He nodded. 'Very well, Constable Perkins. Look after[16] these people. Write down the details in your notebook. I'll take charge of this now.'

I have not yet described this new arrival and find it difficult to do so even now for he was quite simply[17] one of the most reptilian men I have ever encountered, with eyes too small for his face, thin lips and skin so smooth[18] as to be almost featureless[19]. His most prominent feature[20] was a thick

1. repris par
2. au premier rang
3. lui soutenir la tête
4. je découvris la présence
5. me toisait
6. Relevez-vous, je vous prie
7. reculez
8. lieu de résidence
9. Vous, les enfants
10. avant que je ne vous arrête tous
11. votre secteur
12. du bon travail
13. rester concis
14. plus vite nous en aurons fini ici
15. ce qui n'apporta pas grand-chose que je ne sache déjà
16. Occupez-vous de
17. tout simplement
18. une peau si lisse
19. que les traits étaient à peine visibles
20. Le plus frappant chez lui

mane of hair[1] of a most unnatural white, which is to say that it really was completely colourless[2] and might never have had any colour at all. It was not as if he was old – he could not have been more than thirty or thirty-five. The hair was in complete contrast to his wardrobe[3], which consisted of black overcoat, black gloves and black scarf. Although he was not a large man, he had a certain presence, even an arrogance, which I had already witnessed[4] in the way he had taken command of[5] the situation. He spoke softly, but his voice had an edge[6] that left you in no doubt that he was used to being obeyed[7]. But it was his mercurial quality[8] that most unnerved me[9], his refusal to connect emotionally with anyone at all. That was what put me in mind[10] of the snake. From the moment I had first spoken to him, I had felt him slithering[11] around me. He was the sort of person who looked through you or behind you but who would never look *at* you[12]. I had never met anyone quite so in command of themselves[13], living in a world in which the rest of us could be only trespassers, forbidden to come near[14].

'So your name is Dr Watson?' he said.

'Yes.'

'And this is Sherlock Holmes! Well, I rather doubt we'll be reading of this in one of your famous chronicles, will we, unless it comes under the heading[15] of *The Adventure of the Psychotic Opium Addict.* Your colleague was at Creer's Place tonight?'

'He was pursuing an investigation.'

'Pursuing it with a pipe and a needle[16] it would seem. A rather unorthodox method of detection[17], I would have said. Well, you can leave, Dr Watson. There is nothing more you can do tonight. A pretty business[18] we have here! This girl can't be more than sixteen or seventeen years old.'

'Her name is Sally Dixon. She was working at a public house called The Bag of Nails in Lambeth.'

1. une épaisse chevelure
2. incolore
3. tranchait sur ses vêtements
4. que j'avais déjà remarquée
5. pris en main
6. un ton cassant
7. avait l'habitude d'être obéi
8. son côté fuyant
9. me mit si mal à l'aise
10. ce qui m'avait fait penser
11. ramper
12. ne vous regardait jamais en face
13. aussi maître de lui
14. des intrus, soigneusement tenus à l'écart
15. à moins que cela ne paraisse sous le titre
16. une aiguille
17. d'investigation
18. C'est une sacrée affaire

'She was known to her assailant?'

'Mr Holmes was not her assailant!'

'So you would have us think.[1] Unfortunately, there are witnesses who have a different point of view.' He glanced at the Scottish man. 'You are a doctor?'

'Yes, sir.'

'And you saw what happened here tonight?'

'I already told the constable, sir. The girl was begging in the street. This man came from that building over there. I thought he was drunk or out of his mind[2]. He followed the girl into this square and he killed her with a revolver. It's as plain as that.[3]'

'In your opinion, is Mr Holmes well enough[4] to travel with me to Holborn police station[5]?'

'He cannot walk. But there is no reason why he should not travel in a cab.'

'There is one on the way.' The white-haired man, who had still not given me his name, walked slowly over to Holmes who still lay on the ground, a little recovered, fighting to regain his composure[6]. 'Can you hear me, Mr Holmes?'

'Yes.' It was the first word he had spoken.

'My name is Inspector Harriman. I am arresting you for the murder of this young woman, Sally Dixon. You are not obliged to say anything unless you desire to do so, but whatever you do say I shall take down in writing[7] and it may be used as evidence against you[8] hereafter[9]. Do you understand?'

'This is monstrous!' I cried. 'I am telling you that Sherlock Holmes had nothing whatsoever to do[10] with this crime. Your witness is lying. This is some conspiracy[11]—'

'If you do not wish to find yourself arrested for obstruction and also quite possibly sued for slander[12], then I suggest you try to find the wisdom to remain silent[13]. You will have your chance[14] to speak when this comes to court[15]. In the meantime, I will ask

1. C'est ce que vous voulez nous faire croire.
2. ivre ou fou
3. C'est aussi simple que cela.
4. en état
5. poste de police
6. luttant pour reprendre ses esprits
7. je devrai consigner par écrit tout ce que vous direz
8. retenu contre vous
9. ensuite
10. n'a rien à voir du tout
11. Il s'agit d'un complot
12. poursuivi pour calomnie
13. la sagesse de garder le silence
14. l'occasion
15. à l'audience

1. de vous écarter
2. continuer à faire mon travail
3. à quel point
4. lui est redevable
5. cela change quoi que ce soit
6. L'arme du crime
7. bien suffisant pour commencer
8. je ne peux me chamailler
9. en cellule
10. petiote
11. releva Holmes
12. l'emmena [de force]
13. enveloppé dans un linge
14. alors qu'on le faisait monter
15. je fus soulagé
16. devait commencer à s'estomper
17. brancard
18. s'éloigna [à pied]
19. Et soudain
20. l'agrippa
21. il me vint cette idée folle
22. me saisir de lui
23. tout en maintenant
24. à distance

you again to step aside[1] and leave me to get on with my business[2].'

'Do you have no idea who this is and to what extent[3] the police force in this city and, indeed, in this country, are indebted to him[4]?'

'I know very well who he is and I cannot say that it makes any difference[5] to the situation as I find it. We have a dead girl. The murder weapon[6] is in his hand. We have a witness. I think that's enough to be getting on with[7]. It is almost twelve and I cannot be squabbling[8] with you all night. If you have any reason to complain about my behaviour, you can do so in the morning. I hear a cab approaching. Let us get this man into a cell[9] and this poor little mite[10] to the morgue.'

There was nothing more I could do except stand and watch as Constable Perkins returned and, with the help of the doctor, lifted Holmes to his feet[11] and dragged him away[12]. The gun that he had been carrying was wrapped in cloth[13] and taken with him. At the last minute, as he was being helped[14] into the cab, his head turned and our eyes met and I was relieved[15] at least to see that some of the life had returned to them and that whatever drug he had taken – or been given – must be wearing off[16]. More policemen had arrived and I saw Sally covered with a blanket and carried away on a stretcher[17]. Dr Ackland shook hands with Harriman, handed him a business card, and walked off[18]. Before I knew it[19], I was on my own – and in a hostile, insalubrious part of London. I suddenly remembered that I still had the revolver that Holmes had given me, in my coat pocket. My hand closed on it[20] and the mad thought came to me[21] that perhaps I should have used it to rescue Holmes, seizing hold of him[22] and carrying him with me whilst keeping[23] Harriman and the crowd at bay[24]. But such an attempt would have helped neither of us. There were other ways to fight back[1] and, with that in mind and cold steel[2] in my hand, I turned away and hurriedly made for home[3].

I had a visitor, early the next morning. It was the one man I most wanted to see[4] – Inspector Lestrade. As he came striding in[5], interrupting me at my breakfast, my first thought was that he brought news that Holmes had already been released and would be arriving shortly, too. One look at his face, however, was enough to dash my hopes[6]. He was grim[7] and unsmiling and, from the look of him[8], had either risen very early or perhaps had not slept at all. Without asking permission, he sat down so heavily at the table that I might have wondered if he would ever find the strength to rise again.

'Will you have some breakfast, Inspector?' I ventured.

'That would be most kind of you, Dr Watson. I am certainly in need of something to restore me. This business![9] Frankly, it beggars belief[10]. Sherlock Holmes, for goodness sake! Have these people forgotten how much of a good turn we owe him[11] at Scotland Yard? That they should think him guilty! And yet, it doesn't look good[12], Dr Watson. It doesn't look good.'

I poured him a cup of tea, filling the cup which Mrs Hudson had set out[13] for Holmes – she was, of course, unaware[14] of what had taken place the night before. Lestrade sipped noisily[15]. 'Where is Holmes?' I asked.

'They held him overnight[16] at Bow Street.'

'Have you seen him?'

'They wouldn't let me! As soon as I heard what had happened last night, I went straight round[17]. But this man, Harriman, he's a queer one and no mistake[18]. Most of us at Scotland Yard, those of us of the same rank[19], we muddle along together[20] as best

1. d'autres façons de riposter
2. la froideur de l'acier
3. me hâtai de rentrer
4. l'homme que je désirais voir entre tous
5. Lorsqu'il entra à grands pas
6. suffit à anéantir mes espoirs
7. avait l'air sombre
8. vu son air
9. Quelle affaire !
10. c'est incroyable
11. combien de fois il nous a rendu service
12. cela se présente mal
13. sortie
14. dans l'ignorance
15. but bruyamment
16. Il a été écroué pour la nuit
17. j'ai accouru
18. c'est un drôle de type, croyez-moi
19. du même grade
20. on essaie de s'entendre

we can. But not him. Harriman has always kept his own counsel. He has no friends and no family that I know of. He does a good job, I'll give him that[1], but although we've passed[2] in the corridor, I've never spoken more than a few words to him and he's never answered back. As it happens[3], I saw him briefly this morning and asked to visit Mr Holmes, thinking it was the very least I could do[4], but he just walked right past me[5]. A little common courtesy[6] wouldn't have hurt, but that's the man we're up against[7]. He's with Holmes now, interviewing him. I'd give my eye teeth[8] to be in the room with them, for that would be a battle of wits if ever there was one[9]. As far as I can tell, Harriman's already made up his mind, but of course it's all nonsense[10] and so I've come here, hoping you can shed some light on[11] this matter. You were there last night?'

'I was in Bluegate Fields.'

'And is it true that Mr Holmes visited an opium den?'

'He went there, but not to indulge in that hateful practice[12].'

'No?' Lestrade's eyes travelled to the mantelpiece and to the morocco case that contained a hypodermic syringe. I wondered how he had learned of[13] Holmes's occasional habit.

'You know Holmes too well to think otherwise[14],' I chided him[15]. 'He is still investigating the deaths of the man in the flat cap and the child, Ross. That was what took him to East London.'

Lestrade took out his notebook[16] and opened it. 'I think you had better tell me what progress you and Mr Holmes had made, Dr Watson. If I am going to fight on his behalf[17], and it may well be that we have a battle royal on our hands[18], then the more I know the better[19]. I ask you to leave nothing out[20].'

It was strange, really, for Holmes had always thought himself in competition with the police and

1. je le reconnais
2. il nous arrive de nous croiser
3. Justement
4. que c'était la moindre des choses
5. ne m'a pas accordé un regard
6. minimum de politesse
7. voilà à quel genre d'homme nous avons affaire
8. Je donnerais n'importe quoi
9. ça devrait faire de ces étincelles !
10. c'est absurde
11. clarifier un peu
12. se livrer à cette pratique détestable
13. était au courant de
14. pour imaginer le contraire,
15. le tançai-je
16. carnet
17. me battre pour lui
18. que la bataille soit rude
19. il vaut mieux que j'en sache le plus possible
20. ne rien omettre

would, in normal circumstances, have told them none of the details of his investigation. On this occasion, though, I had no choice but to acquaint Lestrade with[1] everything that had happened both before and after the child had been killed, starting with[2] our visit to Chorley Grange School for Boys, which had led us to Sally Dixon and The Bag of Nails. I told him of her attack on me[3], our discovery of the stolen pocket watch, our unhelpful[4] interview with Lord Ravenshaw, and Holmes's decision to place an advertisement in the evening papers. Finally, I described the visit of the man who called himself Henderson and how he had led us to Creer's Place.

'He was a tidewaiter?'

'That was what he said, Lestrade, but I fear he was dissimulating[5], as in the rest of his story.'

'He may be innocent. You cannot say what happened at Creer's Place.'

'It's true that I was not there, but nor was Henderson[6], and his very absence gives me cause for concern[7]. Looking at everything that has occurred, I believe this was a deliberate trap to incriminate[8] Holmes and to bring an end[9] to his investigation.'

'But what is this House of Silk? Why would anyone go to such lengths[10] to keep it secret?'

'I cannot say.'

Lestrade shook his head. 'I am a practical[11] man, Dr Watson, and I have to tell you that all this seems a very long way from the[12] point where we started – a dead man in a hotel room. That man, as far as we know, was Keelan O'Donaghue, a vicious hoodlum[13] and bank robber from Boston, who came to England on a mission of revenge against the[14] picture dealer[15], Mr Carstairs of Wimbledon. So how do you get from there to the deaths of two children, this business[16] of the white ribbon, this mysterious Henderson and all the rest of it[17]?'

1. de mettre Lestrade au courant de
2. à commencer par
3. Je lui racontai qu'elle m'avait agressé
4. infructueuse
5. qu'il ne nous ait menti
6. Henderson non plus
7. c'est cette absence que je trouve inquiétante
8. un piège tendu pour compromettre
9. mettre un terme
10. quelqu'un prendrait-il autant de peine
11. pragmatique
12. très éloigné du
13. truand
14. décidé à se venger du
15. marchand de tableaux
16. histoire
17. et tout ce qui s'ensuit

'That was exactly what Holmes was trying to discover. Can I see him?'

'Harriman is in charge of the case and until Mr Holmes has been formally charged[1], nobody will be allowed to speak with him. They are taking him to a police court this afternoon.'

'We must be there.'

'Of course. You understand that no defence witnesses will be called at this stage[2], Dr Watson, but even so[3] I will try to speak for him[4] and attest to his good character[5].'

'Will they keep him at Bow Street?'

'For the time being[6], but if the judge thinks there's a case to answer[7] – and I can't see him thinking otherwise[8] – he will be put in prison.'

'What prison?'

'I can't say, Dr Watson, but I will do everything in my power on his behalf. In the meantime, is there anyone to whom you can apply[9]? I would imagine that two gentlemen like yourselves must have friends of influence, especially after being involved in so many cases of what you might call a delicate nature. Perhaps among Mr Holmes's clients there is someone to whom you can turn?'

My first thought was of Mycroft. I had not mentioned him, of course, but he had been in my mind before Lestrade had begun to speak. Would he agree to see me? He had issued a warning[10] in this very room, and he had been adamant[11] that he would be powerless if it was ignored[12]. Even so, I made the decision to present myself once more at the Diogenes Club as soon as the opportunity arose[13]. But that would have to wait until after the police court. Lestrade rose to his feet. 'I will call for you[14] at two o'clock,' he said.

'Thank you, Lestrade.'

'Don't thank me yet, Dr Watson. There may be nothing that I can do. If ever a case looked

1. officiellement accusé
2. qu'aucun témoin de la défense ne sera appelé à ce stade
3. néanmoins
4. en sa faveur
5. me porter garant de sa moralité
6. Pour le moment
7. qu'il y a lieu d'engager des poursuites
8. j'ai du mal à croire qu'il pense le contraire
9. que vous pourriez solliciter
10. lancé un avertissement
11. affirmé résolument
12. si l'on passait outre
13. à la première occasion
14. passerai vous prendre

cut and dried[1], this is it.' I remembered that Inspector Harriman had said much the same to me[2] the night before. 'Harriman wants to try Mr Holmes[3] for murder and I think you should prepare yourself for the worst[4].'

1. S'il y a bien une affaire qui semble jouée d'avance

2. m'avait dit à peu près la même chose

3. que M. Holmes soit jugé

4. vous attendre au pire

TWELVE

The Evidence in the Case

Never before had I attended a police court and yet[1], as I approached that solid and austere building on Bow Street in the company of Lestrade, I felt a strange sense of familiarity, as if it was right that I had been summoned[2] and that my coming here was somehow[3] inevitable. Lestrade must have seen the look on my face for he smiled mournfully[4]. 'I don't suppose you expected to find yourself in a place like this, eh, Dr Watson?' I told him that he had taken the very thought from my head[5]. 'Well, you have to wonder how many other men have passed this way[6] thanks to you – by which, of course, I mean[7] you and Mr Holmes.'

He was quite right.[8] This was the end of the process which we had so frequently begun, the first step on the way to the Old Bailey[9] and then perhaps the gallows[10]. It is curious to reflect now, at the very end of my writing career, that each and every one of my chronicles[11] ended with the unmasking or the arrest of a miscreant[12], and that after that point, almost without exception, I simply assumed that their fate[13] would be of no further interest to my readers and gave up on them[14], as if it was their wrongdoing alone that[15] justified their existence and that once the crimes had been solved they were no longer human beings with beating hearts and broken spirits[16]. Never once did I consider the fear and anguish they

1. pourtant
2. je sois convoqué
3. en quelque sorte
4. tristement
5. lu dans mes pensées
6. sont passés par là
7. bien sûr, je veux dire par là
8. Il avait tout à fait raison.
9. la cour d'assises [de Londres]
10. à la potence
11. toutes mes chroniques sans exception
12. avec un scélérat démasqué ou arrêté
13. leur sort
14. je les délaissais
15. seuls leurs méfaits
16. du désespoir

must have endured as they passed through these swing doors[1] and walked[2] these gloomy corridors. Did any of them ever weep tears of repentance[3] or offer prayers for their salvation[4]? Did some of them fight on to the end? I did not care. It was not part of my narrative.

But as I look back on[5] that iron-cold[6] December day when Holmes himself faced the forces that he had so often unleashed[7], I think that perhaps I did them an injustice[8]; even villains as cruel as Culverton Smith or as conniving[9] as Jonas Oldacre. I wrote what are now called detective stories[10]. By chance[11], my detective was the greatest of them all. But in a sense he was defined by the men and, indeed, the women he came up against[12], and I cast them aside all too easily[13]. Entering the police court they all returned very forcibly[14] to mind and it was almost as if I could hear them calling to me: 'Welcome. You are one of us now.'

The courtroom was square and windowless, with wooden benches and barriers[15] and the royal arms emblazoned on[16] the far wall. This is where the magistrate sat, a stiff[17], elderly man whose demeanour had something wooden about it too[18]. There was a railed-off platform[19] in front of him and it was here that the prisoners were brought one after the other, for the process was rapid and repetitive so that, to the onlooker[20] at least, it became almost monotonous. Lestrade and I had arrived early, taking our places in the public gallery with a few other onlookers, and we watched as a forger[21], a burglar[22] and a magsman[23] were all remanded in custody to await trial[24]. And yet the magistrate could also be compassionate. An apprentice[25] accused of drunken and violent behaviour – it had been his eighteenth birthday – was sent away with the details of his crime placed in the Refused Charge Book[26]. And two children, no more than eight or nine years old,

1. portes battantes
2. parcouraient
3. versaient-ils jamais des larmes de repentir
4. leur salut
5. lorsque je repense à
6. d'un froid glacial
7. si souvent déchaînées
8. ai-je été injuste envers eux
9. sournois
10. des romans policiers
11. Le hasard a fait que
12. qu'il affrontait
13. je m'en détournais trop vite
14. brutalement
15. des bancs et des balustrades en bois
16. armoiries royales ornant
17. raide
18. à l'air aussi raide que les bancs
19. box surélevé
20. spectateur
21. faussaire
22. cambrioleur
23. escroc
24. envoyés en détention provisoire dans l'attente de leur procès
25. apprenti
26. registre d'abandon de poursuites

brought in for begging, were handed over to the Police Courts Mission with the recommendation that they should be looked after either by the Waifs[1] and Strays[2] Society[3], by Dr Barnardo's orphanage or by the Society for the Improvement of London's Children. It was odd to hear the last of these three named for this was the organisation responsible for Chorley Grange, which Holmes and I had visited.

Everything had proceeded at a pace[4], but now Lestrade nudged me[5] and I became aware of a new sense of gravity in the courtroom. More uniformed policemen and clerks[6] entered and took their places. The usher[7] of the court, a plump, owl-like man[8] in his black robes[9], approached the magistrate and began to mutter to him in a low voice. Two men whom I recognised came in and sat down a few feet apart[10] on one of the benches. One was Dr Ackland, the other a red-faced[11] man who might have been in the crowd outside Creer's Place but who had made no impression upon me at the time. Behind them, sat Creer himself (Lestrade pointed him out[12]), wiping his hands as if attempting to dry them. They were all here, I saw at once, as witnesses.

And then Holmes was brought in, wearing the same clothes in which he had been arrested, and so unlike himself[13] that had I not known better[14] I might have thought that he had deliberately disguised himself so as to baffle me[15] as he had so often done before. He had clearly not slept. He had been questioned at length[16] and I tried not to imagine the various indignities, all too familiar to common criminals, which must have been heaped upon him[17]. Gaunt at the best of times[18], he appeared positively emaciated[19], but as he was led into the dock[20] he turned and looked at me and I saw a glint in his eye[21] that told me the fight was not over yet[22] and reminded me that Holmes had always been at his most formidable when the odds seemed to be stacked[23]

1. enfants abandonnés
2. errants
3. Association
4. s'était déroulé rapidement
5. me donna un coup de coude
6. des greffiers
7. L'huissier
8. un homme rondelet, à l'allure de chouette
9. toge
10. à quelques pas l'un de l'autre
11. rougeaud
12. me le désigna
13. si altéré
14. si je n'avais pas su qu'il n'en était rien,
15. à un point méconnaissable
16. subi un interrogatoire prolongé
17. dont on avait dû l'accabler
18. Émacié en temps normal
19. véritablement décharné
20. au banc des accusés
21. étincelle dans son regard
22. qu'il n'avait pas abandonné la partie
23. tout semblait jouer

against him. Beside me, Lestrade straightened up[1] and muttered something under his breath[2]. He was angry and indignant on Holmes's behalf, revealing a side of his character I had never seen before.

A barrister[3] presented himself, a well-rounded, diminutive sort[4] with thick lips and heavy eyelids, and it soon became clear that he had assumed the role of prosecutor[5], although ringmaster[6] might be the better description from the manner in which he directed the proceedings[7], treating the court almost as a circus of the law[8].

'The accused is a well-known detective,' he began. 'Mr Sherlock Holmes has achieved public renown through[9] a series of stories which, though gaudy[10] and sensational, are based at least partly on truth.' I bristled at this[11] and might even have protested had Lestrade not reached out and tapped me gently on the arm. 'That said[12], I will not deny that there are one or two less capable[13] officers at Scotland Yard who owe him a debt of gratitude[14] in that, from time to time, he has helped direct their investigations with hints and insights[15] that have borne fruit[16].' Hearing this, it was Lestrade's turn to scowl[17]. 'But even the best of men have their demons and in the case of Mr Holmes it is opium that has turned him from a friend of the law into the basest malefactor[18]. It is beyond dispute[19] that he entered an opium den which goes by the name of Creer's Place in Limehouse just after eleven o'clock last night. My first witness is the owner of that establishment, Isaiah Creer.'

Creer took the witness stand[20]. There was no swearing-in[21] at these proceedings. I could only see the back of his head, which was white and hairless, folding into his neck[22] in a way that made it hard to see where one ended and the other began. Prompted by[23] the prosecutor, he told the following tale[24].

1. se redressa
2. dans sa barbe
3. avocat
4. du genre petit gros
5. procureur
6. Monsieur Loyal
7. présidait l'audience
8. un cirque judiciaire
9. doit sa notoriété à
10. de mauvais goût
11. Je me hérissai à ces mots
12. Cela dit
13. modérément doués
14. peuvent lui être reconnaissants
15. grâce à des indices et une sagacité
16. qui ont porté leurs fruits
17. faire la grimace
18. le pire malfaiteur
19. Il est indiscutable
20. vint à la barre des témoins
21. On ne prêtait pas serment
22. formant un pli dans son cou
23. À l'invitation du
24. fit le récit suivant

Yes, the accused had entered his house – a private and legal establishment, my lord[1], where gentlemen could indulge their habit in comfort and security – just after eleven o'clock. He had said very little. He had demanded a dose of the intoxicant[2], paid for it, and smoked it immediately. Half an hour later, he had asked for a second[3]. Mr Creer had been concerned that Mr Holmes, for it was only later[4] that he had learned his name and, he assured the court, at the time of their meeting he had been a complete stranger[5], had become agitated and aroused[6]. Mr Creer had suggested that a second dose might be unwise[7] but the gentleman had disagreed in the strongest terms[8] and, in order to avoid[9] a scene and to maintain[10] the tranquillity for which his establishment was noted[11], he had provided the essentials[12] in return for another payment. Mr Holmes had smoked the second pipe and his sense of delirium had increased to the extent[13] that Creer had sent a boy out to find a policeman, fearing there might be a breach of the peace[14]. He had attempted to reason with[15] Mr Holmes, to calm him down, but without success. Wild-eyed, beyond control[16], Mr Holmes had insisted that there were enemies in the room, that he was being pursued, that his life was in danger. He had produced[17] a revolver, at which point Mr Creer had insisted that he leave.

'I was afraid for my life,' he told the court. 'My only thought was to have him out[18] of the house. But I see now that I was wrong and that I should have let him remain there until help arrived in the shape[19] of Constable Perkins. For when I released him onto the street[20] he was out of his mind[21]. He didn't know what he was doing. I have seen this happen before, your honour. It is rare, freakish[22]. But it is a side effect[23] of the drug. I have no doubt that when Mr Holmes gunned down[24] that poor girl, he believed he was confronting some grotesque monster. Had I

1. monsieur le Juge
2. stupéfiant
3. en avait demandé une deuxième
4. car ce n'est que plus tard
5. inconnu
6. très agité
7. ne serait peut-être pas raisonnable
8. l'avait contesté avec force
9. éviter
10. préserver
11. réputé
12. fourni le nécessaire
13. s'était accru au point
14. une atteinte à l'ordre public
15. tenté de faire entendre raison à
16. Le regard fou, incontrôlable
17. sorti
18. Je ne voulais qu'une chose : le faire partir
19. en la personne
20. l'ai mis dehors,
21. il avait perdu la tête
22. insolite
23. effet secondaire
24. a abattu

known he was armed, I would never have supplied him with the substance in the first place, so help me God[1]!'

The story was corroborated in every respect[2] by a second witness, the red-faced man I had already noticed. He was languid and overly refined[3], a man of exceedingly aristocratic type with a pinched nose that sniffed at this common air with distaste[4]. He could not have been more than thirty and was dressed in the very latest fashion[5]. He provided no fresh[6] revelations, repeating almost verbatim[7] what Creer had said. He had, he said, been stretched out on a mattress on the other side of the room, and though in a very relaxed state was prepared to swear[8] that he had been perfectly conscious of what had been taking place. 'Opium, for me, is an occasional indulgence[9],' he concluded. 'It provides a few hours in which I can retreat from the anxieties[10] and the responsibilities of my life. I see no shame[11] in it. I know many people who take laudanum[12] in the privacy[13] of their own homes for precisely the same reason. For me, it is no different to smoking tobacco or taking alcohol. But then I[14],' he added, pointedly[15], 'am able to handle it[16].'

It was only when the magistrate asked him his name for the record[17] that the young man created a stir[18] in the court. 'It is Lord Horace Blackwater.'

The magistrate stared at him. 'Do I take it[19], sir, that you are part of the Blackwater family of Hallamshire?'

'Yes,' replied the young man. 'The Earl[20] of Blackwater is my father.'

I was as surprised as anyone. It seemed remarkable, shocking even, that the scion[21] of one of the oldest families in England should have found his way to[22] a sordid drug den in Bluegate Fields. At the same time, I could imagine the weight that his evidence would add to the case[23] against my friend.

1. bonté divine
2. en tous points
3. indolent et raffiné à l'excès
4. avec un air pincé et dégoûté
5. à la dernière mode
6. nouvelles
7. mot pour mot
8. prêt à jurer
9. un petit plaisir occasionnel
10. éloigner mes angoisses
11. honte
12. [préparation à base d'opium, utilisée autref. contre la douleur]
13. dans l'intimité
14. il se trouve que moi
15. insista-t-il
16. je le supporte bien
17. pour mémoire
18. un frémissement
19. Dois-je comprendre
20. comte
21. le descendant
22. ait pu se retrouver dans
23. combien ce témoignage pèserait

1. qu'un misérable marin ou charlatan
2. ruiner sa réputation
3. inutile de le préciser
4. quittait la barre
5. se parler en chuchotant
6. croustillant
7. pain béni
8. en toge noire
9. son casque au côté
10. un fantôme
11. qu'il s'agissait de sa tête
12. C'est lui qui en dit le moins
13. à sa place
14. abordé
15. prié de se rendre
16. en route
17. coups de feu
18. étendu sans connaissance
19. mare de sang
20. à sa tignasse blanche
21. À sa manière de s'exprimer
22. pesé et prononcé distinctement

This was not just some low-life sailor or mountebank[1] giving his version of events. It was a man who could quite possibly ruin himself[2] by even admitting he had been at Creer's Place.

He was fortunate that, this being a police court, there were no journalists present. The same, I hardly need add[3], would be true for Holmes. As Lord Blackwater stepped down[4], I heard the other members of the public muttering to each other[5] and perceived that they were here only for the spectacle and this sort of salacious[6] detail was bread and butter[7] to them. The magistrate exchanged a few words with his black-robed[8] usher as his place was taken by Stanley Perkins, the constable whom I had encountered on the night in question. Perkins stood stiffly, with his helmet at his side[9], holding it as if he were a ghost[10] at the Tower of London and it was his head[11]. He had the least to say[12], but then much of the story had already been told for him[13]. He had been approached[14] by the boy that Creer had sent out and asked to come[15] to the house on the corner of Milward Street. He had been on his way[16] when he had heard two gunshots[17] and had rushed to Coppergate Square which was where he had discovered a man, lying unconscious[18] with a gun, and a girl lying in a pool of blood[19]. He had taken charge of the scene as a crowd had gathered. He had seen at once that there was nothing he could do for the girl. He described how I had arrived and identified the unconscious man as Sherlock Holmes.

'I couldn't believe it when I heard that,' he said. 'I had read some of the exploits of Mr Sherlock Holmes and to think that he might be involved in this sort of thing ... well, it beggared belief.'

Perkins was followed by Inspector Harriman, instantly recognisable on account of that shock of white hair[20]. From the way he spoke[21], with every word measured and carefully delivered[22] for perfect effect, it could be imagined that he had been rehearsing this speech[1] for hours, which may well indeed have been the case. He did not even attempt to keep the contempt out[2] of his voice. The imprisonment, and indeed the execution of my friend, might have been his only mission in life.

'Let me tell the court my movements last night.' Thus he began. 'I had been called to a break-in[3] at a bank on the White Horse Road, which is but a short distance away[4]. As I was leaving[5], I heard the sound of gunshots and the constable's whistle and turned my way south[6] to see if I could assist. By the time I arrived, Constable Perkins was in command[7] and doing an admirable task. I will be recommending Constable Perkins for a promotion. It was he who informed me of the identity of the man who now stands before you. As you have already heard, Mr Sherlock Holmes has a certain reputation. I am sure many of his admirers are going to be disappointed that the true nature of the man, his addiction to drugs and its murderous consequences, should have fallen so far from[8] the fiction which we have all enjoyed[9].

'That Mr Holmes murdered Sally Dixon is beyond question[10]. In fact, even the imaginative powers[11] of his biographer would be unable to raise a shred of[12] doubt in the minds of his readers. At the scene of the crime I observed that the gun in his hand was still warm[13], that there were residues of powder-blackening[14] on his sleeve and several small bloodstains on his coat which could only have arrived there if he had been standing in close proximity[15] to the girl when she was shot. Mr Holmes was semi-conscious, still emerging from an opium trance[16] and barely aware[17] of the horror of what he had done. I say "barely aware" but by that I do not mean that he was completely ignorant. He knew his guilt[18], your honour. He offered no defence. When

1. bien répété son discours
2. taire le mépris
3. un cambriolage
4. à quelques pas d'ici
5. Au moment de partir
6. j'ai bifurqué au sud
7. avait la situation en main
8. soit si éloignée de
9. avons tous appréciée
10. ne fait aucun doute
11. pouvoir de l'imagination
12. susciter le moindre
13. encore chaud
14. des résidus de poudre
15. tout près
16. d'un état second dû à l'opium
17. à peine conscient
18. Il se savait coupable

1. je l'ai averti de ses droits

2. a sorti une histoire à dormir debout

3. non pas mû

4. par le besoin de satisfaire ses appétits

5. de me communiquer

6. à la recherche d'un indice

7. on s'était emparé de lui

8. À titre personnel

9. se plaigne d'avoir été

10. il est impensable que pour cette fois

11. d'en distribuer gratuitement

12. un tissu de mensonges

13. prétend également

14. Je veux bien

15. témoignage

16. la confondre avec

17. Enfin, j'ajouterai

18. victime d'une machination

19. C'est ce que j'appellerais du délire

20. en réalité

I cautioned him[1] and placed him under arrest, he made no attempt to persuade me that the circumstances were anything other than what I have described.

'It was only this morning, after eight hours sleep and a cold shower, that he came up with a cock-and-bull story[2] proclaiming his innocence. He told me that he had visited Creer's Place, not because he was drawn there[3] to feed his unsavoury appetite[4], but because he was investigating a case, the details of which he refused to share with me[5]. He said that a man, known only to him as Henderson, had sent him to Limehouse in pursuit of some clue[6], but that the information had turned out to be a trap and that as soon as he had entered the den he had been overpowered[7] and forced to consume some narcotic. Speaking personally[8], I find it a little strange when a man visits an opium den and then complains that he has been[9] drugged. And since Mr Creer spends his entire life selling drugs to men who wish to buy them, it is unaccountable that on this occasion[10] he should have decided to give them away free[11]. But we know that this is a barrel of lies[12]. We have already heard from a distinguished witness who saw Mr Holmes smoke one pipe and then demand a second. Mr Holmes also claims[13] that he knows the murdered girl and that she, too, was part of this mysterious investigation. I am willing to[14] accept this part of his testimony[15]. It may well be that he had met her before and in his delirium he somehow managed to confuse her with[16] some imaginary master criminal. He had no other motive for killing her.

'It only remains for me to add[17] that Mr Holmes now insists that he is part of a conspiracy[18] which includes me, Constable Perkins, Isaiah Creer, Lord Horace Blackwater and, quite possibly, your honour yourself. I would describe this as delusional[19], but actually[20] it's worse than that. It's a deliberate attempt to extricate himself from the[1] consequences of the delusions he was suffering last night. How unfortunate for Mr Holmes that we have a second witness who actually saw the killing itself. His testimony will, I am sure, bring an end to these proceedings[2]. For my part, I can only say that in my fifteen years with[3] the Metropolitan Police, I have never encountered a case where the evidence has been more cut and dried[4], the guilty party more obvious[5].'

I almost expected him to take a bow[6]. Instead, he nodded respectfully[7] at the magistrate and sat down.

The final witness was Dr Thomas Ackland. I had barely examined him in the darkness and the confusion of the night, but standing in front of me now, he struck me as an unattractive[8] man with curls[9] of bright red hair (he would have been assured of a place[10] in the red-headed league[11]) tumbling unevenly[12] from an elongated head[13] and dark freckles[14] which made his skin seem almost diseased[15]. He had the beginnings of a moustache, an unusually long neck and watery[16] blue eyes. It is possible, I suppose, that I exaggerate his appearance for, as he spoke, I felt a deep and irrational loathing for[17] a man whose words seemed to place the final seal on[18] my friend's guilt. I have gone back to the official transcripts[19] and can therefore[20] present exactly what he was asked and what he himself said so that it cannot be claimed that my own prejudices[21] distort the record[22].

The Prosecutor: Could you please tell the court your name.

Witness: It is Thomas Ackland.

The Prosecutor: You are from Scotland.

Witness: Yes. But I now live in London.

The Prosecutor: Will you please[23] tell us a little of your career, Dr Ackland.

Witness: I was born in Glasgow and studied medicine at the university there. I received my

1. d'échapper aux
2. mettre un terme à cette phase préliminaire
3. dans
4. les preuves étaient aussi confondantes
5. le coupable aussi évident
6. à ce qu'il fasse la révérence
7. inclina respectueusement la tête
8. peu séduisant
9. des boucles
10. aurait eu sa place assurée
11. Ligue des rouquins [aventure de Holmes]
12. retombant en cascade
13. d'une tête tout en longueur
14. des taches de rousseur
15. faisaient presque maladie de peau
16. vitreux
17. répugnance envers
18. sceller pour de bon
19. transcription
20. par conséquent
21. préjugés
22. déforment l'histoire
23. Veuillez

medical degree[1] in 1867. I became a lecturer[2] at the Royal Infirmary School of Medicine in Edinburgh and later the Professor of Clinical Surgery[3] at Edinburgh's Royal Hospital for Sick[4] Children. I moved to London five years ago, following[5] the death of my wife, and was invited to become a governor[6] at the Westminster Hospital, which is where I am now.

The Prosecutor: The Westminster Hospital was established for the poor and is funded by public subscription[7]. Is that right?

Witness: Yes.

The Prosecutor: And you yourself have given generously[8] to the maintenance[9] and enlargement[10] of the hospital, I believe.

Magistrate: I think we should get to the point[11], if you don't mind, Mr Edwards.

The Prosecutor: Very well, your honour. Dr Ackland, could you please tell the court how you happened to be in the vicinity[12] of Milward Street and Coppergate Square last night?

Witness: I had been to visit one of my patients. He is a good, hard-working[13] man, but of a poor family, and after he left the hospital, I was concerned for his well-being[14]. I came to him late[15] because I had earlier attended a[16] dinner at the Royal College of Physicians[17]. I left his house at eleven o'clock, intending to walk some of the way home[18] – I have lodgings in Holborn. However, I became lost in the fog and it was quite by chance[19] that I entered the square a little before midnight.

The Prosecutor: And what did you see?

Witness: I saw the whole thing.[20] There was a girl, poorly dressed against this inclement weather[21], no more than fourteen or fifteen years old. I shudder to think what she might have been doing out in the street at this hour, for this is an area known for all manner of vice[22]. When I first noticed her, her hands were raised and she was quite clearly[23] terrified. She

1. diplôme de médecin
2. professeur
3. chirurgie
4. malades
5. à la suite de
6. administrateur
7. financé par la souscription publique
8. vous-même avez généreusement contribué
9. l'entretien
10. l'extension
11. en venir aux faits
12. comment il se fait que vous vous soyez trouvé à proximité
13. travailleur
14. m'inquiétais de sa santé
15. suis arrivé tard chez lui
16. sortais d'un
17. Collège royal de médecine
18. rentrer en faisant un bout de chemin à pied
19. par hasard
20. J'ai vu toute la scène.
21. insuffisamment couverte par ce mauvais temps
22. un quartier très malfamé
23. manifestement

uttered one word. "Please ... !" Then there were two shots and she fell to the ground. I knew at once that she was dead. The second shot had penetrated the skull and would have killed her instantly.

The Prosecutor: Did you see who fired the shots?

Witness: Not at first, no. It was very dark and I was completely shocked. I was also in fear of my life[1], for it occurred to me that there must be some madman on the loose[2] to wish to bring harm[3] to this wee, defenceless girl[4]. Then I made out a figure[5] standing a short distance away, holding a gun which was still smoking in his hand. As I watched, he groaned and fell to his knees. Then he sprawled, unconscious, on the ground[6].

The Prosecutor: Do you see that figure today?

Witness: Yes. He is standing in front of me in the dock.

There was another stir in the public gallery for it was as clear to all the other spectators as it was to me that this was the most damning evidence[7] of all. Sitting next to me, Lestrade had become very still[8], his lips tightly drawn[9], and it occurred to me that the faith in[10] Holmes which had done him such credit must surely be shaken to the core[11]. And what of me? I confess that I was in turmoil[12]. It was, on the face of it[13], inconceivable that my friend could have killed the one girl he most wanted[14] to interview, for there was still a chance that Sally Dixon could have been told something by her brother which might have led us to the House of Silk. And then there was also the question of what she was doing in Coppergate Square to begin with. Had she been captured and held prisoner[15] before Henderson even visited us and could he have deliberately led us into a trap with this very end in mind[16]? That seemed to me to be the only logical conclusion. But at the same time I recalled something Holmes had said to me many times, namely[17] that when you have

1. Je craignais aussi pour ma vie
2. que seul un fou en liberté
3. pouvait vouloir du mal
4. gamine sans défense
5. j'ai distingué une silhouette
6. est tombé de tout son long, sans connaissance
7. le témoignage le plus accablant
8. s'était figé
9. très serrées
10. sa foi en
11. passablement ébranlée
12. en plein désarroi
13. à première vue
14. qu'il voulait par-dessus tout
15. enlevée et retenue prisonnière
16. dans ce but précisément
17. à savoir

eliminated the impossible, whatever remains, however improbable, must be the truth[1]. I might be able to dismiss[2] the evidence given by Isaiah Creer, for a man like him would certainly be open to bribery[3] and would say anything that was required of him. But it was impossible, or at least absurd to suggest, that an eminent Glaswegian doctor, a senior police officer[4] from Scotland Yard and the son of the Earl of Blackwater, a member of the English aristocracy, should all come together for no obvious reason to fabricate[5] a story and incriminate a man whom none of them[6] had ever met. That was the choice before me[7]. Either all four of them were lying. Or Holmes, under the influence of opium, had indeed committed a terrible crime.

The magistrate needed no such deliberation[8]. Having heard the evidence, he called for the Charge Book[9] and entered[10] Holmes's name and address, his age and the charge that had been preferred against him[11]. To these were added the names and addresses of the prosecutor and his witnesses and an inventory of all the articles found in the prisoner's possession. (They included a pair of pince-nez, a length of string[12], a signet ring[13] bearing the crest[14] of the Duke of Cassel-Felstein, two cigarette ends[15] wrapped in a page torn from the *London Corn Circular*, a chemical pipette[16], several Greek coins[17] and a small beryl[18]. To this day, I wonder what the authorities must have made of it all.) Holmes, who had not uttered a word throughout the entire[19] procedure, was then informed that he would have to remain in custody[20] until the coroner's court, which would be convened[21] after the weekend. After that, he would proceed to trial[22]. And that was the end of the business. The magistrate was in a hurry to get on. There were several more cases to try[23] and the light was already fading. I watched as Holmes was led away.

1. ce qui reste, si improbable que cela paraisse, doit être la vérité
2. rejeter
3. prêt à se laisser soudoyer
4. un policier haut gradé
5. s'accordent tous, sans raison apparente, à concocter
6. qu'aucun d'entre eux
7. qui s'offrait à moi
8. d'autant de réflexion
9. le registre des accusations
10. y inscrivit
11. l'accusation retenue contre lui
12. bout de ficelle
13. chevalière
14. aux armoiries
15. mégots
16. pipette de chimiste
17. pièces de monnaie
18. [pierre précieuse]
19. de toute
20. rester en garde à vue
21. la convocation devant le coroner, qui aurait lieu
22. ce serait son procès
23. d'autres affaires à juger

'Come with me, Watson!' Lestrade said. 'Move sharp[1], now. We don't have a lot of time.'

I followed him out of the main courtroom[2], down a flight of stairs and into a basement area that was utterly without[3] comfort, where even the paint-work was mean and shabby[4], and which might have been expressly designed for[5] prisoners, for men and women who had parted company with the ordinary world above[6]. Lestrade had been here before, of course. He swiftly led me[7] along a corridor and into a lofty[8], white-tiled[9] room with a single window and a bench that ran all the way round[10]. The bench was divided by a series of wooden partitions[11] so that whoever sat there would be isolated and unable to communicate with those on either side. I knew at once that this was the Prisoners' Waiting Room[12]. Perhaps Holmes had been held here before the trial.

We were no sooner in[13] than there was a movement at the door and Holmes appeared, escorted by a uniformed officer. I rushed towards him and might even have embraced him[14] had I not realised that, in his view[15], this would have been just one more indignity piled up on so many[16]. Even so, my voice broke as I addressed him[17]. 'Holmes! I do not know what to say. The injustice of your arrest, the way you have been treated ... it is beyond any imagining[18].'

'It is certainly most interesting,' returned he. 'How are you, Lestrade? A strange turn of events[19], do you not think? What do you make of it?'

'I really don't know what to think, Mr Holmes,' Lestrade muttered.

'Well, that's nothing new[20]. It seems that our friend, Henderson, led us a pretty song and dance[21], hey, Watson? Well, let's not forget that I half-expected it and he has still proved useful to us. Before, I suspected that we had stumbled on to[22] a conspiracy that went far beyond[23] a murder in a hotel room. Now I am certain of it.'

1. Dépêchez-vous
2. la salle d'audience principale
3. totalement dépourvue de
4. les peintures étaient abîmées
5. spécialement prévue pour
6. d'en haut
7. me guida prestement
8. vaste
9. carrelée de blanc
10. qui en faisait tout le tour
11. cloisons
12. salle d'attente
13. à peine arrivés
14. le serrer dans mes bras
15. pour lui
16. ajoutée à tant d'autres
17. en lui parlant
18. cela dépasse l'imagination
19. Les événements ont pris une étrange tournure
20. ce n'est pas nouveau
21. nous a bien menés en bateau
22. étions tombés sur
23. qui dépassait de loin

1. à quoi bon
2. saura s'en accommoder
3. je suis pendu
4. je vous laisse le soin
5. tout cela n'était qu'un malentendu
6. prendre les choses à la légère
7. incontestable
8. attachez plus de crédit à ma parole
9. accueilli comme
10. un mélange de cordialité et de méfiance
11. en effet
12. prendre ma dose à 4 pence
13. éveiller sa méfiance
14. à peine eus-je passé la porte
15. m'ont sauté dessus
16. m'empoignant le cou
17. me maintenant les bras
18. le crâne rasé
19. les avant-bras d'un lutteur
20. et la force qui va avec

'But what good is it[1] to know these things if you are to be imprisoned and your reputation destroyed?' I replied.

'I think my reputation will look after itself[2],' Holmes said. 'If they hang me[3], Watson, I shall leave it to you[4] to persuade your readers that the whole thing was a misunderstanding[5].'

'You may make light of all this[6], Mr Holmes,' growled Lestrade. 'But I should warn you that we have very little time. And the evidence against you seems, in a word, unarguable[7].'

'What did you make of the evidence, Watson?'

'I don't know what to say, Holmes. These men don't appear to know each other. They have come from different parts of the country. And yet they are in complete agreement about what occurred.'

'And yet, surely you would take my word above[8] that of our friend Isaiah Creer?'

'Of course.'

'Then let me tell you at once that what I have told Inspector Harriman is the true version of events. After I entered the opium den, I was approached by Creer and greeted as[9] a new customer – which is to say, with a mixture of warmth and wariness[10]. There were four men lying semi-conscious, or pretending to be, on the mattresses and one of them was indeed[11] Lord Horace Blackwater, although of course I did not know him at the time. I pretended that I had come for my fourpenny worth[12] and Creer insisted that I follow him into his office to make the payment there. Not wishing to raise his suspicions[13], I did as he asked and I was no sooner through the doorway[14] than two men sprang on me[15], seizing hold of my neck[16] and pinioning my arms[17]. One of them, Watson, we know. It was Henderson himself! The other had a shaven head[18] and the shoulders and forearms of a wrestler[19], with the strength to match[20]. I was unable to move. "You have been very unwise[1], Mr Holmes, to interfere in things which do not concern you and unwise to believe that you could take on[2] people more powerful than yourself," Henderson said, or words to that effect[3]. At the same time, Creer approached me carrying a small glass filled with some foul-smelling liquid[4]. It was an opiate of some sort[5], and there was nothing I could do as it was forced between my lips. There were three of them and only one of me.[6] I could not reach my gun. The effect was almost immediate. The room spun[7] and the strength went out of my legs[8]. They released me and I fell to the floor.'

'The devils![9]' I exclaimed.

'And then?' Lestrade asked.

'I remember nothing more until I awoke with Watson beside me. The drug must have been extremely strong.'

'That's all very well, Mr Holmes. But how do you explain the testimonies[10] we have heard from Dr Ackland, from Lord Horace Blackwater and from my colleague Harriman?'

'They have colluded.[11]'

'But why? These are not ordinary men.'

'Indeed not. Were they ordinary I would be more inclined to believe them. But does it not strike you as strange[12] that three such remarkable specimens should have emerged, out of the darkness[13], at exactly the same time?'

'What they said made sense[14]. There was not a single questionable[15] word spoken in this court.'

'No? I beg to differ with you[16], Lestrade, for I heard several. We might start with the good Dr Ackland. Did you not find it surprising that although he said it was too dark for him to see who fired the shot, in the same breath[17] he testified that he could see smoke rising[18] from the gun? He must have a unique sort of vision[19], this Dr Ackland. And then there's Harriman himself. You might find it worthwhile

1. Il est très imprudent de votre part
2. vous en prendre à
3. ou quelque chose d'approchant
4. d'un liquide à l'odeur infecte
5. un genre d'opiacé
6. Nous étions à trois contre un.
7. s'est mise à tourner
8. mes jambes ont cédé
9. Les fumiers !
10. témoignages
11. Ils sont de connivence.
12. cela ne vous paraît pas bizarre
13. aient surgi des ténèbres
14. tenait debout
15. douteux
16. Je ne partage pas votre avis
17. sur sa lancée
18. de la fumée sortant
19. une faculté visuelle exceptionnelle

to confirm[1] that there really was a break-in at a bank on the White Horse Road. It seems to me a touch[2] providential.'

'Why?'

'Because if I were to rob a bank, I would wait until after midnight when the streets were a little less populated. I might also head for[3] Mayfair, Kensington or Belgravia – anywhere where the local residents[4] might have deposited[5] enough money to be worth stealing[6].'

'And what of Perkins?'

'Constable Perkins was the only honest witness. Watson, I wonder if I could trouble you[7] ... ?

But before Holmes could continue, Harriman appeared in the doorway, his face thunderous[8]. 'What the devil is going on[9] here?' he demanded. 'Why is the prisoner not on his way to a cell? Who are you, sir?'

'I am Inspector Lestrade.'

'Lestrade! I know you. But this is my case. Why are you interfering?'

'Mr Sherlock Holmes is very well known to me—'

'Mr Sherlock Holmes is well known to a great many people. Are we going to invite them all in to make his acquaintance[10]?' Harriman turned to the policeman who had brought Holmes from the courtroom, and who had been standing in the room, looking increasingly uncomfortable[11]. 'Officer! I'll take your name and your number[12] and you'll hear more of this in due course[13]. For the present, you can escort Mr Holmes to the back yard[14] where a police van[15] is waiting to take him to his next place of residence[16].'

'And where is that?' Lestrade demanded.

'He is to be held[17] at the House of Correction[18] at Holloway.'

I blanched at this[19], for all of London knew the conditions that prevailed[20] at that grim and imposing[21] fortress. 'Holmes!' I said. 'I will visit you—'

1. Cela vaut peut-être la peine de vérifier
2. un tantinet
3. J'irais aussi du côté de
4. les habitants du quartier
5. déposé
6. pour que cela vaille la peine de le voler
7. cela vous dérangerait-il
8. l'air courroucé
9. Que diable se passe-t-il
10. à faire sa connaissance
11. l'air de plus en plus mal à l'aise
12. matricule
13. en temps utile
14. l'arrière-cour
15. fourgon cellulaire
16. vers son nouveau lieu de séjour
17. Il sera détenu
18. maison d'arrêt
19. Cela me fit blêmir
20. de détention
21. lugubre et imposante

'It distresses me[1] to contradict you, but Mr Holmes will not be receiving visitors until my investigation is complete[2].'

There was nothing more that Lestrade or I could do. Holmes did not attempt to struggle[3]. He allowed the policeman to raise him up[4] and lead him from the room. Harriman followed and the two of us were left alone.

1. Désolé
2. soit finie
3. n'opposa aucune résistance
4. le mettre debout

THIRTEEN
Poison

1. relaté la mort
2. le procès qui avait suivi
3. que du papier de soie, usé par le temps
4. grave et abject
5. se situe près de
6. en patrouille dans le secteur
7. serveuse
8. On présume
9. sortait à l'instant
10. qui font la mauvaise réputation du quartier
11. détective privé
12. mis en état d'arrestation
13. exploite un domaine d'env. 400 ha

All the newspapers had reported on the death[1] of Sally Dixon and the subsequent trial[2]. One account I have before me still, the paper now as fragile as tissue, worn away with age[3]:

> A crime of a serious and despicable character[4] was committed two nights ago in Coppergate Square which lies close to[5] the river and Limehouse Basin. Just before twelve o'clock, Police Constable Perkins of the H Division, patrolling the area[6], heard a gunshot and hurried towards the source of the disturbance. He arrived too late to save the victim, a sixteen-year-old serving girl[7] from a London public house who lived nearby. It has been conjectured[8] that she was on her way home and unexpectedly encountered her assailant who had just emerged[9] from one of the opium dens for which the area is notorious[10]. This man was identified as Mr Sherlock Holmes, a consulting detective[11], and he was immediately taken into police custody[12]. Although he denied all knowledge of the crime, a series of highly respectable witnesses appeared to testify against him, including Dr Thomas Ackland of the Westminster Hospital and Lord Horace Blackwater who farms a thousand acres[13] in Hallamshire. Mr Holmes has now been moved

to the House of Correction at Holloway and this whole, sorry incident[1] once again pinpoints the scourge of drugs[2] in our society and calls into question the continued legality[3] of those dens of[4] vice where they can be freely consumed.

I need hardly say that this made extremely unpleasant reading at the breakfast table on the Monday following Holmes's arrest. There were also aspects of the report that were highly questionable[5]. The Bag of Nails was in Lambeth, so why had the reporter assumed that Sally Dixon was on her way home? It was also curious that no mention had been made of Lord Blackwater's own indulgence in[6] that 'den of vice'.

The weekend had been and gone[7], two days in which I could do little but fret[8] and wait for news. I had sent fresh clothes[9] and food to Holloway, but could not be sure that Holmes had received them. From Mycroft I had heard nothing[10], although he could not possibly[11] have missed the stories in the newspapers and, besides, I had sent repeated messages to the Diogenes Club. I did not know whether to be indignant or alarmed[12]. On the one hand, his lack of response[13] seemed churlish and even petulant[14], for although it was true that he had warned us against precisely the course of action we had taken, surely he would not have hesitated to use his influence, given the seriousness[15] of his brother's situation. But then again, I recalled what he had said – 'There will be nothing I can do for you' – and I wondered at the power[16] of the House of Silk, whatever it might be, that could incapacitate[17] a man whose influence reached to the inner circles[18] of government.

I had resolved to walk round to the club and to present myself in person[19] when the doorbell rang

1. cet incident déplorable
2. pointe le fléau de la drogue
3. remet en question le maintien de la légalité
4. repaires du
5. très discutables
6. qu'il n'y soit pas indiqué que lord Blackwater lui-même fréquentait
7. s'était écoulé
8. au cours desquels je ne fis que me tracasser
9. des vêtements propres
10. je n'avais aucune nouvelle
11. décemment
12. si m'alarmer ou m'indigner
13. absence de réaction
14. marquer sa mauvaise humeur, voire sa colère
15. la gravité
16. j'étais sidéré par le pouvoir
17. à même de neutraliser
18. les plus hautes sphères
19. d'y aller en personne

and, after a short pause, Mrs Hudson introduced a very beautiful woman, well gloved and dressed[1] with simple elegance and charm. So absorbed was I with my thoughts that it took me a few moments to recognise Mrs Catherine Carstairs, the wife of the Wimbledon art dealer whose visit to our office had set in motion[2] these unhappy events. In fact, seeing her, I found it hard to make the necessary connection, which is to say, I was quite lost as to how[3] a gang of Irish hoodlums in an American city, the destruction of four landscapes by John Constable and a shoot-out with a posse of Pinkerton's agents could have possibly led us to our present pass[4]. Here was a paradox indeed. On the one hand, the discovery of the dead man in Mrs Oldmore's Private Hotel had been the cause of everything that had happened but on the other it didn't seem to have anything to do with it. Perhaps it was the writer in me coming to the fore[5], but I might have said that it was as if two of my narratives had somehow got muddled together[6] so that the characters from one[7] were unexpectedly appearing in the other. Such was my sense of confusion[8] on seeing Mrs Carstairs. And there she was, standing in front of me, suddenly sobbing while I simply stared at her like a fool[9].

'My dear Mrs Carstairs!' I exclaimed, leaping to my feet[10]. 'Please, do not distress yourself. Sit down. May I get you a glass of water?'

She was unable to speak. I led her to a chair and she produced a handkerchief which she used to dab at her eyes[11]. I poured her some water and carried it over, but she waved it away[12]. 'Dr Watson,' she murmured at last. 'You must forgive me coming here.'

'Not at all. I am very pleased to see you. When you came in, I was preoccupied but I can assure you that you now have my full attention. Have you further news[13] from Ridgeway Hall?'

'Yes. Horrible news. But is Mr Holmes away?'

1. bien vêtue et gantée
2. déclenché
3. je ne voyais pas comment, avec
4. nous avions pu en arriver là
5. était-ce l'écrivain en moi qui ressortait
6. deux de mes récits s'étaient en quelque sorte télescopés
7. les personnages de l'un
8. C'est cette confusion que je ressentis
9. fondant en larmes alors que je la dévisageais bêtement
10. en me levant d'un bond
11. pour se tamponner les yeux
12. refusa d'un geste
13. d'autres nouvelles

'You have not heard? Have you not seen a newspaper?'

She shook her head. 'I don't interest myself in the news. My husband does not encourage it.'

I considered showing her the piece I had just been reading, then decided against it[1]. 'I'm afraid[2] Mr Sherlock Holmes is indisposed[3],' I said. 'And is likely to be for some time[4].'

'Then it's hopeless. I have no one else to turn to[5].' She bowed her head. 'Edmund does not know I have come here today. In fact, he counselled strongly against it[6]. But I swear to you, I will go mad, Dr Watson. Is there no end to this nightmare[7] that has suddenly come to destroy all our lives?'

She began to cry afresh[8] and I sat, helpless, until at last the tears abated[9]. 'Perhaps it might help if you tell me what brought you here,' I suggested.

'I will tell you. But can you help me?' She suddenly brightened.[10] 'Of course! You're a doctor! We've seen doctors already. We've had doctors in and out of the house. But maybe you'll be different. You'll understand.'

'Is your husband ill?'

'Not my husband. My sister-in-law[11], Eliza. You remember her? When you first met her, she was already complaining of headaches and various pains[12], but since then her condition has suddenly worsened[13]. Now Edmund thinks she may be dying[14] and there is nothing that anyone can do.'

'What made you think you might find help here?'

Mrs Carstairs straightened herself in her chair. She wiped her eyes and suddenly I was aware[15] of the strength of spirit[16] that I had noticed when we first met. 'There is no love between my sister-and-law and me,' she said. 'I'll not pretend otherwise. From the very start, she thought me an adventuress[17] with my talons out[18] to ensnare[19] her brother when he was at his lowest ebb, a fortune hunter[20]

1. puis me ravisai
2. Désolé, mais
3. souffrant
4. il devrait le demeurer un certain temps
5. vers qui me tourner
6. était très contre
7. cauchemar
8. à nouveau
9. désemparé, jusqu'à ce que les pleurs se calment
10. Son regard s'éclaira.
11. belle-sœur
12. de maux de tête et de diverses douleurs
13. son état s'est aggravé subitement
14. qu'elle est peut-être en train de mourir
15. je pris conscience
16. force de caractère
17. a vu en moi une aventurière
18. qui sortait ses griffes
19. pour mettre le grappin
20. une femme intéressée

who planned only to profit from his wealth. Forget the fact that I came to this country with plenty of money of my own[1]. Forget that I was the one who nursed Edmund back to health[2] on board the *Catalonia*. She and her mother would have hated me, no matter who I was[3], and they never gave me a chance. Edmund had always belonged to them, you see – the younger brother, the devoted son[4] – and they could never bear the idea of his finding happiness with anyone else. Eliza even blames me for[5] the death of her mother. Can you believe it? What was a tragic domestic accident – the flame blew out on her gas fire – became in her mind a deliberate suicide, as if the old lady preferred to die than to see me as the new mistress of the house. In a way, they're both mad. I wouldn't dare say that[6] to Edmund, but it's true. Why could they never accept the fact that he loves me and be glad for both our sakes[7]?'

'And this new illness ... ?'

'Eliza thinks she is being poisoned. Worse than that, she insists that I am responsible. Don't ask me how she has arrived at this conclusion. It's madness, I tell you!'

'Does your husband know of this?'

'Of course he does. She accused me while I was there with them in the room. Poor Edmund! I have never seen him so confused. He didn't know how to respond – for if he had taken my side against her[8], who knows what it would have done to her state of mind. He was mortified[9], but the moment we were alone he rushed to my side and begged my forgiveness[10]. Eliza is sick, there's no doubting that[11], and Edmund takes the view[12] that her delusions are part[13] of the sickness and he may well be right[14]. Even so, the situation has become almost intolerable for me. All her food is now prepared separately in the kitchen and carried straight up[15] to her room by Kirby, who makes sure that it never

1. ma propre fortune
2. dont les soins ont guéri Edmund
3. de toute façon
4. le frère cadet, le fils dévoué
5. me reproche même
6. Je n'oserais jamais le dire
7. se réjouir pour nous
8. s'il avait pris mon parti
9. très gêné
10. m'a suppliée de le pardonner
11. cela ne fait aucun doute
12. pense
13. ses délires font partie
14. il se pourrait bien qu'il ait raison
15. montée directement

leaves his sight[1]. Edmund actually shares the dish with her[2]. He pretends he is being companionable[3] but of course he is acting as nothing more than[4] one of those ancient Roman food-tasters[5]. Maybe I should be grateful. For a week now he has eaten everything that she has eaten and he is in perfect health, while she becomes sicker and sicker, so if I am adding deadly nightshade to her diet[6], it's a perfect mystery why only she is affected[7].'

'What do the doctors believe to be the cause of her illness?'

'They are all baffled[8]. First they thought it was diabetes, then blood poisoning[9]. Now they fear the worst and they are treating her for cholera.' She lowered her head and when she raised it again, her eyes were full of tears. 'I will tell you a terrible thing, Dr Watson. Part of me wants her to die. I have never thought that of another human being, not even my first husband when he was at his most drunken and violent[10]. But sometimes I find myself thinking that if Eliza were to go, at least Edmund and I would be left in peace. She seems intent on tearing us apart[11].'

'Would you like me to come with you to Wimbledon?' I asked.

'Would you?' Her eyes brightened. 'Edmund did not want me to see Sherlock Holmes. There were two reasons. As far as he was concerned[12], his business with your colleague was over. The man from Boston who was shadowing him[13] is dead and there seems nothing more to be done. And were we to bring[14] a detective to the house, he feared it would only persuade Eliza that she was right.'

'Whereas[15] you thought ... ?'

'I hoped Mr Holmes would prove my innocence.'

'If it will help to ease your mind[16], I will be glad to accompany you,' I said. 'I should warn you that I am only a general practitioner[17] and my experience is limited, but my long collaboration with Sherlock

1. veille à ne jamais la quitter des yeux
2. mange du même plat qu'elle
3. que c'est pour lui tenir compagnie
4. ne fait que jouer le rôle de
5. ces goûteurs de la Rome antique
6. de la belladone à sa nourriture
7. atteinte
8. ne savent qu'en penser
9. une septicémie
10. dans ses pires accès d'ivresse et de violence
11. déterminée à nous séparer
12. En ce qui le concerne
13. le suivait
14. si nous faisions venir
15. Alors que
16. cela peut vous tranquilliser
17. ne suis qu'un généraliste

Holmes has given me an eye[1] for the unusual[2] and it may be that I notice something that your other advisers have missed[3].'

'Are you sure, Dr Watson? I would be so very grateful. I still sometimes feel such a stranger in this country that it's a blessing[4] to have anyone on my side.'

We left together. I had no wish at all[5] to leave Baker Street but I could see that there was nothing to be gained by sitting there on my own. Although Lestrade was active on my behalf, I had yet to be given permission[6] to visit Holmes at Holloway. Mycroft would not arrive at the Diogenes Club until the afternoon. And despite what Mrs Carstairs had said, the mystery of the man in the flat cap was far from resolved[7]. It would be interesting to see Edmund Carstairs and his sister again, and although I knew that I was a very poor replacement for[8] Holmes himself, it still might be possible that I would see or hear something that might shed a little light on what was happening and hasten my friend's release[9].

Carstairs was not at first pleased to see me when I presented myself in the hallway[10] of his home with its elegant artworks and softly ticking[11] clock. He had been about to leave for lunch and was meticulously dressed in a frock coat, grey satin cravat[12] and well-varnished shoes. His top hat[13] and walking stick were on a table by the door. 'Dr Watson!' he exclaimed. He turned to his wife. 'I thought we had agreed that we would not be resorting[14] to the services of Sherlock Holmes.'

'I am not Holmes,' I said.

'Indeed not. I was just reading in the paper that Mr Holmes has fallen into the most disreputable circumstances[15].'

'He did so in pursuit of the business that you brought to his door[16].'

'A business that has now been concluded.'

1. m'a doté d'une certaine acuité
2. ce qui sort de l'ordinaire
3. ayant échappé à vos autres conseillers
4. une chance
5. Je n'avais aucune envie
6. y travaillait pour moi, j'attendais toujours l'autorisation
7. loin d'être résolu
8. pouvais mal suppléer à l'absence de
9. accélérer la libération de mon ami
10. le vestibule
11. au tic-tac feutré
12. d'une redingote, d'un foulard de satin gris
13. chapeau haut de forme
14. n'aurions plus recours
15. est dans une situation tout à fait déshonorante
16. lui avez confiée

'He does not think so.'

'I beg to disagree.'

'Come[1], Edmund,' Mrs Carstairs cut in. 'Dr Watson has very kindly travelled with me all the way[2] from London. He has agreed to see Eliza and give us the benefit of his opinion.'

'Eliza has already been seen[3] by several doctors.'

'And one more opinion can't hurt[4].' She took his arm. 'You have no idea what it's been like for me these last few days. Please, my dear. Let him see her. It may help her, too, even if it's only to have someone else to whom she can complain.'

Carstairs relented[5]. He patted her hand.[6] 'Very well. But it won't be possible for a while. My sister rose late[7] this morning and I heard her drawing a bath[8]. Elsie is with her now. It will be at least thirty minutes before she is presentable.'

'I am quite happy to wait,' I said. 'But I will use the time, if I may[9], to examine the kitchen. If your sister persists in her belief[10] that her food is being tampered with[11], it may prove useful to see where it is prepared.'

'Of course, Dr Watson. And you must forgive my rudeness just now[12]. I wish Mr Holmes well[13] and I am glad to see you. It's just that this nightmare never seems to stop. First Boston, then my poor mother, that business at the hotel, now Eliza. Only yesterday I acquired a gouache from the school of Rubens, a fine study of Moses[14] at the Red Sea[15]. But now I wonder if I am not afflicted by curses as fearsome[16] as those experienced by the Pharaohs[17].'

We went downstairs and into a large, airy kitchen so filled with pots and pans, steaming cauldrons[18] and chopping boards[19] that it gave the impression of being busy even though there was very little activity in evidence. There were three people in the room. One of them I recognised. The manservant[20], Kirby, who had first admitted us[21] to Ridgeway Hall was sit-

1. Allons
2. fait tout le trajet avec moi
3. examinée
4. ne peut faire de mal
5. se radoucit
6. Il lui tapota la main.
7. s'est levée tard
8. se faire couler un bain
9. j'en profiterai, si vous le permettez
10. à croire
11. l'on touche à sa nourriture
12. d'avoir été grossier à l'instant
13. J'espère que tout ira bien pour M. Holmes
14. une superbe étude de Moïse
15. mer Rouge
16. victime de malédictions aussi effrayantes
17. pharaons
18. de casseroles, de chaudrons fumants
19. planches à découper
20. domestique
21. nous avait fait entrer la première fois

ting at the table, buttering[1] some bread for his lunch. A small, ginger-haired pudding of a woman[2] was standing at the stove[3], stirring[4] a soup, the aroma of which – beef and vegetables[5] – filled the air. The third person was a sly-looking[6] young man, sitting in the corner, idly polishing the cutlery[7]. Although Kirby had risen to his feet the moment we entered, I noticed that the young man remained where he was, glancing over his shoulder as if we were intruders who had no right to disturb him. He had long, yellow[8] hair, a slightly feminine face, and must have been about eighteen or nineteen years old. I remembered Carstairs telling Holmes and me that Kirby's wife had a nephew, Patrick, who worked below stairs and supposed this must be him.

Carstairs introduced me. 'This is Dr Watson, who is trying to determine the cause of my sister's illness. He may have some questions for you and I would be glad if you would answer them as candidly as you can[9].'

Although I had insinuated myself into[10] the kitchen, I was actually unsure[11] what to say but began with the cook who seemed the most approachable[12] of the three. 'You are Mrs Kirby?' I asked.

'Yes, sir.'

'And you prepare all the food?'

'Everything is prepared in this kitchen, sir, by me and by my husband. Patrick scrubs[13] the potatoes and helps with the washing, when he can be so minded[14], but all the food passes through my hands and if there is anything poisoned in this house, Dr Watson, you won't be finding it here. My kitchen is spotless[15], sir. We scrub it[16] with carbolate of lime[17] once a month. You can enter the pantry[18] if you wish. Everything is in its place and there's plenty of fresh air. We buy the food locally and nothing that's not fresh comes through the door.'

1. en train de beurrer
2. une rousse très grasse
3. aux fourneaux
4. touillant
5. bœuf aux légumes
6. à l'air sournois
7. polissant l'argenterie d'un air distrait
8. blonds
9. avec autant de franchise que possible
10. Bien que je me sois faufilé dans
11. en réalité, je ne savais trop
12. la plus avenante
13. brosse
14. le veut bien
15. d'une propreté impeccable
16. On la nettoie
17. un [ancien] détergent à la chaux
18. aller dans l'office

'It's not the food that's the cause of Miss Carstairs's illness, begging your pardon[1], sir,' muttered Kirby with a glance at the master of the house. 'You and Mrs Carstairs have had nothing different to her[2] and you're both well.'

'If you ask me[3], there's something strange what's come[4] into this house,' Mrs Kirby said.

'What do you mean by that, Margaret?' Mrs Carstairs demanded.

'I don't know, ma'am. I don't mean anything by it. But we're all worried to death on account of[5] poor Miss Carstairs and it's just as if somehow there's something wrong about this place[6] but whatever it is, my conscience is clear and I would pack my bags[7] tomorrow and leave if anyone suggested otherwise.'

'Nobody is blaming you[8], Mrs Kirby.'

'But she's right though[9]. There is something wrong in this house.' It was the kitchen boy, speaking for the first time and his accent reminded me[10] that Carstairs had told us that he came from Ireland.

'Your name is Patrick, is it not?' I asked.

'That's right, sir.'

'And where are you from?'

'From Belfast, sir.'

It was surely a coincidence and nothing more but Rourke and Keelan O'Donaghue had also come from Belfast. 'How long have you been here[11], Patrick?' I asked.

'Not long, sir. But they've made me very welcome[12].' And the boy smirked as if at some private joke[13].

It was none of my business[14], but everything about his behaviour – the way he slouched[15] on his stool and even the manner of his speech[16] – struck me as purposefully disrespectful[17] and I was surprised that Carstairs allowed him to get away with it[18]. His wife was less tolerant.

1. si je puis me permettre
2. avez mangé la même chose qu'elle
3. voulez mon avis
4. c'est bizarre, ce qui arrive
5. morts d'inquiétude pour
6. quelque chose ne tournait pas rond ici
7. je suis prête à plier bagage
8. Personne ne vous reproche rien
9. pourtant
10. me rappela
11. Depuis quand êtes-vous là
12. j'ai été très bien accueilli
13. fit un sourire en coin, d'un air entendu
14. Cela ne me regardait pas
15. sa posture avachie
16. sa façon de parler
17. délibérément irrespectueux
18. le laisse faire

'How dare you[1] speak to us like that, Patrick,' she said. 'If you're insinuating something, you should say it. And if you're unhappy here, you should leave.'

'I like it well enough[2], Mrs Carstairs, and I wouldn't say there was anywhere else I would want to go.'

'Such insolence! Edmund, will you not speak to him?'

Carstairs hesitated, and in that brief pause there was a jangle[3] and Kirby looked round at the row of servants' bells[4] on the far wall[5]. 'That's Miss Carstairs, sir,' he said.

'She must have finished her bath,' Carstairs said. 'We can go up to her. Unless you have any more questions, Dr Watson?'

'Not at all,' I replied. The few questions I had asked had been futile and I was suddenly dispirited[6], for it had occurred to me that had Holmes been present, he would probably have solved the entire mystery by now[7]. What would he have made[8] of the Irish serving boy and his relationship with the rest of them? And what would he have seen as his eyes swept across the room[9]? 'You see, Watson, but you do not observe.' He had said it often enough and never had I felt it to be more true. The kitchen knife lying on the table, the soup bubbling on the hearth[10], the brace of pheasants[11] hanging from a hook[12] in the pantry, Kirby casting his eyes downwards[13], his wife standing with her hands on her apron[14], Patrick still smiling ... would they have told him something more than they told me? Undoubtedly. Show Holmes a drop[15] of water and he would deduce[16] the existence of the Atlantic. Show it to me and I would look for a tap[17]. That was the difference between us.

We went back upstairs and all the way to the top floor[18]. As we climbed up, we passed a young girl, hurrying the other way with a bowl[19] and two towels[20]. This was Elsie, the scullery maid. She kept

1. Comment osez-vous
2. Je me plais bien, ici
3. un tintement retentit
4. la rangée de clochettes de service
5. sur le mur du fond
6. démoralisé
7. à cette heure-ci
8. Qu'aurait-il pensé
9. en balayant la pièce du regard
10. mijotant dans l'âtre
11. couple de faisans
12. suspendus à un crochet
13. qui baissait les yeux
14. tablier
15. une goutte
16. il en déduirait
17. chercherais un robinet
18. au dernier étage
19. cuvette
20. serviettes

her head down and I saw nothing of her face. She brushed past us[1] and was gone.

Carstairs knocked gently[2] at the door, then entered his sister's bedroom to see if she would receive a visit from me. I waited outside with Mrs Carstairs. 'I will leave you here, Dr Watson,' said she. 'It will only distress[3] my sister-in-law if I go in. But please let me know if there is anything that you notice that has a bearing[4] on her illness.'

'Of course.'

'And thank you again for coming. I feel so relieved to have you as my friend.'

She swept away[5] just as the door opened and Carstairs invited me in. I entered a close, plushly furnished[6] bedroom built into the eaves[7] with small windows, the curtains partly drawn[8] and a fire burning in the grate. I noticed that a second door opened into an adjoining bathroom and the smell of lavender bath salts[9] was heavy in the air. Eliza Carstairs was lying in bed, propped up with pillows[10] and wearing a shawl. I could see at once that her health had deteriorated rapidly since my last visit. She had the pinched, exhausted quality[11] that I had all too often[12] observed in my more serious[13] patients, and her eyes stared out pitifully over the sharp ridges[14] that her cheekbones had become. She had combed her hair, but it was still[15] dishevelled, spreading around her shoulders[16]. Her hands, resting on the sheet[17] in front of her, might have been those of a dead woman.

'Dr Watson!' she greeted me[18] and her voice rasped in her throat[19]. 'Why have you come to visit me?'

'Your sister-in-law asked me to come, Miss Carstairs,' I replied.

'My sister-in-law wants me dead[20].'

'That is not the impression she gave. May I take your pulse?'

1. nous frôla
2. toqua
3. Cela ne fera qu'affliger
4. ayant une incidence
5. se retira
6. meublée avec luxe
7. dans l'avant-toit
8. partiellement tirés
9. le parfum de sels de bain à la lavande
10. soutenue par des oreillers
11. les traits tirés et l'air épuisé
12. trop souvent
13. les plus atteints
14. au-dessus des arêtes saillantes
15. tout de même
16. ébouriffés, lâchés sur les épaules
17. posées sur le drap
18. me dit-elle, en guise d'accueil,
19. la voix rauque
20. veut ma mort

1. croyez-moi sur parole
2. le suivant
3. Chut
4. la gronda
5. combattre
6. une teinte légèrement bleutée
7. qui m'avaient été décrits
8. des douleurs abdominales
9. les articulations douloureuses
10. mes os se décomposer
11. qui s'occupent de vous
12. Vous laisser mourir de faim ne peut que vous affaiblir.
13. pour que l'air circule bien
14. l'hygiène
15. est primordiale
16. Je prends un bain
17. de vêtements
18. les draps
19. repas
20. alors moi aussi
21. ne veux-tu pas entendre raison
22. se laissa retomber

'You may take what you wish. I have nothing more to give. And when I am gone, take my word for it[1], Edmund will be next[2].'

'Hush[3], Eliza! Don't say such things,' her brother scolded her[4].

I held her pulse which was beating much too rapidly as her body attempted to fight off[5] the disease. Her skin had a slightly bluish tinge[6] which, along with the other symptoms that had been reported to me[7], made me wonder if her doctors might be right in suggesting cholera as the cause of her sickness. 'You have abdominal pain[8]?' I asked.

'Yes.'

'And aching joints[9]?'

'I can feel my bones rotting away[10]. '

'You have doctors in attendance[11]. What drugs have they prescribed?'

'My sister is taking laudanum,' Carstairs said.

'Are you eating?'

'It is the food that is killing me!'

'You should try to eat, Miss Carstairs. Starving yourself will only make you weaker.[12]' I released her. 'There is little more I can suggest. You might open the windows to allow the air to circulate[13], and cleanliness[14], of course, is of the first importance[15].'

'I bath[16] every day.'

'It would help to change your garments[17] and the bed linen[18] every day too. But above all, you must eat. I have visited the kitchen and seen that your meals[19] are well prepared. You have nothing to fear.'

'I am being poisoned.'

'If you are being poisoned, then so am I[20]!' Carstairs exclaimed. 'Please, Eliza! Why will you not see sense[21]?'

'I am tired.' The sick woman fell back[22], closing her eyes. 'I thank you for your visit, Dr Watson. Open the windows and change the bed clothes! I can see that you must be at the very pinnacle[1] of your profession!'

Carstairs ushered me out[2] and, in truth, I was glad to go. Eliza Carstairs had been rude[3] and scornful[4] the first time we had met her and her illness had only exaggerated these aspects of her character. Carstairs and I parted company[5] at the front door. 'Thank you for your visit, Dr Watson,' he said. 'I understand the forces that drove[6] my dear Catherine to your door and I very much hope that Mr Holmes will be able to extricate himself[7] from the difficulties which he is in[8].'

We shook hands. I was about to leave and then I remembered. 'There is just one other thing, Mr Carstairs. Is your wife able to swim?'

'I'm sorry? What an extraordinary question! Why do you wish to know?'

'I have my methods ...'

'Well, as a matter of fact, Catherine cannot swim at all. Indeed, she has a fear of the sea[9] and has told me she will not enter the water under any circumstances[10].'

'Thank you, Mr Carstairs.'

'Good day, Dr Watson.'

The door closed. I had received an answer to the question that Holmes had put to me[11]. Now all I needed to know was why I had asked it.

1. parmi les experts
2. me conduisit hors de la pièce
3. grossière
4. dédaigneuse
5. nous séparâmes
6. les motifs qui ont poussé
7. de se sortir
8. dans lesquelles il se trouve
9. peur de la mer
10. sous aucun prétexte
11. m'avait soumise

FOURTEEN

Into the Dark

A note from Mycroft awaited me on my return[1]. He would be at the Diogenes Club early that evening and would be pleased to see me if I would like to call upon him[2] at around that time. I was almost worn out[3] by my journey to and from[4] Wimbledon on top of[5] the activity of recent days ... it was never possible for me to exert myself to any great extent[6] without being reminded of the injuries[7] I had sustained in Afghanistan. Even so, I decided to go out once again after a short rest[8] for I was acutely aware of the ordeal[9] that Sherlock Holmes must be enduring[10] while I was at liberty, and this outweighed[11] any consideration of my own well-being[12]. Mycroft might not give me a second opportunity to visit him, for he was as capricious as he was corpulent, flitting like some oversized shadow through[13] the corridors of power[14]. Mrs Hudson had laid out a late lunch[15] which I ate before falling asleep in my chair and the sky was already darkening when I set out and caught a cab back to Pall Mall.

He met me once again in the Stranger's Room but this time his manner was more clipped and formal[16] than it had been when I was there with Holmes. He began without any pleasantries[17]. 'This is a bad business. A very bad business. Why did my brother seek my advice[18] if he was not prepared to take it?'

1. m'attendait à mon retour
2. venir le voir
3. exténué
4. mon aller-retour à
5. ajouté à
6. me démener beaucoup
7. sans que cela réveille les blessures
8. repos
9. parfaitement conscient de l'épreuve
10. devait endurer
11. c'était plus important que
12. mon propre bien-être
13. hantant, telle une ombre immense
14. allées du pouvoir
15. disposé un déjeuner tardif
16. le ton était plus pincé et solennel
17. sans les civilités d'usage
18. m'a-t-il demandé conseil

'I think it was information he required from you, not advice,' I countered.

'A fair point.[1] But given that I was able to provide only the one and not the other, he might have done well[2] to listen to what I had to say. I told him that no good would come of it – but that was his character, even when he was very young. He was impetuous. Our mother used to say the same and always feared that he would find himself in trouble[3]. Would that she had lived[4] to see him established as a detective. She would have smiled at that!'

'Can you help him?'

'You already know the answer to that, Dr Watson, for I told you the last time we met. There is nothing I can do.'

'Would you see him hanged[5] for murder?'

'It will not come to that.[6] It cannot come to that. Already I am working behind the scenes[7], and although I am finding a surprising amount of interference and obfuscation[8], he is too well known to too many people of importance for that possibility to arise[9].'

'He is being held at Holloway.'

'So I understand[10], and being well cared for – or at least as well as that grim place will allow.'

'What can you tell me of Inspector Harriman?'

'A good police officer, a man of integrity[11], with not a spot on his record[12].'

'And what of the other witnesses?'

Mycroft closed his eyes and lifted his head as if tasting[13] a good wine. In this way did he give himself pause for thought[14]. 'I know what you are inferring[15], Dr Watson,' he said at length. 'And you must believe me when I say that, despite his reckless[16] behaviour, I still have Sherlock's best interests at heart[17] and am working to make sense of what has happened. I have already, at considerable personal expense, investigated the backgrounds of[18]

1. C'est juste.
2. il aurait mieux fait
3. s'attire des ennuis
4. Si seulement elle avait vécu assez longtemps
5. Voudriez-vous qu'il soit pendu
6. Cela n'ira pas jusque-là.
7. en coulisses
8. d'obstruction
9. pour que cela arrive
10. C'est ce que j'ai compris
11. intègre
12. des états de service irréprochables
13. s'il dégustait
14. le temps de la réflexion
15. ce que vous insinuez
16. téméraire
17. les intérêts de Sherlock me tiennent toujours à cœur
18. d'où viennent

1. n'ont rien à se reprocher
2. célibataires
3. ne sont pas du même club
4. à des lieues l'un de l'autre
5. leur présence simultanée
6. qui les relie
7. de ne pas s'en mêler
8. une confrérie ou un cercle
9. dont on me tait l'existence
10. provoque ma convocation
11. faire comme si je n'avais rien vu
12. de stupides annonces
13. Allez-vous permettre qu'il soit jugé ?
14. que vous ne surestimiez
15. en écailles de tortue
16. une pincée de tabac à priser
17. plaider sa cause
18. en son nom
19. témoin de moralité
20. découragé
21. qui a de la ressource
22. maintenant, en ces heures si difficiles

both Dr Thomas Ackland and Lord Horace Blackwater, and regret to tell you that as far as I can see they are beyond reproach[1], both of good families, both single[2], both wealthy men. The two of them do not club together[3]. They did not go to the same school. For most of their lives, they have lived hundreds of miles apart[4]. Beyond the coincidence of their both being[5] in Limehouse at the same time of night, there is nothing that connects them[6].'

'Unless it is the House of Silk.'

'Exactly.'

'And you will not tell me what it is.'

'I will not tell you because I do not know. This is precisely the reason why I warned Sherlock to stay away[7]. If there is something, a fellowship or a society[8], at the heart of government which is being kept from me[9], and which is so secret that even to mention its name has me summoned[10] instantly to certain offices in Whitehall, then my instinct is to turn and look the other way[11], not to place damn fool advertisements[12] in the national press! I told my brother as much as I could ... indeed more, perhaps, than I should have.'

'So what will happen? Will you allow him to stand trial?[13]

'What I allow or do not allow has nothing to do with the matter. I fear you place too high a value on[14] my influence.' Mycroft produced a tortoiseshell[15] box from his waistcoat pocket and took a pinch of snuff[16]. 'I can be his advocate[17]; no more and no less. I can speak on his behalf[18]. If it really becomes necessary, I will appear as a character witness[19].' I must have looked disappointed, for Mycroft put the snuff away, rose to his feet and came over to me. 'Do not be disheartened[20], Dr Watson,' he counselled. 'My brother is a man of considerable resource[21] and even in this, his darkest hour[22], he may yet surprise you.'

'Will you visit him?' I asked.

'I think not. Such a thing would embarrass him and inconvenience me to no discernible advantage[1]. But you must tell him that you have consulted me and that I am doing what I can.'

'They will not let me see him.'

'Re-apply[2] tomorrow. Eventually, they must let you in. They have no reason not to.' He walked with me to the door. 'My brother is very fortunate to have a staunch ally[3] as well as such a fine chronicler[4],' he remarked.

'I hope I have not written his last adventure.'

'Goodbye, Dr Watson. It would upset me[5] to have to be discourteous to you, so I would be obliged if you did not communicate with me again except, of course, in the most urgent circumstances[6]. I wish you a good evening.'

It was with a heavy heart[7] that I returned to Baker Street, for Mycroft had been even less helpful[8] than I had hoped and I wondered what circumstances he could have been referring to[9] if these were not urgent already. At least he might have gained me admittance[10] to Holloway so the journey had not entirely been wasted[11] but I had a headache, my arm and shoulder were throbbing[12] and I knew that I was close to exhausting my strength[13]. However, my day was not over yet. As I left my cab and walked over to the front door I knew so well, I found my path blocked by[14] a short, solid[15] man with black hair and black coat who loomed at me out of the pavement[16].

'Dr Watson?' he asked.

'Yes?'

I was anxious to be on my way but the little man had imposed himself in front of me[17]. 'I wonder if I might ask you, doctor, to come with me?'

'On what business?'

1. sans réel bénéfice
2. Refaites une demande
3. un allié dévoué
4. un remarquable chroniqueur
5. Cela m'ennuierait
6. en cas de grand péril
7. le cœur lourd
8. encore moins coopératif
9. pouvait faire allusion
10. aurait pu m'obtenir l'accès
11. vain
12. m'élançaient
13. j'arrivais au bout de mes forces
14. en travers de mon chemin
15. massif
16. surgissant vers moi depuis le trottoir
17. s'interposa devant moi

1. qui concerne
2. de plus près
3. À en juger par son apparence
4. commerçant
5. tailleur
6. croque-mort
7. de volontairement lugubre
8. qui tombait sur sa lèvre supérieure
9. chapeau melon
10. en équilibre sur la pointe des pieds
11. à le voir brandir un mètre de couturier
12. cercueil
13. Je ne suis que l'agent
14. de celui qui en est détenteur
15. mais il m'est interdit de le dire
16. pas d'humeur
17. ne vous propose pas de venir
18. Il l'exige.
19. n'a pas l'habitude d'essuyer des refus
20. baisser le regard
21. Ne sursautez pas.
22. ne risquez rien
23. si vous vous voulez bien
24. J'avais fait un pas en arrière, stupéfait
25. pointé sur
26. exécuté
27. tour de magie

'On a matter that relates to[1] your friend, Mr Sherlock Holmes. What other business could there be?'

I examined him more closely[2] and what I saw did not encourage me. To look at[3], I would have taken him for a tradesman[4], perhaps a tailor[5] or even an undertaker[6], for there was something almost studiously mournful[7] about his face. He had heavy eyebrows and a moustache that drooped over his upper lip[8]. He was also wearing black gloves and a black bowler hat[9]. From the way he was standing, poised on the balls of his feet[10], I expected him to whip out a tape measure[11] at any moment. But to measure me for what? A new suit or a coffin[12]?

'What do you know of Holmes?' I asked. 'What information do you have that you cannot tell me here?'

'I have no information at all, Dr Watson. I am merely the agent[13], the very humble servant, of one who does[14], and it is this person who has sent me here to request you to join him.'

'To join him where? Who is he?'

'I regret that I am not at liberty to say[15].'

'Then I'm afraid you're wasting your time. I am in no mood[16] to go out again tonight.'

'You do not understand, sir. The gentleman for whom I work is not inviting your presence[17]. He is demanding it.[18] And although it pains me, I have to tell you that he is not used to being denied[19]. In fact, that would be a horrible mistake. Could I ask you to look down[20], sir? There! Do not start.[21] You are quite safe[22], I assure you. Now, if you would be kind enough to[23] come this way ...'

I had stepped back in astonishment[24] for, on doing as he had asked, I had seen that he was holding a revolver, aimed at[25] my stomach. Whether he had produced it while we talked, or whether he had been holding it all the time, I could not say, but it was as if he had performed[26] some unpleasant magic trick[27] and the weapon had suddenly materialised. He was certainly comfortable with it[1]. The person who has never fired a revolver holds it in a certain way, as does[2] the man who has used one many times. I could easily tell to which category my assailant belonged.

'You will not shoot me in the middle of the street[3],' I said.

'On the contrary, Dr Watson, I am instructed to do exactly that[4] should you choose to make difficulties for me. But let us be frank with each other. I do not wish to kill you any more[5] than you, I am sure, wish to die. It may help you to know – and I give you my solemn word[6] on this – that we mean you no harm[7], although I suppose it may not seem that way at the moment. Even so, after a while, all will be explained and you will understand why these precautions are necessary.'

He had an extraordinary manner of speaking, both[8] obsequious and extremely threatening[9]. He gestured with the gun[10] and I observed a black carriage standing by with two horses and a coachman in place. It was a four-wheeler with windows of frosted glass[11], and I wondered if the man who had demanded to meet me was sitting inside. I walked over and opened the door. The interior was empty, the fittings[12] elegant and of rich quality[13]. 'How far are we travelling?' I asked. 'My landlady is expecting me for dinner.'

'You'll get a better dinner where we're going. And the sooner you get in[14], the sooner we can be on our way.'

Would he have really shot me down outside[15] my own home? I quite believed he would. He had an implacable quality[16]. At the same time, were I to climb into this carriage, I might be carried away[17] and never seen again[18]. Suppose he had been sent by the same people who had killed both Ross and his sister and who had dealt so cunningly with[19] Holmes?

1. très à l'aise avec
2. tout comme
3. en pleine rue
4. j'ai précisément ordre de le faire
5. pas plus vous tuer
6. ma parole d'honneur
7. ne vous voulons aucun mal
8. à la fois
9. menaçante
10. fit un geste de son arme
11. en verre dépoli
12. la décoration
13. de belle facture
14. plus vite vous monterez
15. devant
16. un côté implacable
17. on pouvait m'emmener
18. me faire disparaître
19. qui s'étaient si habilement occupés de

1. tendus de soie
2. gris perle
3. Quelle que soit la façon d'aborder les choses
4. à la suite de quoi
5. m'empêcher de voir à l'intérieur
6. à l'extérieur
7. la lueur filante
8. s'évanouirent
9. j'en couvris mes genoux
10. souvent en décembre
11. dodelinant en avant
12. l'arme abandonnée sur ses genoux
13. paysage
14. se redressa subitement
15. comme s'il grondait un élève turbulent
16. vous cacher son adresse
17. très secret
18. de laisser vos mains où elles sont
19. de laisser les fenêtres fermées
20. Combien de temps va durer le trajet ?
21. Le temps qu'il faudra.

I noticed that the walls of the carriage were lined with silk[1] – not white, but pearl grey[2]. At the same time, I reminded myself, the man had said that he represented someone with information. Whichever way I looked at it[3], it seemed to me I had no choice. I climbed in. The man followed me and closed the door whereupon[4] I saw that I had certainly been foolish in one respect. I had assumed that the opaque glass had been placed there to prevent me looking in[5] when, obviously, it was actually there to stop me looking out[6].

The man had climbed in opposite me and at once the horses were whipped up and we set off. All I could see was the passing glow[7] of the gas lamps and even those fell away[8] once we left the city, travelling, I would have said, north. A blanket had been placed on the seat for me and I drew it over my knees[9] for, like every other December night[10], it had become very cold. My companion said nothing and seemed to have fallen asleep, his head rolling forward[11] and the gun resting loosely in his lap[12]. But when, after about an hour, I reached out to open the window, wondering if I might see something in the landscape[13] that would tell me where I was, he jerked up[14] and shook his head as if chiding a naughty schoolboy[15]. 'Really, Dr Watson, I would have expected better of you. My master has taken great pains to keep his address from you[16]. He is a man of a very retiring nature[17]. I would ask you to keep your hands to yourself[18] and the windows closed[19].'

'For how long are we going to travel?[20]'

'For as long as it takes.[21]'

'Do you have a name?'

'I do indeed, sir. But I fear that I am not at liberty to reveal it to you.'

'And what can you tell me of the man who employs you?'

'I could talk my way to the North Pole on that subject[1], sir. He is a remarkable person. But he would not appreciate it. All in all, the less said the better[2].'

The journey was almost unendurable to me. My watch showed me that it lasted two hours, but there was nothing to tell me in which direction we were going nor how far, as it had occurred to me that we might well be going round and round in circles[3] and our destination could in fact have been very close. Once or twice the carriage changed direction and I felt myself swinging to the side[4]. Most of the time, the wheels seemed to be turning over smooth[5] asphalt but occasionally there would be a rattle[6] and I would feel that we had passed onto a paved causeway[7]. At one point[8] I heard a steam train[9] passing above us. We must be under a bridge. Otherwise, I felt swallowed up by[10] the darkness that surrounded me and finally dozed off[11], for the next thing I knew[12] we had come to a shuddering halt[13] and my travelling companion was leaning across me, opening the door.

'We will go straight into the house, Dr Watson,' he said. 'These are my instructions. Pray do not linger outside. It is a cold and a nasty night. If you do not go straight in, I fear it might be the death of you.'

I glimpsed only a massive, uninviting[14] house, the front draped in ivy[15], the garden overrun with weeds[16]. We could have been in Hampstead or Hampshire, for the grounds were surrounded by high walls with heavy, wrought-iron gates[17] which had already been closed behind us. The building itself put me in mind of[18] an abbey[19] with crenulated windows[20], gargoyles[21] and a tower stretching above[22] the roof. All the windows upstairs were dark but there were lamps burning in some of the rooms below. A door stood open beneath the porch, but there was nobody to welcome me, if such a place as this could ever, even on the most sunlit[23] summer's

1. en raconter jusqu'au pôle Nord
2. moins j'en dis, mieux je me porte
3. pouvions très bien tourner en rond
4. basculer de côté
5. lisse
6. vibration
7. chaussée pavée
8. Une fois,
9. train à vapeur
10. englouti dans
11. je m'assoupis
12. tout de suite après, j'eus l'impression
13. que nous nous étions arrêtés brutalement
14. peu attrayante
15. drapé de lierre
16. envahi de mauvaises herbes
17. grilles en fer forgé
18. me fit penser à
19. abbaye
20. des fenêtres crénelées
21. des gargouilles
22. surplombant
23. ensoleillé

evening, be described as welcoming[1]. Urged on by my fellow passenger[2], I hurried in. He closed the door hard[3] behind me and its boom echoed[4] down the gloomy corridors.

'This way, sir.' He had taken up a lamp and I followed him down a passageway[5], past windows of stained glass[6], oak panelling[7], paintings so dark and faded that, but for the frames[8], I might barely have noticed them at all. We came to a door. 'In here. I will let him know you have arrived. He won't be long. Touch nothing. Go nowhere. Show restraint![9]' And after having delivered this strange directive[10], he backed out the way he had come.

I was in a library with a log fire[11] burning in a stone fireplace[12] and candles arranged on the mantel[13]. A round table of dark wood with several chairs occupied the centre of the room and there were more candles burning here. There were two windows, both heavily curtained[14], and a thick rug on the otherwise bare, wooden floor[15]. The library must have held[16] several hundred volumes. Shelves rose from the floor to the ceiling[17] – a considerable distance – and there was a ladder, on wheels[18], that could be tracked[19] from one end of the shelves to the other. I took a candle and examined some of the covers[20]. Whoever owned this house must be well versed in[21] French, German and Italian, for all three languages were evident[22] as well as English. His interests encompassed physics[23], botany, philosophy, geology, history and mathematics. There were no works[24] of fiction as far as I could see. Indeed, the selection of books put me very much in mind of Sherlock Holmes, for they seemed quite accurately to reflect his tastes[25]. From the architecture of the room, the shape of the fireplace, the ornate[26] ceiling, I could see that the house must be of Jacobean design. Obeying the instructions I had been given, I sat down on one of the chairs and stretched

1. qualifié d'accueillant
2. Pressé par mon compagnon de voyage
3. violemment
4. le coup résonna
5. un couloir
6. des vitraux
7. des boiseries de chêne
8. sans les cadres
9. Faites preuve de retenue !
10. injonction
11. feu de bois
12. cheminée en pierre
13. des bougies disposées sur le dessus
14. aux lourdes tentures
15. à même le plancher
16. devait contenir
17. Des étagères s'élevaient du sol au plafond
18. une échelle, sur roues
19. que l'on pouvait faire glisser
20. les dos de certains livres
21. devait bien maîtriser
22. bien visibles
23. Ses centres d'intérêt couvraient la physique
24. d'ouvrages
25. ses goûts
26. ouvragé

my hands in front of the fire. I was grateful for the warmth[1] for, even with the blanket, the journey had been merciless[2].

There was a second door in the room, opposite the one I had entered, and this opened suddenly to reveal a man so tall and thin that he seemed out of proportion to the frame[3] that surrounded him and might actually have to stoop[4] to come in. He was wearing dark trousers, Turkish slippers[5] and a velvet smoking jacket. As he entered, I saw that he was almost bald, with a high forehead and deep, sunken eyes. He moved slowly, his stick-like arms folded across his chest[6], clinging on to each other[7] as if they were holding him together[8]. I noticed that the library connected with a chemical[9] laboratory and that was where he had been occupying himself while I waited. Behind him, I saw a long table cluttered with test tubes, retorts[10], bottles, carboys[11] and hissing[12] Bunsen lamps. The man himself smelled strongly of chemicals[13], and although I wondered about the nature of his experiments, I thought it better not to ask.

'Dr Watson,' he said. 'I must apologise for keeping you waiting[14]. There was a delicate matter that required my attention but which I have now brought to a fruitful conclusion[15]. Have you been offered wine? No? Underwood, assiduous in his duties though he undoubtedly is[16], cannot be described as the most considerate[17] of men. Unfortunately, in my line of work, one cannot pick and choose[18]. I trust that he looked after you on the long journey here.'

'He did not even tell me his name.'

'That is hardly surprising. I do not intend[19] to tell you mine. But it is already late and we have business to attend to[20]. I am hoping you will dine with me.'

'It is not my habit[21] to take dinner with men who refuse even to introduce themselves.'

1. de cette chaleur
2. éprouvant
3. trop grand pour l'embrasure
4. se courber
5. des babouches
6. ses bras maigres croisés sur la poitrine
7. se tenant l'un l'autre
8. le maintenaient d'un seul tenant
9. de chimie
10. encombrée de tubes à essai, de cornues
11. de bonbonnes
12. sifflantes
13. avait une forte odeur de produits chimiques
14. de vous avoir fait attendre
15. réglée
16. même s'il est, à n'en point douter, sérieux dans son travail
17. prévenant
18. faire le difficile
19. Je n'ai pas l'intention
20. des choses à faire
21. dans mes habitudes

1. réfléchir à ceci
2. il peut tout vous arriver
3. n'en saurait rien
4. Le couvert est mis dans la pièce d'à côté.
5. me ramena
6. passer en face
7. la totalité d'une aile
8. tribune [loggia] des musiciens
9. de réfectoire
10. avec assez de place
11. jadis
12. assis autour
13. flambant
14. un interminable ballet de plats
15. Une seule lampe à abat-jour
16. jetait un halo
17. de la charcuterie
18. encerclés par les ombres
19. voûtées
20. tassé
21. peu pratique pour un corps si dégingandé
22. [Les Hêtres rouges]
23. je la trouve très réussie

'Perhaps not. But I would ask you to consider this[1]: anything could happen to you[2] in this house. To say that you are completely in my power may sound silly and melodramatic, but it happens to be true. You do not know where you are. Nobody saw you come here. If you were never to leave, the world would be none the wiser[3]. So I would suggest that, of the options open to you, a pleasant dinner with me may be one of the more preferable. The food is frugal but the wine is good. The table is laid next door.[4] Please come this way.'

He led me back out[5] into the corridor and across[6] to a dining room that must have occupied almost an entire wing[7] of the house, with a minstrel's gallery[8] at one end and a huge fireplace at the other. A refectory[9] table ran the full distance between the two, with room enough[10] for thirty people, and it was easy to imagine it in bygone times[11] with family and friends gathered round[12], music playing, a fire roaring[13] and an endless succession of dishes being carried back and forth[14]. But tonight it was empty. A single shaded lamp[15] cast a pool of light[16] over a few cold cuts[17], bread, a bottle of wine. It appeared that the master of the house and I were to eat alone, hemmed in by the shadows[18], and I took my place with a sense of oppression and little appetite. He sat at the head of the table, his shoulders stooped[19], hunched up[20] in a chair that seemed ill-designed for a frame as ungainly[21] as his.

'I have often wanted to meet you, Dr Watson,' my host began as he served himself. 'It may surprise you to learn that I am a great admirer of yours and have every one of your chronicles.' He had carried with him a copy of the *Cornhill Magazine* and he opened it on the table. 'I have just finished this one here, the *Adventure of the Copper Beeches*[22], and I think it very well done[23].' Despite the bizarre circumstances of the evening, I could not help but feel a certain satisfaction, for I had been particularly pleased with the way this story had turned out. 'The fate[1] of Miss Violet Hunter was of no interest to me,' he continued. 'And Jephro Rucastle was clearly a brute of the worst sort. I find it remarkable that the girl should have been so credulous[2]. But, as always, I was most gripped by[3] your depiction[4] of Mr Sherlock Holmes and his methods. A pity that you did not set out the seven separate explanations of the crime that he mentioned to you. That would have been most insightful[5]. But, even so, you have opened the workings[6] of a great mind to the public and for that we should all be grateful. Some wine?'

'Thank you.'

He poured two glasses, then continued. 'It is a shame[7] that Holmes does not devote himself exclusively to this sort of wrongdoing, which is to say, domestic crime where the motives are negligible and the victims of no account[8]. Rucastle was not even arrested for his part[9] in the affair, although he was badly disfigured?'

'Horribly.'

'Perhaps that is punishment enough. It is when your friend turns his attention to larger matters[10], to business enterprises organised by people such as myself, that he crosses the line[11] and becomes an annoyance[12]. I rather fear that recently he has done precisely that, and if it continues it may well be that the two of us have to meet, which, I can assure you, would be not at all to his advantage.'

There was an edge to his voice that caused me to shudder.[13] 'You have not told me who you are,' I said. 'Will you explain *what* you are?'

'I am a mathematician, Dr Watson. I do not flatter myself when I say that my work on the Binomial Theorem[14] is studied in most of the universities of Europe. I am also what you would doubtless term a criminal, although I would like to think that I have

1. Le sort
2. naïve
3. J'ai trouvé captivante
4. description
5. très instructif
6. dévoilé le fonctionnement
7. Quel dommage
8. les victimes sans importance
9. pour son rôle
10. à des affaires plus conséquentes
11. qu'il va trop loin
12. devient gênant
13. Son ton cassant me fit trembler.
14. [formule du binôme de Newton]

made a science out of crime[1]. I try not to dirty my own hands[2]. I leave that for the likes of Underwood[3]. You might say I am an abstract thinker[4]. Crime in its purest form is, after all, an abstract, like music. I orchestrate. Others perform[5].'

'And what do you want with me? Why have you brought me here?'

'Other than[6] the pleasure of meeting you? I wish to help you. More to the point[7], and it surprises me to hear myself say it, I wish to help Mr Sherlock Holmes. It was a great pity[8] that he did not pay attention to me two months ago when I sent him a certain keepsake[9], inviting him to look into the business[10] which has now caused him such grief[11]. Perhaps I should have been a little more direct.'

'What did you send him?' I asked, but I already knew.

'A length of white ribbon.'

'You are part of the House of Silk!'

'I have nothing to do with it!' For the first time he sounded angry. 'Do not disappoint me, please, with your foolish syllogisms[12]. Save them[13] for your books.'

'But you know what it is.'

'I know everything. Any act of wickedness[14] that takes place in this country, no matter how great or small, is brought to my attention[15]. I have agents in every city, in every street. They are my eyes. They never so much as blink[16].' I waited for him to continue, but when he did so, it was on another tack[17]. 'You must make me a promise, Dr Watson. You must swear on everything that is sacred to you that you will never tell Holmes, or anyone else, of this meeting. You must never write about it. You must never mention it. Should you ever learn[18] my name, you must pretend that you are hearing it[19] for the first time and that it means nothing to you.'

'How do you know I will keep such a promise?'

1. j'ai transformé le crime en science
2. de ne pas me salir les mains
3. à Underwood et ses semblables
4. théoricien
5. jouent
6. Hormis
7. Plus précisément
8. Il est fort regrettable
9. souvenir
10. à examiner l'affaire
11. est aujourd'hui la cause de ses malheurs
12. vos stupides syllogismes
13. Gardez-les
14. Tout acte répréhensible
15. m'est signalé
16. Des yeux qui ne clignent même pas
17. à propos d'autre chose
18. Si jamais vous appreniez
19. faire semblant de l'entendre

'I know you are a man of your word[1].'

'And if I refuse?'

He sighed[2]. 'Let me tell you now that Holmes's life is in great danger. More than that[3], he will be dead within[4] forty-eight hours unless you do as I ask. I alone[5] can help you, but will only do so on my terms[6].'

'Then I agree.[7]'

'You swear?'

'Yes.'

'On what?'

'On my marriage.'

'Not good enough.'

'On my friendship with Holmes.'

He nodded. 'Now we understand each other.'

'Then what is the House of Silk? Where will I find it?'

'I cannot tell you. I only wish I could, but I fear Holmes must discover it for himself. Why? Well, in the first instance[8] because I know he is capable and it will interest me to study his methods, to see him at work. The more I know of him, the less formidable he becomes[9]. But there is also a broader point of principle at stake[10]. I have admitted to you that I am a criminal, but what exactly does that mean? Simply that there are certain rules[11] which govern society but which I find a hindrance[12] and therefore choose to ignore. I have met perfectly respectable bankers and lawyers[13] who would say exactly the same. It is all a question of degree. But I am not an animal, Dr Watson. I do not murder children. I consider myself a civilised man and there are other rules which are, to my mind[14], inviolable.

'So what is a man like myself to do when he comes across[15] a group of people whose behaviour – whose criminality – he considers to be beyond the pale[16]? I could tell you who they are and where you can find them. I could have already told the police. Alas[17],

1. de parole
2. soupira
3. Pire
4. d'ici
5. Moi seul
6. sous certaines conditions
7. Alors j'accepte.
8. en premier lieu,
9. moins son génie m'effraie
10. une question de principe qui est en jeu
11. règles
12. je considère comme une entrave
13. des banquiers et des juristes
14. de mon point de vue
15. croise
16. qu'il estime inadmissible
17. Hélas

such an act would cause considerable damage[1] to my reputation among many of the people I employ who are less high-minded than me[2]. There is such a thing as a criminal code[3] and many criminals of my acquaintance take it very seriously. In fact, I tend to concur[4]. What right have I to judge[5] my fellow criminals[6]? I would certainly not expect to be judged by them.'

'You sent Holmes a clue.'

'I acted on impulse, which is very unusual for me and shows how annoyed I had become[7]. Even so, it was a compromise, the very least I could do in the circumstances. If it did spur him into action[8], I could console myself with the thought that I had done very little and was not really to blame. If, on the other hand, he chose to ignore it, no damage had been done, and my conscience was clear[9]. That said, you have no idea how sorry I was that he chose the latter course of action[10] – or inaction, I should say. It is my sincere belief that the world would be a much better place[11] without the House of Silk. It is still my hope that this will come to pass[12]. That is why I invited you here tonight.'

'If you cannot give me information, what can you give me?'

'I can give you this.' He slid something across the table towards me. I looked down and saw a small, metal key.

'What is this?' I asked.

'It is the key to his cell.'

'What?' I almost laughed aloud[13]. 'You expect Holmes to escape? Is that your master plan[14]? You want me to help him break out[15] of Holloway?'

'I do not know why you find the notion[16] so amusing, Dr Watson. Let me assure you that there is no possible alternative.'

'There is the coroner's court. The truth will come out.[17]'

1. nuirait considérablement
2. n'ont pas ma noblesse d'esprit
3. Il y a bien un code, chez les criminels,
4. j'y adhère volontiers
5. De quel droit pourrais-je juger
6. camarades
7. à quel point j'étais contrarié
8. cela l'incitait à agir
9. j'avais la conscience tranquille
10. cette dernière ligne de conduite
11. bien meilleur
12. cela arrivera
13. faillis éclater de rire
14. plan génial
15. à s'évader
16. cette idée
17. La vérité éclatera.

His face darkened. 'You still have no conception of the sort of people you are up against[1], and I begin to wonder if I'm not wasting my time. Let me make it clear to you[2]: Sherlock Holmes will never leave the House of Correction alive. The coroner's court has been set[3] for next Thursday, but Holmes will not be there. His enemies will not allow it. They plan[4] to kill him while he is in jail.'

I was horrified. 'How?'

'That I cannot tell you. Poisoning or strangulation would be the easiest methods, but there are a hundred accidents they could arrange. Doubtless they will find a way to make the death appear natural[5]. But trust me[6]. The order has already been given. His time is running out.[7]'

I picked up the key. 'How did you get this?'

'That is immaterial[8].'

'Then tell me how I am to get it to him. They won't let me see him.'

'That is for you to arrange. There is nothing more I can do without revealing my part in this. You have Inspector Lestrade on your side. Speak to him.' He stood up suddenly, pushing his chair back from the table. 'There is nothing more to be said, I think. The sooner you return to Baker Street, the sooner you can begin to consider what must be done.' He relaxed a little. 'I will add only this. You have no idea how keenly I have felt the pleasure of making your acquaintance[9]. Indeed, I quite envy Holmes having[10] such a staunch biographer at his side. I, too, have certain stories of considerable interest to share[11] with the public and I wonder if I might one day call on[12] your services. No? Well, it was an idle thought[13]. But, this meeting aside, I suppose it is always possible that I may turn up as a character in one of your narratives[14]. I hope you will do me justice[15].'

1. n'avez toujours pas compris à qui vous avez affaire
2. Je vais être très clair avec vous
3. fixée
4. Ils ont l'intention
5. pour que la mort paraisse naturelle
6. vous pouvez me croire
7. Le temps lui est compté.
8. sans importance
9. comme je suis heureux d'avoir fait votre connaissance
10. j'envie vraiment Holmes d'avoir
11. à partager
12. faire appel à
13. une idée en l'air
14. j'apparaisse dans l'un de vos récits
15. que vous me rendrez justice

1. fait un signe
2. dispositif
3. Je vidai
4. je jetai un regard derrière moi
5. piquant sa nourriture
6. la lueur de la bougie
7. Hormis une fois où je l'aperçus

They were the last words he spoke to me. Perhaps he had signalled[1] with some hidden contrivance[2], for at that moment the door opened and Underwood appeared. I drained[3] my glass for I needed the wine to fortify me for the journey. Then, taking the key, I stood up. 'Thank you,' I said.

He did not reply. At the door, I took one look back[4]. My host was sitting on his own at the head of that huge table, poking at his food[5] in the candlelight[6]. Then the door closed. And apart from one brief glimpse[7] at Victoria Station, a year later, I never saw him again.

FIFTEEN

Holloway Prison

My return to London was, in some respects, even more of an ordeal[1] than had been my departure. Then I had found myself little more than a captive, in the hands of people who quite possibly meant harm to me, being carried towards an unknown destination on a journey that could have lasted[2] half the night. Now, I knew I was returning home and had only a few hours to endure, but it was impossible to find any sort of equanimity[3]. Holmes was to be murdered! The mysterious forces that had conspired to have him arrested were still not content[4] and only his death would suffice[5]. The metal key that I had been given was clutched so tightly[6] in my hand that I could have made a duplicate from the impression squeezed into my flesh[7]. My only thought was to reach[8] Holloway, to warn Holmes of what was afoot[9] and to assist in his immediate exit[10] from that place. And yet how was I to reach him? Inspector Harriman had already made it clear that he would do everything in his power to keep the two of us apart. On the other hand, Mycroft had said I could approach him[11] again 'in the most urgent circumstances', which was what these surely were[12]. But just how far[13] would his influence extend, and

1. encore plus pénible
2. aurait pu durer
3. un semblant de sérénité
4. restaient insatisfaits
5. les comblerait
6. serrée si fort
7. en faire faire un double à partir de la marque sur ma paume
8. Je n'avais qu'une idée : me rendre à
9. ce qui se tramait
10. l'aider à sortir sur-le-champ
11. le contacter
12. ce qui était sûrement le cas
13. jusqu'où exactement

by the time he got me into the House of Correction, might it already be too late?

With these thoughts raging in[1] my mind, and with nothing but the silent Underwood leering at me[2] from the seat opposite and darkness on the other side of the frosted windows, the journey seemed to stretch on for ever[3]. Worse still, part of me knew that I was being deceived[4]. The coach was surely going round and round in circles, purposefully exaggerating[5] the distance between Baker Street and the strange mansion where I had been invited to dinner. It was particularly vexing[6] to reflect that had Holmes been in my place, he would have taken note of all the different elements – the chime of a church bell[7], the blast of a steam whistle[8], the smell of stagnant water, the changing surfaces beneath the wheels, even the direction of the wind rattling against[9] the windows – and drawn a perfectly detailed map of our journey[10] at the end of it. But I was most certainly not up to the challenge[11] and could only wait for the glow of gas lamps to reassure me that we were back in the city and, perhaps half an hour later, the slowing down[12] of the horses and the final, jolting halt[13] that signalled we were at the end of our journey. Sure enough, Underwood threw open the door and there, across the road, were my familiar lodgings.

'Safely home[14], Dr Watson,' said he. 'I apologise once again for inconveniencing you[15].'

'I will not forget you easily, Mr Underwood,' I replied.

He raised his eyebrows. 'My master has told you my name? How curious.'

'Perhaps you would care to tell me his.'

'Oh no, sir. I concede that I am but a speck on a canvas[16]. My life is of little significance[17] in comparison with his greatness[18] but nonetheless I am at-

1. faisant rage dans
2. qui me lorgnait
3. durer une éternité
4. que l'on cherchait à me leurrer
5. rallongeant à dessein
6. contrariant
7. carillon d'une église
8. son d'un sifflet à vapeur
9. claquant contre
10. tracé le chemin exact que nous avions parcouru
11. pas à la hauteur de la tâche
12. ralentissement
13. le dernier arrêt, dans une secousse,
14. Vous voilà chez vous, sain et sauf
15. de vous avoir dérangé
16. quantité négligeable
17. n'est rien
18. ce grand homme

tached to it and would wish it to continue for a while yet[1]. I will wish you a good night.'

I climbed down. He signalled to the driver and I watched as the carriage rattled away, then hurried in.

But there was to be no rest for me that night. I had already begun to formulate a plan by which[2] the key might safely be delivered[3] to Holmes, along with a message alerting him to the danger he was in even if, as I feared, I was not permitted to visit him myself. I had already concluded that a straightforward letter would do no good[4]. Our enemies were all around us and there was every chance[5] that they would intercept it. If they discovered that I was aware of[6] their intentions, it might spur them on to strike all the faster[7]. But I could still send him a message – and some sort of code was required[8]. The question was, how could I indicate that it was there to be deciphered[9]? There was also the key. How could I deliver it into his hand? And then, casting my eye[10] around the room, I fell upon the answer[11]: the very same book[12] that Holmes and I had been discussing only a few days before, *The Martyrdom of Man* by Winwood Reade. What could be more natural than to send my friend something to read while he was confined[13]? What could appear more innocent?

The volume was leather-bound[14] and quite thick. Upon[15] examining it, I saw that it would be possible to slip the key into the space between the spine and the bound edges[16] of the pages. This I did and, taking up the candle, I carefully poured liquid wax into the two ends, in effect gluing it in place[17]. The book still opened normally and there was nothing to suggest that it had been tampered with[18]. Taking up my pen, I then wrote the name, Sherlock Holmes, on the frontispiece[19] and, beneath it, an address: 122B Baker Street. To a casual observer[20] it would appear that nothing was amiss[21] but Holmes

1. qu'elle dure encore un peu
2. à fomenter un plan selon lequel
3. remise
4. qu'une simple lettre ne servirait à rien
5. il était quasi certain
6. connaissais
7. les décider à agir encore plus vite
8. était nécessaire
9. qu'il s'agissait d'un code
10. promenant mon regard
11. j'eus la réponse
12. ce livre même
13. enfermé
14. relié en cuir
15. En
16. le dos et la reliure
17. de telle sorte qu'elle soit bien collée
18. trafiqué
19. frontispice
20. À voir comme ça,
21. qu'il n'y avait rien d'anormal

would recognise my hand at once and would see that the number of our lodgings had been inverted. Finally, I turned to page 122 and, using a pencil, placed a series of tiny dots[1], almost invisible to the naked eye[2], under certain letters in the text so that a new message was spelled out[3]: YOU ARE IN GREAT DANGER. THEY PLAN TO KILL YOU. USE KEY TO CELL. I AM WAITING. JW.

Satisfied with my work, I finally went to bed and fell into a troubled sleep[4] punctured by[5] images of the girl, Sally, lying in the street with blood all around her, of a length of white ribbon looped around[6] a dead boy's wrist and of the man with the high-domed forehead[7], looming at me across the refectory table.

1. tout petits points
2. à l'œil nu
3. afin de rédiger un autre message
4. sombrai dans un sommeil agité
5. émaillé d'
6. enroulé autour
7. le front en pain de sucre

I awoke early the next day and sent a message to Lestrade, urging him once again[8] to help arrange a visit to Holloway, no matter what Inspector Harriman had to say[9]. To my surprise, I received a reply informing me that I could enter the prison at three o'clock that afternoon, that Harriman had concluded his preliminary investigation and that the coroner's court had indeed been set for Thursday, two days hence[10]. On first reading, this struck me[11] as good news. But then I thought of a more sinister explanation. If Harriman was part of the conspiracy, as Holmes believed and as everything about his manner[12] and even his appearance suggested, he might well have stood aside[13] for a quite different reason. My host of the night before had insisted that Holmes would never be allowed to stand trial. Suppose the assassins were preparing to strike[14]! Could Harriman know that it was already too late?

I could barely contain myself[15] throughout the morning and left Baker Street well before the appointed hour[16], arriving at Camden Road before the clocks had struck the half-hour. The coachman

8. lui redemandant instamment
9. quoi qu'en dise l'inspecteur Harriman
10. dans deux jours
11. je le pris
12. dans son attitude
13. laissé faire
14. s'apprêtaient à frapper
15. J'eus du mal à tenir en place
16. bien avant l'heure dite

left me in front of the outer gate[1] and, despite my protestations, hurried away, leaving me in the cold and misty[2] air. All in all I couldn't blame him. This wasn't a place where any Christian soul would have chosen to linger[3].

The prison was of Gothic design; on first appearance a sprawling, ominous[4] castle, perhaps something out of a fairy story[5] written for a malevolent[6] child. Constructed from Kentish ragstone[7], it consisted of a series of turrets and chimneys, flagpoles and castellated walls[8], with a single tower soaring above[9] and seeming almost to disappear into the clouds. A rough, muddy track[10] led to the main entrance, which was purposefully[11] designed to be as unwelcoming[12] as possible, with a massive wooden gate and steel portcullis[13] framed by a few bare and withered[14] trees on either side. A brick wall, at least fifteen feet[15] high, surrounded the entire complex, but above it I could make out[16] one of the wings, with two lines of small, barred windows whose rigid uniformity somehow hinted at[17] the emptiness and misery of life inside. The prison had been built at the foot of a hill and, looking beyond it, it was possible to make out the pleasant pastures and slopes[18] that rose up to Highgate. But that was another world, as if the wrong backdrop[19] had been accidentally lowered onto the stage[20]. Holloway Prison stood on the site of a former[21] cemetery, and the whiff of death and decay still clung to the place, damning[22] those who were inside, warning those without to stay away.

It was as much as I could bear[23] to wait thirty minutes in the dismal light with my breath frosting and the cold spreading upwards through my feet[24]. At last I walked forward, clutching the book with the key concealed[25] in its spine, and as I entered the prison it occurred to me that were I to be discovered, this horrid place could well become my home.

1. la grille extérieure
2. brumeux
3. un quidam aurait envie de s'attarder
4. menaçant et tentaculaire
5. sorti d'un conte de fées
6. malfaisant
7. moellon du Kent [calcaire gris-bleu]
8. de tourelles et de cheminées, de mâts et de murs crénelés
9. qui s'élançait au-dessus
10. sentier sommaire et boueux
11. volontairement
12. rébarbative
13. une herse en acier
14. maigres et rabougris
15. d'au moins 4,50 m
16. distinguai
17. donnait une idée de
18. pâtures et versants
19. mauvais décor
20. descendu sur scène
21. ancien
22. relents de mort et de décomposition y persistaient, accablant
23. Il me fut très pénible
24. me gagnant par les pieds
25. cachée

I think it is true to say that I broke the law[1] at least three times in the company of Sherlock Holmes, always for the best of reasons, but this was the high point of my criminal career. Strangely, I was not even slightly nervous. It did not occur to me that anything could possibly go wrong. All my thoughts were focused on the plight[2] of my friend.

I knocked on a door which stood inconspicuously[3] beside the outer gate and it was opened almost at once by a surprisingly bluff and even jovial[4] officer, dressed in dark blue tunic and trousers with a bunch[5] of keys hanging from a wide, leather belt[6]. 'Come in, sir. Come in. It's more pleasant in than out and there's not many days you could say *that* with any truth[7].' I watched him lock the door behind us, then followed him across a courtyard to a second gate, smaller, but no less secure[8], than the first. I was already aware of an eerie[9] silence inside the prison. A ragged, black crow perched[10] on the branch of a tree but there was no other sign of life. The light was fading rapidly but as yet no lamps had been lit[11] and I had a sense of shadows within shadows[12], of a world with almost no colour at all.

We had entered a corridor with an open door to one side, and it was through here that I was taken, into a small room with a desk, two chairs and a single window looking directly on to a brick wall. To one side stood a cabinet[13] with perhaps fifty keys suspended on hooks[14]. A large clock faced me and I noticed the second hand[15] moved ponderously[16], pausing between each movement, as if to emphasise[17] the slow passage of time for all those who had come this way. A man sat beneath it. He was dressed similarly to[18] the officer who had met me, but his uniform had a few trimmings of gold[19], on his cap[20] and shoulders, denoting his senior rank[21]. He was elderly, with grey hair cut short and steely[22] eyes.

1. j'ai enfreint la loi
2. tout entières à la détresse
3. à peine visible
4. franc, voire enjoué
5. trousseau
6. ceinture
7. et que ce soit vrai
8. pas moins sécurisée
9. inquiétant
10. Une pauvre corneille était perchée
11. aucune lampe n'était encore allumée
12. une impression d'ombres parmi les ombres
13. D'un côté, il y avait un placard
14. des crochets
15. trotteuse
16. pesamment
17. pour souligner
18. tout comme
19. parements dorés
20. képi
21. indiquant un grade supérieur
22. gris acier

As he saw me, he scrambled to his feet[1] and came round from behind the desk.

'Dr Watson?'

'Yes.'

'My name is Hawkins. I am the chief warder[2]. You have come to see Mr Sherlock Holmes?'

'Yes.' I uttered the word with a sudden sense of dread[3].

'I am sorry to have to inform you that he was taken ill[4] this morning. I can assure you that we have done everything we can to accommodate him[5] in a manner appropriate to a man of his distinction, despite the very serious crime of which he is accused. He has been kept away[6] from the other prisoners. I have personally visited him on several occasions and have had the pleasure of conversing[7] with him. His illness came suddenly and he was given treatment at once[8].'

'What is wrong with him?'

'We have no idea. He took his lunch at eleven o'clock and rang the bell for assistance[9] immediately after. My officers found him doubled up on the floor[10] of his cell in evident pain[11].'

I felt an ice-cold tremor[12] in the very depth of my heart. It was exactly what I had been fearing. 'Where is he now?' I asked.

'He is in the infirmary. Our medical officer, Dr Trevelyan, has a number of private rooms[13] which he reserves for desperate cases. After examining Mr Holmes, he insisted on moving him there.'

'I must see him at once,' I said. 'I am a medical man myself ...'

'Of course, Dr Watson. I have been waiting to take you there[14] now.'

But before we could leave, there was a movement behind us and a man whom I knew all too well appeared, blocking our way. If Inspector Harriman had been told the news[15], he did not look surprised

1. se leva précipitamment
2. gardien chef
3. appréhension
4. tombé malade
5. pour l'installer
6. tenu à l'écart
7. de m'entretenir
8. il a été soigné aussitôt
9. a sonné pour demander de l'aide
10. se tordant sur le sol
11. visiblement en proie à des douleurs
12. frisson glacial
13. chambres particulières
14. Je vous attendais pour vous y conduire
15. avait appris la nouvelle

by it. In fact, his attitude was quite languid, leaning against the door frame, with his attention half-fixed on a gold ring[1] on his middle finger[2]. He was dressed in black as always, carrying a black walking stick. 'So what's this all about[3], Hawkins?' he asked. 'Sherlock Holmes ill?'

'Seriously ill,' Hawkins declared.

'I am distraught[4] to hear it!' Harriman straightened up. 'You're sure he's not deceiving you[5]? When I saw him this morning, he was in perfect health.'

'Both my medical officer and I have examined him and I assure you, sir, that he is gravely stricken[6]. We are just on our way to see him.'

'Then I will accompany you.'

'I must protest—'

'Mr Holmes is my prisoner and the subject[7] of my investigation. You can protest all you like[8], but I will have my way[9].' He smiled malevolently. Hawkins glanced at me and I could see that, decent man though he was, he dared not argue[10].

The three of us set off through the depths[11] of the prison. Such was my state of mind that I can recall[12] few of the details, although my overall impressions[13] were of heavy flagstones[14], of gates that creaked and clashed[15] as they were unlocked and locked behind us, of barred windows too small and too high up to provide a view and of doors ... so many doors, one after another, each identical, each sealing up[16] some small facet of human misery[17]. The prison was surprisingly warm and had a strange smell, a mixture of oatmeal[18], old clothes and soap. We saw a few warders standing guard[19] at various intersections, but no prisoners apart from two very old men struggling past[20] with a basket of laundry[21]. 'Some are in the exercise yard[22], some on the treadwheel or in the oakum shed[23],' Hawkins replied to a question I had not asked. 'The day begins early and ends early here.'

1. une bague en or
2. majeur
3. Alors, de quoi s'agit-il
4. Je suis bouleversé
5. qu'il ne simule pas
6. très mal en point
7. l'objet
8. autant que vous voudrez
9. il en sera fait comme je l'entends
10. malgré sa bonne volonté, il n'osait pas protester
11. dans les entrailles
12. me rappelle
13. impression générale
14. d'imposantes dalles
15. grinçaient et claquaient
16. chacune renfermant
17. une facette de la misère humaine
18. mêlant le gruau d'avoine
19. montant la garde
20. qui nous croisèrent péniblement
21. panier de linge sale
22. cour
23. hangar

'If Holmes has been poisoned, he must be sent immediately to a hospital,' I said.

'Poison?' Harriman had overheard me[1]. 'Who said anything about poison?'

'Dr Trevelyan does indeed suspect severe food poisoning[2],' returned Hawkins. 'But he is a good man. He will have done everything within his power ...'

We had reached the end of the central block from which the four main wings stretched out[3] like the blades of a windmill[4] and found ourselves in what must be a recreation area[5], paved with Yorkshire stone, with a lofty ceiling[6] and a corkscrew metal staircase[7] leading to a gallery that ran the full length of the room above. A net had been stretched[8] across our heads so that nothing could be thrown down[9]. A few men, dressed in grey army cloth[10], were sorting through[11] a pile of infants' clothes which were heaped up[12] on a table in front of them. 'For the children of St Emmanuel Hospital,' Hawkins said. 'We make them here.' We passed through an archway and up a matted[13] staircase. By now I had no idea where I was and would never have been able to find my way out again[14]. I thought of the key that I was still carrying, concealed in the book. Even if I had been able to deliver it into Holmes's hands, what good would it have been? He would have needed a dozen keys and a detailed map to get out of this place.

There was a pair of glass-panelled doors[15] ahead of us. Once again, these had to be unlocked, but then swung open into a very bare, very clean room with no windows but skylights up above[16] and candles already lit on two central tables, for it was almost dark. There were eight beds, facing each other in two rows of four, the coverlets blue and white check[17], the pillowcases striped calico[18]. The room reminded me at once of my old army hospital where I had often watched men die with the same discip-

1. m'avait entendu
2. grave intoxication alimentaire
3. rayonnaient
4. ailes d'un moulin à vent
5. une salle de loisirs
6. une belle hauteur de plafond
7. un escalier métallique en colimaçon
8. Un filet avait été tendu
9. jeté en bas
10. de treillis gris
11. triaient
12. entassés
13. recouvert d'un tapis
14. retrouver la sortie
15. portes vitrées
16. des lucarnes très hautes
17. les dessus de lit étaient à carreaux bleus et blancs
18. les taies d'oreiller en calicot rayé

line and lack of complaint[1] that had been expected of them in the field[2]. Only two of the beds were occupied. One contained a shrivelled[3], bald man whose eyes I could see were already focusing on the next world[4]. A hunched-up shape[5] lay, shivering, in the other. But it was too small to be Holmes.

A man dressed in a patched and worn[6] frock coat rose up from where he had been working and came over to greet us[7]. From the very first[8] I thought I recognised him, just as – it occurred to me now – his name had also been familiar to me. He was pale and emaciated, with sandy whiskers[9] that seemed to be dying on his cheeks and cumbersome spectacles[10]. I would have said he was in his early forties but the experiences of his life wore heavily upon him, giving him a pinched, nervous disposition[11] and ageing him[12]. His slender[13], white hands were folded across his wrists. He had been writing and his pen had leaked[14]. There were blotches of ink[15] on his forefinger and thumb[16].

'Mr Hawkins,' he said, addressing the chief warder. 'I have nothing further to report to you[17], sir, except that I fear the worst[18].'

'This is Dr John Watson,' Hawkins said.

'Dr Trevelyan.' He shook my hand. 'It is a pleasure to make your acquaintance, although I would have asked for happier circumstances.'

I was certain I knew the man. But from the way he had spoken and the firmness of his handshake[19], he was making it clear that, even if we were not meeting for the first time, this was the impression he wished to give.

'Is it food poisoning?' Harriman demanded. He had not troubled[20] to introduce himself.

'I am quite positive that[21] poison of one sort or another is responsible,' Dr Trevelyan replied. 'As to how it came to be administered[22], that is not for me to say.'

1. le même courage muet
2. au combat
3. ridé
4. regardaient déjà vers l'au-delà
5. Une forme recroquevillée
6. rapiécé et usé
7. vint nous accueillir
8. D'emblée,
9. portait des favoris blond-roux
10. d'encombrantes lunettes
11. l'avaient marqué au point qu'il était hagard et nerveux
12. le vieillissant
13. fines
14. fui
15. des taches d'encre
16. son index et son pouce
17. rien de plus à vous communiquer
18. je crains le pire
19. la fermeté de sa poignée de main
20. n'avait pas pris la peine
21. Je suis formel :
22. il a pu être administré

'Administered?'

'All the prisoners in the wing[1] eat the same food. Only he has become ill.'

'Are you suggesting foul play?[2]'

'I have said what I have said, sir.'

'Well, I don't believe a word of it. I can tell you, doctor, that I was rather expecting something of this sort. Where is Mr Holmes?'

Trevelyan hesitated and the warder stepped forward[3]. 'This is Inspector Harriman, Dr Trevelyan. He is in charge of your patient.'

'I am in charge of my patient while he is in my infirmary,' the doctor retorted[4]. 'But there is no reason why you should not see him, although I must ask you not to disturb him. I gave him a sedative and he may well be asleep. He is in a side-room[5]. I thought it better that he be kept apart from the other prisoners.'

'Then let us waste no more time.'

'Rivers!' Trevelyan called out to[6] a lanky, round-shouldered fellow[7] who had been almost invisible but was sweeping the floor in one corner. He was wearing the uniform of a male nurse[8] rather than that of a prisoner. 'The keys ...'

'Yes, Dr Trevelyan.' Rivers lumbered over to[9] the desk, took up a key-chain[10] and carried it over to an arched door[11] set on the far side[12] of the room. He appeared to be lame, dragging one leg behind him[13]. He was sullen[14] and rough-looking, with unruly ginger hair spilling down[15] to his shoulders. He stopped in front of the door and, taking his time, fitted a key into the lock[16].

'Rivers is my orderly[17],' Trevelyan explained in a low voice. 'He's a good man, but simple[18]. He takes charge of[19] the infirmary at night.'

'Has he been in communication with Holmes?' Harriman asked.

1. de cette aile
2. Insinuez-vous qu'il y a eu tentative de meurtre ?
3. s'avança
4. rétorqua
5. une chambre à part
6. interpella
7. type dégingandé, aux épaules tombantes,
8. un uniforme d'infirmier
9. se dirigea pesamment vers
10. récupéra un trousseau de clefs
11. porte voûtée
12. à l'autre bout
13. boiter, traînant la patte
14. maussade
15. ses cheveux roux indisciplinés cascadant
16. inséra une clef dans la serrure
17. aide-infirmier
18. simplet
19. veille sur

1. communique rarement
2. les gorges basculer
3. verrous externes
4. qu'il fallut tirer
5. monacale
6. des murs bruts
7. des latrines
8. Il arracha les couvertures.
9. Il n'y avait nulle part où se cacher.
10. toujours en place
11. tour de passe-passe
12. rugit-il
13. regardai à l'intérieur

'Rivers is seldom in communication[1] with anyone, Mr Harriman. Holmes himself has not uttered a word since he was brought here.'

At last Rivers turned the key. I heard the tumblers fall[2] as the lock connected. There were also two bolts on the outside[3] that had to be drawn back[4] before the door could be opened to reveal a small room, almost monastic[5] with plain walls[6], a square window, a bed and a privy[7].

The bed was empty.

Harriman plunged inside. He tore off the covers.[8] He knelt down and looked under the bed. There was nowhere to hide.[9] The bars on the window were still in place[10]. 'Is this some sort of trick[11]?' he roared[12]. 'Where is he? What have you done with him?'

I moved forward and looked in[13]. There could be no doubting it. The cell was empty. Sherlock Holmes had disappeared.

SIXTEEN

The Disappearance

Harriman rose to his feet[1] and almost fell upon[2] Dr Trevelyan. For once his carefully cultivated *sang-froid* had deserted him. 'What game is going on[3] here? ' he cried. 'What do you think you're doing?'

'I have no idea ...' the hapless[4] doctor began.

'I beg of you to show some restraint[5], Inspector Harriman.' The chief warder imposed himself[6] between the two men, taking charge. 'Mr Holmes was in this room?'

'Yes, sir,' Trevelyan replied.

'And it was locked and bolted[7], as I saw just now, from the outside?'

'Indeed so, sir. It is a prison regulation[8].'

'Who was the last to see him?'

'That would have been[9] Rivers. He took him a mug[10] of water, upon my request[11].'

'I took it but he didn't drink it,' the orderly grumbled. 'He didn't say nothing, neither. He just lay there.'

'Asleep?' Harriman walked up to Dr Trevelyan until the two of them were but inches apart[12]. 'Are you really telling me he was ill, doctor, or was it perhaps, as I believed from the outset[13], that he was dissembling[14] – first so that he would be brought here, second so that he could choose his moment to walk out[15]?'

1. se releva
2. faillit se jeter sur
3. À quoi joue-t-on
4. malheureux
5. Je vous prie de vous modérer
6. s'interposa
7. fermée à clef et verrouillée
8. règle pénitentiaire
9. Ce doit être
10. grand verre
11. à ma demande
12. ne plus être qu'à quelques centimètres
13. dès le début
14. qu'il simulait
15. le bon moment pour s'enfuir

'As to the first[1], he was most certainly ill,' replied Trevelyan. 'At least, he had a high fever, his pupils were dilated and the sweat was pouring from his brow[2]. I can attest to that[3], for I examined him myself. As to the second, he could not possibly have walked out of here, as you suggest. Look at the door, for heaven's sake! It was locked from the outside. There is but one key[4] and it has never left my desk. There are the bolts, which were fastened[5] until Rivers drew them back just now. And even if, by some bizarre and inexplicable means[6], he had been able to leave the cell, where do you think he would go? To begin with, he would have had to cross this ward[7] and I have been at my desk all afternoon. The door through which you three gentlemen entered was locked. And there must be a dozen more[8] locks and bolts between here and the front gate. Are you to tell me that he somehow spirited himself through all of them[9] too?'

'It is certainly true that walking out of Holloway would be nothing short of impossible[10],' Hawkins agreed.

'Nobody can leave this place,' muttered Rivers, and he seemed to smirk as if at some private joke. 'Unless his name is[11] Wood. Now, he left here only this afternoon. Not on his own two legs though, and I don't think anyone would have had a mind to ask him[12] where *he* was going, nor when he was coming back.'

'Wood? Who is Wood?' Harriman asked.

'Jonathan Wood was here in the infirmary,' Trevelyan replied. 'And you're wrong to make light of it[13], Rivers. He died last night and was carried out in a coffin[14] not an hour ago.'

'A coffin? Are you telling me that a closed coffin was taken from this room?' I could see the detective working things out[15] and realised, as did he[16], that it presented[17] the most obvious, indeed the only

1. En ce qui concerne le premier point
2. la sueur ruisselait de son front
3. le certifier
4. Il n'y a qu'une clef
5. mis
6. moyens
7. traverser cette salle
8. de plus
9. qu'il les aurait tous traversés par enchantement
10. tout bonnement impossible
11. À moins de s'appeler
12. n'aurait pensé à lui demander
13. vous avez tort de le prendre à la légère
14. emporté dans un cercueil
15. commencer à comprendre
16. me rendis compte, comme lui
17. cela constituait

method for Holmes's escape[1]. He turned on the orderly. 'Was the coffin here when you took in the water?' he demanded.

'It might have been.'

'Did you leave Holmes on his own[2], even for a few seconds?'

'No, sir. Not for one second. I never took my eyes off him.[3]' The orderly shuffled on his feet[4]. 'Well, maybe I attended to[5] Collins when he had his fit[6].'

'What are you saying, Rivers?' Trevelyan cried.

'I opened the door. I went in. He was sound asleep[7] on the bed. Then Collins began his coughing[8]. I put the mug down and ran out to him.'

'And what then? Did you see Holmes again?'

'No, sir. I settled Collins.[9] Then I went back and locked the door.'

There was a long silence. We all stood there, staring at each other[10] as if waiting to see who would dare to speak first[11].

It was Harriman. 'Where is the coffin?' he exclaimed.

'It will have been[12] carried outside,' Trevelyan replied. 'There will be a wagon[13] waiting to carry it to the undertaker[14] in Muswell Hill.' He grabbed[15] his coat. 'It may not be too late. If it's still there, we can intercept it before it leaves.'

I will never forget the progress that we made through[16] the prison. Hawkins went first[17] with a furious Harriman at his side. Trevelyan and Rivers came next[18]. I followed last[19], the book and the key still in my hand. How ridiculous they seemed now, for even if I had been able to deliver them to my friend, along with a ladder and a length of rope[20], he would never have been able to get out of this place on his own. It was only because of Hawkins, signalling[21] at the various guards, that we ourselves were able to leave. The doors were unlocked and swung open, one after another. Nobody stood in our way.

1. seul mode d'évasion possible pour Holmes
2. seul
3. Je ne l'ai pas quitté des yeux.
4. passa d'un pied sur l'autre
5. sauf peut-être pour aller m'occuper de
6. sa crise
7. dormait profondément
8. s'est mis à tousser
9. J'ai calmé
10. à nous dévisager
11. lequel oserait parler en premier
12. Il a dû être
13. un chariot
14. aux pompes funèbres
15. saisit
16. notre parcours à travers
17. était en tête
18. suivaient
19. Je fermais la marche
20. avec une échelle et de la corde
21. qui faisait signe

We took a different path to that which I had come originally, for this time we passed a laundry with men sweating at giant tubs[1] and another room filled with boilers[2] and convoluted metal tubes[3] that supplied the prison's heating[4], finally crossing a smaller, grassy[5] courtyard and arriving at what was evidently a side entrance[6]. It was only here that a guard attempted to block our passage, demanding our letters of authority[7].

'Don't be a damn fool[8],' Harriman snapped[9]. 'Do you not recognise your own chief warder?'

'Open the gate!' Hawkins added. 'There's not a moment to lose.'

The guard did as he was bidden[10] and the five of us passed through.

And yet, even as we went, I found myself reflecting[11] on the number of strange circumstances that had come together[12] to effect my friend's escape[13]. He had feigned illness[14] and managed to fool a trained doctor[15]. Well, that was easy enough. He had done much the same to me. But he had inveigled himself[16] into a room in the infirmary at exactly the same time as a coffin had been delivered and had, moreover, been able to count on an open door, a coughing fit[17] and the clumsiness[18] of a mentally backward[19] orderly. It all seemed too good to be true. Not, of course, that I cared one way or another.[20] If Holmes had truly found a miraculous way out of this place, I would be nothing but overjoyed[21]. But even so I was sure that something was wrong, that we had leapt to a false conclusion[22] and, perhaps, that was exactly what he had intended.

We found ourselves in a broad, rutted avenue[23] that ran along the side of the prison with the high wall on one side and a line of trees on the other. Harriman let out a cry and pointed[24]. A wagon stood waiting while two men loaded[25] a box into the back: from the size and the shape it was evidently a make-

1. suant devant des baquets gigantesques
2. de chaudières
3. de tuyaux métalliques biscornus
4. le chauffage
5. herbeuse
6. une entrée latérale
7. nos laissez-passer
8. Ne soyez pas idiot
9. aboya Harriman
10. obtempéra
11. je réfléchissais
12. réunies
13. pour permettre l'évasion de mon ami
14. feint d'être malade
15. duper un docteur chevronné
16. il avait rusé pour se trouver
17. accès de toux
18. maladresse
19. un peu attardé
20. Non que cela m'importât de toute façon.
21. fou de joie
22. nous avions tiré une conclusion hâtive
23. large avenue défoncée
24. poussa un cri en montrant quelque chose
25. chargeaient

shift coffin[1]. I must confess that I felt a moment of relief[2] at the sight of it. I would have given almost anything right then to see Sherlock Holmes and to reassure myself that his illness had indeed been feigned and not the result of deliberate poisoning. But as we hurried forward, my brief euphoria was replaced by utter dismay[3]. If Holmes were found and apprehended, he would be dragged back into the prison and Harriman would make sure that he was never given a second opportunity and that he remained well beyond my reach[4].

'Hold there![5]' cried he. He strode up to the two men who had manhandled[6] the box into a diagonal position and were holding it, about to lever it[7] into the wagon. 'Lower the coffin back to the ground![8] I wish to examine it.' The men were rough and grimy labourers[9], a father and son from the look of them, and they glanced at each other quizzically before they obeyed[10]. The coffin lay flat upon the gravel[11]. 'Open it!'

This time the men hesitated – to carry a dead body was one thing[12] but to look on it quite another[13].

'It's all right,' Trevelyan assured them, and the strange thing is that it was at that very moment that I realised how I knew him, where we had met before.

His full name was Percy Trevelyan and he had come to our Baker Street lodgings six or seven years before, urgently in need[14] of my friend's services. I remembered now that there had been a patient, Blessington, who had behaved in a mysterious fashion[15] and who had eventually been found hanged[16] in his room ... the police had assumed that it was suicide, an opinion with which Holmes had at once disagreed. It was strange that I had not recognised him immediately for I had admired Trevelyan and had studied his work on nervous diseases[17] – he had won the Bruce Pinkerton prize[18], no less[19]. But circumstances had not been kind to him then[20], and

1. un cercueil de fortune
2. soulagement
3. consternation totale
4. hors de ma portée
5. Un instant !
6. placé
7. la hisser
8. Reposez le cercueil par terre !
9. ouvriers frustes et crasseux
10. d'un air perplexe avant d'obéir
11. était maintenant à plat sur le gravier
12. c'était une chose de porter un cadavre
13. en était une autre
14. ayant besoin de toute urgence
15. s'était comporté curieusement
16. qu'on avait retrouvé pendu
17. maladies nerveuses
18. le prix
19. rien que ça
20. ne l'avaient pas épargné, alors

had clearly become worse since, for he had aged considerably, with a look of exhaustion[1] and frustration that had changed his appearance. As I recalled, he had not worn spectacles when we first met. His health had clearly deteriorated. But it was certainly he, reduced to the role of prison doctor, a position that was well beneath a man of his capabilities[2], and it occurred to me, with a sense of excitement that I was careful to conceal[3], that he must have colluded[4] in this attempted escape[5]. He certainly owed Holmes a debt of gratitude[6] and why else[7] would he have pretended not to know me? Now I understood how Holmes had got into the coffin in the first place[8]. Trevelyan had placed his orderly in charge quite deliberately. Why else would he have trusted[9] a man who was evidently unfit for any such responsibility[10]? The coffin would have been placed nearby. Everything would have been planned in advance. The pity of it was[11] that the two labourers had been so slow in their work[12]. They should have been half-way to[13] Muswell Hill, by now. Trevelyan's assistance had been to no avail[14].

One of the labourers had produced a crowbar[15]. I watched as it was placed under the lid[16]. He pressed down[17] and the lid of the coffin was torn free, the wood splintering[18]. The two of them stepped forward and lifted it off[19]. As one[20], Harriman, Hawkins, Trevelyan and I moved closer.

'That's him,' Rivers grunted[21]. 'That's Jonathan Wood.'

It was true. The corpse that lay staring up[22] was a grey-faced, worn-out[23] figure who was definitely not Sherlock Holmes and who was definitely[24] dead.

Trevelyan was the first to recover his composure. 'Of course it's Wood,' he exclaimed. 'I told you. He died in the night – a coronary[25] infection.' He nodded at the undertakers. 'You may close the coffin and take him up.'

1. d'épuisement
2. un poste bien en dessous de ses capacités
3. je pris soin de cacher
4. être complice
5. tentative d'évasion
6. devait une grande reconnaissance à Holmes
7. sinon, pourquoi
8. pour commencer
9. fait confiance à
10. inapte
11. Quel dommage
12. si lents à accomplir leur tâche
13. à mi-chemin de
14. vaine
15. pied-de-biche
16. sous le couvercle
17. Il appuya
18. céda, le bois se fissurant
19. l'enlevèrent
20. Comme un seul homme
21. grogna
22. le regard fixant le ciel
23. éreinté, au visage gris
24. bel et bien
25. coronarienne

'But where is Sherlock Holmes?' Hawkins cried.

'He cannot have left the prison!' Harriman replied. 'Somehow he tricked us, but he must still be inside, waiting his opportunity[1]. We must raise the alarm[2] and search the place from top to bottom[3].'

'But that will take all night!'

Harriman's face was as colourless as his hair. He spun on his heel, almost kicking out in his vexation[4]. 'I don't care if it takes all week! The man must be found.'

He wasn't. Two days later, I was alone in Holmes's lodgings, reading a report of the events that I had myself witnessed.

> Police are still unable to explain[5] the mysterious disappearance of the well-known consulting detective Sherlock Holmes, who was being held at Holloway Prison in connection with the[6] murder of a young woman in Coppergate Square. Inspector J. Harriman who is in charge of the inquiry has accused the prison authorities of a dereliction of duty[7], a charge that has been strenuously denied[8]. The fact remains that Mr Holmes somehow managed to spirit himself out[9] of a locked cell and through a dozen locked doors in a manner that would appear to deny the laws of nature[10] and the police are offering a reward of £50 to anyone who can supply information leading to his discovery and apprehension[11].

Mrs Hudson had responded[12] to this strange state of affairs[13] with a remarkable degree of indifference. She had, of course, read the newspaper accounts[14] and had spoken but one brief sentence when she had served my breakfast. 'It's a lot of nonsense[15], Dr Watson.' She seemed personally offended[16] and it is somehow comforting to me[17], all these years later, to

1. à guetter le bon moment
2. donner l'alerte
3. de fond en comble
4. Il fit volte-face, tapant presque du pied tant il était excédé
5. ne s'explique toujours pas
6. dans le cadre du
7. manquement au devoir
8. vigoureusement démentie
9. s'évader
10. défier les lois de la nature
11. permettant de le retrouver et de l'appréhender
12. réagi
13. état de choses
14. récits dans les journaux
15. un tissu d'absurdités
16. offensée
17. rassurant pour moi

1. une foi absolue
2. pensionnaire
3. supporté
4. toutes sortes de bizarreries
5. son violon
6. crises dues à
7. accès
8. généreusement
9. Bien qu'elle apparaisse ici et là dans mes récits
10. était devenue propriétaire
11. ce qui lui était arrivé
12. J'aurais dû plus parler avec elle
13. et moins la considérer comme faisant partie des meubles
14. séjour
15. un pas
16. je n'avais pas prêté attention à ces bruits
17. je ne m'attendais pas à
18. d'un regard ahuri
19. emmitouflé dans
20. lui couvrant le menton
21. rondelet
22. en se débarrassant
23. vêtements d'extérieur
24. rafraîchit la mémoire

reflect that she had complete faith[1] in her most famous lodger[2], but then she perhaps knew him better than anyone and had put up with[3] all manner of peculiarities[4] during the lengthy period that he was with her, including desperate and often undesirable visitors, the violin-playing[5] late into the night, the occasional seizures induced by[6] liquid cocaine, the long bouts[7] of melancholy, the bullets fired into the wallpaper and even the pipe smoke. True, Holmes paid her handsomely[8], but she hardly ever complained and remained loyal to the end. Although she flits in and out of my pages[9], I actually knew very little about her, not even how she came to occupy the property[10] at 221 Baker Street (I believe she inherited it from her husband, although what became of him[11] I cannot say). After Holmes left, she lived alone. I wish I had conversed[12] with her more and taken her for granted a little less[13].

At any event, my sojourn[14] was interrupted by the arrival of that lady, and with her, another visitor. I had indeed heard the doorbell ring and a footfall[15] on the stair but preoccupied as I was, these sounds had barely registered[16] so I was unprepared for[17] the arrival of the Reverend Charles Fitzsimmons, the principal of Chorley Grange School, and greeted him, I am afraid, with a look of blank puzzlement[18], as if we had never met before. The fact that he was wrapped in[19] a thick black coat with a hat and scarf across his chin[20] did help to make a stranger of him. His clothes made him look even more rotund[21] than he had before.

'You will forgive me interrupting you, Dr Watson,' he said, divesting himself[22] of these outer garments[23] and revealing the clerical collar which would have at once jogged my memory[24]. 'I was unsure whether to come but felt I must ... I must! But first I need to ask you, sir. This extraordinary business with Mr Sherlock Holmes, is it true?'

'It is true that Holmes is suspected of a crime of which he is completely innocent,' I replied.

'But I read now that he has escaped, that he has managed to spring himself from the confinement of the law[1].'

'Yes, Mr Fitzsimmons. He has also managed to evade his accusers[2] in a manner which is a source of mystery, even to me.'

'Do you know where he is?'

'I have no idea.'

'And the child, Ross, do you have any news of him?'

'In what sense?[3]'

'Have you found him yet?'

Evidently, Fitzsimmons had somehow missed the reports of the boy's terrible death – although, it occurred to me, sensational though they had been, Ross had not actually been named[4]. It therefore fell to me[5] to tell him the truth. 'I am afraid we were too late. We did find Ross, but he was dead.'

'Dead? How did it happen?'

'Somebody had beaten him very badly. He was left to die by the river, close to Southwark Bridge.'

The headmaster's eyes fluttered[6] and he fell heavily into a chair. 'Dear God in Heaven![7]' he exclaimed. 'Who would do such a thing to a child? What wickedness is there[8] in this world? Then my visit to you is redundant[9], Dr Watson. I thought I might be able to help you find him. I had come upon a clue[10] – or rather, my dear wife, Joanna, had discovered it. I brought it to you in the hope that you might know the whereabouts of[11] Mr Holmes and pass it to him[12] and that even given his own exigencies[13], he might ...' His voice trailed off.[14] 'But it is too late. The child should never have left Chorley Grange. I knew no good would come of it.'

'What is this clue?' I asked.

'I have it with me. It was, as I say, my wife who found it in the dormitory. She was turning the mat-

1. se soustraire à la réclusion pénale
2. échapper à ses accusateurs
3. De quel point de vue ?
4. le nom de Ross n'avait pas été cité
5. Il m'incomba donc
6. cligna des paupières
7. Dieu du ciel !
8. vilenie règne
9. superflue
10. J'étais tombé sur un indice
11. où se trouvait
12. le lui transmettre
13. qu'en dépit de sa situation critique
14. Il n'acheva pas sa phrase.

1. de temps à autre
2. les aérer et faire une fumigation
3. des poux
4. nous leur livrons un combat permanent
5. cahier
6. couverture grossière, pâlie et froissée
7. d'une écriture enfantine
8. entrepris
9. qu'il a négligé ses exercices
10. brouillon
11. à gribouiller
12. important
13. une feuille bien pliée
14. il la déplia et l'étala
15. une publicité, un dépliant bon marché
16. fleuri à une époque
17. un tatou
18. merveilles
19. nains, jongleurs
20. squelette vivant
21. Un penny l'entrée

tresses – we do it now and then[1] to air and fumigate them[2]. Some of the boys have lice[3] ... we wage a constant war against them[4]. At any event, the bed occupied by Ross is now taken by another child, but there was a copybook[5] concealed there.' Fitzsimmons took out a thin book with a rough cover, faded and crumpled[6]. There was a name written in a childish hand[7], in pencil on the front.

Ross Dixon

'Ross could not read or write when he came to us, but we had endeavoured[8] to teach him the rudiments. Each child in the school is given a copybook and a pencil. You will see inside his that he has forsaken his exercises[9]. It is all very messy[10]. He seems to have passed much of his time scribbling[11]. But on examining it, we discovered this and it seemed to us to have significance[12].'

He had opened the book in the middle to show a sheet of paper, neatly folded[13] and slipped inside as if the intention had been deliberately to conceal it. Taking it out, he unfolded it and spread it[14] on the table for me to see. It was an advertisement, a cheap flyer[15] for an attraction of the sort that I knew had once sprung up[16] around such areas as Islington and Cheapside but which had since become rarer. The text was decorated by images of a snake, a monkey and an armadillo[17]. It read:

DR SILKIN'S HOUSE OF WONDERS[18]
MIDGETS, JUGGLERS[19], THE FAT LADY
AND THE LIVING SKELETON[20].
A cabinet of curiosities from the four corners
of the globe
ONE PENNY ENTRANCE[21]
Jackdaw Lane, Whitechapel

'I would, of course, discourage my boys from ever entering such a place,' the Reverend Fitzsimmons said. 'Freak shows[1], music halls, one penny gaffs[2] ... it astonishes me that a great city such as London will tolerate[3] such entertainments[4], where everything that is vulgar and unnatural is celebrated[5]. The lessons of Sodom and Gomorrah[6] spring to mind[7]. I say this to you, Dr Watson, as it may be that Ross concealed this advertisement for no other reason[8] than that he knew it was against the very spirit of Chorley Grange. It may have been an act of defiance[9]. He was, as my wife told you, a very wilful[10] boy—'

'But it may also have a connection for him,' I broke in. 'After he left you, he sought refuge with[11] a family in King's Cross and also with his sister. But we have no idea where he was before. It could be that he fell in with this crowd[12].'

'Exactly. I feel sure it is worthy of investigation[13] which is why[14] I brought it to you.' Fitzsimmons collected his things[15] and got to his feet. 'Is there any possibility that you will be in communication with Mr Holmes?'

'I am still hoping that he will contact me in some way[16].'

'Then perhaps you will see what he makes of it. Thank you for your time, Dr Watson. I am very, very shocked about young Ross. We will pray for him in the school chapel this Sunday. No. There is no need to show me out[17]. I will find my way.'

He took up[18] his coat and scarf and left the room. I stared at the page, allowing my eyes to travel across[19] the gaudy lettering[20] and the crude[21] illustrations. I think I must have read it two or three times before I saw what should have been obvious to me[22] from the start. But there was no mistaking it[23]. Dr Silkin's House of Wonders. Jackdaw Lane. Whitechapel.

I had just found the House of Silk.

1. Des exhibitions de monstres
2. des foires à deux sous
3. tolère
4. divertissements
5. vulgaire et contre nature est mis en avant
6. Sodome et Gomorrhe
7. viennent à l'esprit
8. pour la simple raison
9. de défi
10. obstiné
11. s'est réfugié chez
12. qu'il a fréquenté ces gens
13. que cela mérite d'être élucidé,
14. c'est pourquoi
15. ramassa ses affaires
16. d'une manière ou d'une autre
17. me raccompagner
18. reprit
19. balayant du regard
20. caractères tapageurs
21. grossières
22. aurait dû me sauter aux yeux
23. on ne pouvait s'y tromper

SEVENTEEN

A Message

My wife returned to London the following day. She had sent me a telegram from Camberwell to inform me of her arrival and I was waiting for her at Holborn Viaduct when her train drew in[1]. I have to say that I would not have left Baker Street for any other reason. I was still certain that Holmes would attempt to reach me[2] and dreaded the idea of[3] his making his way to his lodgings[4], with all the dangers that would entail[5], only to find me not in[6]. But nor could I consider allowing Mary to cross the city unattended[7]. One of her greatest virtues was her tolerance, the way she put up with my long absences in the company of Sherlock Holmes. Never once did she complain, although I know she worried that I was putting myself in danger, and I owed it to her now to explain[8] what had happened while she had been away and to inform her that, regretfully[9], it might be a while yet before we could be permanently reunited. And I had missed her. I looked forward[10] to seeing her again.

It was now the second week in December and, after the bad weather that had begun the month, the sun was out and although it was very cold, everything was ablaze with a sense of prosperity[11] and good cheer[12]. The pavements were almost invisible beneath the bustle[13] of families arriving from the countryside and bringing with them wide-eyed children in numbers[14] that might have populated a small city themselves. The ice-rakers[15] and the

1. entra en gare
2. me joindre
3. redoutais
4. que, parvenu à rentrer chez lui
5. que cela supposait
6. il ne m'y trouve pas
7. laisser Mary traverser la ville seule
8. je me devais de lui expliquer
9. malheureusement
10. Il me tardait
11. éclatait la prospérité
12. la bonne humeur
13. la cohue
14. dans des proportions
15. personnes récupérant la glace [avec de longs râteaux]

crossing-sweepers[1] were out. The sweetmeat and grocer shops[2] were gloriously festooned[3]. Every window carried advertisements for goose clubs, roast beef clubs and pudding clubs[4] and the very air was filled with the aroma of[5] burned sugar and mincemeat[6]. As I climbed down from my brougham[7] and made my way into the station, pushing against the crowd[8], I reflected on the circumstances that had alienated me[9] from all this activity, from the day-to-day[10] pleasures of London in the festive season. That was perhaps the disadvantage of my association with Sherlock Holmes. It drew me into dark places where, in truth, nobody would choose to go.

The station was no less crowded[11]. The trains were on time[12], the platforms[13] filled with young men carrying parcels[14], packages and hampers[15], scurrying around as excitably[16] as Alice's white rabbit[17]. Mary's train had already arrived and I was briefly unable to locate her[18] as the doors opened and yet more souls poured[19] into the metropolis[20]. But then I saw her and, as she climbed down from her carriage, an event occurred that caused me a moment of disquiet[21]. A man appeared, shuffling across[22] the platform as if about to accost her. I could only see him from the back[23] and, apart from an ill-fitting[24] jacket and red hair, would have been unable to identify him again. He seemed to speak briefly to her, then boarded[25] the train, disappearing from sight. But perhaps I was mistaken. As I approached her she saw me and smiled and then I had taken her in my arms and together we were walking towards the entrance where I had told my driver to wait.

There was much that Mary wanted to tell me of her visit. Mrs Forrester had been delighted to see her and the two of them had become the closest of companions[26], their relationship of governess and employer being long behind them[27]. The boy, Richard, was polite and well behaved[28] and, once he had

1. balayeurs [aux carrefours]
2. confiseries et les épiceries
3. brillamment décorées
4. [clubs permettant des achats groupés pour les fêtes]
5. l'air embaumait
6. [mélange fruits secs-épices, pour tartelettes]
7. [voiture à chevaux]
8. me frayant un chemin dans la foule
9. m'avaient éloigné
10. quotidiens
11. était aussi bondée
12. à l'heure
13. les quais
14. colis
15. panières
16. courant partout, aussi excités
17. le lapin blanc d'Alice [au pays des merveilles]
18. la repérer
19. encore plus de monde se déversait
20. capitale
21. d'inquiétude
22. traversant
23. de dos
24. trop serrée
25. monta dans
26. des amies très proches
27. depuis longtemps derrière elles
28. bien élevé

begun to recover from his sickness, charming company. He was also an avid reader of my stories! The household was just as she remembered it, comfortable and welcoming. The whole visit had been a success, apart from a slight headache and sore throat[1] that she had herself picked up[2] in the last few days and which had been exacerbated[3] by the journey. She looked tired and, when I pressed her[4], she complained of a sense of heaviness[5] in the muscles of her arms and legs. 'But don't fuss over me[6], John. I'll be quite my old self[7] after a rest and a cup of tea. I want to hear all your news. What is this extraordinary business I've been reading about with Sherlock Holmes?'

I wonder to what extent I should blame myself for not examining Mary more closely. But I was preoccupied and she herself made light of her illness[8]. And I was thinking also of the strange man who had approached her. It is quite likely that, even had I known, there would have been nothing that I could do. But even so, I have always had to live with the knowledge that I took her complaints too lightly and failed to recognise the early signs[9] of the typhoid fever which would take her from me[10] all too soon.

It was she who brought up the message, just after we set off. 'Did you see that man just now?' she asked.

'At the train? Yes, I did see him. Did he speak to you?'

'He addressed me by name.[11]'

I was startled. 'What did he say?'

'Just "Good morning, Mrs Watson." He was very uncouth[12]. A working man[13], I would have said. And he pressed this[14] into my hand.'

She produced a small cloth bag[15] which she had been clutching all the time but which she had almost forgotten in the pleasure of our reunion and our necessary haste leaving[16] the station. Now she

1. une légère migraine et un mal de gorge
2. qu'elle-même avait contractés
3. aggravés
4. je voulus en savoir plus
5. d'une sensation de lourdeur
6. Ne vous en faites pas pour moi
7. J'irai beaucoup mieux
8. prenait sa maladie à la légère
9. je n'ai pas reconnu les premiers symptômes
10. allait me l'enlever
11. Il m'a appelée par mon nom.
12. rustre
13. Un ouvrier
14. il a placé ceci
15. sac en toile
16. la nécessité de sortir rapidement de

handed it to me. There was something heavy inside the bag, and I thought at first that it might be coins for I heard the clink of metal[1], but on opening it and pouring the contents into the palm of my hand, I found myself holding three solid nails[2].

'What is the meaning of this?' I asked. 'Did the man say nothing more? Can you describe him?'

'Not really, my dear. I barely glanced at him[3] as I was looking at you. He had chestnut[4] hair, I think. And a dirty, unshaven[5] face. Does it matter?'

'He said nothing else? Did he demand money?'

'I told you. He greeted me by name; nothing more.'

'But why on earth[6] would anyone give you a bag of nails?' The words were no sooner out of my mouth than[7] I understood and let out a cry of exultation. 'The Bag of Nails! Of course!'

'What is it, my dear?'

'I believe, Mary, that you may have just met Holmes himself.'

'It looked nothing like him.'

'That is exactly the idea![8]'

'This bag of nails means something to you?'

It meant a great deal. Holmes wanted me to return to one of the two public houses that we had visited when we were searching for Ross. Both had been called The Bag of Nails, but which one did he have in mind[9]? It would surely not be the second one, in Lambeth, for that was where Sally Dixon had worked and it was known to the police. All in all, the first one, in Edge Lane, was more likely. For he was certainly afraid of being seen; that much was implicit in[10] the manner he had chosen to communicate with me. He had been in disguise[11] and if anyone had seen the approach[12] and tried to apprehend Mary or myself on the station platform, they would have found nothing but a[13] cloth bag with three carpenter's nails[14] and no indication at all that a message had been passed.

1. le tintement du métal
2. gros clous
3. Je l'ai à peine regardé
4. châtains
5. mal rasé
6. pourquoi diable
7. C'est en prononçant ces mots que
8. C'était le but !
9. à laquelle pensait-il
10. cela au moins se devinait à
11. était déguisé
12. la rencontre
13. rien trouvé d'autre qu'un
14. clous de menuisier

'My dear, I'm afraid I am going to have to abandon you the moment we are home[1],' I said.

'You are not in any danger are you, John?'

'I hope not.'

She sighed. 'Sometimes I think you are fonder of Mr Holmes than you are of[2] me.' She saw the look[3] on my face and patted my hand gently[4]. 'I'm only being pleasant with you.[5] And you don't need to come all the way[6] to Kensington. We can stop at the next corner. The driver can bring in my bags[7] and I can see myself home[8].' I hesitated and she looked at me more seriously. 'Go to him, John. If he resorted to such lengths[9] to send a message, then he must be in trouble and needs you as he has always needed you. You cannot refuse.'

And so I parted company from her, not just taking my life in my hands but almost losing it as I slipped out in the traffic[10], coming close to being run over by an omnibus[11] in the Strand. For it had occurred to me that, if Holmes was afraid of being followed, I should be too, and it was therefore vital that I should not be seen. I dodged[12] between various carriages and finally reached the safety of the pavement where I looked carefully about me[13] before turning back the way I had come[14], arriving in that forlorn and sorry[15] part of Shoreditch about thirty minutes later. I remembered the public house well. A run-down[16] place that looked little better[17] in the sunlight than it had in the fog. I crossed the street and went in.

There was one man sitting in the saloon bar[18] and it was not Sherlock Holmes. To my great surprise and somewhat to my mortification, I recognised the man called Rivers who had assisted Dr Trevelyan at Holloway Prison. He was no longer wearing his uniform, but his vacant expression[19], sunken eyes and unruly ginger hair were unmistakable[20]. He was slouching[21] at a table with a glass of stout[22].

1. dès que nous serons rentrés
2. que vous êtes plus attaché à M. Holmes qu'à
3. l'expression
4. me tapota la main
5. Je vous taquine.
6. de faire tout le chemin
7. porter mes bagages à l'intérieur
8. rentrer seule à la maison
9. S'il s'est donné autant de mal
10. dans la circulation
11. manquant me faire renverser par un omnibus
12. Je me faufilai
13. autour de moi
14. de revenir sur mes pas
15. triste et désolée
16. délabré
17. n'avait pas meilleure allure
18. la salle du bar
19. air vague
20. reconnaissables entre tous
21. affalé
22. bière brune

'Mr Rivers!' I exclaimed.

'Sit down with me, Watson. It's very good to see you again.'

It was Holmes who had spoken – and in that second I understood how I had been deceived[1] and how he had effected his escape from prison in front of my very eyes[2]. I confess that I almost fell into the seat that he had proffered[3], seeing, with a sense of haplessness, the smile that I knew so well beaming at me from beneath the wig and the make-up[4]. For that was the wonderment[5] of Holmes's disguises. It wasn't that he used a great deal of theatrical trickery[6] or camouflage. It was more that he had a knack of[7] metamorphosing into whatever character he wished to play and that if he believed it, you would believe it too, right up to the moment of revelation. It was like gazing at an obscure point on a distant landscape[8], at a rock or a tree which had taken on the shape[9], perhaps, of an animal. And yet once you had drawn closer[10] and seen it for what it was, it would never deceive you again[11]. I had sat down with Rivers. But now it was obvious to me that I was with Holmes.

'Tell me—' I began.

'All in good time[12], my dear fellow,' he interrupted. 'First, assure me that you were not followed here.'

'I am certain I am alone.'

'And yet there were two men behind you at Holborn Viaduct. Policemen, from the look of them[13], and doubtless in the employ of[14] our friend Inspector Harriman.'

'I didn't see them. But I took great care leaving my wife's carriage when it was halfway down the Strand. I didn't allow it to come to a complete stop[15] and slipped behind a barouche[16]. I can assure you that if there were two men with me at the station, they are now in Kensington and wondering what became of me.'

1. que je n'y avais vu que du feu

2. sous mon nez

3. qu'il m'avait avancé

4. m'adressant ce sourire rayonnant, si familier, sous la perruque et le maquillage

5. le côté merveilleux

6. accessoires de théâtre

7. le don de savoir

8. un point sombre au loin

9. qui aurait pris la forme

10. une fois qu'on l'a vu de près

11. on ne s'y trompe plus

12. Chaque chose en son temps

13. apparemment

14. travaillant pour

15. ne l'ai pas laissé s'arrêter totalement

16. [type de calèche]

'My trusty[1] Watson!'

'But how did you know that my wife was arriving today? How did you even come to be[2] at Holborn Viaduct at all[3]?'

'That is simplicity itself. I followed you from Baker Street, realised which train you must be meeting[4] and managed to get ahead of you[5] in the crowd.'

'That is only the first of my questions, Holmes, and I must insist that you satisfy me on all counts[6], for it makes my head spin simply to[7] see you sitting here. Let us start with Dr Trevelyan. I assume you recognised him and persuaded him to help you escape.'

'That is exactly the case. It was a happy coincidence that our former client should have found employment at the prison although I would like to think that any medical man would have been persuaded to my cause[8], particularly when it became clear that there was a plan to murder me.'

'You knew of that?'

Holmes glanced at me keenly[9], and I realised that if I were not to break the pledge I had given[10] to my sinister host, two nights before, then I must pretend to know nothing at all. 'I expected it from the moment I was arrested. It was clear to me that the evidence against me would begin to fall apart[11] as soon as I was allowed to speak and so, of course, my enemies would not permit it. I was waiting for[12] an attack of any description[13] and took particular care to examine my food. Contrary to popular belief[14], there are very few poisons that are completely tasteless[15] and certainly not the arsenic which they hoped would finish me[16]. I detected it in a bowl of meat broth[17] which was brought to me on my second evening ... a particularly foolish attempt, Watson, and one that I was grateful for, as it gave me exactly the weapon that I needed.'

'Was Harriman part of this plot?' I asked, unable to keep the fury out of my voice.

1. fidèle
2. vous êtes-vous retrouvé
3. en fait
4. quel train vous deviez attendre
5. passer devant vous
6. en tous points
7. j'en ai le vertige, rien qu'à
8. tout médecin se serait laissé convaincre de m'aider
9. me lança un regard perçant
10. briser le serment que j'avais fait
11. à s'effondrer
12. Je m'attendais à
13. de n'importe quel type
14. Contrairement à une idée reçue,
15. vraiment indécelables au goût
16. avec lequel ils espéraient m'achever
17. bouillon de viande

'Inspector Harriman has either been paid well or is at the very heart of the conspiracy that you and I have uncovered[1]. I suspect the latter.[2] I thought of going to Hawkins. The chief warder had struck me as a civilised man and he had taken pains to ensure that my stay at the House of Correction had not been any more uncomfortable than it had to be[3]. However, to have raised the alarm too soon might have been to precipitate[4] a second, more lethal[5] attack, and so instead, I requested an interview[6] with the medical officer and, after being escorted to the hospital, was delighted to discover that we were already acquainted, for it made my task considerably easier. I showed him the sample[7] of the soup that I had kept back[8] and explained to him what was afoot[9], that I had been falsely arrested[10] and that it was my enemies' intention that I should never leave Holloway alive. Dr Trevelyan was horrified. He would have been inclined to believe me anyway for he still felt himself to be in debt to me following that business in Brook Street.'

'How did he come to be in Holloway?'

'Needs must[11], Watson. You will recall that he lost his employment after the death of his resident patient[12]. Trevelyan is a brilliant man, but one whom fortune has never favoured[13]. After drifting several months[14], the position at Holloway was the only one he could find and, reluctantly[15], he took it. We must try to help him one day.'

'Indeed so, Holmes. But continue ...'

'His first instinct was to inform the chief warder, but I persuaded him that the conspiracy against me was too entrenched[16], my enemies too powerful, and that although it was critical[17] for me to regain my liberty, we could not risk involving anybody else and it would have to be achieved[18] by other means. We began to discuss what these might be[19]. It was obvious to Trevelyan, as it was to me, that I could

1. découverte
2. Je penche pour la seconde hypothèse.
3. que nécessaire
4. aurait peut-être accéléré
5. mortelle cette fois-ci
6. à m'entretenir
7. l'échantillon
8. gardé
9. ce qui se tramait
10. arrêté sous un faux prétexte
11. Nécessité fait loi
12. son patient hospitalisé
13. à qui la fortune n'a jamais souri
14. quelques mois d'incertitude
15. à contrecœur
16. trop bien établie
17. bien qu'il soit crucial
18. qu'il faudrait y parvenir
19. à discuter en quoi ils pourraient consister

1. sortir par la force
2. C'est-à-dire
3. de creuser
4. d'escalader
5. Il n'y avait pas moins de
6. le monde extérieur
7. sans rencontrer de résistance
8. je craignais
9. rendre plus crédible
10. un pauvre diable
11. gravement
12. me ferait sortir clandestinement
13. je l'ai rejetée tout de suite
14. trop de failles
15. notamment
16. grandissants
17. ne m'avait pas tué
18. je me méfiais d'eux
19. la réaction qu'ils attendaient de moi
20. remarqué
21. façons débraillées
22. concevoir un autre plan

not physically force my way out[1]. That is[2], there was no question of digging[3] a tunnel or climbing[4] the walls. There were no fewer than[5] nine locked doors and gates between my cell and the outside world[6], and even with the best of disguises, I could not hope to walk through them unchallenged[7]. Clearly, I could not consider the use of violence. For about an hour we spoke together and all the time I was anxious[8] that Inspector Harriman might reappear at any moment for he was still continuing to interview me to lend credence to[9] his empty and fraudulent investigation.

'And then Trevelyan mentioned Jonathan Wood, a poor wretch[10] who had spent most of his life in prison and who was about to end it there for he had fallen grievously[11] ill and was not expected to survive the night. Trevelyan suggested to me that when Wood died, I could be admitted to the prison hospital. He would conceal the body and smuggle me out[12] in the coffin. That was his idea but I dismissed it with barely a second thought[13]. There were too many impracticalities[14], not the least of which must be[15] the growing[16] suspicions of my persecutors who would be wondering already why the poison administered in my evening meal had failed to finish me[17] and who might already suspect that I was wise to them[18]. A dead body leaving the prison at such a time would be too obvious. It was exactly the sort of move they would expect me to make[19].

'But during my time in the hospital I had already taken note of[20] the orderly, Rivers, and in particular the good fortune of his appearance: his slovenly manner[21] and bright red hair. I saw at once that all the necessary elements – Harriman, the poison, the dying man – were in place and that it would be possible to devise an alternative scheme[22], using one against the other. I told Trevelyan what I would need and to his eternal credit[1] he did not question my judgement[2] but did as I requested.

'Wood died shortly before midnight. Trevelyan came to my cell and told me personally what had come to pass[3], then returned home to collect the few items[4] which I had requested and which I would need. The following morning, I announced that my own illness had worsened. Trevelyan diagnosed[5] severe food poisoning and admitted me to the hospital where Wood had already been laid out[6]. I was there when his coffin arrived and even helped lift him into it. Rivers, however, was absent. He had been given the day off[7] and now Trevelyan produced the wig and the change of clothes[8] which would allow me to disguise myself as Rivers. The coffin was removed[9] shortly before three o'clock and at last everything was in place. You must understand the psychology, Watson. We needed Harriman to do our work for us[10]. First of all[11], we would reveal my extraordinary and inexplicable disappearance from a securely locked[12] cell. Then, almost immediately, we would inform him of a coffin and a dead body that had just left the place. Under the circumstances[13], I had no doubt that he would jump to the wrong conclusion, which is precisely what he did. So confident was he[14] that I was in the coffin, that he did not take so much as a second glance at[15] the slow-witted[16] orderly who was seemingly[17] responsible for what had occurred. He rushed off, in effect easing my passage out[18]. It was Harriman who ordered the doors to be unlocked and opened. It was Harriman who undermined the very security[19] that should have kept me in.'

'It's true, Holmes,' I exclaimed. 'I never looked at you. All my attention was focused on the coffin.'

'I have to say that your sudden appearance was the one eventuality[20] that I had never considered and I was afraid that at the very least you might reveal

1. je lui en saurai gré éternellement,
2. n'a pas mis en doute mon jugement
3. ce qui était arrivé
4. prendre les quelques accessoires
5. a diagnostiqué
6. le corps de Wood était déjà exposé
7. Il bénéficiait d'un jour de congé
8. les vêtements
9. retiré
10. que Harriman fasse le travail à notre place
11. Tout d'abord
12. solidement verrouillée
13. Dans ces circonstances
14. Il était tellement sûr
15. qu'il a à peine regardé
16. faible d'esprit
17. semblait
18. facilitant ainsi ma sortie
19. déjoué toute cette sécurité
20. la seule éventualité

your acquaintanceship with[1] Dr Trevelyan. But you were magnificent, Watson. I would say that having both you and the warder there actually added to the sense of urgency[2] and made Harriman more determined to chase down[3] the coffin before it left.'

There was such a twinkle in his eye[4] as he said this that I took it as a compliment, although I understood the role I had actually played in the adventure. Holmes liked an audience[5] as much as any actor on the stage and the more there were of us present[6], the easier he would have found it[7] to play the part.

'But what are we to do now?' I asked. 'You are a fugitive. Your name is discredited. The very fact[8] that you have chosen to escape will only help to persuade the world of your guilt[9].'

'You paint a bleak picture[10], Watson. For my part, I would say that circumstances have immeasurably improved[11] since last week.'

'Where are you staying?'

'Have I not told you? I keep rooms[12] all over London for eventualities just such as this[13]. I have one nearby, and I can assure you that it is a great deal more agreeable than the accommodation I have just left.'

'Even so, Holmes, it seems that you have inadvertently made[14] many enemies.'

'That does indeed seem to be the case. We have to ask ourselves what it is that unites such disparate bodies[15] as Lord Horace Blackwater, scion of one of England's oldest families, Dr Thomas Ackland, benefactor of the Westminster Hospital and Inspector Harriman, who has fifteen years unblemished service[16] in the Metropolitan Police. This is the question that I put to you[17] in the less than congenial surroundings[18] of Bow Street. What do these three men have in common? Well, the fact that they are all men is a start[19]. They are all wealthy and well connected[20]. When brother Mycroft spoke of a scandal,

1. ne révéliez connaître
2. a amplifié l'impression d'urgence
3. à courir remettre la main sur
4. Il avait l'œil si pétillant
5. aimait avoir un auditoire
6. plus l'assistance était nombreuse
7. plus il avait dû trouver facile
8. Le fait même
9. culpabilité
10. Vous brossez un tableau bien noir
11. se sont infiniment améliorées
12. Je dispose de pied-à-terre
13. précisément pour ce genre de cas
14. sans le vouloir, vous vous êtes fait
15. ce qui relie des êtres aussi différents
16. d'impeccables états de service
17. je vous ai posée
18. le cadre pour le moins inhospitalier
19. un début
20. ils ont des relations

these are the very sort of people who might be damaged[1]. I understand, by the by[2], that you returned to Wimbledon.'

I could not possibly conceive how, or from whom Holmes could have heard this but it was not the time to go into such details. I merely assented[3] and briefly told him of the circumstances of my last visit. He seemed particularly agitated by the news of[4] Eliza Carstairs, the rapid decline[5] in her health. 'We are dealing with a mind of unusual cunning and cruelty[6], Watson. This matter cuts very deep[7] and it is imperative that we conclude this business so that we can visit Edmund Carstairs again.'

'Do you think that the two are connected?' I asked. 'I cannot see how the events in Boston and even the stabbing of Keelan O'Donaghue at a private hotel here in London could possibly have led to the horrible business with which we are now occupied.'

'But that is only because you are assuming[8] that Keelan O'Donaghue is dead,' replied Holmes. 'Well, we shall have more news of that soon enough[9]. While I was in Holloway, I was able to send a message to Belfast—'

'They permitted you to wire[10]?'

'I had no need for the post office. The criminal underworld[11] is faster and less expensive and available to anyone who happens to find themselves[12] on the wrong side of the law. There was a man in my wing, a forger[13] by the name of Jacks, whom I met in the exercise yard and who was released two days ago. He carried my enquiry[14] with him, and as soon as I have a reply, you and I shall return to Wimbledon together. In the meantime[15], you have not answered my question.'

'What connects the three men? The answer is obvious. It is the House of Silk.'

'And what is the House of Silk?'

1. à qui cela pourrait nuire
2. au fait
3. Je me contentai d'acquiescer
4. les nouvelles concernant
5. dégradation
6. exceptionnellement ingénieux et cruel
7. Toute cette histoire va très loin
8. vous partez du principe
9. à ce propos très bientôt
10. télégraphier
11. Le milieu criminel
12. à la portée de quiconque se trouve
13. faussaire
14. a emporté ma demande
15. En attendant

'Of that I have no idea.[1] But I think I can tell you where to find it.'

'Watson, you astonish me.'

'You do not know?'

'I have known for[2] some time. Nonetheless[3], I will be fascinated to know your own conclusions – and how you arrived at them[4].'

By good fortune, I had been carrying the advertisement with me[5] and now unfolded it and showed it to my friend, relating[6] my recent interview with the Reverend Charles Fitzsimmons. 'Dr Silkin's House of Wonders,' he read. For a moment he seemed puzzled, but then his face brightened[7]. 'But of course. This is exactly what we have been looking for. Once again I must congratulate you[8], Watson. While I have been languishing in confinement[9], you have been busy.'

'This was the address that you had expected?'

'Jackdaw Lane? Not exactly. Nonetheless, I am confident[10] that it will provide all the answers that we have been searching for[11]. What time is it? Almost one o'clock. I would imagine we would do better[12] to approach such a place under cover of darkness[13]. Would you be amenable[14] to meeting me here again in, shall we say[15], four hours?'

'I would be happy to, Holmes.'

'I knew I could count on you. And I would suggest you bring your service revolver, Watson. There are many dangers afoot[16] and I fear it is going to be a long night.'

1. Je n'en ai pas la moindre idée.
2. Je le sais depuis
3. Néanmoins
4. vous y êtes parvenu
5. Par chance, j'avais la publicité sur moi
6. en lui racontant
7. s'éclaira
8. vous féliciter
9. je languissais en prison
10. sûr
11. que nous recherchons
12. qu'il vaudrait mieux
13. à la faveur de l'obscurité
14. Seriez-vous disposé
15. disons
16. De nombreux dangers nous guettent

EIGHTEEN

The Fortune-Teller[1]

There are, I think, occasions when you know that you have arrived at the end of a long journey[2], when, even though your destination is still concealed from sight[3], you are somehow aware that when you turn the corner that lies just ahead of you[4], there it will be. That was how I felt as I approached The Bag of Nails a second time, just before five o'clock, with the sun already down[5] and a chill, unforgiving darkness descending[6] on the city. Mary had been asleep when I returned home and I had not disturbed her, but as I had stood there in my consulting room[7], weighing[8] my revolver in my hand and checking that it was fully loaded[9], I wondered what a casual observer would make[10] of the scene: a respectable doctor in Kensington arming himself and preparing to set out in pursuit of a conspiracy that had so far encompassed[11] murder, torture, kidnap and the perversion of[12] justice. I slipped the weapon into my pocket, reached for my greatcoat and went out.

Holmes was no longer in disguise, apart from a hat and a scarf which he had drawn across the lower part of his face[13]. He had ordered[14] two brandies[15] to brace us[16] against the bitterness[17] of the night. I would not have been surprised if it had snowed, for there had already been a few flakes blowing in the breeze[18] as I arrived. We barely spoke, but I remember that as we set the glasses down[19] he glanced

1. diseuse de bonne aventure
2. voyage
3. n'est pas encore visible
4. qu'au détour du chemin que vous prenez
5. alors que le soleil commençait déjà à se coucher
6. qu'une obscurité implacable et glaciale s'abattait
7. cabinet
8. soupesant
9. entièrement chargé
10. ce qu'un passant penserait
11. englobait déjà
12. des entraves à
13. qu'il avait ramené sur le bas de son visage
14. commandé
15. cognacs
16. nous armer
17. la rigueur
18. quelques flocons volant dans la brise
19. reposions nos verres

at me, and I saw all the good humour and resoluteness[1] that I knew so well positively[2] dancing in his eyes and understood that he was as eager as I[3] to have this done with[4].

'So, Watson ... ?' he asked.

'Yes, Holmes,' I said. 'I am ready.'

'And I am very glad to have you once again at my side.'

A cab carried us east and we descended on the Whitechapel Road, walking the remaining distance to Jackdaw Lane. These travelling fairs[5] could be found all over the countryside during the summer months but came into the city as soon as the weather turned[6] and they were notorious[7] for the late hours they kept and the din[8] that they made – indeed, I wondered how the local populace[9] could possibly endure Dr Silkin's House of Wonders, for I heard it long before I saw it[10]; the grinding of an organ[11], the beat of a drum[12], and a man's voice shouting into the night. Jackdaw Lane was a narrow passageway running between the Whitechapel and Commercial Roads, with buildings, mainly shops and warehouses[13], rising three storeys[14] on either side with windows that seemed too small for the amount[15] of bricks that surrounded them. An alleyway opened out about halfway down[16] and it was here that a man had imposed himself, dressed in a frock coat, an old-fashioned four-in-hand necktie[17] and a top hat so beaten about[18] that it seemed to be perched on the side of his head as if trying to throw itself off[19]. He had the beard, the moustache, the pointed nose[20] and the bright eyes of a pantomime[21] Mephistopheles[22].

'One penny entrance!' he exclaimed. 'Step inside[23] and you will not regret it. Here you will see some of the wonders of the world from Negros to Esquimaux and more besides[24]. Come, gentlemen! Dr Silkin's House of Wonders. It will amaze you. It will aston-

1. la détermination
2. véritablement
3. aussi déterminé que moi
4. d'en finir avec tout cela
5. foires itinérantes
6. dès le changement de saison
7. mal vues
8. pour leur ouverture tardive et le vacarme
9. riverains
10. bien avant de la voir
11. le grincement d'un orgue
12. battement d'un tambour
13. des entrepôts
14. s'élevant sur trois étages
15. par rapport à la quantité
16. s'ouvrit devant nous, à mi-parcours environ,
17. une cravate démodée à nœud simple
18. si défoncé
19. de perdre l'équilibre
20. nez pointu
21. de pantomime
22. Méphistophélès [incarnation du diable]
23. Entrez
24. plus encore

ish you. Never will you forget what you see here tonight.'

'You are Dr Silkin?' Holmes asked.

'I have that honour, sir. Dr Asmodeus Silkin, late of India[1], late of the Congo. My travels have taken me all over the world and all that I have experienced you will find here for the sum of a single penny.'

A black dwarf[2] in a pea jacket[3] and military trousers stood next to him, beating out a rhythm[4] on a drum and adding a loud roll[5] every time the penny was mentioned. We paid over two coins and were duly ushered through[6].

The spectacle that awaited us took me quite by surprise. I suppose in the harsh light[7] of the day it might have been revealed in all its tawdry shabbiness[8] but the night, held at bay[9] by a ring of burning braziers[10], had lent it a certain exoticism[11] so that if you did not look too closely you really could believe that you had been transported to another world ... perhaps one in a storybook.

We were in a cobbled[12] yard, surrounded by buildings in such a state of disrepair[13] that they were partly open to the elements[14] with crumbling[15] doorways and rickety[16] staircases dangling precariously from the brickwork[17]. Some of these entranceways had been hung[18] with crimson[19] curtains and signs advertising entertainments that a further payment of a halfpence or farthing would provide. The man with no neck. The world's ugliest[20] woman. The five-legged[21] pig. Others were open, with waxworks[22] and peep shows providing a glimpse of the sort of horrors that I knew all too well from my time with Holmes. Murder seemed to be the predominant theme. Maria Martin was there, as was Mary Ann Nichols, lying with her throat slit[23] and her abdomen open just as she had been when she was discovered not far from here, two years before. I heard the crack of rifles[24]. A shooting gallery had been set

1. originaire des Indes
2. nain
3. vareuse
4. battant la cadence
5. un roulement de tambour
6. on nous fit entrer
7. à la lumière crue
8. médiocrité tapageuse
9. tenue à distance
10. un cercle de braseros allumés
11. lui conférait un certain exotisme
12. pavée
13. état de délabrement
14. exposés aux intempéries
15. qui s'écroulaient
16. branlants
17. pendant dangereusement de la maçonnerie
18. portes d'entrée étaient tendues de
19. pourpres
20. la plus laide
21. à cinq pattes
22. des statues de cire
23. sa gorge tranchée
24. des coups de fusils

up inside one of the buildings, I could make out the gas flames jetting[1] and the green bottles standing at the far end.

These attractions and others were contained in[2] the outer perimeter[3], but there were also gypsy wagons[4] parked in the courtyard itself, with platforms[5] constructed between them for performances that would continue throughout the night. A pair of identical twins[6], orientals, were juggling[7] a dozen balls, hurling them between them[8] with such fluidity that they made it seem automatic. A black man in a loincloth[9] held up a poker[10] that had been made red-hot in a charcoal burner[11] and licked it with his tongue[12]. A woman in a cumbersome, feathered[13] turban read palms[14]. An elderly magician performed parlour tricks[15]. And all around, a crowd, far larger than I would have expected – there must have been more than two hundred people there – laughed and applauded, wandering aimlessly[16] from performance to performance while a barrel organ jangled ceaselessly[17] around them. I noticed a woman of monstrous girth[18] strolling before me and another so tiny[19] that she could have been a child, but for her elderly appearance[20]. Were they spectators or part of the spectacle? It was hard to be sure.

'So, what now[21]?' Holmes asked me.

'I really have no idea,' I replied.

'Do you still believe this to be the House of Silk?'

'It seems unlikely, I agree.' I suddenly realised the import[22] of what he had just said. 'Are you telling me that you do not think it is?'

'I knew from the outset that there was no possibility of it so being[23].'

For once, I could not hide my irritation. 'I have to say, Holmes, that there are times when you try my patience to the limit[24]. If you knew from the start that this was not the House of Silk then perhaps you can tell me – why are we here?'

1. jaillissant
2. massées
3. le pourtour
4. des roulottes de tsiganes
5. des estrades
6. jumeaux
7. jonglaient avec
8. se les lançant
9. vêtu d'un pagne
10. tisonnier
11. chauffé à blanc dans un poêle à charbon
12. le léchait
13. à plumes
14. lisait les lignes de la main
15. des tours de passe-passe
16. déambulant
17. un orgue de Barbarie jouait de son crincrin
18. monstrueusement grosse
19. menue
20. si elle n'avait pas eu l'air âgé
21. que faisons-nous
22. la signification
23. que ce soit le cas
24. mettez ma patience à rude épreuve

'Because we are supposed to be[1]. We were invited.'

'The advertisement ... ?'

'It was meant[2] to be discovered, Watson. And you were meant[3] to give it to me.'

I could only shake my head at these enigmatic answers and decided that, following his ordeal in Holloway prison, Holmes had returned entirely to his old self[4] – secretive, over-confident[5] and thoroughly annoying[6]. And still I was determined to prove him wrong[7]. Surely it could not be a coincidence, the name of Dr Silkin on the advertisements, the fact that one had been found concealed beneath Ross's bed. If it was meant to be discovered, why place it there? I looked around me, searching for anything that might be worth my attention, but in the whirl of activity[8], with the flames of the torches flickering and dancing[9], it was almost impossible to settle on anything that might be relevant[10]. The jugglers were throwing swords[11] at each other now. There was another rifle shot and one of the bottles exploded, showering glass[12] over the shelf. The magician reached into the air[13] and produced a bouquet of silk flowers. The crowd, standing around him, applauded.

'Well, we might as well ...' I began.

But then, at that very moment[14], I saw something and my breath caught in my throat[15]. It could, of course, be a coincidence. It might mean nothing at all. Perhaps I was trying to read some significance into a tiny[16] detail simply to justify our presence here. But it was the fortune-teller. She was sitting on a sort of raised platform[17] in front of her caravan behind a table on which were spread out the tools of her trade[18]: a deck of tarot cards[19], a crystal ball, a silver pyramid and a few sheets[20] of paper with strange runes[21] and diagrams. She had been gazing in my direction and, as I caught her eye[22], it seemed to me that she raised a hand in salutation, and there

1. sommes censés y être
2. Elle était destinée
3. vous étiez censé
4. totalement redevenu lui-même
5. présomptueux
6. très contrariant
7. de lui prouver qu'il avait tort
8. le tourbillon général
9. à la lueur vacillante des torches
10. de choisir un détail éventuellement pertinent
11. des sabres
12. projetant du verre
13. fit un large mouvement du bras
14. à cet instant précis
15. qui me coupa le souffle
16. infime
17. haute estrade
18. étalés ses instruments de travail
19. un jeu de tarot
20. feuilles
21. [anciens caractères germaniques, à portée magique]
22. comme je croisai son regard

it was, tied[1] around her wrist: a length of white, silk ribbon.

My immediate thought was to alert Sherlock Holmes but almost at once I decided against it. I felt I had been ridiculed[2] enough for one evening. And so, without explanation, I left his side[3], wandering forward as if drawn by idle curiosity[4] and then climbed the few steps to the platform. The gypsy woman surveyed me[5] as if she had not just expected me to come but had foreseen it[6]. She was a large, masculine woman with a heavy jaw[7] and mournful, grey eyes.

'I would like to have my fortune told,' I said.

'Sit down,' she replied. She had a foreign accent and a manner of speech that was surly and unwelcoming[8]. There was a footstool[9] opposite her in the cramped space[10] and I lowered myself onto it.

'Can you see the future?' I asked.

'It will cost you a penny.'

I paid her the money and she took my hand, spreading it in her own[11] so that the white ribbon was right before me. Then she stretched out a withered[12] finger and began to trace the lines on my palm as if she could smooth them out with her touch[13]. 'A doctor?' she asked.

'Yes.'

'And married. Happily. No children.'

'You are quite correct on all three counts[14].'

'You have recently known the pain of a separation.' Was she referring to my wife's sojourn in Camberwell or to the brief imprisonment of Holmes? And how could she possibly know of either[15]? I am now, and was then, a sceptic. How could I fail to be?[16] In my time with Holmes I found myself investigating a family curse[17], a giant rat and a vampire – and all three turned out to have[18] perfectly rational explanations. I therefore waited for[19] the gypsy to reveal to me[20] the source of her trickery.

1. noué
2. ridiculisé
3. je m'éloignai de lui
4. si j'étais animé par la simple curiosité,
5. m'inspecta du regard
6. qu'elle l'avait prévu
7. mâchoire forte
8. bourrue et revêche
9. repose-pieds
10. cet espace exigu
11. la posant, ouverte, dans la sienne
12. flétri
13. les effacer en passant le doigt
14. avez raison sur ces trois points
15. de l'un ou de l'autre
16. Comment ne pas l'être ?
17. une malédiction familiale
18. pour les trois, il s'avéra qu'il y avait
19. J'attendis donc que
20. me révèle

'Have you come here alone?' she asked.

'No. I am with a friend.'

'Then I have a message for you. You will have seen a shooting range[1] contained in the building behind us.'

'Yes.'

'You will discover all the answers that you seek in the rooms above it. But tread carefully[2], doctor. The building is condemned and the floor is lousy[3]. You have a long lifeline[4]. You see it here? But it has weaknesses[5]. These creases[6] ... They are like arrows being fired towards you[7] and there are still many more to come. You should beware lest one of them should hit[8] ...'

'Thank you.' I took my hand back[9] as if snatching it from the flames[10]. As sure as I was that the woman was a fake[11], there was something about her performance that had unnerved me[12]. Perhaps it was the night, the scarlet shadows writhing[13] all about me, or it could have been the constant cacophony, the music and the crowds, that were overwhelming my senses[14]. But I had a sudden instinct that this was an evil place and that we should never have come. I climbed back down to Holmes and told him what had just transpired[15].

'So are we now to be guided by fortune-tellers?' was his brusque response. 'Well, Watson, there are no other obvious alternatives. We must see this through to the end[16].'

We made our way past a man with a monkey on his shoulder and another, naked to the waist[17], exposing a myriad of lurid tattoos[18] which he animated by flexing his various muscles[19]. The shooting gallery[20] was before us, with a staircase twisting unevenly[21] above. There was a volley of rifle shots[22]. A group of apprentices were trying their luck at the bottles, but they had been drinking and their bullets disappeared harmlessly[23] into the darkness. With

1. stand de tir
2. marchez prudemment
3. le plancher est pourri
4. ligne de vie
5. des faiblesses
6. plis
7. des flèches qui vous visent
8. vous méfier, une flèche pourrait vous atteindre
9. Je retirai ma main
10. je l'arrachais aux flammes
11. une fausse cartomancienne
12. m'avait perturbé
13. les ombres écarlates se tordant
14. obnubilaient mes sens
15. ce que je venais d'apprendre
16. aller jusqu'au bout
17. torse nu
18. d'horribles tatouages
19. en faisant jouer ses différents muscles
20. stand de tir
21. sinueux et irrégulier
22. une salve de coups de fusils
23. sans rien toucher

Holmes leading the way, we climbed up, treading carefully, for the wooden steps gave every impression of being on the edge of collapse[1]. Ahead of us, an irregular gap[2] in the wall – it might once have been a door – loomed open[3], with only darkness beyond. I looked back and saw the gypsy woman sitting in her caravan, watching us with an evil eye[4]. The white ribbon still dangled[5] from her wrist. Before I reached the top[6] I knew that I had been deceived, that we should not have come here.

We entered the upper floor[7] which must once have been used for the storage of coffee[8] for the smell of it was still apparent[9] in the grimy air[10]. But now it was empty. The walls were mouldering[11]. The dust was thick on[12] every surface. The floorboards creaked[13] beneath our feet. The music from the barrel organ seemed distant now and cut off[14] and the murmur of the crowd had disappeared altogether[15]. There was still enough light reflecting from the torches which blazed[16] all around the fair to illuminate the room but it was uneven, constantly moving in such a way as to cast distorted shadows[17] all around us, and the further we went in, the darker it would become.

'Watson ...' Holmes muttered, and the tone of his voice was enough to tell me what he desired. I produced my gun and found comfort in its weight[18], in the touch of cold metal[19] against my palm.

'Holmes,' I said. 'We are wasting our time. There is nothing here.'

'And yet a child has been here before us,' replied he.

I looked beyond him and saw, lying on the floor in the far corner, two toys[20] that had been abandoned there. One was a spindle top[21], the other a lead soldier standing stiffly to attention[22] with most of its paint worn away[23]. There was something infinitely pathetic about them. Had they once belonged to Ross? Had this been a place of refuge for him before he was

1. sur le point de s'écrouler
2. trou
3. était béant
4. un regard mauvais
5. pendait toujours
6. Avant d'avoir atteint le haut
7. dernier étage
8. pour stocker du café
9. flottait encore
10. l'atmosphère crasseuse
11. moisissaient
12. Une épaisse couche de poussière recouvrait
13. grinçaient
14. très lointaine
15. totalement disparu
16. flambaient
17. qu'elle projetait des ombres déformées
18. fus réconforté par son poids
19. par le contact du métal froid
20. jouets
21. sorte de toupie
22. soldat de plomb au garde-à-vous
23. effacée

killed and these the only souvenirs of a childhood he had never really had? I found myself drawn[1] towards them, walking away from the entrance, just as had been intended, for too late did I see[2] the man step out from behind an alcove, nor could I avoid the cudgel[3] that came sweeping through the air towards me[4]. I was struck on the arm below the elbow and felt my fingers jerk open in a blaze of white pain[5]. The gun clattered[6] to the ground. I lunged for it[7], but was struck a second time, a blow that sent me sprawling[8]. At the same time, a second voice came out of the darkness.

'Don't either of you move or I'll shoot you where you stand.'

Holmes ignored the instruction. He was already at my side, leaning over me[9]. 'Watson, are you all right? I will never forgive myself if they have done you serious injury.'

'No, no.' I clasped[10] my arm, searching for any break[11] or fracture and knew at once that I had only been badly bruised[12]. 'I'm not hurt.'

'Cowards![13]'

A man with thinning hair[14], an upturned[15] nose and heavy, round shoulders stepped towards us, allowing the light from outside to fall across his face. I recognised Henderson, the tidewaiter (or so he claimed) who had sent Holmes into the trap at Creer's opium den. He had told us that he was an addict, and that must have been one of the only true parts of his story, for he still had the bloodshot eyes and sickly pallor[16] that I remembered. He was holding a revolver. At the same time, his accomplice[17] picked up my own weapon and shuffled forward, keeping it trained on us[18]. This second man I did not know. He was burly, toad-like[19], with close-cropped hair and swollen[20] ears and lips, like those of a boxer after a bad fight[21]. His cudgel was actually a heavy walking stick[22], which still dangled from his left hand.

1. Je me sentis attiré
2. car je vis trop tard
3. et je ne pus non plus éviter le gourdin
4. arriva sur moi, fendant l'air
5. ma main s'ouvrir d'un coup, les doigts saisis d'une douleur fulgurante
6. tomba avec fracas
7. Je me précipitai pour le récupérer
8. coup qui me jeta à terre
9. penché sur moi
10. Je tâtai
11. fêlure
12. n'avais que de mauvaises contusions
13. Lâches !
14. un début de calvitie
15. en trompette
16. les yeux rougis et cette pâleur maladive
17. complice
18. pointée sur nous
19. baraqué, avec une allure de crapaud
20. enflées
21. dur combat
22. en fait une lourde canne

'Good evening, Henderson,' Holmes remarked in a voice in which I could detect nothing more[1] than equanimity. From the way he spoke, he could have been casually greeting an old acquaintance[2].

'You are not surprised to see me, Mr Holmes?'

'On the contrary, I had fully expected it[3].'

'And you remember my friend, Bratby?'

Holmes nodded. He turned to me. 'This was the man who held me down in the office at Creer's Place, when the opiate was forced on me,' he explained. 'I had rather hoped[4] he might be here too.'

Henderson hesitated, then laughed. Gone was any pretence of the weakness[5] or inferiority that he had displayed[6] when he had come to our lodgings. 'I don't believe you, Mr Holmes. I am afraid that you are all too easily gulled[7]. You did not find what you were looking for at Creer's. You haven't found it here, either. It seems to me that you will go off like a firework ... in any direction[8].'

'And what are your intentions?'

'I would have thought that would be obvious to you. We thought we'd dealt with you[9] at Holloway Prison, and it would have been better for you, all in all, if you'd stayed there. So this time our methods are going to be a little more direct. I have been instructed[10] to kill you, to shoot you like a dog.'

'In that event[11], would you be so kind as to satisfy my curiosity on just a couple of points[12]? Was it you who killed the girl at Bluegate Fields?'

'As a matter of fact it was.[13] She was stupid enough to return to the public house where she worked and it was easy enough to pick her up[14].'

'And her brother?'

'Little Ross? Yes, that was us. It was a horrible thing to have to do[15], Mr Holmes, but he brought it upon himself[16]. The boy stepped out of line[17] and we had to make an example of him.'

'Thank you very much. It is exactly as I thought.'

1. déceler rien d'autre
2. simplement en train de saluer une vieille connaissance
3. je m'y attendais tout à fait
4. J'espérais bien
5. Il n'y avait plus trace de la faiblesse
6. qu'il avait montrée
7. vraiment trop facile à duper
8. comme un feu d'artifice, vous partez au quart de tour
9. On pensait vous avoir réglé votre compte
10. J'ai ordre
11. Dans ce cas
12. sur deux ou trois points
13. C'est moi, oui.
14. ne fut pas difficile de l'y cueillir
15. horrible d'avoir à faire ça
16. il l'a cherché
17. a dépassé les bornes

Henderson laughed a second time but never had I seen an expression more devoid[1] of good humour. 'Well, you're a cool enough customer[2], aren't you, Mr Holmes? And I suppose you've got it all figured out[3], haven't you!'

'Of course.'

'And when that old bird[4] sent you up here, you knew she'd been waiting for you?'

'The fortune-teller spoke to my colleague, not to me. I assume you paid her to do your bidding[5]?'

'Cross her palm with sixpence[6] and she'd do anything.'

'I expected another trap, yes.'

'Let's get it over with[7],' the man called Bratby urged.

'Not yet, Jason. Not quite yet.'

For once, I did not need Holmes to explain why they were waiting. I saw it all too clearly for myself.[8] When we had been climbing the stairs, there had been a crowd gathered around the shooting gallery with the shots ringing out below[9]. Now, for the moment, it was silent. The two assassins were waiting for the crack of the rifles to recommence[10]. The sound would mask two further[11] gunshots up here. Murder is the most horrible crime of which a human being is capable, but this cold-blooded, calculated[12], double murder struck me as particularly vile[13]. I was still clutching my arm. All sense of feeling had left me[14] where I had been struck, but I dragged myself to my feet[15], determined that I would not be killed by these men while I was on my knees[16].

'You might as well put down your weapons and give yourselves up[17] now,' Holmes remarked. He was utterly calm and I began to wonder if he had indeed known all along[18] that the two men would be here.

'What?'

1. aussi dépourvue
2. quelqu'un qui a du sang-froid
3. vous avez tout compris
4. la vieille
5. pour qu'elle vous obéisse
6. Mettez-lui 6 pence dans la main
7. Finissons-en
8. Ce n'était que trop clair pour moi.
9. les tirs qui retentissaient en bas
10. reprenne
11. de plus
12. calculé, de sang-froid
13. abominable
14. Je ne sentais plus rien
15. je me remis péniblement debout
16. alors que j'étais à genoux
17. vous rendre
18. toujours su

'There is going to be no killing tonight. The shooting gallery is closed. The fair is over.[1] Do you not hear?'

For the first time, I realised that the barrel organ had stopped. The crowd seemed to have departed[2]. Outside this empty and derelict[3] room, all was silent.

'What are you talking about?'

'I did not believe you the first time we met, Henderson. But then it was expedient[4] to walk into your trap, if only to see[5] what you were planning. But do you really believe I would do the same[6] a second time?'

'Put those guns down![7]' a voice cried out.

In the next few seconds, there was such a confusion of events[8] that, at the time, I was barely able to make any sense of them[9]. Henderson brought his gun round[10], meaning to fire either at me or past me[11]. I will never know, for his finger was never able to tighten on the trigger[12]. At the same moment, there was a fusillade of shots, the muzzle of a gun flashing white[13], and he was literally thrown off his feet[14], a fountain of blood bursting[15] from his head. Henderson's associate[16], the man he had referred to as Bratby, spun round[17]. I do not think he intended to fire but it was enough that he was armed. A bullet hit him in the shoulder and another in the chest. I heard him cry out as he was thrown back[18], my gun flying out[19] of his hand. There was a clatter as his walking stick hit the wooden floorboards and rolled away. He was not dead. Wheezing[20], sobbing in pain[21] and shock, he crumpled[22] to the ground. There was a brief pause, the silence almost as shocking as the violence that had gone before[23].

'You left that very late[24], Lestrade,' Holmes remarked.

'I was interested to hear[25] what the villain said,' the same replied. I looked round and saw that Inspector Lestrade was indeed here, and three police

1. La fête est finie.
2. être partie
3. à l'abandon
4. il était opportun
5. ne serait-ce que pour voir
6. que je ferais la même chose
7. Déposez vos armes !
8. les événements furent si confus
9. y comprendre quelque chose
10. tourna son arme
11. tirer soit sur moi, soit derrière moi
12. presser la détente
13. le canon d'un revolver lançant un éclair blanc
14. projeté en l'air
15. jet de sang jaillissant
16. acolyte
17. fit volte-face
18. crier en tombant à la renverse
19. s'envolant
20. La respiration sifflante
21. pleurant de douleur
22. s'effondra
23. qui avait précédé
24. Vous avez pris votre temps
25. Je tenais à entendre

officers with him, already entering the room, checking on[1] the men who had been shot.

'You heard him confess to[2] the murders?'

'Yes, indeed, Mr Holmes.' One of his men had reached Henderson. He examined him briefly and shook his head. I had seen the wound[3]. I was not surprised. 'I'm afraid he will not face justice for his crimes[4] .'

'Some might say he already has.'

'Even so, I would have preferred him alive, if only as a witness. I've put my neck on the line[5] for you, Mr Holmes, and this night's work could still cost me dear[6].'

'It will cost you another commendation[7], Lestrade, and well you know it[8].' Holmes turned his attention to me. 'How are you bearing up[9], Watson? Are you hurt?'

'Nothing that a little embrocation[10] and a whisky and soda won't cure[11],' I replied. 'But tell me, Holmes. You knew all along[12] that this was a trap?'

'I strongly suspected it. It seemed inconceivable to me that an illiterate[13] child would keep an advertisement folded beneath his bed. And as our late friend[14], Henderson, said, we had already been deceived once. I am beginning to learn how our enemies work[15].'

'Meaning ... ?[16]'

'They used you to find me. The men who followed you to Holborn Viaduct were not police officers. They were in the employ of our enemies, who had provided you with what appeared to be an irresistible clue in the hope that you would know of my whereabouts[17] and would deliver it to me[18].'

'But the name, Dr Silkin's House of Wonders. Are you telling me that he has nothing to do with it?'

'My dear Watson! Silkin is not so uncommon a name[19]. They could have used Silkin the bootmaker[20] in Ludgate Circus or Silkin the timber

1. examinant
2. avouer
3. la blessure
4. qu'il ne réponde pas de ses crimes devant la justice
5. J'ai pris de gros risques
6. me coûter cher
7. décoration
8. vous le savez très bien
9. Comment vous en sortez-vous
10. [préparation huileuse antalgique]
11. ne guériraient
12. Vous saviez depuis le début
13. illettré
14. feu notre ami
15. fonctionnent nos ennemis
16. C'est-à-dire ?
17. sauriez où j'étais
18. me le remettriez
19. un nom si rare que ça
20. bottier

yard[1] in Battersea. Or Silkman or Silk Way or anything that would have us believe[2] we were closing in on[3] the House of Silk. It was only necessary to draw me into the open[4] so that they could finally be rid of me[5].'

'What of you, Lestrade? How did you come to be here?'

'Mr Holmes approached me[6] and asked me to come, Dr Watson.'

'You believed in his innocence!'

'I never doubted it from the start. And when I looked into that matter[7] at Coppergate Square it soon became clear that there was something crooked[8] about the affair. Inspector Harriman said he was on his way from a bank robbery[9] on the White Horse Road, but there was no such robbery. I looked in the report book[10]. I visited the bank. And it seemed to me that if Harriman was prepared to lie[11] about that in court, he might be prepared to lie about quite a few other things too.'

'Lestrade took a gamble[12],' Holmes cut in. 'For his first instinct was to return me[13] to the prison authorities. But he and I know each other well, whatever our differences[14], and have collaborated too often to fall out over[15] a false accusation. Is that not true, Lestrade?'

'Whatever you say, Mr Holmes.'

'And at heart, he is as eager as I to bring an end to this affair and to bring the true culprits to[16] justice.'

'This one is alive!' one of the police officers exclaimed. While Holmes and I had been talking, they had been examining our two assailants.

Holmes crossed over to where Bratby lay and knelt beside him. 'Can you hear me, Bratby?' he asked. There was silence, then a soft whining[17] like a child in pain. 'There is nothing we can do for you but you still have time to make some amends[18], to atone for[19] some of your crimes before you meet your maker[20].'

1. scierie
2. qui pourrait nous faire croire
3. que nous nous rapprochions dangereusement de
4. m'attirer à découvert
5. se débarrasser de moi
6. m'a contacté
7. j'ai creusé cette histoire
8. de louche
9. venait d'un cambriolage de banque
10. le registre des rapports
11. prêt à mentir
12. a fait un pari risqué
13. de me remettre
14. quelles que soient nos divergences
15. nous brouiller pour
16. les véritables coupables devant
17. un léger gémissement
18. pour vous racheter un peu
19. expier
20. avant d'affronter votre Créateur

Very quietly, Bratby began to sob[1].

'I know everything about the House of Silk. I know what it is. I know where it is to be found ... indeed, I visited it last night but found it empty and silent. That is the one piece of information[2] which I have no way of discovering for myself and yet it is vital[3] if we are to bring an end to this business once and for all. For the good of your own salvation[4], tell me. When does it next meet?[5]'

There was a long silence. Despite myself, I felt a surge of pity[6] for this man who was about to breathe his last[7] even though he had intended to kill me – and Holmes with me – just a few minutes before. For all men are equal at the moment of death and who are we to[8] judge them when a much greater judge awaits[9]?

'Tonight,' he said. And died.

Holmes straightened up[10]. 'At last fortune is on our side[11], Lestrade,' he said. 'Will you accompany me a little further[12]? And do you have at least ten men with you? They will need to be steadfast and resolute[13] for, I promise you, they will not forget what we are about to reveal.'

'We're with you, Holmes,' Lestrade replied. 'Let's get this over with.'

Holmes had my gun. I had not seen when he had retrieved it[14], but once again he pressed it into my hand, looking me[15] in the eyes. I knew what he was asking. I nodded and together we set off.

1. sangloter
2. la seule information
3. elle est pourtant essentielle
4. Si vous voulez trouver le salut
5. Quand est sa prochaine réunion ?
6. un élan de pitié
7. sur le point d'expirer
8. qui sommes-nous pour
9. juge autrement plus puissant les attend
10. se redressa
11. La chance est enfin de notre côté
12. encore un instant
13. fermes et résolus
14. l'avait récupéré
15. en me regardant

NINETEEN

The House of Silk

We returned to the highest reaches[1] of Hamworth Hill, to Chorley Grange School for Boys. Where else[2] could the investigation have taken us[3]? It was from here that the flyer had come and it was obvious now that somebody had placed it under the mattress of Ross's bed for the headmaster to find, knowing that he would bring it to us, drawing us into the trap at Dr Silkin's winter fair. It was, of course, always possible that Charles Fitzsimmons had been lying all along[4] and that he was part of the conspiracy, too. And yet, even now I found that hard to believe, for he had struck me as the very model of propriety[5] with his sense of duty, his concern for the welfare[6] of his boys, his respectable wife, the anguish[7] with which he had greeted the death[8] of Ross. It was hard to imagine that all this had been no more than a masquerade and I felt sure, even now, that if he had been drawn into[9] something dark and evil, it had been against his knowledge or inclination[10].

Lestrade had brought ten men with him in four separate carriages that had followed each other, silently climbing the hill that seemed to rise endlessly[11] from the northern edge[12] of London. He was still carrying a revolver, as were Holmes and I, but the rest of his men were unarmed[13], so that if it was the case that we were preparing for a physical confrontation, speed and surprise[14] would be

1. tout en haut
2. Dans quel autre endroit
3. nous conduire
4. ait menti depuis le début
5. un vrai modèle de rectitude
6. son souci du bien-être
7. la peine
8. reçu la nouvelle de la mort
9. entraîné dans
10. à son insu ou à son corps défendant
11. s'élever à l'infini
12. depuis la frange nord
13. n'étaient pas armés
14. la rapidité et l'effet de surprise

of the very essence[1]. Holmes gave the signal and the carriages stopped a short distance from our target[2], which was not the school itself, as I had imagined, but the square building[3] on the other side of the lane which had once been a coach-builder's factory. Fitzsimmons had told us that it was used for musical recitals[4] and in this, at least, he must have been telling the truth for there were several coaches[5] parked outside and I could hear piano music coming from within[6].

We took up our positions behind a clump of trees[7] where we could remain unobserved[8]. It was half past eight and it had begun to snow, fat white feathers[9] falling out of the night sky. The ground was already white and it was markedly colder[10] up here, at the brow of the hill[11], than it had been in the city. I was in considerable pain from the blow that had been inflicted on me[12] at the fair, my entire arm throbbing[13] and my old wound twitching in sympathy[14], and I feared I might have the beginnings of a fever. But I was determined to show none of it. I had come this far and I would see it through to the end. Holmes was waiting for something and I had infinite faith in his judgement, even if we had to stand here all night.

Lestrade must have been aware of my discomfort[15] for he nudged me[16] and handed me a silver hip flask[17]. I raised it to my lips and took a sip[18] of brandy before handing it back to the little detective. He wiped it on his sleeve, drank some himself and put it away[19].

'What's the plan, Mr Holmes?' he asked.

'If you want to catch these people red-handed[20], Lestrade, then we must learn how to enter without raising the alarm.'

'We're going to break into a[21] concert?'

'It is not a concert.'

1. absolument essentiels
2. non loin de notre cible
3. le bâtiment carré
4. des concerts
5. véhicules
6. venant de l'intérieur
7. un bouquet d'arbres
8. rester sans être vus
9. un épais duvet blanc
10. il faisait nettement plus froid
11. ici, au sommet de la colline
12. du coup reçu
13. avec des élancements dans tout le bras
14. se réveillant pour faire bonne mesure
15. dut voir mon malaise
16. me donna un petit coup de coude
17. flasque
18. bus une gorgée
19. la rangea
20. la main dans le sac
21. débarquer en plein

I heard the soft rattle of yet another approaching carriage and turned to see a brougham pulled by a fine, grey mare[1]. The driver was whipping it on[2], for the hill was steep[3] and the ground underfoot[4] already treacherous[5], mud and snow causing the wheels to slip[6]. I glanced at Holmes. There was a look in his face quite different from any that I had seen before. I would describe it as a sort of cold satisfaction, a sense that he had been proven right[7] and that now, at last, he could seek vengeance[8]. His eyes were bright but the bones in his cheek drew dark lines[9] below them and I thought not even the angel of death would appear quite so menacing[10] when finally we met.

'Do you see, Watson?' he whispered.

Concealed behind the trees, we could not be seen but at the same time we had an uninterrupted view[11] both of the school building and of the lane as it ran in both directions. Holmes pointed and, in the moonlight[12], I saw a symbol painted in gold on the side of the brougham; a raven and two keys. It was the family crest of Lord Ravenshaw and I remembered the arrogant man with the swollen eyes[13] whose watch had been stolen and whom we had met in Gloucestershire. Was it possible that he was involved in this too? The coach turned into the driveway and stopped. Lord Ravenshaw descended, clearly recognisable[14] even at this distance, dressed in a black cloak and top hat. He walked to the front door and knocked on it. It was opened by an unseen figure[15], but as the yellow light spilled out[16], I saw him holding something which dangled from his hand. It resembled a long strip[17] of paper but of course it was no such thing[18]. It was a white silk ribbon. The new arrival[19] was admitted. The door closed.

'It is exactly as I thought,' Holmes said. 'Watson, are you prepared to accompany me? I must warn you that what you will encounter on the other side[20]

1. belle jument grise
2. usait de son fouet pour l'encourager
3. raide
4. sous les sabots
5. glissant
6. faisant patiner les roues
7. le sentiment d'avoir vu juste
8. se venger
9. traçaient des lignes sombres
10. même l'ange de la mort n'aurait pas eu l'air si menaçant
11. une vue panoramique
12. au clair de lune
13. aux yeux gonflés
14. très reconnaissable
15. silhouette invisible
16. le seuil fut éclairé
17. bande
18. ce n'était rien de tel
19. arrivant
20. ce que vous verrez de l'autre côté

of that door may cause you great distress[1]. This case has been an interesting one and I have long feared that it could lead[2] to only one conclusion. Well, there is no helping it[3]. We must see what has to be seen. Your gun is loaded? A single shot, Lestrade. That will be the signal for you and your men to come in.'

'Whatever you say[4], Mr Holmes.'

We left the protection of the trees and crossed the road, our feet already crunching[5] on an inch of freshly laid snow[6]. The house loomed up in front of us, the windows heavily curtained[7] and allowing only a soft rectangle of light to show through[8]. I could still hear the piano playing but it no longer suggested to me a formal recital[9] – someone was performing an Irish ballad[10], the sort of music that might have been performed in the lowest public house[11]. We passed the line of carriages still waiting for their owners, and reached the front door. Holmes knocked. The door was opened by a young man whom I had not met on my last visit to the school, with black hair pressed close to[12] his head, arched eyebrows[13] and a manner that was both supercilious and deferential[14]. He was dressed in a vaguely military style with a short jacket, peg-top trousers[15] and buttoned boots[16]. He also wore a lavender waistcoat and matching[17] gloves.

'Yes?' The house steward[18], if that was what he was, had failed to recognise us and regarded us with suspicion.

'We are friends of Lord Horace Blackwater,' Holmes said, and I was astonished to hear him name one of his accusers at the police court.

'He sent you here?'

'He very much recommended you to me.'

'And your name?'

'It is Parsons. This is a colleague of mine, Mr Smith.'

1. beaucoup vous affliger
2. je crains depuis longtemps qu'il ne mène
3. nous n'y pouvons rien
4. Comme vous voudrez
5. crissant
6. deux ou trois centimètres de neige fraîchement tombée
7. couvertes de lourdes tentures
8. ne laissant passer qu'un léger rectangle de lumière
9. concert classique
10. ballade irlandaise
11. jouée dans des pubs de dernière catégorie
12. plaqués sur
13. des sourcils arqués
14. une attitude à la fois hautaine et respectueuse
15. un fuseau
16. des bottes à boutons
17. assortis
18. L'intendant

'And did Lord Blackwater provide you with any token or means[1] of identification? It is not normally our practice[2] to admit strangers in the middle of the night.'

'Most certainly. He told me to give you this.' Holmes reached into his pocket and withdrew[3] a length of white silk ribbon. He held it in the air for a moment, then handed it across.

The effect was immediate. The house steward bowed his head[4] and opened the door a little wider, gesturing with one hand. 'Come in.'

We were admitted into a hallway that took me quite by surprise, for I had been remembering the austere and gloomy nature[5] of the school on the other side of the lane and had been expecting more of the same[6]. Nothing could have been further from the truth[7], for I was surrounded by opulence, by warmth[8] and bright light. A black and white tiled[9] corridor, in the Dutch[10] style, led into the distance, punctuated by elegant mahogany[11] tables with curlicues and turned legs[12] resting against the walls between the various doors. The gas lamps were themselves installed in highly ornate fitments[13] and had been turned up to allow the light to pour onto[14] the many treasures that the house possessed. Elaborate rococo mirrors[15] with brilliant silver frames hung on the walls, which were themselves draped with heavily embossed scarlet and gold wallpaper[16]. Two marble statues from ancient Rome stood opposite each other in niches and, although they might have seemed unremarkable[17] in a museum, they seemed shockingly inappropriate[18] in a private home. There were flowers and potted plants everywhere, on the tables, on pilasters and on wooden plinths[19], their scent hanging heavy in the overheated air[20]. The piano music was coming from a room at the far end. There was nobody else in sight.

1. fourni un symbole quelconque
2. Il n'est pas dans nos habitudes
3. fouilla dans sa poche et en retira
4. inclina la tête
5. l'aspect lugubre
6. quelque chose de similaire
7. n'était moins vrai
8. de chaleur
9. dallé de noir et blanc
10. hollandais
11. en acajou
12. à fioritures et aux piètements tournés
13. des éléments richement décorés
14. bien éclairer
15. Des miroirs rococo sophistiqués
16. papier peint rouge et or chargé de reliefs
17. banales
18. totalement déplacées
19. des socles
20. saturant l'air surchauffé

'If you would like to wait in here, gentlemen, I will inform the master of the house that you are here.'

The house steward led us through a door and into a drawing room as well appointed[1] as the corridor outside. It was thickly carpeted.[2] A sofa and two armchairs, all upholstered in[3] dark mauve, had been arranged around a fireplace where several logs were blazing. The windows were covered by thick velvet curtains with heavy pelmets[4], which we had seen from outside, but there was a glass door where the curtain had been drawn back and which led into a conservatory[5] filled with ferns[6] and orange trees[7] with a large brass cage[8] containing a green parakeet[9] at the very centre. One side of the room was taken up with bookshelves[10], the other with a long sideboard[11] on which were displayed all manner of ornaments[12], from blue and white Delft pottery[13] and photographs in frames, to a tableau of two stuffed kittens[14] sitting on miniature chairs, their paws pressed together[15] as if they were husband and wife. An occasional table with spandrels[16] stood beside the fire with a number of bottles and glasses.

'Please make yourselves comfortable[17],' the house steward said. 'Can I offer you gentlemen a drink?' We both declined[18]. 'Then if you would like to remain here, I will return very shortly.' He left the room, his feet making no sound on the carpet, and closed the door. We were alone.

'For Heaven's sake, Holmes!' I cried. 'What is this place?'

'It is the House of Silk,' he replied, grimly.

'Yes. But what ... ?'

He held up a hand. He had gone over to the door and was listening for anyone[19] outside. Having satisfied himself[20], he carefully opened it and signalled to me. 'We have an ordeal ahead of us[21],' he whispered. 'I am almost sorry to have brought you here, old friend. But we must see an end to it.'

1. aussi bien meublée
2. Le sol était recouvert d'un épais tapis.
3. le tout revêtu de
4. de lourdes cantonnières
5. jardin d'hiver
6. de fougères
7. d'orangers
8. grande cage en laiton
9. perruche
10. occupé par des rayonnages de livres
11. buffet
12. d'objets décoratifs
13. faïence de Delft
14. chatons en peluche
15. les pattes jointes
16. une table d'appoint à pans ouvragés [angles]
17. installez-vous
18. refusâmes tous les deux
19. écoutait pour savoir s'il y avait quelqu'un
20. Rassuré
21. Une épreuve nous attend

We slipped outside. The house steward had disappeared, but the music was still playing, a waltz[1] now, and it struck me that the keys were a little out of tune[2]. We made our way down the corridor, moving further into the building, away from the front door. Somewhere, far above us, I heard someone cry out very briefly and my blood froze[3], for I was sure it was the sound of a child[4]. A clock, suspended on the wall and ticking heavily, showed ten to nine but so enclosed were we[5], so cut off[6] from the outside world, that it could have been any time of the night or day. We reached a staircase and began to make our way up. Even as we took the first steps[7], I heard a door open somewhere along the corridor and a man's voice which I thought I recognised. It was the master of the house. He was on his way to see us.

We hurried forward, turning the corner[8] just as two figures – the house steward who had greeted us and another – passed below[9].

'Onwards[10], Watson,' Holmes whispered.

We came to a second corridor, this one with the gas lamps turned down[11]. It was carpeted, with floral wallpaper and there were many more doors with, on either side, oil paintings in heavy frames[12] which proved to be tawdry imitations of classical works[13]. There was an odour in the air that was sweet[14] and unpleasant. Even though the truth had still not fully dawned on me[15], my every instinct was to leave this place, to wish that I had never come.

'We must choose a door,' Holmes muttered. 'But which one?'

The doors were unmarked[16], identical, polished oak[17] with white porcelain handles[18]. He chose the one closest to him and opened it. Together, we looked in. At the wooden floor, the rug, the candles, the mirror, the jug and the basin[19], the bearded man we had never seen before, sitting, dressed only in a

1. valse
2. les touches étaient quelque peu désaccordées
3. se glaça
4. une voix d'enfant
5. nous étions si confinés
6. si coupés
7. Dès les premières marches
8. tournant à l'angle
9. passaient en bas
10. En avant
11. éteintes
12. des peintures à l'huile aux cadres surchargés
13. d'œuvres classiques
14. doucereuse
15. la vérité ne s'imposât pas encore à moi
16. anonymes
17. en chêne poli
18. poignées
19. le broc et la cuvette

white shirt open at the collar[1], at the boy on the bed behind him.

It could not be true. I did not want to believe it. But nor could I disavow the evidence of my own eyes[2]. For that was the secret of the House of Silk. It was a house of ill-repute, nothing more, nothing less[3]; but one designed for men with a gross[4] perversion and the wealth to indulge it[5]. These men had a predilection for young boys and their wretched[6] victims had been drawn from those same schoolchildren[7] I had seen at Chorley Grange, plucked off the[8] London streets with no families or friends to care for them[9], no money and no food, for the most part ignored by a society to which they were little more than an inconvenience[10]. They had been forced or bribed into a life of squalor[11], threatened with torture or death if they did not comply[12]. Ross had briefly been one of them. No wonder[13] he had run away. And no wonder his sister had tried to stab me, believing I had come to take him back. What sort of country did I live in, at the end of the last century, I wonder, that could so utterly abandon its young[14]? They could fall ill. They could starve. And worse. Nobody cared.

All these thoughts raced through my consciousness[15] in the few seconds that we stood there. Then the man noticed us. 'What the devil do you think you're doing?' he thundered[16].

Holmes closed the door. At that very moment, there was a cry from downstairs as the master of the house entered the drawing room and found that we had gone. The piano music stopped. I wondered what we should do next[17], but a second later the decision was taken from us[18]. A door opened further down the corridor and a man stepped out, fully dressed but with his clothes in disarray[19], his shirt hanging out at the back[20]. This time I knew him at once. It was Inspector Harriman.

1. d'une chemise blanche au col ouvert
2. je ne pouvais pas non plus nier ce que j'avais sous les yeux
3. une maison close, ni plus, ni moins
4. répugnante
5. la fortune permettant de s'y livrer
6. malheureuses
7. choisies parmi ces mêmes écoliers
8. arrachés aux
9. pour se soucier d'eux
10. embarras
11. On les avait contraints par la force ou l'appât du gain à avoir une vie sordide
12. s'ils ne se soumettaient pas
13. Pas étonnant
14. sa jeunesse
15. ces pensées se bousculèrent dans mon esprit
16. tonna-t-il
17. comment réagir
18. ne nous appartint plus
19. en désordre
20. pendant dans le dos

He saw us. 'You!' he exclaimed.

He stood, facing us. Without a second thought, I took out my revolver and fired the single shot[1] that would bring Lestrade and his men rushing to our aid. But I did not fire into the air as I could have done. I aimed at Harriman and pulled the trigger with a murderous intent[2] which I had never felt before and have never felt since. For the only time in my life, I knew exactly what it meant to wish to kill[3] a man.

My bullet missed[4]. At the last second, Holmes must have seen what I intended and cried out, his hand leaping[5] towards my gun. It was enough to spoil my aim[6]. The bullet went wild, smashing[7] a gas lamp. Harriman ducked[8] and ran away, reaching a second staircase and disappearing down it. At the same time, the gunshot had set off an alarm throughout the building. More doors flew open[9] and middle-aged men lurched[10] into the corridor, looking around them, their faces filled with panic and consternation as if they had been secretly waiting many years for their sins to be uncovered[11] and had guessed, at once, that the moment had finally come. Down below, there was the crash[12] of wood and the sound of shouting as the front door was forced open[13]. I heard Lestrade calling out. There was a second gunshot. Somebody screamed.

Holmes was already moving forward, pushing past anyone who[14] happened to get in his way, following in Harriman's path[15]. The Scotland Yard man had clearly decided that the game was up[16], but it seemed inconceivable that he would be able to escape. Lestrade had arrived. His men would be everywhere. And yet, that was evidently what Holmes feared, for he had already reached the staircase and was hurrying down[17]. I followed, and together we reached the ground floor with its black and white tiled corridor. Here, everything was chaos. The front

1. cet unique coup de feu
2. une volonté meurtrière
3. ce que signifiait avoir envie de tuer
4. manqua sa cible
5. levant brusquement la main
6. pour que je vise mal
7. dérapa, brisant
8. se baissa pour l'éviter
9. D'autres portes s'ouvrirent d'un coup
10. arrivèrent en titubant
11. que leurs péchés soient révélés
12. Tout en bas, il y eut un craquement
13. on enfonçait la porte d'entrée
14. bousculant quiconque
15. sur les traces de Harriman
16. la partie était finie
17. descendait à toute allure

door was open, an icy wind blowing[1] through the corridors and the gas lamps flickering. Lestrade's men had already begun their work. Lord Ravenshaw, who had removed his cloak to reveal a velvet smoking jacket, ran out of one of the rooms, a cigar still in his hand. He was seized by an officer[2] and pinned back[3] against the wall.

'Get your hands off me![4]' he shouted. 'Don't you know who I am?'

It had not yet dawned on him[5] that the whole country would soon know who he was, and would doubtless hold him and his name in revulsion[6]. Other clients of the House of Silk were already being arrested, bumbling around the place[7] without courage or dignity, many of them weeping tears of self-pity[8]. The house steward was sitting slumped[9] on the floor, with blood trickling[10] from his nose. I saw Robert Weeks, the teacher who had been a graduate from Balliol College, being dragged out[11] of a room with his arm twisted behind his back[12].

There was a door at the very back of the house. It was open and led into a garden. One of Lestrade's men was lying in front of it, blood pumping out[13] of a bullet wound in his chest. Lestrade was already attending to him[14] but seeing Holmes he looked up, his face flushed with anger[15]. 'It was Harriman!' he exclaimed. 'He fired as he came down the stairs.'

'Where is he?'

'Gone!' Lestrade pointed at the open door.

Without another word, Holmes plunged after[16] Harriman. I followed, partly because my place was always at his side but also because I wanted to be there when scores were finally settled[17]. Harriman might only be a servant of the House of Silk, but he had made this business personal[18], falsely[19] imprisoning Holmes and conniving in his murder[20]. I would gladly have shot him. I was still sorry I had missed.

1. un vent glacial soufflait
2. Un officier le saisit
3. le plaqua
4. Ne me touchez pas !
5. Il n'avait pas encore réalisé
6. n'aurait sans doute que dégoût pour lui
7. allant et venant, l'air empoté,
8. pleurant sur leur propre sort
9. assis affalé
10. un filet de sang coulant
11. être traîné hors
12. un bras bloqué dans le dos
13. du sang jaillissant
14. auprès de lui
15. rouge de colère
16. se rua à la poursuite de
17. on réglerait les comptes
18. il en avait fait une affaire personnelle
19. à tort
20. complotant pour l'assassiner

Out into the darkness and the swirling snow[1]. We followed a path round the side of[2] the house. The night had become a maelstrom of black and white and it was hard even to make out[3] the buildings on the other side of the lane. But then we heard the crack of a whip[4] and the whinny[5] of a horse, and one of the carriages shot forward, racing[6] towards the gate. There could be no doubt who was behind the reins[7]. With a heavy heart and a bitter taste[8] in my mouth, I realised that Harriman had got away, that we would have to wait in the hope that he would be found and apprehended[9] in the days that followed.

But Holmes was having none of it[10]. Harriman had taken a curricle, a two-wheeler drawn by[11] two horses. Without stopping to choose from the vehicles that were left, he leapt into the nearest one, a flimsy[12] dog cart[13] with but one[14] horse – and not the healthiest specimen at that[15]. Somehow I managed to clamber into the back[16] and then we were off in pursuit, ignoring the cries of the driver who had been smoking a cigarette nearby and hadn't noticed us until it was too late. We burst through the gates, then swept round into the lane. With Holmes whipping it on, the horse proved to have more spirit[17] than we might have expected and the little dog cart simply flew over[18] the snow-covered surface. We might have one horse less than Harriman, but our vehicle was lighter and more agile. Perched high up, I could only cling on for dear life[19], thinking that if I fell off I would surely break my neck.

This was no night for a chase[20]. The snow was sweeping at us horizontally[21], punching at us in a series of continuous bursts[22]. I could not begin to[23] understand how Holmes could see, for every time I tried to peer into[24] the darkness I was instantly blinded[25] and my cheeks were already numb with cold[26]. But there was Harriman, no more than fifty

1. les flocons tourbillonnants
2. contournant
3. distinguer
4. le claquement d'un fouet
5. hennissement
6. partit en trombe
7. tenait les rênes
8. un goût amer
9. arrêté
10. pour Holmes, il n'en était pas question
11. carrick, un attelage à deux roues, à
12. léger
13. [véhicule découvert, pour le transport des chiens menés à la chasse]
14. un seul
15. guère fringant, en plus
16. me hisser à l'arrière
17. d'entrain
18. volait littéralement au-dessus
19. m'accrocher vaille que vaille
20. poursuite
21. venait droit sur nous
22. bourrasques
23. J'étais loin de
24. scruter
25. aveuglé
26. engourdies par le froid

yards ahead of us. I heard him cry out with vexation, heard the lash[1] of his whip. Holmes was sitting in front of me, crouched[2] forward, holding the reins with both hands, keeping his balance[3] only with his feet. Every pothole[4] threatened to throw him out. The slightest curve[5] caused us to skid[6] madly across the icy surface of the road. I wondered if the splinter bars[7] could possibly hold, and in my mind's eye I saw[8] imminent catastrophe as our steed[9], excited by the chase, ended up dashing us to pieces[10]. The hill was steep and it was as if we were plunging into a chasm[11] with the snow swirling all around us and the wind sucking us down[12].

Forty yards, thirty ... somehow we were managing to close the gap[13] between us. The hooves[14] of the other horses were thundering down[15], the wheels of the curricle madly spinning[16], the entire structure rattling and shaking[17] as if it would tear itself apart at any time[18]. Harriman was aware of us now. I saw him glance back, his white hair a mad halo[19] around his head. He reached for something. Too late did I see what it was. There was a tiny flash of red, a gunshot that was almost lost in the cacophony of the chase. I heard the bullet strike wood. It had missed Holmes by inches and me by even less. The closer we were, the easier a target we became[20]. And yet still we hurtled down[21].

Now there were lights in the distance, a village or a suburb. Harriman fired a second time. Our horse screamed and stumbled[22]. The entire dog cart flew into the air, then came crashing down[23], jarring my spine[24] and setting my shoulder ablaze[25]. But fortunately the animal had been wounded and not killed and, if anything, the near calamity[26] only made it all the more determined[27]. Holmes cried out wordlessly. Thirty yards, twenty. In a few seconds we would overtake[28].

1. cinglement
2. accroupi
3. se maintenant en équilibre
4. nid-de-poule
5. La moindre courbe
6. déraper
7. brancards de l'attelage
8. j'imaginais déjà
9. fier coursier
10. nous précipitait vers l'abîme
11. abîme
12. qui nous aspirait
13. réduire la distance
14. sabots
15. dévalaient la pente avec fracas
16. tournant frénétiquement
17. bringuebalant
18. se désintégrer à tout moment
19. formant un halo dément
20. plus nous devenions une cible facile
21. dévalions toujours
22. trébucha
23. s'écrasa
24. heurtant ma colonne vertébrale
25. me brûlant l'épaule
26. au contraire, avoir frôlé la catastrophe
27. renforça sa détermination
28. le dépasser

But then Holmes was dragging on the reins and I saw a sharp bend ahead[1]– the lane veered round to the left[2], and if we tried to take it at this speed we would be killed for sure. The dog cart sluiced across the surface[3], ice and mud spitting out[4] from beneath the wheels. I must surely be thrown off[5]. I tightened my grip, the wind battering me, the whole world barely more than a blur[6]. There was a sharp crack ahead of me – not a third bullet, but the sound of splintering[7] wood. I opened my eyes to see that the curricle had taken the corner[8] too quickly. It was on one wheel and that had placed an unimaginable strain[9] on the wooden frame which broke apart[10] even as I watched[11]. Harriman was jerked out of his seat and into the air[12], the reins pulling him forward[13]. For a brief second he was suspended there. Then the whole thing toppled onto its side[14], with Harriman disappearing from sight. The horses kept running, but they had become separated from the carriage and took off[15] into the darkness. The curricle slithered[16] and spun[17], finally coming to a halt right in front of us, and for a moment I thought we would crash into it[18]. But Holmes still had the reins. He guided our steed around the obstacle, drawing it into a halt[19].

Our horse stood there, panting[20]. There was a bloody streak[21] along its flank and I felt as if my every bone[22] had become dislocated. I had no coat and I was shivering with cold.

'Well, Watson,' Holmes rasped, breathing heavily[23]. 'Do you think I have a future as a cab driver?'

'You might have one indeed,' I replied. 'But don't expect too many tips[24].'

'Let us see what we can do for Harriman.'

We climbed down – but one glance told us that the pursuit was over in every sense. Harriman was covered in blood. His neck was so badly broken[25] that, although he lay sprawled out[26] with his palms

1. virage serré, devant
2. virait à gauche
3. traversa tout d'un trait
4. jaillissant
5. éjecté
6. ne voyant que du flou
7. qui se fend
8. pris le virage
9. soumis à une tension incroyable
10. se brisa
11. sous mes yeux
12. éjecté de son siège et expédié dans les airs
13. le tirant en avant
14. versa sur le côté
15. décampèrent
16. vira
17. tournoya
18. allions foncer dedans
19. et l'amena à l'arrêt
20. haletant
21. traînée de sang
22. tous mes os
23. essoufflé, articula d'une voix rauque
24. trop de pourboires
25. tellement brisé
26. était étendu de tout son long

down on[1] the surface of the lane, his sightless eyes stared up at[2] the sky and his entire face was contorted by a[3] hideous grimace of pain. Holmes took one look at him, then nodded. 'This was no more than he deserved[4],' he said.

'He was a wicked[5] man, Holmes. These are all evil people.'

'You put it quite succinctly[6], Watson. Can you bear to return to Chorley Grange?'

'Those children, Holmes. Those poor children.'

'I know. But Lestrade should by now have taken charge of the situation. Let us see what can be done.'

Our horse was full of fire and resentment, its nostrils steaming[7] in the night. With difficulty we managed to turn it round and drove slowly back up the hill. I was surprised how far we had come[8]. The journey down had been a matter of a few minutes.[9] It took us more than half an hour to return. But the snow seemed to be gentler[10] and the wind had dropped[11]. I was glad to have time to collect myself[12], to be alone with my friend.

'Holmes,' I said. 'When did you first know?'

'About the House of Silk? I suspected that something was amiss[13] the first time we came to Chorley Grange. Fitzsimmons and his wife were consummate[14] actors but you will recall[15] how angry he became when the child that we questioned – a fair-haired boy by the name of Daniel – mentioned that Ross had a sister who worked at The Bag of Nails. He covered it well[16] and tried to make us believe that he was annoyed[17] that this information had not come to us sooner. But in fact he was furious that anything had been told to us at all[18]. I was also puzzled[19] by the nature of the building opposite the school. I could see at a glance[20] that the wheel tracks belonged to a number of different carriages, including a brougham and a landau. Why should the owners of such expensive vehicles be coming to a

1. plaquées sur
2. son regard fixe était levé vers le ciel
3. tordue en une
4. Il ne méritait pas moins
5. méchant
6. Voilà qui est bien résumé
7. plein de fougue et de rancune, les naseaux fumants
8. de la distance parcourue
9. L'aller n'avait pris que quelques minutes
10. se calmer
11. était retombé
12. le temps de reprendre mes esprits
13. ne tournait pas rond
14. d'excellents
15. rappelez-vous
16. l'a bien caché
17. fâché
18. que l'on nous ait dit quoi que ce soit
19. intrigué
20. tout de suite

musical recital by a group of anonymous, deprived boys[1]? It made no sense.'

'But you did not realise ...'

'Not then. It is a lesson that I have learned, Watson, and one that I shall remember for the future. In the pursuit of a crime, a detective must occasionally be guided by his worst imaginings[2] – which is to say that he must put himself in the mind[3] of the criminal. But there are limits beyond which any civilised man will not allow himself to stoop[4]. Such was the case here. I did not imagine what Fitzsimmons and his cohorts[5] might be involved in for the simple reason that I did not wish to. Like it or not[6], in future I must learn to be less fastidious[7]. It was only when we discovered the body of poor Ross that I began to see that we had entered an arena different to anything we had formerly experienced[8]. It was not just the cruelty of his injuries. It was the white ribbon tied around his wrist. Anyone who could have done such a thing to a dead child must have a mind that was utterly, completely corrupt[9]. To such a man, anything would be possible.'

'The white ribbon ...'

'As you saw, it was the token[10] by which these men recognised each other and which would allow them entrance to the House of Silk. But it had a second purpose[11]. By looping it around the child's wrist, they made an example of him. They knew that it would be reported in the papers and would therefore act as a warning[12], that this is what would happen to anyone who dared cross their path[13].'

'And the name, Holmes. Is that why they called it the House of Silk?'

'It was not the only reason, Watson. I fear the answer has been in front of us[14] all the time, although perhaps it only became obvious in retrospect[15]. You will recall the name of the charity which Fitzsimmons told us supported[16] his work? The Society

1. donné par un groupe de garçons défavorisés et inconnus
2. se laisser guider par ses pires supputations
3. se mettre dans la tête
4. que tout homme civilisé se refuse à envisager
5. sa clique
6. Que je le veuille ou non
7. à moins consulter mes goûts
8. tout ce que nous connaissions
9. foncièrement corrompu
10. le symbole
11. raison d'être
12. servirait ainsi d'avertissement
13. osant se mettre en travers de leur route
14. sous nos yeux
15. ce ne soit devenu évident qu'a posteriori
16. finançait

for the Improvement of London's Children. I rather think we have been pursuing[1] the House of SILC – and not Silk. That must surely have been its origin at any rate[2]. The charity could have been constructed[3] precisely for these people. It gave them the mechanism[4] to find the children and the mask behind which[5] they could exploit them.'

We had reached the school. Holmes handed the dog cart back[6] to its driver with an apology[7]. Lestrade was waiting for us at the door. 'Harriman?' he asked.

'He is dead. His curricle overturned[8].'

'I can't say I'm sorry.'

'How is your officer, the man who was shot?'

'Badly hurt[9], Mr Holmes. But he'll live.'

Unwilling though I was to[10] enter the building a second time, we followed Lestrade back inside. Some blankets had been brought down and used to cover the police officer who had been shot by Harriman, and the piano, of course, was silent. But apart from that the House of Silk was much as it had been[11] when we had first entered it. It made me shudder to return[12], but I was aware that we still had unfinished business[13].

'I have sent for more men[14],' Lestrade told us. 'It's a nasty business we have here, Mr Holmes, and it's going to take someone a lot more senior[15] than me to sort it out[16]. Let me tell you that the children have been sent back to the school on the other side of the lane and I have two officers keeping an eye on them, for all the teachers in this horrible place are implicated in what's been going on and I have them all under arrest[17]. Two of them – Weeks and Vosper – I think you met.'

'What of Fitzsimmons and his wife?' I asked.

'They're in the drawing room and we'll see them shortly, although there's something I want to show you first, if you can stomach it[18].' I could hardly be-

1. que nous cherchions
2. en tout cas
3. constituée
4. Cela leur a fourni l'infrastructure
5. le masque derrière lequel
6. restitua le dog-cart
7. en s'excusant
8. s'est renversé
9. Très mal en point
10. Malgré ma réticence à
11. telle que nous l'avions trouvée
12. Je frémissais en y retournant
13. qu'il y avait encore des choses à régler
14. demandé des renforts
15. de bien plus haut placé
16. pour le régler
17. je les ai tous mis en état d'arrestation
18. le supporter

lieve that the House of Silk could hold any further secrets[1] but we followed Lestrade back upstairs, he talking all the while[2]. 'There were another nine men here. What am I to call them? Clients? Customers? They include Lord Ravenshaw and another man who will be well known to you, a certain doctor by the name of Ackland. Now I can see why he was so keen to perjure himself against you[3].'

'And what of Lord Horace Blackwater?' asked Holmes.

'He was not present here tonight, Mr Holmes, although I'm sure we'll find that he was a frequent visitor. But come this way[4]. I'll show you what we've found and see if you can make sense of it[5].'

We walked along the corridor where we had encountered Harriman. The doors were now open, revealing bedrooms, all of which were luxuriously appointed[6]. I had no wish to enter any of them – my very skin recoiled[7] – but I went in after Holmes and Lestrade and found myself in a room draped in blue silk[8] with a cast-iron bed[9], a low sofa and a door leading into a bathroom with piped water[10]. The opposite wall was taken up by a low cabinet on which stood a glass tank[11] containing a number of rocks and dried flowers arranged in what amounted to a miniature landscape[12], the possession of a naturalist, perhaps, or a collector.

'This room was not in use when we entered it,' Lestrade explained. 'My men continued along the corridor to the next room, which is nothing more than a storage cupboard, and they only opened it quite by chance. Now, look over here. This is what we found.'

He drew our attention to the tank and at first I could not see why we were examining it. But then I realised that there was a small aperture cut into[13] the wall behind it, perfectly concealed by the glass so that it was virtually invisible.

1. receler d'autres secrets
2. lui ne cessant de parler
3. si disposé à se parjurer en témoignant à charge contre vous
4. venez par ici
5. vous y comprenez quelque chose
6. aménagées avec luxe
7. j'en avais la chair de poule
8. tendue de soie bleue
9. lit en fonte
10. l'eau courante
11. un aquarium
12. disposés en paysage miniature
13. ouverture pratiquée dans

'A window!' I exclaimed. And then I grasped its significance[1]. 'Anything that happened[2] in this room could be observed.'

'Not just observed,' Lestrade muttered, grimly.

He took us back out into the corridor, then threw open the door of the cupboard. It was empty inside but for[3] a table on which stood a mahogany box[4]. At first, I was not sure what I was seeing but then Lestrade unfastened[5] the box which opened like a concertina[6] and I realised that it was in fact a camera[7] and that its lens[8], at the end of a sliding tube[9], was pressed against the other side of the window that we had just seen.

'A quarter plate[10] Le Merveilleux, manufactured[11] by J. Lancaster and Son of Birmingham, if I am not mistaken,' Holmes remarked.

'Is this part of their depravity[12]?' Lestrade demanded. 'That they had to keep a record[13] of what took place?'

'I think not,' Holmes replied. 'But I now understand why my brother, Mycroft, was given such a hostile reception when he began his enquiries and why he was unable to come to my aid[14]. You say you have Fitzsimmons downstairs?'

'And his wife.'

'Then I think it is time we had our reckoning[15].'

The fire was still burning in the drawing room and the room was warm and close[16]. The Reverend Charles Fitzsimmons was sitting on the sofa with his wife and I was glad to see that he had exchanged his clerical garb[17] for a black tie and dinner jacket. I do not think I could have borne any more of his pretence that he was part of the church[18]. Mrs Fitzsimmons sat rigid and withdrawn[19] and refused to meet our eyes. She did not utter a word throughout the interview that followed. Holmes sat down. I stood with my back to the fire[20]. Lestrade remained by the door.

1. j'en saisis la signification
2. Tout ce qui se passait
3. hormis
4. était posée une boîte en acajou
5. ouvrit
6. accordéon
7. un appareil photo
8. son objectif
9. l'extrémité d'un tube coulissant
10. Un quart de plaque
11. fabriqué
12. dépravation
13. garder trace
14. me venir en aide
15. de solder nos comptes
16. chaleureuse et intime
17. ses vêtements religieux
18. simulacre d'appartenance à l'Église
19. roide et impassible
20. dos au feu de cheminée

'Mr Holmes!' Fitzsimmons sounded pleasantly surprised[1] to see him. 'I suppose I must congratulate you, sir. You certainly have proven yourself to be every bit[2] as formidable[3] as I was led to believe[4]. You managed to escape from the first trap that we set you. Your disappearance from Holloway was extraordinary. And as neither Henderson nor Bratby have returned to this establishment, I will assume that you got the better of them[5] at Jackdaw Lane and they are both under arrest?'

'They are dead,' Holmes said.

'They would have ended up being hanged[6] anyway, so I suppose it makes no great difference.'

'Are you prepared to answer my questions?'

'Of course. I see absolutely no reason why not. I am not ashamed of what we have been doing here at Chorley Grange. Some of the policemen have treated us very roughly[7] and ...' Here he called out to Lestrade at the door. '. . . I can assure you I will be making an official complaint[8]. But the truth is that we have only been providing[9] what certain men have been requesting for centuries[10]. I am sure you have studied the ancient civilisations of the Greeks, the Romans and the Persians? The cult of Ganymede[11] was an honourable one, sir. Are you repulsed[12] by the work of Michelangelo or even by the sonnets of William Shakespeare? Well, I'm sure you have no wish to discuss the semantics of the matter[13]. You have the upper hand[14], Mr Holmes. What do you wish to know?'

'Was the House of Silk your idea?'

'It was entirely mine. I can assure you that the Society for the Improvement of London's Children and the family of our benefactor, Sir Crispin Ogilvy who, as I told you, paid for the purchase of Chorley Grange, have no knowledge[15] of what we have been doing and would, I am sure, be as dismayed[16]

1. avait l'air agréablement surpris
2. en tous points
3. redoutable
4. que ce que je croyais
5. avez eu raison d'eux
6. fini pendus
7. avec beaucoup de rudesse
8. que je déposerai plainte
9. n'avons fait que fournir
10. demandent depuis des siècles
11. Ganymède [jeune prince enlevé par Zeus]
12. choqué
13. discuter des finesses de la question
14. l'avantage
15. ne savent rien
16. consternés

as you. I have no need to protect them. I am merely telling you the truth.'

'It was you who ordered[1] the killing of Ross?'

'I will confess to it, yes. I am not proud of it, Mr Holmes, but it was necessary to ensure my own safety[2] and the continuation[3] of this enterprise. I am not confessing to the murder itself, you understand. That was carried out[4] by Henderson and Bratby. And it might be as well to add that you would be deluding yourself if you thought of Ross as[5] some innocent, a little angel who fell into bad ways[6]. Mrs Fitzsimmons was right. He was a nasty piece of work[7] and brought his end entirely upon himself[8].'

'I believe you have been keeping a photographic record[9] of some of your clients.'

'You have been into the blue room?'

'Yes.'

'It has been necessary from time to time.'

'I assume your purpose was blackmail[10].'

'Blackmail, occasionally, and only when absolutely necessary, for it will not surprise you to learn that I have made a considerable amount of money[11] from the House of Silk and had no particular need for any other form of revenue[12]. No, no, no, it was more to do with self-protection[13], Mr Holmes. How do you think I was able to persuade Dr Ackland and Lord Horace Blackwater to appear in a public court[14]? It was an act of self-preservation[15] on their part. And it is for this very same reason that I can tell you now that my wife and I will never stand trial[16] in this country. We know too many secrets about too many people, some of whom are in the very highest positions[17], and we have the evidence carefully tucked away[18]. The gentlemen whom you found here tonight were but a small selection of my grateful clients. We have ministers and judges, lawyers and lords. More than that, I could name one member of the noblest family in the country who has been a

1. avez commandité
2. pour garantir ma propre sécurité
3. continuité
4. exécuté
5. vous tromperiez en voyant en Ross
6. a mal tourné
7. C'était un vaurien
8. il a bien cherché ce qui lui est arrivé
9. des traces photographiques
10. votre but était le chantage
11. j'ai tiré des sommes considérables
12. d'autres sources de revenus
13. pour ma protection personnelle
14. au tribunal
15. par instinct de conservation
16. ne serons jamais jugés
17. les plus hautes fonctions
18. bien à l'abri

frequent visitor here, but of course he relies on[1] my discretion, just as I can rely on his protection should the need arise[2]. You take my point[3], Mr Holmes? They will never allow you to bring this matter to light[4]. Six months from now[5] my wife and I will be free and, quietly, we will begin again. Perhaps it will be necessary to look to[6] the Continent. I have always had a certain penchant for the South of France. But wherever and whenever[7], the House of Silk will re-emerge[8]. You have my word on it.[9]'

Holmes said nothing. He stood up and together he and I left the room. He did not mention Fitzsimmons again that night and nor did he have anything further to say[10] on the subject the following morning. But by then, we were busy again[11], for the entire adventure had of course begun at Wimbledon and it was to there that we now returned[12].

1. il compte sur
2. si besoin était
3. Vous me comprenez
4. étaler cette affaire au grand jour
5. D'ici six mois,
6. de nous tourner vers
7. quels que soient le lieu et le moment
8. refera surface
9. Croyez-moi.
10. il n'eut rien à rajouter non plus
11. avions à nouveau à faire
12. c'est là que nous sommes retournés

TWENTY

Keelan O'Donaghue

The snowfall[1] of the night before had transformed Ridgeway Hall in a way that was quite startling[2], accentuating its symmetry and rendering it somehow timeless[3]. I had thought it handsome on both occasions that I had visited, but as I approached it for the last time, in the company of Sherlock Holmes, I thought it as perfect as the miniature houses one might see behind the window of a toy shop[4] and it almost felt like an act of vandalism to scour the white driveway[5] with our carriage wheels.

It was early in the afternoon of the following day and I must confess that, had I been given a chance[6], I would have postponed[7] this visit at least for another twenty-four hours[8], for I was exhausted from the night before and my arm, where I had been struck, was aching to the extent[9] that I could barely close the fingers of my left hand. I had passed a wretched[10] night, desperate to fall asleep[11] in order to put out of my mind everything I had seen at Chorley Grange, yet unable to do so[12] precisely because it was still so fresh in my memory. I had come to the breakfast table and had been irked[13] to see Holmes, quite fresh[14], restored in every way to his old self, greeting me in that clipped, precise way of his[15] as if nothing untoward[16] had occurred. It was he who had insisted on this visit, having already sent a wire[17] to Edmund Carstairs before

1. chute de neige
2. spectaculaire
3. quelque peu intemporel
4. que l'on voit dans la vitrine d'un magasin de jouets
5. zébrer l'allée blanche
6. si j'avais pu
7. reporté
8. d'au moins 24 heures
9. me faisait si mal
10. très mauvaise
11. à chercher désespérément le sommeil
12. mais incapable de le faire
13. agacé
14. tout reposé
15. à sa façon, précise et heurtée
16. rien de fâcheux
17. télégramme

I had risen[1]. I remembered our meeting at The Bag of Nails when I had described what had befallen[2] the family, and Eliza Carstairs in particular. He was as concerned now as he had been then and clearly placed great significance on[3] her sudden illness. He insisted on seeing her for himself[4], although quite how he might be able to help her when I and so many other doctors had failed was beyond my comprehension.

We knocked on the door. It was opened by Patrick, the Irish scullery boy whom I had met in the kitchen. He looked blankly[5] at Holmes, then at me. 'Oh, it's you,' he scowled[6]. 'I wasn't expecting to see you back here again.'

Never had I been greeted on a doorstep[7] with quite such insolence but Holmes seemed amused. 'Is your master in?' he asked.

'Who shall I say is calling?[8]'

'My name is Sherlock Holmes. We are expected. And who are you?'

'I'm Patrick.'

'That's a Belfast accent if I'm not mistaken.'

'What's it to you?[9]'

'Patrick? Who is it? Why is Kirby not here?' Edmund Carstairs had appeared in the hallway and came forward, clearly agitated. 'You must forgive me, Mr Holmes. Kirby must still be upstairs with my sister. I did not expect the door to be opened by the kitchen boy. You can go now, Patrick. Go back to your place.'

Carstairs was as immaculately attired[10] as he had been on every occasion that I had seen him, but the lines that days of anxiety had drawn[11] were clearly visible on his face and, like me, I suspected that he had not been sleeping well.

'You received my wire,' Holmes said.

'I did. But you evidently did not receive mine. For I clearly stated[12], as I had already intimated[13] to Dr Watson, that I had no further need[14] of your ser-

1. mon lever
2. ce qui était arrivé à
3. accordait une grande importance à
4. pour la voir lui-même
5. d'un air ahuri
6. dit-il, en grimaçant
7. à la porte
8. Qui dois-je annoncer ?
9. Qu'est-ce que ça peut vous faire ?
10. impeccablement vêtu
11. les rides creusées par ces journées difficiles
12. j'y disais clairement
13. l'avais laissé entendre
14. je n'avais plus besoin

vices. I am sorry to say it[1], but you have not been helpful to[2] my family, Mr Holmes. And I must add that I understood that you had been arrested and were in serious trouble with the law.'

'Those matters have been resolved. As to your wire, Mr Carstairs, I did indeed receive it, and read what you had to say with interest.'

'And you came anyway[3]?'

'You first came to me because you were being terrorised by a man in a flat cap, a man you believed to be[4] Keelan O'Donaghue from Boston. I can tell you that I am now in command of the facts of the matter[5] which I am happy to share[6] with you. I can also tell you who killed the man that we found at Mrs Oldmore's Private Hotel. You may try to persuade yourself that these things are no longer important, and if that is the case, let me put it very simply[7]. If you wish your sister to die, you will send me away[8]. If not, you will invite me in and hear what I have to say.'

Carstairs hesitated and I could see that he was fighting with himself, that in some strange way he seemed almost afraid of us, but in the end his better sense prevailed[9]. 'Please,' he said. 'Let me take your coats. I don't know what Kirby is doing. It sometimes seems to me that this entire household is in disarray[10].' We removed our outer garments and he gestured towards the drawing room where we had been received on our first visit.

'If you will permit me, I would like to see your sister before we sit down,' Holmes remarked.

'My sister is no longer able to see anyone. Her sight has failed her.[11] She can barely speak.'

'No speech[12] will be necessary. I wish merely to see her room. Is she still refusing to eat?'

'It is no longer a question of refusal. She is unable to consume[13] solid food. It is the best I can do to[14] make her take a little warm soup from time to time.'

1. Navré de vous le dire
2. vous n'avez été d'aucune aide pour
3. malgré tout
4. que vous preniez pour
5. j'ai à présent une pleine connaissance des faits
6. de partager
7. le choix est simple, croyez-moi
8. alors demandez-moi de quitter les lieux
9. la raison l'emporta
10. part à vau-l'eau
11. Elle a perdu la vue.
12. Aucune parole
13. incapable de consommer
14. Tout ce que je peux faire, c'est de

'She still believes she is being poisoned.'

'In my view, it is this irrational belief[1] that has become the main cause of her illness, Mr Holmes. As I told your colleague, I have tasted every single morsel[2] that has passed her lips with no ill-effect at all[3]. I do not understand the curse that has come upon me. Before I met you, I was a happy man.'

'And hope to be again, I am sure.'

We climbed back up to the attic room[4] that I had been in before. As we arrived at the doorway, the manservant, Kirby, appeared with a tray of soup, the plate untouched[5]. He glanced at his master and shook his head, indicating that once again the patient had refused to eat. We went in. I was at once dismayed by the sight of[6] Eliza Carstairs. How long had it been since I had last seen her? Hardly more than a week and yet in that time she had visibly deteriorated to the extent[7] that she put me in mind of the living skeleton that I had seen advertised[8] at Dr Silkin's House of Wonders. Her skin was stretched[9] in that horrible way that attends upon patients[10] only when they are close to the end[11], her lips drawn back to expose her gums[12] and teeth. The shape of the body beneath the covers was tiny and pathetic. Her eyes stared at us but saw nothing. Her hands, folded across her chest, were those of a woman thirty years older than Eliza Carstairs.

Holmes examined her briefly. 'Her bathroom is next door[13]?' he asked.

'Yes. But she is too weak to walk there[14]. Mrs Kirby and my wife bathe her where she lies[15] ...'

Holmes had already left the room. He entered the bathroom, leaving Carstairs and myself in an uneasy silence[16] with the staring woman. At last he reappeared. 'We can return downstairs,' he said. Carstairs and I followed him out, both of us bemused[17], for the entire visit had lasted less than thirty seconds.

1. idée absurde
2. le moindre morceau
3. sans aucun problème
4. la chambre mansardée
5. intacte
6. en voyant
7. son état s'était si manifestement dégradé
8. dont j'avais vu la réclame
9. tirée
10. caractéristique des malades
11. leur fin est proche
12. gencives
13. dans la pièce d'à côté
14. pour y aller
15. la lavent dans son lit
16. silence inconfortable
17. déconcertés

We went back down to the drawing room where Catherine Carstairs was sitting in front of a cheerful fire, reading a book. She closed it the moment[1] we entered and rose quickly to her feet. 'Why, Mr Holmes and Dr Watson! You are the last two people I expected to see.' She glanced at her husband. 'I thought ...'

'I did exactly as we agreed[2], my dear. But Mr Holmes chose to visit us anyway.'

'I am surprised that you did not wish to see me, Mrs Carstairs,' Holmes remarked. 'Particularly as you came to consult me a second time after your sister-in-law fell ill.'

'That was a while ago, Mr Holmes. I don't wish to be rude[3], but I have long since given up any hope[4] that you can be of assistance to us. The man who came uninvited to[5] this house and stole money and jewellery from us is dead. Do we want to know who stabbed him[6]? No! The fact that he can trouble us no more[7] is enough. If there is nothing you can do to help poor Eliza, then there is no reason for you to stay.'

'I believe I can save Miss Carstairs. It may still be not too late.'

'Save her from what?'

'From poison.'

Catherine Carstairs started[8]. 'She is not being poisoned! There is no possibility of that. The doctors do not know the cause of her illness but they are all agreed on that[9].'

'Then they are all wrong. May I sit down? There is much that I have to tell you and I think we would all be more comfortable seated[10].'

The wife glared at him[11] but this time the husband took Holmes's side[12]. 'Very well, Mr Holmes. I will listen to what you have to say. But make no mistake[13]. If I believe that you are attempting to deceive me, I will have no hesitation in asking you to leave[14].'

1. dès que
2. comme nous en étions convenus
3. Je ne veux pas être grossière
4. il y a longtemps que je n'espère plus
5. s'est introduit dans
6. l'a poignardé
7. ne puisse plus nous importuner
8. sursauta
9. sont tous d'accord là-dessus
10. tous plus à l'aise assis
11. le fustigea du regard
12. se rangea du côté de Holmes
13. attention
14. à vous prier de partir

1. Mon but
2. c'est tout le contraire
3. le plus éloigné

'My aim[1] is not to deceive you,' returned Holmes. 'In fact, quite the contrary[2].' He sat down in the armchair furthest[3] from the fire. I took the chair next to him. Mr and Mrs Carstairs sat together on the sofa opposite. Finally he began.

4. si mes souvenirs sont bons
5. lorsque vous m'avez quitté
6. le premier acte

'You came to my lodgings, Mr Carstairs, on the advice of your accountant, because you were afraid that your life might be threatened by a man you had never met. You were on your way that evening to the opera, to Wagner, as I recall[4]. But it was late by the time you left me[5]. I imagine you missed the first curtain[6].'

'No. I arrived on time.'

7. Peu importe.
8. justicier
9. si c'était bien lui
10. dans le but précis
11. très liés
12. ensuite
13. avaient localisé
14. sous une pluie de balles
15. je vous prie

'No matter.[7] There were many aspects of your story that I found quite remarkable, the principal one being the strange behaviour of this vigilante[8], Keelan O'Donaghue, if indeed it was he[9]. I could well believe that he had followed you all the way to London and found out your address here in Wimbledon, with the express purpose[10] of killing you. You were, after all, responsible – at least in part – for the death of his twin brother, Rourke O'Donaghue, and twins are close[11]. And he had already taken vengeance on Cornelius Stillman, the man who had purchased the oil paintings from you and who subsequently[12] paid for the Pinkerton's agents who tracked down[13] the Flat Cap Gang in Boston and put an end to their careers in a hail of bullets[14]. Remind me, if you will[15]. What is the name of the agent you employed?'

'It was Bill McParland.'

16. ait cherché à vous tuer
17. ne vous a-t-il pas assailli et poignardé
18. un navire repartant

'Of course. As I say, twins are often very close and it is no surprise that Keelan should have sought your death[16]. So why did he not kill you? Once he had discovered where you lived, why did he not spring out and put a knife in you[17]? That is what I would have done. Nobody knew he was in this country. He could have been on a ship back[18] to America before you were even in the morgue. But, in fact, he did the exact opposite of that. He stood outside your house, wearing the flat cap that he knew would identify him. Worse than that, he appeared again, this time when you and Mrs Carstairs were leaving the Savoy. What was in his mind, do you think? It is almost as if he were daring you[1] to go to the police, to get him arrested.'

'He wished to frighten us,' Mrs Carstairs said.

'But that was not the motive on[2] his third visit. This time he returned to the house with a note which he pressed into your husband's hand. He asked for a meeting[3] at your local church[4] at midday.'

'He did not show up[5].'

'Perhaps he never intended to. His final intervention in your life came when he broke into[6] the house and stole fifty pounds and jewellery from your safe. By now[7], I am finding his behaviour more than remarkable[8]. Not only does he know exactly which window to choose, he has somehow got his hands[9] on a key lost by your wife several months before he arrived in the country. And it is interesting, is it not, that he is now more interested in money than in murder, for he is actually standing in this very house in the middle of the night. He could climb the stairs and kill you both in your bed—'

'I woke up and heard him.'

'Indeed so, Mrs Carstairs. But by that time he had already opened the safe. I take it[10] that you and Mr Carstairs sleep in separate rooms[11], by the way?'

Carstairs flushed[12]. 'I do not see that our domestic arrangements have any bearing[13] on the case.'

'But you do not deny it. Very well, let us stay with our strange and somewhat indecisive intruder[14]. He makes his getaway to a private hotel[15] in Bermondsey. But now events take a surprising turn[16] when a second assailant, a man about whom we know nothing, catches up with[17] Keelan O'Donaghue – again, we must assume it is he[18] – stabs him to death, and

1. vous défiait
2. son intention lors de
3. Il demandait une rencontre
4. église de quartier
5. n'est jamais venu
6. a cambriolé
7. Aujourd'hui
8. plus qu'incroyable
9. on ne sait comment, mis la main
10. suppose
11. faites chambre à part
12. rougit
13. aient une incidence
14. drôle d'intrus pour le moins indécis
15. Il file dans un hôtel
16. une tournure imprévue
17. rattrape
18. supposer qu'il s'agit bien de lui

1. puisqu'il porte
2. Où voulez-vous en venir avec tout cela
3. Je ne fais que vous dire clairement
4. ne tient pas debout
5. à moins, en fait, de partir de l'hypothèse
6. si simple
7. de loin
8. la glisser dans la fente de la porte d'entrée
9. est destinée
10. la tenir en l'air
11. de façon qu'on puisse la lire depuis
12. plus tôt que d'habitude
13. quelques instants avant que
14. ait pu agir
15. au-dessus de sa tête

takes not only his money but anything that might identify him, apart from a cigarette case which is in itself unhelpful as it bears[1] the initials WM.'

'What do you mean by all this[2], Mr Holmes?' Catherine Carstairs asked.

'I am merely making it clear to you[3], Mrs Carstairs, as it was to me from the very start, that this narrative makes no sense whatsoever[4] – unless, that is, you start from the premise[5] that it was not Keelan O'Donaghue who came to this house, and that it was not your husband with whom he wished to communicate.'

'But that's ridiculous. He gave my husband that note.'

'And failed to appear at the church. It may help if we put ourselves in the position of this mysterious visitor. He seeks a private interview with a member of this household but that is not such a simple matter[6]. Apart from yourself and your husband, there is your sister-in-law, various servants ... Mr and Mrs Kirby, Elsie and Patrick, the kitchen boy. To begin with, he watches from a distance[7] but finally he approaches with a note written in large letters and neither folded nor in an envelope. Clearly, his intention cannot be to post it through the door[8]. But is it possible, perhaps, that he hopes to see the person for whom this correspondence is intended[9], simply to hold it up[10] so that it can be read through[11] the window of the breakfast room? No need to ring the bell. No need to risk the message falling into the wrong hands. It will be known to just the two of them and they can discuss their business later. Unfortunately, however, Mr Carstairs returns unexpectedly early[12] to the house, moments before[13] our man has had the chance to achieve his aim[14]. So what does he do? He raises the note high above him[15] and hands it to Mr Carstairs. He knows he is being watched from the breakfast room and his meaning now is rather different. "Find me," he is saying. "Or I will tell Mr Carstairs everything I know. I will meet him in the church. I will meet him anywhere I please[1]. You cannot prevent me." Of course, he does not turn up at the assignation[2]. He has no need to. The warning is enough.'

'But with whom did he wish to speak if not with me?' Carstairs demanded.

'Who was in the breakfast room at the time[3]?'

'My wife.' He frowned as if anxious to[4] change the subject. 'Who was this man, if he was not Keelan O'Donaghue?' he asked.

'The answer to that is perfectly simple, Mr Carstairs. He was Bill McParland, the Pinkerton's detective. Consider for a moment.[5] We know that Mr McParland was injured[6] during the shoot-out in Boston and the man we discovered in the hotel room had a recent scar[7] on his right cheek. We also know that McParland had fallen out[8] with his employer, Cornelius Stillman, who had refused to pay him the amount of money he felt he was owed[9]. He therefore had a grievance[10]. And then there is his name. Bill, I would imagine, is short for[11] William and the initials we found on the cigarette case were—'

'WM,' I interjected.

'Precisely, Watson. And now things begin to fall into place[12]. Let us begin by considering the fate[13] of Keelan O'Donaghue himself. First, what do we know about this young man? Your narrative was surprisingly comprehensive[14], Mr Carstairs, and for that I am grateful to you. You told us that Rourke and Keelan O'Donaghue were twins but that Keelan was the smaller of the two. They carried each other's initials, tattooed on their arms, proof, if any were needed, of the extraordinary closeness of their relationship[15]. Keelan was clean-shaven[16] and taciturn. He wore a flat cap which, one would imagine, would have made it difficult to see very much of his face[17].

1. où bon me semblera
2. rendez-vous clandestin
3. à ce moment-là
4. comme s'il voulait
5. Réfléchissez un instant.
6. a été blessé
7. cicatrice récente
8. s'était fâché
9. la somme d'argent qui, pensait-il, lui était due
10. un grief
11. le diminutif de
12. le puzzle se met en place
13. le sort
14. étonnamment complet
15. l'étroitesse de leur lien
16. imberbe
17. bien voir son visage

1. de carrure frêle
2. Lui seul
3. se faufiler dans le caniveau
4. réussir ainsi à s'enfuir
5. dans la saleté de cet immeuble
6. la chance d'avoir sa propre chambre
7. ce qui pouvait justifier cela
8. les éléments que je viens d'exposer
9. blanchisserie
10. a mis au monde
11. Le calme
12. pénétrait dans la pièce
13. retenir leur souffle
14. avec étonnement
15. ses lèvres esquissant un sourire mièvre
16. Chef de gang ?
17. Tous les indices convergent vers
18. Il n'y a pas d'autre explication possible.
19. pâlir
20. se figea
21. les statues de cire aperçues

We know that he was of slender build[1]. He alone[2] was able to squeeze through the gulley[3] that led to the river and so effect his escape[4]. But I was particularly struck by one detail that you mentioned. The gang all lived together in the squalor of the tenement[5] in South End – all, that is, apart from Keelan who had the luxury of his own room[6]. I wondered from the very start why that might be[7].

'The answer, of course, is quite obvious, given all the evidence I have just laid out[8] and I am happy to say that I have had it confirmed by no less than Mrs Caitlin O'Donaghue who still lives in Sackville Street in Belfast where she has a laundry[9]. It is this. In the spring of 1865 she gave birth[10], not to twin brothers but to a brother and a sister. Keelan O'Donaghue was a girl.'

The silence that greeted this revelation was, in a word, profound. The stillness[11] of the winter's day pressed in on the room[12] and even the flames in the fireplace, which had been flickering cheerfully, seemed to be holding their breath[13].

'A girl?' Carstairs looked at Holmes in wonderment[14], a sickly smile playing around his lips[15]. 'Running a gang?[16]'

'A girl who would have had to conceal her identity if she were to survive in such an environment,' Holmes returned. 'And anyway, it was her brother, Rourke, who ran the gang. All the evidence points to[17] this single conclusion. There can be no alternative.[18]'

'And where is this girl?'

'That is simple, Mr Carstairs. You are married to her. '

I saw Catherine Carstairs turn pale[19] but she said nothing. Sitting next to her, Carstairs was suddenly rigid[20]. The two of them reminded me of the waxworks I had glimpsed[21] at the fair at Jackdaw Lane.

'You do not deny it, Mrs Carstairs?' Holmes asked.

'Of course I deny it! I have never heard anything quite so preposterous[1].' She turned to her husband and suddenly there were tears in her eyes. 'You're not going to allow him to speak to me in this way, are you, Edmund? To suggest that I might have some connection with a hateful brood of criminals[2] and evil-doers[3]!'

'Your words, I think, fall on deaf ears[4], Mrs Carstairs,' Holmes remarked.

And it was true. From the moment that Holmes had made his extraordinary declaration, Carstairs had been gazing in front of him with an expression of peculiar horror[5] that suggested to me that some small part of him must have always known the truth, or at least suspected it[6], but now, at last, he was being forced to stare it straight in the face[7].

'Please, Edmund ...' She reached out to him, but Carstairs flinched[8] and turned away.

'May I continue?' Holmes asked.

Catherine Carstairs was about to speak but then relaxed. Her shoulders slumped[9] and it was as if a silken veil had been torn from her face[10]. Suddenly she was glaring at us with a hardness and an expression of hatred[11] that would have been unbecoming[12] in[13] any English gentlewoman[14] but which had surely sustained her throughout[15] her life. 'Oh yes, oh yes,' she snarled[16]. 'We might as well hear the rest of it.'

'Thank you.' Holmes nodded in her direction, then went on. 'After the death of her brother, and the destruction of the Flat Cap Gang, Catherine O'Donaghue – for that was her given name[17] – found herself in a situation that must have seemed quite desperate. She was alone, in America, wanted[18] by the police. She had also lost the brother who had been closer to her than anyone on this planet, and whom she must have dearly loved[19]. Her first thoughts were of revenge. Cornelius Stillman had been foolish enough

1. d'aussi grotesque
2. une horrible bande de malfrats
3. de scélérats
4. ne sont pas entendus
5. d'un air étrangement horrifié
6. la subodorait
7. obligé d'envisager carrément l'hypothèse
8. tressaillit
9. s'affaissèrent
10. un voile de soie tombait de son visage
11. haine
12. inconvenante
13. chez
14. dame de la bonne société
15. nourri
16. dit-elle, hargneuse
17. tel était son prénom
18. recherchée
19. aimer tendrement

1. pour se vanter de ses exploits
2. Reprenant son personnage de femme
3. d'une bonne
4. tout l'argent qu'elle avait pu amasser
5. se trouverait face à face
6. en haute mer
7. totale
8. tel qu'il était
9. de l'autre sexe
10. de vous lier avec lui
11. l'attirer dans vos filets
12. contre l'avis
13. c'était une vengeance ô combien plus douce
14. au départ
15. que vous haïssiez
16. l'épouse dévouée
17. la supercherie
18. facilitée
19. j'imagine
20. en état de nudité
21. Il y avait l'inconvénient de ce tatouage

to boast of his exploits[1] in the Boston press. Still in disguise, she tracked him down to the garden of his house in Providence and shot him dead. But he was not the only person mentioned in the advertisement. Reverting now to her female persona[2], Catherine followed Edmund Carstairs onto the Cunard liner, the *Catalonia*. It is clear what was on her mind. She no longer had any future in America. It was time to return to her family in Belfast. Nobody would suspect her, travelling as a single woman, accompanied by a maid[3]. She took with her what profits she had been able to save[4] from her past crimes. And somewhere in the middle of the Atlantic she would come face to face[5] with Carstairs. It is easy enough to commit murder on the high seas[6]. Carstairs would disappear and her revenge would be complete[7].'

Holmes now addressed Mrs Carstairs directly. 'But something changed your mind. What was it, I wonder?'

The woman shrugged. 'I saw Edmund for what he was[8].'

'It is precisely as I thought. Here was a man with no experience of the opposite sex[9] apart from a mother and a sister who had always dominated him. He was ill. He was afraid. How amusing it must have been for you to come to his aid, to befriend him[10] and finally to draw him into your net[11]. Somehow you persuaded him to marry you in defiance[12] of his own family – and how much sweeter this revenge[13] than the one you had originally[14] planned. You were intimately connected to a man you loathed[15]. But you would play the part of the devoted wife[16], the charade[17] made easier[18] by the fact that you have chosen to sleep in separate rooms and, I fancy[19], you have never allowed yourself to be seen in a state of undress[20]. There was the inconvenience of that tattoo[21], was there not. So were you ever to visit a pleasure beach[1], you would naturally be unable to swim[2].

'All would have been well but for the arrival[3] of Bill McParland from Boston. How had he picked up your trail[4] and learned your new identity? We will never know, but he was a detective, a very good one, and doubtless had his methods. It was not your husband he was signalling[5] outside this house and at the Savoy. It was you. By this stage[6], he was no longer interested in arresting you. He had come here for the money he was owed[7] and his desire for it[8], his sense of injustice[9], his recent wound – all this drove him to desperation[10]. He met with you, did he not?'

'Yes.'

'And he demanded money from you. If you paid him enough, he would let you keep your secret. When he handed your husband that note, he was effectively warning you. At any time, he could reveal everything he knew.'

'You have it all[11], Mr Holmes.'

'Not all, not quite yet. You needed to give McParland something to keep him quiet[12] but had no resources of your own. It was therefore necessary to create the illusion of a burglary. You came down in the night and guided him to the correct window[13] with a light. You opened that window from inside and allowed him to climb in[14]. You opened the safe, using a key which you had never in fact lost. And even here you could not resist a touch of malice[15]. As well as the money, you gave him a necklace which had belonged to the late Mrs Carstairs and which you knew had great sentimental value to your husband. It seems to me that any chance you had[16] to hurt him was irresistible to you and you always seized it with alacrity[17].

'McParland made one mistake. The money that you gave to him – fifty pounds – was only a first

1. vous rendre à la plage
2. vous seriez bien incapable d'aller nager
3. sans l'arrivée
4. retrouvé votre trace
5. à qui il faisait signe
6. À ce stade
7. qui lui était dû
8. qu'il voulait toucher
9. sentiment d'injustice
10. l'a poussé au désespoir
11. avez tout compris
12. pour le faire taire
13. l'avez guidé vers la bonne fenêtre
14. grimper à l'intérieur
15. à un mouvement de méchanceté
16. chaque fois que vous aviez l'occasion
17. la saisissiez toujours promptement

payment. He had demanded more[1] and, foolishly[2], he gave you the name of the hotel where he was staying[3]. It is possible that the sight of you in all the finery of a[4] wealthy English lady deceived him and he forgot the creature you had once been[5]. Your husband was at the gallery in Albemarle Street. You chose your moment, slipped out of the house and climbed into the hotel through a back window. You were waiting in McParland's room when he returned and struck from behind, stabbing him in the neck. I wonder, incidentally[6], how you were dressed?'

'I was dressed in my old style[7]. Petticoats[8] and crinolette[9] would have been a little cumbersome[10].'

'You silenced[11] McParland and removed any trace[12] of his identity, missing only the cigarette case. And with him gone, there was nothing to stand in the way of the rest of your scheme[13].'

'There is more?' Carstairs rasped. All the blood had left his face and I thought he might be about to faint[14].

'Indeed so, Mr Carstairs.' Holmes turned back to the wife. 'The cold-blooded marriage[15] that you had arranged for yourself was only the means to an end[16]. It was your intention to kill Edmund's family one at a time: his mother, his sister and then him. At the end of it, you would inherit everything that had been his. This house, the money, the art ... all of it would be yours[17]. It is hard to imagine the hatred that must have been driving you forward, the relish[18] with which you went about your task[19].'

'It has been a pleasure, Mr Holmes. I have enjoyed every minute of it.'

'My mother?' Carstairs gasped the two words[20].

'The most likely explanation was the one you first suggested to me, that the gas fire in her bedroom blew out[21]. But it was not one that stood up to scrutiny[22]. For your manservant, Kirby, told us that he blamed himself for the death as he had stopped up[23]

1. en voulait plus
2. bêtement
3. il était descendu
4. que vous voyant dans vos tenues raffinées de
5. la délinquante que vous aviez été
6. soit dit en passant
7. comme avant
8. Des jupons
9. une petite tournure [jupon à armature]
10. encombrants
11. avez réduit au silence
12. effacé toute trace
13. ne gênait la suite de votre plan
14. s'évanouir
15. Ce mariage froidement planifié
16. qu'un moyen de parvenir à vos fins
17. tout vous appartiendrait
18. la délectation
19. vous avez agi
20. émit ces deux mots dans un souffle
21. s'est éteint
22. une explication résistant à l'examen
23. bouché

every crack and crevice in the room. Your mother disliked draughts[1] so it was impossible that a draught could have blown out the fire. Your sister, however, had come to another conclusion. She believed that the late Mrs Carstairs had taken her own life, so distraught was she at[2] your marriage. But as much as Eliza loathed your new wife and instinctively knew her to be dissembling[3], even she was unable to arrive at the truth, which is that Catherine Carstairs entered the room and deliberately blew out the flame, leaving the old lady to perish[4]. There could be no survivors, you see. For the property to be hers, everyone had to die.'

'And Eliza?'

'Your sister is being slowly poisoned.'

'But that's impossible, Mr Holmes. I told you—'

'You told me that you have carefully examined everything she has eaten, which only suggests to me that she is being poisoned in another way. The answer, Mr Carstairs, is the bath. Your sister insists on bathing regularly and uses strong, lavender bath salts[5]. I must confess that this is a most novel way[6] of administering poison, and I am frankly surprised that it has been so effective[7], but I would say that a small measure[8] of aconitine has been added, regularly, to the bath salts. It has entered Miss Carstairs's system through her skin and also, I would imagine, through the moisture and the fumes[9] which she has, of necessity, absorbed. Aconitine is a highly toxic alkaloid which is soluble in water and which would have killed your sister instantly if a large dose had been used. Instead, you have noted this slow but remorseless decline[10]. It is a striking and innovative[11] method of murder, Mrs Carstairs, and one which I am sure will be added to the annals of crime[12]. It was also quite daring of you, incidentally[13], to visit my colleague while I was incarcerated, although you naturally pretended you knew nothing of that.

1. détestait les courants d'air
2. tellement elle était bouleversée par
3. qu'elle se livrait à une imposture
4. laissant mourir la vieille dame
5. sels de bain
6. une façon toute nouvelle
7. efficace
8. dose
9. les vapeurs
10. cette lente mais inexorable dégradation
11. frappante et originale
12. aux annales du crime
13. À propos, c'était très audacieux de votre part

It doubtless persuaded your husband of your devotion to[1] your sister-in-law while, in fact, you were actually laughing at them both[2].'

'You devil![3]' Carstairs twisted away from her[4] in horror. 'How could you? How could anyone?'

'Mr Holmes is right, Edmund,' his wife returned and I noticed that her voice had changed. It was harder, the Irish accent now prominent[5]. 'I would have put all of you in your graves.[6] First your mother. Then Eliza. And you have no idea what I was planning for you[7]!' She turned to Holmes. 'And what now, clever Mr Holmes? Do you have a policeman waiting outside? Should I go upstairs and pack a few things[8]?'

'There is indeed a policeman waiting, Mrs Carstairs. But I have not finished yet.' Holmes drew himself up and I saw a coldness and a vengefulness[9] in his eyes that went beyond anything I had ever seen before. He was a judge about to deliver sentence, an executioner[10] opening the trapdoor[11]. A certain chill had entered the room[12]. A month from now[13], Ridgeway Hall would be empty, unoccupied – and am I too fanciful[14] to suggest that something of its fate was already being whispered[15], that somehow the house already knew? 'There is still the death of the child, Ross, to be accounted for[16].'

Mrs Carstairs burst out laughing. 'I know nothing about Ross,' she said. 'You have been very bright, Mr Holmes. But now you go beyond yourself[17].'

'It is no longer you I am addressing, Mrs Carstairs,' Holmes replied and turned instead to her husband. 'My investigation into your affairs took an unexpected turn[18] on the night that Ross was murdered, Mr Carstairs, and that is not a word I use often, for it is my habit to expect everything[19]. Every crime that I have ever investigated has had what you might call a narrative flow[20] – it is this invisible thread[21] that my friend Dr Watson has always unerringly[22] identified.

1. dévouement envers
2. alors qu'en réalité vous vous moquiez des deux
3. Espèce de monstre !
4. s'écarta d'elle
5. très perceptible à présent
6. J'aurais eu votre peau à tous.
7. ce que je vous réservais
8. faire mes bagages
9. une expression vindicative
10. bourreau
11. la trappe
12. L'atmosphère s'était refroidie de façon caractéristique
13. D'ici un mois
14. est-ce exagéré de ma part
15. se murmurait déjà
16. à expliquer
17. vous allez trop loin
18. un tour imprévu
19. d'habitude, je m'attends à tout
20. une fluidité narrative
21. fil [conducteur]
22. infailliblement

It is what has made him such an excellent chronicler of my work. But I have been aware that this time I have been diverted[1]. I was following one line of investigation and it took me[2], suddenly and quite accidentally, onto another. From the moment I arrived at Mrs Oldmore's Private Hotel, I had left Boston and the Flat Cap Gang behind me. Instead, I was moving in a new direction and one that would eventually take me[3] to the unveiling[4] of a crime more unpleasant than any I had ever encountered.'

Carstairs flinched when he heard this. His wife was regarding him curiously.

'Let us go back[5] to that night, for you, of course, were with me. I knew very little[6] about Ross, except that he was one of the band of street urchins that I have affectionately named[7] the Baker Street Irregulars and who have helped me from time to time. They have been of use to me[8] and I have recompensed them. It seemed a harmless[9] arrangement, at least until now. Ross was left to watch the hotel while his companion, Wiggins, came for me[10]. We drove, the four of us – you, me, Watson and Wiggins – over to Blackfriars. Ross saw us. And at once I perceived that the boy was terrified. He asked who we were, who *you* were. Watson attempted to reassure him and, in doing so[11], both named you[12] and gave the boy your address. That, I rather fear, was to be the death of him[13] – though do not blame yourself, Watson, for the mistake was equally mine.

'I had assumed that Ross was frightened because of what he had seen at the hotel. It was a natural assumption[14] to make for, as things turned out[15], a murder had taken place. I was convinced that he must have seen the killer and, for reasons of his own[16], had decided to keep silent. But I was wrong. What had frightened and amazed the boy was nothing to do with it at all. It was the sight of *you*[17], Mr Carstairs. Ross was determined to know who you

1. quelque chose m'a fait bifurquer
2. elle m'a emmené
3. m'amènerait finalement
4. découverte
5. Revenons
6. J'en savais peu
7. affectueusement baptisés
8. Ils m'ont été utiles
9. inoffensif
10. venait me chercher
11. ce faisant
12. a donné votre nom
13. allait signer son arrêt de mort
14. supposition
15. on le sut ensuite
16. qui lui appartenaient
17. parce qu'il vous avait vu, vous

were and where he could find you because he recognised you. God knows what you had done to that child, and even now I refuse even to consider it[1]. But the two of you had met at the House of Silk.'

Another dreadful[2] silence.

'What is the House of Silk?' Catherine Carstairs asked.

'I will not answer your question, Mrs Carstairs. Nor do I need to address myself to you again except to say this: your entire scheme[3], this marriage of yours, would only have worked with[4] a certain sort of man – one who wanted a wife to spite[5] his family, to give him a certain standing in society, not for reasons of love or affection. As you put it so delicately yourself, you knew him for what he was. I myself wondered exactly what sort of creature I was dealing with on the very first day that we met for it always fascinates me to meet a man who tells me he is late for a Wagner opera on an evening when no Wagner is being played[6] in town.

'Ross recognised you, Mr Carstairs. It was the very worst thing[7] that could have happened, for I can imagine that anonymity[8] was the watchword[9] at the House of Silk. You came in the night, you did what you had to do, and you left. Ross was, in all this, the victim. But he was also old beyond his years[10] and poverty and desperation had driven him inexorably to crime. He had already stolen a gold pocket watch from one of the men who had preyed on him[11]. As soon as he got over the[12] shock of encountering you, he must have seen the possibilities of considerably more[13]. Certainly, that is what he told his friend, Wiggins. Did he visit you the next day? Did he threaten to expose you[14] if you did not pay him a fortune? Or had you already scuttled off to[15] Charles Fitzsimmons and his gang of thugs[16] and demanded that they take care of the situation?'

1. d'y penser
2. redoutable
3. tout votre plan
4. ne pouvait fonctionner qu'avec
5. pour contrarier
6. un soir où aucune représentation de Wagner n'est donnée
7. C'est le pire
8. l'anonymat
9. la règle
10. plus mûr que son âge
11. avaient abusé de lui
12. Dès qu'il s'est remis du
13. la possibilité d'obtenir beaucoup plus
14. de vous dénoncer
15. filé chez
16. voyous

'I never asked them to do anything,' Carstairs muttered in a voice that seemed to be straining to bring the words to his lips[1].

'You went to Fitzsimmons and told him that you were being threatened. Acting on[2] his instructions, you sent Ross to a meeting where he believed he would be paid for his silence. He had left for that meeting moments before Watson and I arrived at The Bag of Nails and by then we were too late. It was not Fitzsimmons or yourself whom Ross met. It was the two thugs who called themselves Henderson and Bratby. And they made sure he would not trouble you again[3].' Holmes paused. 'Ross was tortured to death for his audacity, a white ribbon placed around his wrist as a warning to any other of these wretched children who might have the same ideas. You may not have commanded it, Mr Carstairs, but I want you to know that I hold you personally responsible. You exploited him. You killed him. You are a man as debased and as vile[4] as any I have ever met.'

Holmes rose to his feet.

'And now I will leave this house, for I do not wish to tarry here any longer[5]. It occurs to me that, in some ways, your marriage was not perhaps as ill-judged as might be thought[6]. The two of you are made for each other[7]. Well, you will find police carriages waiting outside for both of you, although they will be taking you their separate ways[8]. You are ready, Watson? We will show ourselves out.[9] '

Edmund and Catherine Carstairs sat motionless[10] on the sofa together. Neither of them spoke. But I felt them watching us intently[11] as we left.

1. avoir du mal à articuler
2. Suivant
3. ont veillé à ce qu'il ne vous cause plus de soucis
4. aussi abject et vil
5. m'attarder ici plus longtemps
6. aussi incongru qu'on pourrait le croire
7. l'un pour l'autre
8. vers des destins différents
9. Nous sortons.
10. étaient assis, immobiles
11. je sentis qu'ils nous regardaient fixement

Afterword

It is with a heavy heart that I draw to the end of my task[1]. While I have been writing this, it is as if I have been reliving it, and although there are some details I would wish to forget, still it has been good to find myself back at Holmes's side, following him from Wimbledon to Blackfriars, to Hamworth Hill and Holloway, always one step behind him (in every sense)[2] and yet enjoying the rare privilege[3] of observing, at close quarters[4], that unique[5] mind. Now that the final page draws near[6], I am aware once again[7] of the room in which I find myself, the aspidistra on the windowsill[8], the radiator that is always a little too hot. My hand is aching and all my memories are skewered on the page[9]. Would that there was more to tell[10], for once I am finished I will find myself alone once again.

I should not complain. I am comfortable here. My daughters visit me occasionally and bring my grandchildren too. One of them was even christened[11] Sherlock. His mother thought she was paying homage[12] to my long friendship, but it is a name he never uses. Ah well, they will come at the end of the week and I will give them this manuscript with directions for its safe lodging[13] and then my work will be done[14]. All that remains is to read it one last time and perhaps take the advice of the nurse who attended upon me[15] this morning.

1. j'achève ma tâche
2. avec un temps de retard (au propre et au figuré)
3. jouissant pourtant du privilège rare
4. de très près
5. exceptionnel
6. approche
7. je reprends conscience
8. rebord de la fenêtre
9. souvenirs sont couchés sur le papier
10. J'aimerais tant que mon histoire ne s'arrête pas là
11. baptisé
12. rendait hommage
13. des instructions pour le mettre sous clef
14. fini
15. qui s'est occupée de moi

'Nearly finished, Dr Watson? I'm sure there are still a few loose ends that need tying up[1]. Dot the i's and cross the t's[2], and then you must let us all read it. I've been talking to the other girls and they can hardly wait!'

There is a little more to add.

Charles Fitzsimmons – I forbear[3] to use the word Reverend – was quite correct in what he said to us on that final night in the House of Silk. He never did come to trial.[4] But on the other hand, he was not released as he had so fondly[5] expected. Apparently there was an accident at the prison where he was being held. He fell down a flight of stairs and was found with a fractured skull. Was he pushed? It would seem very likely for, as he had boasted, he knew some unpleasant secrets about a number of important people and, unless I misunderstood him[6], even went so far as to suggest[7] that he might have connections with the royal family. Absurd, I know, and yet I remember Mycroft Holmes and his extraordinary visit to our lodgings. From what he said to us, and from the way he behaved, it was evident that he had come under considerable pressure[8] and ... But no, I will not even consider the possibility. Fitzsimmons was lying. He was attempting to inflate[9] his own importance before he was arrested and carried away. There's an end to it.[10]

Let us just say that there were people in government who knew what he was doing but who were afraid to expose him for fear of the scandal, backed[11], of course, by photographic evidence – and it is true that in the weeks that followed, there was a series of resignations[12] at the highest level that both astonished and alarmed[13] the country. I very much hope[14], though, that Fitzsimmons was not assassinated. He was without any doubt a monster but no country can afford to throw aside the rule of law[15] simply for the sake of expediency[16]. This seems even

1. quelques détails à peaufiner
2. Apportez la touche finale
3. Je m'abstiens
4. Il ne fut jamais jugé, en effet.
5. si naïvement
6. à moins que j'aie mal compris
7. avait même sous-entendu
8. qu'il subissait de fortes pressions
9. d'exagérer
10. Un point c'est tout.
11. étayé qu'il était
12. démissions
13. inquiétèrent
14. J'espère vivement
15. de totalement ignorer l'autorité de la loi
16. parce que ça l'arrange

more clear to me now, while we are at war[1]. Perhaps his death was just an accident, though a lucky one for all concerned[2].

Mrs Fitzsimmons disappeared. Lestrade told me that she went mad after the death of her husband and was transferred to a lunatic asylum[3] in the far north. Again, this was a fortunate outcome[4], as there she could say what she liked and nobody would believe her. For all I know[5], she is still there to this day[6].

Edmund Carstairs was not prosecuted[7]. He left the country with his sister who, though she recovered, remained an invalid[8] for the rest of her life. The firm of Carstairs and Finch ceased to trade[9]. Catherine Carstairs was tried[10] under her maiden name[11], found guilty and sentenced to life imprisonment. She was fortunate to escape the noose[12]. Lord Ravenshaw went into his study with a revolver and blew his brains out[13]. There may have been one or two other suicides, too, but Lord Horace Blackwater and Dr Thomas Ackland both escaped justice. I suppose one has to be pragmatic about these things, but it still annoys me[14], particularly after what they tried to do to Sherlock Holmes.

And then, of course, there is the strange gentleman who accosted me that night and gave me such an unusual supper. I never did tell Holmes about him and, indeed, have never mentioned him again until now. Some might find this odd, but I had given my word and even though he was a self-acclaimed[15] criminal, as a gentleman I felt I had no choice but to keep it. I am quite certain, of course, that my host was none other than Professor James Moriarty, who was to play such a momentous[16] role in our lives a short while later, and it was the devil's own work[17] to pretend that I had never met him. Holmes talked about him in detail shortly before we left for the Reichenbach Falls, and even then I was

1. alors que nous sommes en guerre
2. pour toutes les personnes concernées
3. asile d'aliénés
4. un heureux dénouement
5. À ma connaissance
6. à ce jour
7. poursuivi
8. resta infirme
9. ses activités
10. jugée
11. nom de jeune fille
12. à la potence
13. se fit sauter la cervelle
14. tout de même cela me dérange
15. de son propre aveu
16. historique
17. j'ai eu un mal fou

fairly sure[1] it was the same man. I have often reflected on this unusual aspect of Moriarty's character[2]. Holmes spoke with horror of his malevolence and the vast number of crimes in which he had been involved. But he also admired his intelligence and, indeed, his sense of fair play. To this day[3] I believe that Moriarty genuinely[4] wanted to help Holmes and wanted to see the House of Silk shut down[5]. As a criminal himself, he had learned of its existence but felt it inappropriate, against the grain[6], for him to take action personally. But it offended his sensibilities[7] and so he sent Holmes the white ribbon and provided me with the key to Holmes's cell in the hope that his enemy would do his work for him[8]. And that, of course, is what happened, although to the best of my knowledge[9] Moriarty never sent a note of thanks[10].

I did not see Holmes over Christmas for I was home with my wife, Mary, whose health had by now become a serious concern to me[11]. However, in January she left London to stay a few days with friends and, at her suggestion, I returned to my old lodgings once again to see how Holmes was bearing up[12] after our adventure. It was during this time that one last incident took place which I must now record.

Holmes had been completely exonerated[13], and any record of the accusations made against him annulled[14]. He was not, however, in an easy state of mind. He was restless[15], irritable and, from his frequent glances at the mantelpiece (I did not need his powers of deduction), I could tell that he was tempted by the liquid cocaine that was his most lamentable habit. It would have helped if he was on a case, but he was not and, as I have often noted, it was when he was idle[16], when his energies were not being directed towards[17] some insoluble mystery, that he became distracted and prone to long moods of depression[18]. But this time, I realised, it was some-

1. quasi certain
2. personnage de
3. Aujourd'hui encore,
4. sincèrement
5. que la Maison de Soie ferme
6. contre nature
7. heurtait sa sensibilité
8. ferait le travail à sa place
9. à ma connaissance
10. un mot de remerciement
11. m'inquiétait sérieusement
12. tenait le coup
13. disculpé
14. toute charge contre lui abandonnée
15. était agité
16. oisif
17. canalisées vers
18. sujet à de longs accès de dépression

thing more. He had not mentioned the House of Silk or any of the details associated with it, but reading the newspaper one morning, he drew my attention to[1] a brief article[2] concerning Chorley Grange School for Boys which had just been closed down[3].

'It's not enough,' he muttered. He crumpled[4] the paper in both hands and set it aside, then added: 'Poor Ross!'

From this, and from other indications in his behaviour – he mentioned, for example, that he might never call upon the services[5] of the Baker Street Irregulars again – I gathered that he still blamed himself, in part, for the boy's death, and that the scenes we had witnessed that night on Hamworth Hill had left an indelible mark[6] on his consciousness. Nobody knew evil like[7] Holmes, but there are some evils that it is better not to know, and he could not enjoy even the rewards of[8] his success without being reminded of the dark[9] places to which it had taken him. I could understand this. I had bad dreams myself. But I had Mary to consider[10], and a medical practice to run[11]. Holmes found himself trapped in his own particular world, forced to dwell on[12] things he would rather forget.

One evening, after we had taken dinner together, he suddenly announced that he was going out. The snow had not returned, but January was as glacial as December had been, and though I had no desire at all for this late[13] expedition, I nonetheless asked him if he would like me to accompany him.

'No, no, Watson. It's kind of you. But I think I would be better alone.'

'But where are you going at this late hour, Holmes? Let's go back to the fire and enjoy a whisky peg[14] together. Any business you may have can surely wait until the day.'

'Watson, you are the very best of friends and I am aware that I have been poor company[15]. What I

1. attira mon attention sur
2. un court article
3. venait d'être fermée
4. froissa
5. ne recourrait sans doute plus jamais aux services
6. une marque indélébile
7. aussi bien que
8. même pleinement jouir de
9. ténébreux
10. dont il fallait que je m'occupe
11. mon cabinet médical à diriger
12. de réfléchir à
13. tardive
14. verre de whisky
15. d'avoir été de piètre compagnie

need is a little time alone. But we will have breakfast tomorrow and I am sure you will find me in better spirits[1].'

We did and he was.[2] We spent a pleasant and companionable[3] day visiting the British Museum and lunching at Simpson's, and it was only as we were returning home that I saw in the newspapers a report of the great fire on Hamworth Hill. A building that had once been occupied by a charitable school had been razed to the ground[4], and apparently the flames had leapt so high[5] into the night sky that they had been visible as far afield[6] as Wembley. I said nothing about it to Holmes and asked no questions. Nor had I remarked[7] that morning that his coat, which had been hanging in its usual place, had carried about it[8] the strong smell of cinders[9]. That evening, Holmes played his Stradivarius for the first time in a while. I listened with pleasure to the soaring tune[10] as we sat together on either side of the hearth.

I hear it still. As I lay down[11] my pen and take to my bed[12], I am aware of the bow[13] being drawn across the bridge[14] and the music rises[15] into the night sky. It is far away and barely audible but – there it is! A pizzicato. Then a tremolo. The style is unmistakable[16]. It is Sherlock Holmes who is playing. It must be. I hope with all my heart that he is playing for me ...

1. avec meilleur moral
2. C'est ce qui se passa.
3. détendu
4. réduit en cendres
5. étaient montées si haut
6. d'aussi loin
7. Je ne lui ai pas fait la remarque, non plus
8. véhiculait
9. une forte odeur de cendres
10. la mélodie qui montait en puissance
11. Alors que je pose
12. vais me coucher
13. l'archet
14. chevalet
15. s'élève
16. reconnaissable entre tous

La collection Yes you can!

Faux débutants

Ken Follett *The Modigliani Scandal*

Mary Higgins Clark *A Stranger is Watching*

Mary Higgins Clark *Where are the Children?*

Anthony Horowitz *The House of Silk*

Yann Martel *Life of Pi*

Nicholas Sparks *Message in a Bottle*

Intermédiaires

Harlan Coben *Play Dead*

Harlan Coben *Stay Close*

Harlan Coben *Tell No One*

Michael Connelly *The Black Box*

Michael Connelly *The Drop*

Ken Follett *Paper Money*

Mary Higgins Clark *A Cry in the Night*

P.D. James *A Mind to Murder*

Douglas Kennedy *The Big Picture*

John le Carré *A Most Wanted Man*

Avancés

Paul Auster *Oracle Night*

Julian Barnes *The Sense of an Ending*

Michael Cunningham *The Hours*

Elizabeth George *A Great Deliverance*

Stephen King *Misery*

Imprimé en Italie par La Tipografica Varese Srl
Dépôt légal : février 2015
315089-01/11028607-février 2015